S0-ATY-166

James stirred in his slur  ;
hard body was stretched quite unselfconsciously before
Phillipa, and she realized that for once she could look her fill.

She leaned toward him to stare into his face, close enough to
detect the brandy on his breath and the sandalwood on his
skin. She shut her eyes for a moment and breathed deeply.
Brandy and sandalwood and James.

Opening her eyes, she gazed at the structure of his face. The
firelight bronzed the strong cheekbone and jaw, and shadowed that dent just below his full bottom lip. Stubble darkened his cheeks, giving him a dangerous air even in sleep.
Her fingertips itched to feel that manly roughness. Then, with
great serenity, she noticed her hand reaching toward him.

"Why, thank you, I do believe I will," she whispered to herself.

The *Spy*
(Book Three in the Liar's Club)

Celeste Bradley

St. Martin's Paperbacks

THE SPY

For information address St. Martin's Press, 175 Fifth Avenue, New York, NY 10010.

ISBN: 978-0-312-38160-8

Printed in the United States of America

St. Martin's Paperbacks edition / February 2004

St. Martin's Paperbacks are published by St. Martin's Press, 175 Fifth Avenue, New York, NY 10010.

10 9 8 7

This book is for Bill
"forever and ever, and then an extra day"

I must thank Monique Patterson and the family at St. Martin's Press for believing in the Liars and in me. There are no words.

And thank you—always—to the women who keep me moving forward when I want to fall back: Darbi Gill, Robyn Holiday, Cheryl Lewallen, Joanne Markis, Jennifer Smith, Cindy and Alexis Tharp. Your capacity for listening to my whining is astonishing.

Last, but always first, my family—who remind me that it is, after all, just a book. (See, you *are* in here every time.)

The Liar's Creed

In the guise of knaves we operate on the fringes of the night, forsaking home, hearth, and love for the protection of all.

We are the invisible ones.

Prologue

England 1813
Midsummer . . .

The wedding march began. James Cunnington took his place beside the bride and felt her trembling fingers clutch at his arm. Beautiful harmonies danced in the high rafters of the chapel that had served his ancestral home for hundreds of years.

If he closed his eyes, he could imagine all the unions that had occurred in this lovely place—all the optimistic grooms, all the joyful brides.

James felt as though he were about to vomit.

His vision swam and his temples throbbed an ugly counterpoint to the strains of music. The shimmering echoes of it seemed to stretch his last nerve to the breaking point. He'd like to blame it on a soaked head, yet he couldn't deny there was much more to it than that.

Only a portion of his problem stemmed from the evening before when all the men present had toasted the groom with enthusiasm. Primarily, his own uneasy heart poisoned his feelings.

This wedding was an excellent thing. He glanced at the

shining face of the woman beside him. She returned his look lovingly. He should be happy today. He should be thinking of devotion and unity and forever.

Instead, all he could think of as he walked down the aisle was betrayal and shame and abiding never-ending guilt.

His guilt.

There was no need to marry, his panic informed him. He could simply choose an heir—even adopt that little chimneysweep boy who'd been hanging about his club. There was no reason for him to go through all this.

He stopped before the vicar and none too soon. He was definitely going to be sick. With a feeling of impending doom, he took the bride's hand and placed it in the groom's.

It was a good thing this was his sister Agatha's wedding and not his own.

Chapter One

One month later . . .

Faint radiance from the nearest street lamps gleamed on the silken skin of a single exposed thigh. Long, ivory, and elegant, it was framed by a ruffle of underthings hiked high and the dark tease of stocking gartered low over the knee. Only a pale flash, a voyeuristic moment in time, yet the sight held the impact of a fist to the gut.

James Cunnington's mouth went dry in that moment and his brisk progress through the park came to a sudden halt. His brain slowed as his pulse quickened, startled into abrupt arousal by the very unexpectedness of his accidental glimpse of creamy female flesh. How long had it been since he had seen a woman's bare thigh? Three months? Four?

Not since the night his mistress had seen fit to kidnap and imprison him. He'd been walking home sated and nearly weak-kneed from yet another evening of astonishingly wicked pleasure at the skilled hands of the most intoxicating woman he had ever met. He'd been jumped by more men than he could defeat alone and had woken as a prisoner of the lovely and devious Lady Lavinia Winchell, French spy and amateur assassin. He'd eventually escaped and managed to foil her plan to assassinate the Prime Minister. The half-healed bullet wound in his shoulder ached at the memory. Lavinia was now imprisoned upon the mercy of the Crown, and if James had anything to say about it, it would not be long before she was hanged for the murders she had committed.

As his mind traveled back down the road of his unquenched desires, the woman before him used the slender limb she had exposed to step up onto a stone park bench. Her aim seemed to be to peer over the high hedge that delineated the borders of the park in the center of the square. James watched mournfully as yards of petticoat, skirt, and dark cloak tumbled back down over the most sexually satisfying experience he'd had in months.

What a pity.

Then he blinked. Pulling himself forcefully from his straying thoughts, James took a moment to notice the lateness of the evening hour. Twilight was long past and only the lamps burning around the square illuminated the darkness.

Odd. Before him was a woman alone in a shadowy park in the middle of London. True, they were in Mayfair—but even this enclave of the wealthy and elite held its dangers. He himself had been set upon in this very park on that fateful night.

A night very much like this one.

James moved forward carefully until he could see the entire dark-cloaked figure silhouetted against the shadows of the hedge. The woman still hadn't seen him or heard his footsteps on the brick-paved walk. Obviously she was far more interested in what lay on the other side of the boxwood.

As far as James knew, the only thing directly beyond the hedge and street was a house.

His house.

Continuing his silent progress, James approached directly behind the woman, who had gone up on tiptoe in her determination to see beyond.

"So, at what are we peeking?"

Phillipa Atwater's heart stopped at the sound of the deep

voice behind her. She jerked backward in her surprise. One of her worn shoes lost its footing on the dew-dampened stone and she felt herself begin to fall—

Only to find herself clasped in a pair of strong arms that cradled her close to a broad hard chest. Naturally, her first response to being grasped by a strange man was to struggle.

A chuckle rumbled from the chest she squirmed against, a sound so deep it went clear through her.

"Now is that any way to reward your hero?"

Her captor's grasp was not harsh, but quite implacable. Her struggles were as effective as a moth fluttering in a boy's hand. With a last frustrated jab of her elbow into the bastard's rock-hard abdomen, she gave up to lie quietly in his hold with her head ducked and her arms crossed.

He laughed again and she felt the warmth of his breath across her check and ear. Bloody rotten hell. Her hood had fallen back during her struggles. Luckily, her hair had come unpinned as well and now hung down about her shoulders. With a shake of her head, her face was well curtained.

"Who are you?" The man's voice was low, but not particularly gentle. In fact, he sounded downright suspicious. "What are you doing about so late?"

Phillipa remained silent. There was nothing to do but wait for her captor to let his grip loosen. It would only take a moment, for she had by necessity become very swift in the last months. The world was full of the groping hands of men. A woman on her own must learn to dodge.

Although she must grudgingly admit that this fellow didn't seem inclined to snatch an illicit caress. His large hands, unyielding as they were, remained most correct—one wrapped firmly around her upper arm, the other politely not gripping her knee.

She felt herself hefted easily, as if he were gauging her weight. His strength would be frightening if it were not for the painless clasp of his muscular arms. For a moment she longed for such secure arms to hide within, just once in a while. It had been so long since she'd had someone strong on her side . . .

"You aren't one for words, are you? That does not disturb me. I feel quite able to stand here all night."

Although his statement was meant to be mildly intimidating, James found it to be somewhat true. She was no burden at all. Or perhaps it was simply the feel of a woman in his arms. Her fragrant hair spread across his chest and shoulder, draping him in a sensuous veil that glinted red in the lamplight. He felt the urge to bury his face in that hair, to feel it on his naked chest . . .

He cleared his throat and shifted his weight, but that only pressed her hip against the hungriest part of him. Swallowing hard, James decided that the best place for the woman was on her own feet. He bent to drop her legs gently down, never letting free his grip on her stiffened shoulders.

There. Much better.

Except that now her side pressed to his and he could feel the small curve of her breast against his extended arm. His fingers tightened involuntarily at the surge of yearning that rolled through him.

His captive whimpered, and instinctively James eased his grip—only to find himself clutching empty air.

She ducked away with astonishing swiftness, her cloak a dark flutter as she whirled. He stepped forward to catch her arm once more, but she dashed to the side, then turned to run into the shadowy trees. He pursued her instantly, his longer legs assuring his success. She dodged tree trunks before him, but he followed the coppery flag of her hair in the dimness. He was her shadow, almost able to reach—

She ran beneath a limb which he didn't see until too late. His brow struck wood. Hard. By the time he'd recovered himself, she was gone.

"Damn." He'd never catch her now. The darkness swallowed her as if she'd never been.

To be quite frank, his powerful arousal had him mistrusting his own instinct to chase her down. What had she done that was so terrible that he ought to pursue her? Stand on a bench in the park?

So, with a rueful shake of his head he remained where he

stood, listening to the fading brush of running feet in the night.

James had a powerful hunch that he was going to regret losing her.

The next afternoon, Phillipa found herself at the house once more. She raised the heavy knocker, took a deep breath, then let it fall. Within moments, the door swung open to reveal a small man in green and black livery. His gaze traveled down, then back up.

Cool dismissal flickered in his eyes. "State your business, then."

Phillipa was startled by the fellow's common speech. She would have thought such a fine house would have nothing less than top-drawer staff. "I—" *Too high and girlish, blast it!* She cleared her throat. "I've come to interview for the position."

"Humph." The butler shrugged and cast her a sour glare. He stepped back and held open the door. "Well, come on then. Or be you wantin' the weather to come in as well?"

Phillipa stepped quickly over the threshold, then winced. After less than an hour as a man, she had decided that the worst thing about wearing trousers was the chafing of her ah . . . thighs. The second worst thing was the fact that she looked entirely too convincing as a male.

She'd once been proud of her willowy figure but the past months of poverty had thinned her down to what could only be described as desperately starved. Her borrowed trousers and frock coat didn't fit at all properly, and the waistcoat was so thoroughly pinned that she could scarcely move her arms without stabbing herself. She smoothed her coat with one hand, feeling the crackle of paper from inside. Ah, yes. In her pocket was the advertisement that had brought her here today.

"Tutor required for a boy of perhaps nine years," the advertisement in her pocket read. *"Patient and agreeable gentlemen should please apply to Mr. James Cunnington, 28 Ashton Square, London."*

James Cunnington.

A familiar name, a name she'd seen in her father's notes. *"Keep a close watch on James Cunnington."* What her father meant by that, she had no idea. That was why she'd been watching this house last night. That was why she was here, dressed in borrowed male clothing that fit about as well as the gender did.

She knew she looked odd, but she was hoping it would pass as scholarly forgetfulness. After all, a young man interviewing for a position as a tutor was hardly required to be the first stare of fashion.

So it was quite a blow when, as she caught a glimpse of herself in the shining surface of an entrance-hall table, she was dismayed to see that she appeared quite plausibly male. A thin, badly dressed fellow stared back at her, features gone bony with starvation—looking entirely neuter.

Apparently she'd quite lost her looks.

This had all seemed a much better idea yesterday. It was as though some madness had seized her on the previous day as she'd stared at the advertisement in her hand.

She'd just been turned down again in her search for a governess position. It was difficult to obtain a position in charge of young ladies when a young lady had no references and no experience of her own. The service agencies of London would not even touch her for that reason.

But that refusal had been the last of the advertisements for a governess, and the last chance she'd had to avoid going into an even lower service. Not that she was too proud, not at this stage of desperation. She would do anything to survive and to discover if Papa still lived.

There'd been no help for it. Phillipa had dug out the three-day-old section of advertisements from beneath her mattress and had begun to peruse all the pages. She passed over her favorite column, the Voice of Society, with little interest. Ever since the Voice had stopped writing about the Griffin, England's Gentleman Spy, Phillipa had lost her taste for gossip.

If only she had someone like the Griffin to turn to . . . but she had only herself to depend on. She must make her own way now. Was there any work out there for a young woman of her varied but inconsistent skills?

Then she had seen the name. *James Cunnington.* Her vision had passed over it, snagged on some snippet of memory, and turned back. She'd run her fingers lightly over the words on the sheet of newsprint. Where had she seen that name before?

After a moment of thought, she'd scrambled off her cot where she'd been bundled up against the damp and chill. With a grunt and a pull, she'd moved the bed a few feet to the left, just enough to kneel down behind it. There she had flipped back the threadbare carpet and run her fingertips over the time-worn planks below.

There was one that sat slightly higher than the others— there. She'd edged her nails over the ridge and lifted carefully, working the plank from its place by dint of much wiggling.

Beneath the plank, down in the hole between the floor supports, had lain an elderly, stained satchel. With one eye on the rather pitifully latched door and an ear alert to the sound of her landlady's heavy footsteps on the stairs, Phillipa had pulled the satchel from beneath the floor and lain it carefully on the cot.

The heavy book within was equally stained and the pages were rippled from the dampness, but Phillipa had ignored the musty smell that rose from it to handle it with such care it was almost a caress. With an almost superstitious compulsion, she ran her fingers over the Greek emblem that was stamped as decoration into the leather cover. The letter Phi, a squat circle bisected by a vertical line.

Then she'd opened it. Quickly she had scanned the pages. If she was not mistaken, she had seen the name from the paper written on the margin of a page—

Yes, there it was, scrawled in Papa's handwriting in that half-legible way he used when it was meant to be read only by himself.

"Keep a close watch on James Cunnington."

Nothing else. No reason *why* James Cunnington should be watched. For his own safety? For reasons of Crown security? For that had been what her father had worked in, before his retirement. He'd never told her specifics, and indeed, she'd never seen this book of notes before the night of her escape from the marauding French soldiers who had broken into her home and stolen her father away . . .

No time for memories or regrets now. She firmly put the recent past from her mind. Pulling the page of advertisements across the cot, she laid it next to her father's open book.

There was no mistake. The name was the same. Friend or foe, it remained to be seen. The best way to determine that would be to get to know this Mr. Cunnington firsthand.

And James Cunnington was advertising for household help.

A tutor to be exact. The very work Phillipa had been looking for, with one small difference.

James Cunnington wanted to hire a man.

Phillipa Atwater. Phillip A. Walters. The name had turned and twisted through her mind. *Phillip.*

If changing her last name slightly had rendered her less visible to those pursuing her, imagine how she'd completely disappear if she—

God, she'd been mad to think what she had been thinking!

Then again, the requirements were slightly less stringent for tutors of boys. In addition, there were far more advertisements asking for tutors than for governesses.

Finally, the fact that taking a male identity might finally throw any pursuers from her back permanently had decided the matter.

Once upon a time she would have scoffed at living such a lie and would have stoutly declared she would die first. Now dying had a realistic ring to it that she'd never before experienced.

There was nothing left. Her rent was overdue and she was down to bread and broth once a day. It wouldn't be much longer before she was on the streets. Her landlady was not a sympathetic sort.

Mrs. Farquart had ordered one of the other residents carted away to Bedlam last week when the poor woman had begun to carry on loud conversations with her dead soldier husband while alone in her room. The woman's things stood in a trunk in the hall, still waiting to be claimed. Her clothes . . . and her husband's clothes.

Phillipa had only borrowed a few things. Just long enough to attend the interview, after which she planned to return them. Then she'd traded her hair to a wigmaker for a pair of boots and changed the color with a bottle of cheap dye that had cost her last pair of whole stockings.

In the mirrored surface, one hand rose to her short mottled brown locks in unconscious mourning. Her waist-length copper hair had been her best feature. Without it, she was merely a thin freckled girl with no figure.

Phillipa shook off that thought and followed the butler through the halls of her prospective employer's house, looking about her with curiosity. Although she had watched the house carefully for hours last night, she'd seen nothing of those who lived within.

She had remained in the park far later than was wise, still hoping for some glimpse of Mr. Cunnington, who she imagined a stout and dour fellow, secretive and unreliable. Perhaps even a bit gouty, for the entry in her father's journal had been from years ago. The man might even be elderly and frail.

Unlike her mysterious captor last night. Heavens, he'd been anything but frail. His broad chest had been like a wall of brick . . .

Phillipa blinked herself back to the present. It was a very fine house, beautifully kept and furnished, yet it had the distinct air of a house not lived in, until she was shown into the study. There reigned the comforting chaos of manly doings, reminding her very much of her father's study in Arieta. The sweet smell of pipe smoke was the only thing missing, besides her father's rumbling chuckle.

Then a rumbling chuckle emerged from the high-backed chair before the fire, so deep it seemed to resonate through her belly—

Phillipa's gasp was covered by the butler's announcement. "Mr. Phillip Walters to interview for the tutor's position, sir."

A tousled head of brown hair emerged around the high winged sides of the chair. "Oh, hell, I forgot."

Her gut shivered further as she recognized the deep voice from the previous evening. Phillipa caught a glimpse of brown eyes and a square jaw before the occupant unfolded himself to his full height.

The man turned toward her, displaying wide shoulders and thick-hewn arms that tapered down to square hands, one of which held the small leather-bound book he had been reading. That same broad chest she remembered from last night tapered to a trim waist, emphasized by the fact that his frock coat lay abandoned over the back of his chair. His fitted waistcoat and fine shirt gave credence to her suspicion that no padding created that form.

Oh, *merde*.

Phillipa forced herself to swallow. So the mysterious James Cunnington was the man who had held her so easily in his arms last night. Would he recognize her now, though she was much changed and she'd been careful not to let him see her face?

He made no sign of it. Perhaps she was in no danger. At least, not from that encounter.

She forced her gaze from his magnificent structure to his face. To her relief, he was not distractingly handsome. Oh, it was a fine face, square and strong, and he did have those deep brown eyes that made him seem rather comfortable—but she was quite able to keep her bearings while looking at his face.

She had always preferred a more poetic sort, pale and haunted by fine feelings. Mr. Cunnington seemed rather like a brown and burly farmer, the sort that named his cow Mabel and knew when to plant by sniffing the soil.

Then again, poets didn't usually come fitted out with a pair of shoulders that blocked the light . . .

". . . Mr. Walters?"

Phillipa jerked to alertness. Her hunger must be making her simple. She must concentrate! Her very life and quite possibly her father's life depended on obtaining this position. She strode forward to shake the wide hand that still hung in the air, waiting for her. At least the fellow seemed to have no trouble believing her to be male.

She tried not to whimper when he nearly crushed her bones. Good heavens, did men always do this to each other? Being one of them was not going to be as easy as she had thought.

After nodding to his manservant—"Thank you, Denny"—James Cunnington waved her to an overstuffed chair facing the one he'd occupied. "The advertisement wasn't very informative, I'm afraid." He seemed almost apologetic. "I've never done this before."

Following his gesture inviting her to sit, Phillipa was enchanted. Not only did he show no sign of associating her with last night, but here was a man who obviously had no idea how to interview a tutor. How perfectly lovely.

"We've had several applicants walk away when they've learned that I'm a single gentleman with no visible means of support, hiring them to teach an ignorant guttersnipe child who lives with me in this house."

He sat back in the chair behind his massive desk, obviously waiting for her to respond.

She nodded and cleared her throat. *Speak deeply.* "I appreciate your candor, Mr. Cunnington. In return, perhaps I should inform you that the last four positions for which I've interviewed have turned me down for reasons of youth, inexperience, and complete lack of references."

She leaned back in her own chair and crossed her legs in imitation of him, although she had to fight a wriggle as the trousers chafed her inner thighs. She must secure some drawers—and soon.

Mr. Cunnington tilted his head. "Do you like children?"

She hesitated. In all honesty, she didn't know any. "It depends upon the child. Not all of them, I'm sure."

"How about discipline?"

"I'm for it, in general. Yet again, the punishment depends on the crime."

"Ah. Interesting, but evasive. What would you do if he, say . . . stole an apple from the neighbor's tree? Would you take the switch to him?"

Phillipa tried to recall how she would have responded to that as a child. "No, that likely wouldn't do any good. He'd only go out and take another, just to prove he wasn't scared of me. Perhaps a day peeling apples in the neighbor's kitchen would be more appropriate?"

Mr. Cunnington grinned. "That would be a sight. If there's a kitchen in London that could hold him." He looked at her for a long moment. She refused to shift and wiggle, despite her nervousness.

"Hmm. What can you offer in lieu of experience and references?"

This answer had been well practiced at least. "Latin, botany, geography, dancing, manners and mores, et cetera. In other words, everything a young la—gentleman should know."

His mouth twitched. "Latin and botany, eh?"

He didn't believe her. She wouldn't get this position, her last chance. Her stomach protested and her head swam.

"I speak seven languages!" she blurted desperately. It was almost true. She could curse fluently in seven languages. She'd paid close attention to the intemperate porters of every country in which her family had traveled over the past ten years.

Mr. Cunnington stood. "I think you should meet my charge before you promise any more wonders, Mr. Walters."

He crossed to a window looking onto what appeared to be the back garden and threw it wide. "Robbie!" he bellowed. "Come have a look at your new tutor!"

Phillipa's knees threatened to give out. She was hired?

She didn't care if her student was a spider monkey, she would teach it everything it needed to know if it would help her return her life to the way it used to be.

She stood and turned to the door, waiting for the boy to enter. She mustn't get off on the wrong foot. If the lad was spoiled, Mr. Cunnington might send her packing on the child's request.

A thrashing of boughs and a scrambling on the windowsill caused her to turn. Her eyes went wide as a small filthy creature clambered into the room from outside the window.

After dusting himself off a bit, a process that did no good as far as Phillipa could see, the child glanced at her, then around the room.

"What, is that him?"

Robbie perused her slowly, from her boots to her carefully cut hair. Then he shot a glance at his guardian and snickered. "I guess he'll do all right. What's 'is name then?"

Mr. Cunnington rolled his eyes at the lack of manners and gave the boy a fond cuff on one ear. "Watch yourself, Rob. Mr. Walters gets you for five hours a day, so I wouldn't plague him off if I were you."

The boy slid knowing eyes to Phillipa and gave her a tiny smirk. She stiffened. Could he *know*? It wasn't possible! Was it?

"Oh, I think me and the perfesser'll get along all right, once we come to an understandin'."

Bloody rat-catching hell. Whether he knew or not, the little anarchist thought he had the upper hand already. If she didn't nip that in the bud, her stay here could become unbearable.

She stepped forward and held out her hand. "I am Phillip Walters, Master Robert. You may call me Mr. Walters. We will begin lessons first thing tomorrow morning after breakfast. I shall expect you on time—and bathed. If not, I shall have to oversee the bathing process myself." She sent Robbie a warning look. "Won't I, Master Robert?"

The poor boy went absolutely ashen with horror. Phillipa

had to stifle a laugh. She didn't think he'd be giving her any trouble for a while.

Mr. Cunnington rumpled Robbie's hair and grinned. "Good. We're settled then. I've been told to offer twenty pounds per annum, and you'll likely earn every penny twice over."

He glanced over her, his sharp eyes taking in the details of her dress. Phillipa knew her clothing was an ill fit and her bartered boots were quite nearly disgraceful. She hoped that was all he could see.

He looked away, pretending interest in the fire. "Perhaps a small advance? You must have some expenses . . ."

Thank God. She'd not had the nerve to ask, but she wouldn't turn it down. "Well, my landlady is due a bit, but I'm sure I could wait . . ." She couldn't wait. *Please don't make me wait.*

He shoved a hand in his pocket. "I've only a five-pound note on me. Will that do?" He pulled it out and pressed it into her hand.

She couldn't believe it. An entire quarter's advance? Even Robbie was surprised. She caught him staring open-mouthed from her hand to his guardian's face. She couldn't blame the boy a bit. Did this man have no concept of the value of the pound?

She delivered a creditable bow to Mr. Cunnington. "Thank you, sir. If I may return to my rooms and gather my things, I should like to move in this evening."

"Excellent. You'll be up for an early start tomorrow then." Mr. Cunnington showed her to the door. "Will you be joining us for dinner as well?"

She was counting on it. If not, she was likely to be nothing but a shrunken bag of bones by morning. However, she hesitated. The less exposure she had to her new employer, the less likelihood of her slipping up and betraying herself.

"If I might have a tray in my room this evening? I should like to—"

"Certainly. Of course you'll want to unpack and settle

in." He opened the door for her and Phillipa reminded herself to put her hat back on her head. "We'll see you in the morning then."

Morning. As the door closed behind her and Phillipa finally allowed herself to breathe, she felt her courage begin to slip away. What had she got herself into?

And what if she couldn't get herself out?

Chapter Two

James shut the front door behind his newest employee and listened as the sound echoed hollowly in the halls. For a brief moment, he'd forgotten how oppressive this place was. The interview with the skinny tutor had quite distracted him.

Phillip Walters. An odd duck, to be certain. He looked as though he dressed from a rubbish bin and cut his hair with a hacksaw. And if James was not mistaken, Mr. Walters was hiding something. Not for a second had James believed his claim to be a man of twenty years. No fellow of that age was entirely beardless, no matter how fine his razor.

No, Mr. Walters was more likely sixteen, or even fifteen. He'd not yet filled out his scrawny frame. Of course, the fellow was starving—James had seen that immediately. The poor bloke had nearly passed out at his feet.

So hungry and desperate that he had lied about his age. James probably would have hired him on that alone, even if the young man hadn't come laden with such remarkable skills. James himself had bounced back quickly enough from his turn a few months ago as a starving prisoner on a French ship, but he remembered hunger well.

"Latin," murmured James. He chuckled. "Dancing."

Still laughing to himself, he returned to the study. Robbie stood in the center of the carpet waiting for him.

Immediately, James felt the usual discomfort that Robbie's presence brought with it. Robbie seemed to want something from him but James never truly knew what it was.

When he'd resolved never to marry, he'd realized his need for some sort of heir. His sister Agatha wanted no part of the estate so she had approved his plan whole-heartedly. A starveling climbing boy for an abusive chimneysweep gang, Robbie had been taken in by the members of James's club after he'd saved Agatha's life, and it had seemed fated that James adopt the young orphan.

He'd taken the lad in to be his heir, and to improve Robbie's life. In the past weeks, good food had begun to fill those sunken cheeks and a safe home had swept away that heartbreaking caution that had once marked his expression.

Yet a hunger still lurked in the boy's eyes, as it did at this moment, and James had no idea how to feed it. He turned away from those demanding eyes and stepped behind the barrier of his desk.

The way his father always had. For a split second, James almost grasped the darkness still lurking in Robbie. Then he dismissed the notion. His own father—a prominent scholar and mathematician—had always been distracted and busy, but James had not suffered from it.

Then again, he'd had his sister Aggie.

Well, now Robbie would have Phillip. Not a sibling but a comrade of sorts. That should take care of things nicely for Robbie, and he would stop looking at James the way he was looking at him right now.

Suddenly James felt an overwhelming desire to be at the club. Away from those hungry eyes. Away from the feeling that he was failing Robbie in some vital but incomprehensible way.

Odd. James had faced imprisonment by Napoleon's henchmen, torture and daily danger, but he couldn't face those relentless blue eyes.

He picked up the journal and the file he'd been copying from when Mr. Walters had arrived and grabbed his frock coat from its roost on the back of his chair. Shrugging it on, he made for the hat residing on the side table in the entry hall. "I'm off, lad. Tell Denny I'll not be home for dinner, will you?"

Robbie followed him slowly. His stony little face did not change expression. "Take me with you."

"Can't do it, Rob." James flashed a desperate smile at him. Robbie didn't alter the intensity of his gaze one iota. James looked away. "I've got business to attend to. Besides, Phillip will be returning soon. You'll want to show him around, won't you?"

Robbie didn't answer and didn't move as James turned to go. When he glanced back, the sight of that small grimy figure standing alone in the hallway made James feel like the lowest growth of scum.

He left all the faster for it.

The colors of the streets of Cheapside faded behind the chill mist like a much-washed print. The few hunched figures scurrying to their destinations faded in and out of Phillipa's vision like memories. The air was cold and damp and she huddled deeper into the worn velvet seat of the cab.

She stole a look behind her as the carriage she'd hired rolled through the late-summer drizzle. Once she'd left the interview, she'd dashed into an alley to pull her dress on over her waistcoat and trousers and her bonnet over her ruined hair before making the journey back to the boardinghouse.

She didn't trust her landlady, Mrs. Farquart, not to interfere with her plan and she honestly didn't know how to make her way across town as a man.

As it was, her one shabby dress had caused most of the carriage drivers to pass her by for richer fare. She'd been fortunate to catch this cabbie whose tattered vehicle was even more disreputable-looking than herself. He'd still asked her to show him her purse before he'd taken the fare.

Now she wished she'd kept Phillip's masculine armor for a bit longer. Was someone following her again? She wasn't sure, nor was she sure about the previous occasions either.

Ever since she had come to London on the run from Napoleon's soldiers and searching for the one man her father had trusted, the city had played tricks on her vision, her memory, and her pocketbook.

Of course, it was possible that there was no one after her at all. She might be jumping at shadows, seeing things that weren't there—French spies around every corner—

Yet they had come before. In the night, tramping through the Spanish village of Arieta, pounding on the door of the villa where she lived so quietly with Papa.

Papa had known precisely what the soldiers had wanted somehow. Without so much as peering through a window, he had acted.

As she had stood at the foot of the stairs in her nightdress, shivering more from a sense of unreality than from cold, he'd rushed to his study where he'd flicked open his wall safe with one motion and emptied it into a bag.

He had directed her to fetch traveling clothes and boots from her room, then ordered her into a small opening that had somehow appeared next to the fireplace in the back parlor.

It was not much bigger than a sea chest, not high enough to stand in, not wide enough to lie down. He'd stuffed her in with her things in her lap and his satchel at her feet.

"It's Napoleon's men. Stay still. Not a word. I'll let you out soon. If . . . if I don't, go to London," he'd whispered. "Change your name. Travel quietly. There's a little money in the bag, enough for your passage. Go to Martin Upkirk, in Cheapside High Street."

"But Papa, what—"

He'd put a finger to her lips, dropped a kiss on her brow, then shut her into the darkness. She'd stayed, her long habit of obedience fighting her impulse to burst from hiding as she'd covered her face with her hands and listened to the muffled sounds outside her tiny cell.

Her father's voice, seemingly calm and unconcerned. A

deeper voice, rough and impatient. Angry words, not quite understandable. Then a series of crashing sounds, as if someone were throwing their things about the rooms and against the walls.

A scuffle of feet . . . a cry of pain . . .

Then the tramping footsteps had retreated and the house had become silent. Still she waited for Papa to open the panel and release her, to take her into his arms and tell her everything was going to be all right.

He hadn't come. That's when she'd known that nothing would ever be all right again.

It had seemed to take hours to discover the tiny ridge between the panels that held the trigger to the door of her little prison, then even longer for her to activate it.

Finally the small panel had sprung open and she had crawled from her hiding place, her back and legs aching from their cramped confinement.

The house was a shambles. Her mother's china lay in shards on the stained and littered carpet. Shredded pages of their precious library lay scattered, while more books smoldered sadly in the grate. Barefoot, Phillipa picked her way through the empty house, her careful calls for Papa resounding in the silence.

Her own clothing had been shredded on the floor of her bedchamber. In fact, her room and Papa's study seemed to have taken the worst of the damage. It was as if the intruders had been looking for something they had not found, and had taken their frustrations out on the empty rooms.

And perhaps on Papa.

That last cry of pain echoed through Phillipa's mind again as she sat in the rocking carriage. She blinked, tearing her thoughts from the past to look about her. Some sound from the street around her had startled her, but she could not say what. These streets were always filled with the sounds of violence and suffering.

She had no proof of her suspicions of being hunted. None but for the way her chamber in Arieta had been targeted and later the way her uncle had fearfully rushed her from his home.

As well as that feeling—the one that set the hairs on her neck to tingling. The one that never truly went away.

The hired carriage pulled to a rough stop a block away from her boardinghouse, just as she'd requested. "'Ere you go, miss." The driver didn't bother to help her from her seat on the shabby cushions.

Phillipa hopped down on her own, then turned back to the driver. "I'll only be a moment. If you'll wait, I'll pay you extra to take me back to Mayfair."

The driver nodded indifferently. "Mind you, don't keep me long, then. I'll not waste the daylight on ye."

His dull eyes sent her a glare that said, *Return or rot in hell, it's all the same to me.* She shivered, reminded that London was a hard place of cobbles and stone, where death occurred daily and danger even more often.

Well, there'd be no more of that, for she now had a mission and a safe place to stay. Thank heavens for Mr. Cunnington's naiveté in this matter.

Phillipa ducked into a shop and turned her flimsy blue summer cloak to show the brown lining. That left the clammy wet side against her, but if she were being followed, it might just break the trail. She also slouched deeply and affected a slight limp, just to confound any possible pursuers further.

Finally she reached the house where she had taken a room and breathed a sigh of relief. With determination, she reminded herself that today was the last time she'd have to come to this dreary place or travel through those lawless streets.

Phillipa paid Mrs. Farquart the back rent she was owed with her chin high, daring the sour-faced woman to challenge her sudden wealth. The landlady only scowled and counted out her change as if it hurt to let go of every copper.

The woman held on to the last coin, pinching it thoughtfully between her thumb and finger. "Got something you might like to know."

Phillipa continued to hold out her hand. "My change please, Mrs. Farquart."

The woman shrugged. "Since you paid in full, I'll give you a hint." A smirk passed over her thin lips. "Someone was here today, looking for you. A bloke, a real gent."

Phillipa somehow kept her outstretched hand from trembling. "I'm sure there must have been a mistake. I know no one in London."

"Well, he knew you. Described you right to your hair, even knew about when you moved in."

Phillipa withdrew her hand to twine her fingers together. Let the woman keep the penny. "Someone who saw me on the street, no doubt."

The coin disappeared with breathtaking swiftness. Mrs. Farquart began to turn away, losing interest now that the money was hers. Phillipa stopped her.

"This man—what did you tell him about me?"

Mrs. Farquart shrugged but there was a dark glint in her sour gaze. "Huh. Told him nothing. Think I wanted you hauled off afore I got my back rent?"

Meaning that now there was no counting on further secrecy. Nor was there a moment to lose.

Phillipa dashed to her small dank room. There was no fire, nor had there ever been one, despite the pre-autumn chill. This sort of room didn't come with amenities like coal or plentiful blankets.

It didn't take long to toss her few belongings into the bag she had carried with her in her flight from Arieta. She hesitated as she fingered the wool of her borrowed frock coat.

It was time to return these things to Bessie's trunk. Yet Phillipa knew it would be difficult to buy new things before she must return to Mr. Cunnington's.

Well, she would simply have to find new clothing on her own. It was bad enough to tell the necessary lies, she would not add stealing to her sins.

When she checked for the trunk that had sat in the hall that morning, however, it was gone. Had Bessie returned?

Mrs. Farquart knew the answer. She stood with her arms crossed in the front hall, sour disapproval etched on her craggy face. "She's not returnin'. Kilt herself, she did. Flung herself right out the window of the hospital."

"Oh, dear Bessie." Phillipa pressed one hand to her breast. Her neighbor had been grief-stricken, it was true, but Phillipa had never suspected that the woman would do something so drastic.

"Her family come to take her things," Mrs. Farquart continued, flicking her glance to Phillipa's own small bag.

"Oh," Phillipa said faintly. She felt terrible that she had removed the clothing from the trunk now. "Well, it's good that her loved ones can benefit from her husband's pay."

It had merely been an innocent comment, but Mrs. Farquart's reaction was harsh and immediate. She grabbed Phillipa's wrist in her talons.

"What d'you know about the pay?"

Astonished, Phillipa could only blink as she stammered an answer. "B—Bessie had t-two years of pay saved in her trunk. She and her husband were going to open a shop when he returned home."

Evident fury and fear washed Mrs. Farquart's face white. "That money weren't in the trunk when her family come for it."

Phillipa didn't grasp her meaning at first. Then her own fury spilled over and she wrenched her arm from the landlady's grasp. "Well, *I* didn't take it out."

"You must have!" shouted the woman. "Yes, it was you. You took it! I knew you were a liar and a thief the minute I laid eyes on you!"

"If anyone took it, it was you! You're a harsh and wicked woman, Mrs. Farquart, and I'm mightily glad to be quit of this house!" Phillipa grabbed up her bag in one hand and her skirts in the other and made a run for the door. Mrs. Farquart had always been sour and rude, but this was downright frightening.

"I'll call the law down on you, thief!" shrieked the woman as Phillipa dashed down the street to where her conveyance still waited. "I'll call the watch to take you clean away!"

The absurdity of the woman's fury and her own flight into the darkening afternoon suddenly struck Phillipa as laughable. Mrs. Farquart thought to strike fear into Phillipa's heart with threats of the lazy, bounty-chasing London watchmen?

That should be alarming when Napoleon himself was after her?

Chapter Three

By the time James approached the Liar's Club where it stood on the edge of the fashionable part of town—a sector where the underworld and upper classes mingled in pursuit of pleasure and entertainment—dusk was overshadowing the already gray sky and the lanterns hanging from all the carriages and carts had been lighted.

At the corner just before the club, James spotted a familiar figure. A tattered little man stood with one shoulder leaning into an unmarked doorway, just barely out of the rain. James couldn't see his face, but that practiced air of inoffensiveness was very Feebles. The wiry little pickpocket was one of the less house-broken of the Liars. Oh, he was loyal to the core, but he worked best on his own, scorning the club environs yet gathering information in seemingly magical ways. And there was none better at tailing a suspect, for swift and nimble Feebles could become even more invisible at will.

Feebles didn't take a bit of notice of James, but James knew the fellow saw him. He raised a finger to his hat brim, ostensibly to pull it down to block the wet. Feebles was looking in an altogether different direction, but he responded with a slight shrug. Grinning slightly to himself, James went on.

James contemplated taking a more discreet route to the club—say, down the back alley and up the side of the building—but with the misting dampness, the ledge that led to the secret "back door" of the club was not likely to be too comfortable at the moment.

At any rate, his hat was pulled low and his collar had been turned up for blocks, like every other bloke fool enough to walk in this weather.

Deciding to risk an open entry this time, James dashed across the street to where a plump doorman stood under a nondescript awning. The doorman's eyes widened, but he opened the door quickly, then followed James in to help him remove his coat.

In the process, Stubbs leaned close to whisper in James's ear, although there were no members yet gracing the outer rooms of the public Liar's Club. "Himself is waitin' for ye in the cry—the cryptol—the code room."

James sighed at Stubbs's stumbling words. The fellow was officially his apprentice, but the former street orphan had never had the merest lick of schooling. "Have you been practicing your letters and your mathematics like I told you, Stubbs?"

"I tried, sir. I just can't make no sense of that primer book." Stubbs's earnest face had reddened when James turned around.

James nodded, praying that he at least appeared patient. "I know it's difficult. But you cannot operate as a saboteur if you cannot read and add, Stubbs. You'll blow up mutton instead of muskets. And how will you make your explosives if you cannot mix and measure?"

Stubbs nodded miserably, his pale blue eyes defeated. James clapped him on the shoulder and added heartily, "You can do it, man! Just keep at it!"

With that James turned away, hoping Stubbs wouldn't pursue the subject. He didn't know how to teach someone to

read, for pity's sake. He could barely get Robbie to bathe
semiregularly.

Perhaps he ought to send Stubbs to school, now that
Agatha and her husband, Sir Simon Raines, had opened a
spy-training academy across the street. Although it stood under the guise of a charity school for the less fortunate, the
newest recruits would be coming into the Liar's Club with
all the advantages of education and deportment that
Agatha's considerable persistence could drum into their
heads.

A boon for the future Liars to be sure, but not likely to be
much help to poor Stubbs. James didn't think that the nearly
thirty-year-old Stubbs would take well to sitting out lessons
with the younger blokes now being trained. The man had
been a working Liar for years, and had a phenomenal mechanical aptitude.

Perfect for a saboteur and entirely trainable, if James
could only get him past the barrier of his extensive ignorance.

I shall add it to my list. Feeling rather bowed under the
weight of it all, James tried to think of something else as he
climbed the stair to the next floor.

Like the surprising appeal of long red locks when he'd always been partial to golden tresses.

James ran a hand over his face, self-disgust rising anew.
Last night had been something of a revelation. He'd thought
his baser impulses had been quelled by his experience with
Lavinia. Apparently he'd only been lying to himself. It was a
good thing he would never see the anonymous flame-haired
woman again.

Jackham was coming down as James was going up, his
grizzled head bent as he managed the stairs one at a time.
"Hullo, Cunnington."

The club's manager was getting about more slowly than
usual this afternoon. Bones broken in a fall long ago had
taken one of London's finest jewel thieves out of the profes-
sion forever. The previous spymaster, Simon Raines, had
hired his old friend to run the public portion of the club,

while carefully keeping the admittedly greedy Jackham out of the inner circle.

Jackham knew the Liars, every one, but believed the club was a front for thieves. All the resources behind the wall had been explained to Jackham as tools for the elaborately planned jobs that fueled all their fortunes. The men were thieves, or thieves in training. The map room was for storing the building plans of all the finest houses—which in fact it did, along with secret routes in and out of Paris and Napoleon's many properties. The code room took a bit more explaining, of course. But Jackham didn't worry much about the details, not as long as his cut was littered with jewels and the club continued to turn a profit.

Jackham enjoyed his work, for he was a fine hand with making money and he knew his whisky, and keeping up the "thieves' den" secret made him feel part of his old life.

James smiled slightly. He'd always been fond of the openly larcenous older fellow. "Feeling the weather, Jackham?"

The man stopped to tug his usual hideous waistcoat into place. "Had worse, I have. Had better too before this summer." Jackham had taken the deaths of the Liars hard, as had they all.

James nodded and moved on. He wasn't in the mood for casual conversation, even with such an old friend as Jackham.

The hallway above led to a number of rooms that were used by various Liars when needed, a good place to bed down for a few nights between missions when things were hectic, the way they always were these days.

To someone off the street, the rooms would seem to be nothing more than the usual rather monastic bedchambers common to gentlemen's clubs around the city.

The difference lay behind these rooms. James walked to the end of the hall, to where the carpet ended at a wall elaborately paneled in gleaming oak. With one hand he pressed upon a single small panel above his head. With the other, he pressed on another panel at waist height.

The wall before him shifted with a click, then retreated a few inches, enough for James to slide it to one side and step through the opening. The door returned to its former position on its carefully calibrated springs and clicked back into being a featureless wall.

On this side, the hallway was slightly less gleaming, slightly more threadbare and—as the smell of old books and slightly damp wool carpet rose to meet him—far more welcoming.

This was his home, not the fine London house he'd purchased at his sister's behest, nor even Appleby, the Lancashire estate he'd inherited on the death of his father.

This club was home, these men his family. What there was left of them . . .

In his mind he heard the voice of Simon Raines. *"We've never had all the men we've needed. We've certainly never had enough specialists. We're now down to two pickpockets, one knife man, four scouts, three rooftop men, and one saboteur, without you."*

Without him.

If not for James, there would be no such deficiency. No empty bed-chambers, no half-filled meetings. No missions going undone because of the shortage of heroes . . .

James closed his eyes. He would not wallow in his guilt. There was no time for mawkish self-blame. He must take the pain and regret he felt at his monumental error and direct it to finding the killers responsible.

He entered the cryptography room. The chamber was large, but had little room in it. Most of the space was filled with stacks of papers, books, and even scrolls. Every code known to the British military and even a few that weren't was held safe within these walls.

There were a number of desks in the room, but only one was occupied by a gentleman. Another, younger man sat across from him.

Fisher, the only one left . . .

Because of Napoleon's obsession with secret codes, the first Liars targeted during the recent betrayal were the brilliant code-breakers. The only remaining cryptographer was Fisher, who had been an apprentice at the time.

Now he was head of his own tiny division.

James looked at the empty seats. Giving those lost men their silent due, he closed his eyes and repeated his secret vow.

"My life for yours."

Yet no matter how many years he devoted himself to his colleagues and his country, he could never erase what he had done.

"James? I hate to disturb you but—"

James gave his head a quick shake and pasted a lying smile on his face. "Sorry. Daydreaming a bit, that's all." He pulled a chair up and sat on it backward, facing the desk. There sat the imposing figure of Dalton Montmorency, Lord Etheridge, the spymaster of the Liar's Club. Code name, the Gentleman.

Or, as Dalton's nephew Collis referred to him behind his back—and never above a whisper—the Grand High Oompah of Everything. James, being neither intimidated nor related, merely called him "sir."

Dalton nodded to him. "How's the shoulder?"

The last thing James wanted to think about now was his injury. "Fine," he said.

"Have you been keeping up with the retraining Kurt set you to?"

"Yes, Mother." James tried to crack a careless grin. He very much feared it came out a sour grimace.

Dalton's cool gaze didn't waver. "Pray take your recovery seriously. We need the Griffin back in action. The club has only one other saboteur—"

"This I know," James snapped. The Liar name once worn proudly now fit ill, like a suit of armor made for another man. "Wouldn't you like to know what our search revealed?"

Dalton raised a brow. "So, what's the news on our target?"

"Good and bad," James said. "We found him."

Fisher straightened in his chair. "Where? When can we get him here?"

"Feebles brought me the new information just this morning." James tossed the file onto the desk in frustration.

"Where? In France. When? Likely never, for it seems he's been working for Napoleon for months now."

"For Napoleon?" Fisher seemed to shrink. "D'you mean I'm up against *Rupert Atwater*?" The thin young man swallowed. "I—but he's *Atwater*! He's brilliant. Matchless. Everything I know, I learned from someone who learned it from him!" Fisher looked as though he might cry. "He was a Liar. One of us. How *could* he?"

James looked away from Fisher's disillusionment. "Who knows?" he said bitterly. "Money? Power?" He glared at the floor, his jaw clenching. "A woman?"

Dalton picked up the file and skimmed the contents quickly. "Was he the sort to fall for bribery?"

James shrugged one shoulder. "I didn't know him well. He retired from the Liars shortly after I began. Simon worked with him. Kurt probably knew him as well, although I doubt Cryptography and Wet-work ever spent much time together, even then."

Fisher snorted. "I should hope not! Consorting with assassins, indeed!"

Dalton eyed the young man coolly. "We are all Liars, Fisher. We serve the Crown equally, for each of us has only one life to offer up. Every man in this club fulfills a vital purpose. They are all your comrades, from illiterate pickpockets to assassins—to overly educated gentleman farmers." He shot a reproving glance James's way.

James stiffened, but stifled further harsh comments speculating on Atwater's probable bedroom preferences and likely inhuman ancestry. Dalton was quite correct. Atwater had been a member of the Liar's Club for years, and according to his file, had only retired when he found that his beloved wife had developed consumption.

The man had then apparently taken his savings and his family on a world tour in desperate search of a cure. The club had lost touch with him after a few years, for he'd moved on as fast as any rumor of a medical miracle could reach him.

Indeed there might be mitigating circumstances that would explain Atwater's sudden reappearance as Napoleon's primary code-breaker and, worse, encoder. Atwater's genius laid at the enemy's disposal *might* not mean the man was guilty of treason . . .

But James wouldn't wager a broken copper on it.

Dalton squinted at the report once more. "Where's the daughter?"

James looked up, startled. "There's no daughter with him in Napoleon's retinue, by our informant's report."

"Our records say that at the time he left the club, he had one young child, a girl." Dalton flipped a page, then another. "No name for her. I wonder where she is now?"

James closed his eyes to think. Atwater had barely registered in his awareness all those years ago, for the younger James had had no interest in the studious pursuits of the code room, not when there was danger and adventure to be found in the realm of the saboteur.

Furthermore, the daughter would have been nigh invisible to a young man of twenty. "Well, Atwater's wife is likely deceased, if she was diagnosed ten years ago. Perhaps the daughter developed consumption as well. They do say it runs in families. That would explain why Atwater's alone now."

Dalton looked at the file. "Poor bloke," he said quietly.

James knew Dalton was thinking of his own beloved wife Clara and the child they both hoped to have. Fighting down sympathy of his own, James reminded himself why it was a good idea never to marry. Too much to lose.

He cleared his throat. "Perhaps we can backtrack. Find out where Atwater was before he joined up with Napoleon. He may have left his daughter there, may have even let a few things slip to her that we can use."

"I hope he left her a bloody handbook," said Fisher glumly, "for that's the only way I'll ever be able to break his codes."

James sat up off the base of his spine. "Might there be such a thing?"

Fisher shrugged. "Could be. Some keep notes on paper,

some keep it in their heads. Atwater is brilliant, but his codes are complex and intricate. If I were him I would keep a book, a key."

Dalton nodded. "Find the daughter and we might just learn more about that key, if it exists. It's worth a try."

James was overwhelmed with the need to act. "I'll go."

Dalton didn't even look his way. "You'll stay. We've a scout in place who can backtrack Atwater."

"But this is my case."

"Your task at this time is to heal. If you wish to return to full duty, you'll need all your strength." Dalton glanced up, indicating James's injured shoulder with a pointed look. "If you recall, the last time you went up against someone, you nearly didn't make it because you weren't fully healed."

James scoffed. "That isn't fair. My hands were tied behind me. And I did prevail . . . eventually."

"Eventually might be too late next time." Dalton closed the file with a snap. "This is not your case. You have no case. You are on half-duty training Stubbs and there you'll remain until I say differently."

James clenched his jaw but did not protest further. There would be no moving Dalton until James proved himself to be well. In the meantime, James did not want Dalton to discern his current investigations into the treasonous career of Lady Lavinia Winchell.

Furthermore, he now had something new to look for. Or rather, someone. Atwater's daughter might be anywhere in the world, but Atwater had been a Brit and a Londoner for more years than he had been a nomad. Miss Atwater could very well be secreted right here in England, under their very noses.

And if she was, James intended to find her.

Dalton nodded as if they had come to some sort of agreement. "Good. Now rest. Heal. And teach Stubbs what you know so that I have even more excellent saboteurs at the Crown's disposal."

Fisher looked up at that. James had quite forgotten the man was in the room, he'd sat so quietly during the short conflict. Handy trick, that.

"Speaking of apprentices," Fisher said, "have you found a likely boy who can read and is quick with sums? I need help and I need it immediately."

Dalton raised a brow at Fisher's tone, causing the younger man to flush although he held the spymaster's gaze.

"No disrespect, sir, but I've not had more than a bit of sleep for days. It's been weeks since I've been back to my own rooms. If I keep this pace up, the club won't have *any* code-breakers."

Dalton only gazed levelly at the man. James didn't envy Fisher. Those silver eyes were a bit too sharp. "I thought you'd be far too busy to train someone up right now," Dalton said.

James frowned. "And what could an untrained lad help you with?"

"Well, some of the simpler codes can be taught quickly," Fisher explained. "Or at least the ability to spot them in use. If nothing else, he can run through the backlog of documents and eliminate the need for me to try every system on every item." His urgency ran down, and Fisher returned to his usual glumness. "It would help. A little."

Satisfied, Dalton nodded. "I'll talk to Lady Raines. I'm sure she can find an apprentice for you from the current class."

"Someone who can read," Fisher reminded him. "And who can count past his toes."

Dalton nodded again, rather patiently, James thought. They all stood. After the spymaster had left the code room, James clapped Fisher on the shoulder. "Now Fish, about those letters you've been working on—"

"I just can't keep working on a closed case, James. I'm sorry."

James rubbed his face. "It isn't closed, not officially. We suspect Lady Winchell is the one who penetrated our security. We know she kidnapped and drugged me. We are sure she fired a pistol at the Prime Minister. Now, we must prove it."

He threw himself into the empty chair opposite Fisher and sighed. "We need evidence. Evidence that does not compromise the secrecy of the club. Evidence that Lavinia cannot charm her way free of, nor lie herself out of. We can't close this case until justice is done upon the one who murdered our comrades, Fisher. As long as we can't prove that shooting me was more than the act of a jilted lover, we cannot question her properly—as a traitor should be. Her letters from prison to her lover are all we have. They must be coded somehow!"

Fisher tapped his pen nib on his nose thoughtfully. James decided not to tell him that his nose already looked like a chimneysweep's.

"Now, don't get angry, James, but you may not be seeing her clearly, not after what you went through. What if she truly was just a jilted lover having an attack of jealousy?"

James raised his brow. "She kidnapped my sister and told her everything before she tried to kill her. Are you sure you want to call Agatha's word into question?"

Since James's sister Agatha was now the bride of the previous spymaster of the Liar's Club and ran the school that secretly trained the next generation of England's spies, Fisher paled and gave his head a nervous little shake.

"I thought not." James rose. "I know you're overworked. I know this case is low priority right now. But please, whenever you have a moment to spare . . ."

Fisher sighed. "I know. I'll go over it again. Who knows? Maybe she'll slip up and we'll spot the code in one of her letters."

"Thanks, Fish."

Fisher groaned. "My name is Fisher, *Jamie*. Not Fish, not Fishy, not bloody Fish-eye. Must you rename *everyone*?"

"I don't rename everyone," James protested virtuously. "I haven't renamed Kurt."

"And the knife rack in Kurt's kitchen has nothing to do with that, I suppose?"

James grinned. "It isn't the knives, it's the trifle. If I anger Kurt, he'll never feed me berry trifle again."

Fisher narrowed his eyes at James. "If you make *me* angry, I'll tell Kurt to put apples in everything he feeds you."

James shuddered. "No-thank-you-very-much."

Fisher smiled slowly. "Apple tarts. Pork with stewed apples. Bangers and applesauce."

James held up both hands in surrender. "Fine. I won't hound you further. Just tell me when you find anything, anything at all, all right?"

Fisher sighed and shook his head. "All right, James."

James gave the thinner man a sound clap on the shoulder that rocked him in his boots. "Good man." Turning to leave, James gave Fisher a last teasing salute. "You're a most excellent fellow, Fish."

As he retraced his earlier path, this time with a smile on his face and Atwater's daughter on his mind, James heard Fisher call out behind him.

"Don't call me Fish!"

Chapter Four

On her first morning in the Cunnington household, Phillipa stretched luxuriously in her new—and comparatively huge—bed. She was warm, she was fed, and she was refreshed after a wonderful night's sleep in her new *safe* abode. Not a scream, not a shouted argument, not a single clatter of rubbish bins had marred her rest.

She dressed quickly, for the scent of cooking food had wafted under her door. It seemed she had some catching up to do, even after polishing off the manly serving that Mr. Cunnington's manservant had brought to her room last night.

There didn't seem to be much staff in this house. She'd only seen one so far. She breathed deeply. Eggs. *Ham*. There must be a cook as well, a good one. Getting up every morning to such reward would be well worth donning men's clothing.

Still, Phillipa tugged at her woolen trousers and thought wistfully of fine batiste underthings and Belgian lace. She missed being a girl, missed the soft fabrics and the sweet scents.

And in this house of men, she found that she missed her mother's voice more than ever. The studied English with the

Castilian lilt. The torrent of liquid Spanish she would release in moments of high emotion.

Phillipa's father had loved his wife with a profound devotion, wrapped in lifelong British reserve. But her mother had known. Everyone in Arieta had known, for Rupert Atwater had a way of coming to life in his wife's presence, as if every other moment were merely filled with waiting for her.

When Isabella Atwater had finally drifted away from them, something in Phillipa's father had died as well. In the past few years, he had yet to come to life again. When France had invaded Spain three years before, Papa hadn't so much as commented upon it, other than to note that Arieta was too isolated to come to any harm in the conflict. It was as if he were merely a walking husk of the man he had been.

Perhaps that was why he had not put up more of a struggle when Napoleon's men had come for him. Or perhaps he'd hoped it would aid Phillipa's own escape, which it had.

She'd passed the next two nights after the raid walking the road alone, taking cover during the day, until she reached her uncle's home. Her mother's brother had reluctantly traveled into the village to make inquiries, for no one wanted to draw the wrong attention. His face when he returned was pale, and he would not look at her.

Rupert Atwater had disappeared, he told her. Then he pressed a wad of notes into her hand and told her to return to England, for she was endangering them all with her presence. He never met her eye, not even once.

She understood his shame, and his fear. Making her way to the coast to board a ship for London had been difficult and lonely, though the money from her father and uncle lubricated many a reluctant cog. Still, she'd concentrated on the fact that soon she would be safe at the home of her father's friend in Cheapside.

But Mr. Upkirk had not been there.

"Dead," a neighbor had explained when Phillipa had found the house dark and the knocker removed. Somewhat reluctantly, the lady had invited her in and served her tea and the story of Upkirk's demise.

"The poor gentleman ran afoul of a footpad most likely. Decent people aren't safe on the streets anymore. When I was a girl, I went out at my pleasure, with only a footman or two. These days, I hardly dare go out at all, except to Bond Street of course." The woman had sipped her tea, probably contemplating her next adventure in shopping, Phillipa had thought wildly.

"At any rate, they pulled poor Mr. Upkirk from the river a few weeks ago." The woman had frowned. "I don't know what's to happen to the house." She had eyed Phillipa's well-made but battered traveling dress with mild distress. "I do hope someone unsuitable won't be moving in."

Phillipa had been too stunned to do anything but thank the lady and leave. *This cannot be taking place*, had been her only coherent thought. She'd come so far, and had freely spent her funds to bribe her way. She'd not worried at the state of her purse, but had only thought of getting Papa's documents to Mr. Upkirk as Papa had wanted.

She had stood on that unfamiliar street and realized that she had nowhere to go. No home in the world. No friends, no resources, no net of paternal safety. She was entirely alone. Fear and anxiety near consumed her.

She'd once held a secret belief that had she lived a different life, she would have been a different, bolder, more exciting person. It seemed that she was only Phillipa after all.

Survival became her primary concern. She had been forced to push her worry for Papa and her own loneliness to the small dark cellar of her mind, where it only showed itself in those barren moments when she awoke from yet another nightmare.

But there had been no nightmares last night in this fine house. Surely she had broken her trail this time. And now that she no longer had to worry about being hunted, she could concentrate on finding out what happened to Papa. Now she might be in a position to do more for him, if Mr. Cunnington turned out to be on the right side. Phillipa shook off her reverie, deciding to concentrate instead on the present.

Especially when the present included food.

Hesitating outside the breakfast room door, Phillipa tugged nervously at her cravat and looked down at herself to check that she'd not forgotten any masculine accouterments.

Cravat neatly tied—bloody awful thing, but it hid her lack of Adam's apple nicely—waistcoat, boots newly shined, hair slicked back, hands authentically roughened by months without cream.

She was well equipped. At least, as well as she could be without . . . equipment.

Standing as tall as possible and squaring her shoulders, she reminded herself for the thousandth time to speak deeply and sit rudely. Then she opened the door with a nervous smile to greet—

No one. Not a soul. Her shoulders slumped. All that bloody work to get ready. Why, she'd risen two hours early just so the servants wouldn't catch her before she'd bound her breasts and stuffed her trousers!

There was no one here to see. Well, then, she might as well eat. At least she wouldn't have to watch herself every minute for fear of behaving strangely.

And she could eat whatever she wanted. *All* she wanted.

What a lovely thought.

Immensely cheered, Phillipa strode forward to prepare a plate for herself from the steaming trays on the sideboard. Eggs! She hadn't seen an egg in weeks. And ham, wonderful salty flavorful ham. Eagerly, she filled her plate, led from one fragrant dish to another.

"Kippers!" she sighed aloud. "I shall simply die now, for I can only be in heaven." .

"Good Lord, Phillip, it's only food."

Phillipa jerked, her thumb slid into the gravy from the ham, and the plate flew from her grip as if she'd thrown it. All the lovely food spattered the table and several chairs, and there seemed to be a bit on the ceiling as well.

James Cunnington stood next to the table, picking egg from his shirtfront. "At least, it *used* to be food." He peered mournfully about the room. "Did you leave any for me, Phillip? Or did you feed it all to the furniture?"

Dear God. The room was simply showered in food. The elegant furnishings were likely ruined. The ceiling plaster certainly was. Not to mention that her employer's fine linen shirt was worth more than the entire balance of her wages.

Stunned, Phillipa could only stand there and watch her last chance to retrieve her father evaporate along with the smears of liquid on the mahogany tabletop. She'd be thrown out before she even got a bite of those kippers dangling so reproachfully from the chandelier.

She couldn't breathe. She could only watch as Mr. Cunnington rounded the table and raised his hand—

To lift another plate from the stack in the warmer. He handed it to her, using his hands to wrap both sets of her fingers around the china rim. "Let's start you out with two hands, Sir Flip-the-plate," he said. Then he smiled.

Phillipa's throat went dry. He was letting her stay, after what she had done? He was *jesting* about it? She sent a last wild glance around the room, but the devastation truly was as bad as she'd thought.

"But—I—"

"Had better stay out of Denny's way for a few days. He won't say a word, but he'll 'humph' at you until it drives you mad."

"Denny?"

"My manservant. Butler, housekeeper, and all-around nursemaid. You recall, the fellow in the grass-green monkey suit?" He turned to extract his own plate from the warmer. "The livery wasn't my idea. My sister wanted apple red, but I refused. So she went behind my back and ordered apple green." He filled his plate and took it to the table. "I hate bloody apples."

The statement struck Phillipa oddly, jolting her from her stupor. "Everyone likes apples." Good, her voice was only a tiny bit shaky.

She put a few items on her plate but her appetite had gone

clean off. Gingerly she sat across from Mr. Cunnington, who had cleared half the table with one grand and largely useless sweep of a napkin.

"Not everybody. I don't."

"I love apples." She shook out her own napkin. Egg rained down anew. Phillipa looked away quickly. "I cannot get enough of them, frankly."

"Good. You eat them all."

"All?"

"All twelve thousand bushels of them. Red ones, green ones, red and green ones . . ." He shuddered. "Can't abide them, not a one."

"You have twelve thousand bushels of apples? Whyever for?"

He sighed. "Because my sister wanted us to be the largest apple growers in Lancashire and I wasn't there to tell her not to plant endless more acres of orchard." He set his fork down as if he could no longer stomach his food. "It's close to harvest, so right now the place reeks of apples. Soon it will be applesauce, apple cider, apple tarts as far as the eye can see—which is why we are in London instead of Lancashire."

So he was landed and undoubtedly wealthy. Had some of that wealth come as payment for treasonous deeds? "We?"

"Robbie and I. And now you, of course."

Phillipa took a bite of her eggs and savored them slowly. Perhaps she would be able to eat after all. Was it too soon to express more curiosity about her employer? Yesterday she'd gotten the impression that he didn't appreciate too many questions.

Then again, as the one responsible for Robbie's education, it would be in keeping with her role to want to know more. She cleared her throat and tried to deepen her voice a bit. "If I may ask, sir, where is Robbie's mother?"

Mr. Cunnington shrugged and forked another bite of ham to his mouth. "Don't know," he said when he swallowed, then he tucked into his eggs with enthusiasm. His square jaw worked quickly and his muscular brown throat contracted, drawing Phillipa's attention to the fact that his ruined shirt was unbuttoned halfway down his chest and she could see glimpses of the springy brown pelt on his chest.

Oh, yes, she remembered that chest . . .

Phillipa looked away, then forced herself to look back. Perhaps this was how men behaved when there were no ladies present to embarrass them. Fascinated by the concept, she wondered what else these mysterious creatures got up to when there were no women around.

"He's an orphan, as far as we know," her employer continued. "He says he has no parents, and by his mistreatment before he came to us, I don't doubt his story. No one has ever stepped up to claim him." Mr. Cunnington grinned fiercely. "Not that they could. Robbie has friends now."

Phillipa blinked but did not comment. There was something strange about this man, with his amiable exterior and steely inner glint. "Do you know his precise age?"

Mr. Cunnington shook his head as he chewed and swallowed. "Even Robbie doesn't know. Sometimes he claims twelve years but I think it is closer to nine. It's difficult to tell. He can be a canny little scamp, a true cynic of the streets—then suddenly be so lost . . ."

His voice trailed off, then he shrugged and cleared his throat as if uncomfortable with his own notion.

Tossing his napkin alongside his empty plate, he stood. "Eat up, Sir Flip. You'll need your strength today, I think." He hesitated. "Only don't . . . don't expect too much from Robbie at first, will you? The poor little bloke's had a hell of a time."

Phillipa only nodded at her employer, then swallowed as Mr. Cunnington turned away. She opened her mouth to assure him of her patience—and forgot to close it. Without his coat, Mr. Cunnington's broad figure was neatly outlined in his soft shirt and snug trousers. And good gracious, what trousers!

Directly at her eye level, his rear was muscled and sculpted, flexing in a most fascinating way as he strode to the door. What a finely made creature he was!

He turned. Phillipa jerked her gaze up before she found

herself eyeing the front of his trousers from the same altitude. She'd apparently been a bit too late, for Mr. Cunnington gazed at her oddly for a moment, then shook his head. "If there's anything you need to purchase for the schoolroom, simply charge it to me."

With those words he was gone, thankfully before Phillipa's blush hit full glow. As the door swung shut, she pressed her palms to her face, trying to check the blood in her cheeks. It was such a burden being a redhead.

She suspected that her lifelong curse of coloring easily was about to be put to the test. Living here would put the blush to any sensible woman. She felt her cheeks cool under her palms. Good.

Now if she could only curb her straying gaze . . .

Chapter Five

Phillipa was ready to teach the world after two good meals from the Cunnington kitchens. Unfortunately, her school-room was not nearly as well prepared as she was.

In truth, the chamber was little more than an old nursery with bookshelves. The only furnishings were two child-sized chairs that had seen better days. There were a number of tall windows to let in good light and the place had been well dusted, but that was about all she could say for it.

Where were the books, the slates, the primers? For that matter, where were pen nibs and ink?

She was standing in the middle of the rather useless space, turning slowly as she examined every inch. Her hopes of finding anything with which to teach her student were lost when Robbie bounded in.

"What's to do, then?" His gaze was wary, but expectant. She suspected that he was interested in learning in spite of his facade of indifference.

"I must go to the study for a moment to find something for you to read from—"

"Won't do no good."

She stopped. "Are you saying you refuse to read for me?"

He shrugged. His head was bent and his gaze fixed on the

toe of his shoe as it worried the rug. "Not sayin' so, not sayin' no."

Wonderful. Her first student was an uncooperative—

Wait a moment. She sat on one of the small chairs, careful to keep her knees wide in a masculine fashion. "Are you trying to tell me that you cannot read?"

Her eyes were level with his, but he shifted his gaze away again. "Readin's for ponces."

She sat up, thinking. "Wellington can read. Are you calling our own leader a ponce?"

"What? You say that again and you'll take your lickin', lady or no!"

"So, you do know my secret."

"You got no gullet," Robbie said, pointing to her throat. "Every bloke's got a gullet."

Ah. No Adam's apple. Phillipa self-consciously twitched her cravat higher with one hand. Blasted noose. Give her a well-made corset any day. "I suppose you'd like to know why I'm dressed so."

Robbie nodded, his arms folded and his eyes narrowed.

How to put it in terms he would understand, without giving too much away? "There is a man—a very powerful man—who I am hiding from."

Robbie looked skeptical. "More powerful than James?"

Although Mr. Cunnington undoubtedly outclassed Napoleon in physical power—heavens, those shoulders!— Phillipa didn't hesitate. "Yes, I fear so. Will you help me stay hidden, just for a while?"

Robbie considered her for a moment, then nodded. "But you're going to need a bit of schooling yourself," he said. He pointed at her chair. "Blokes don't sit like that."

Phillipa looked down at herself to see that while she'd been speaking, her knees had come together and her feet had slipped sideways, offering a demure glimpse of her booted ankles from beneath her slightly tatty trousers. If a gentleman were to see her now, he'd think her decidedly odd. "Quite right. I thank you for pointing that out." She shifted

back, although prying her knees apart went against a lifetime of habit. "How's that?"

Robbie tilted his head. "Not bad. Now you need to
scratch."

She blinked. "I will not!"

"You want to learn this or not?"

"But—but gentlemen don't scratch! Only common—"
She halted as she remembered that Robbie was as common
as they came.

He scratched his nose. "You might be right about that.
Never did see James scratching . . ."

"So I needn't scratch?"

"Guess not. Spitting now . . ."

"*No*. I won't do it."

He considered her. "Not much, but you'd best do it once,
just to be sure you can."

"I'm sure I'll manage, should the need arise." Never.
Ever.

"Well, best keep it in mind. It does come up."

"Well, then, now that you know my secret, it's only fair if
I know one of yours, isn't it?" She leaned closer to the boy
and whispered, "If you can't read, shake your head."

She waited. The dust motes danced in the moments that
stretched between her and the boy standing before her. Finally, his tousled head shook slowly from left to right.

"All right then. Your secret will not leave this room. Will
mine?"

His head came up and he gave her a calculating look.
"You're right clever for a bird."

"Thank you." She rested her elbows on her knees once
more and tapped her chin, thinking. "If you cannot read,
then there is no point in starting with books. This afternoon
I shall find you a slate. We'll begin your letters in the morning. Until then, what would you like to do?"

He was up in a flash and at the door.

"Hold on there, Master Robert! I didn't say you were free
to go."

His shoulders sagged and he came back to stand before her with a sigh. "Almost bloody made it too," he mourned.

She shook her head. It wouldn't do to laugh at his horrid language, for it would only encourage him. That gave her an idea.

"Perhaps for this first day, we shall practice some common phrases that a young gentleman needs during the course of his day."

His eyes narrowed and his little jaw went mulish. "Like what d'you mean?"

"Why don't we begin with 'Good morning, Mr. Walters. It seems we are in for fine weather today. I trust you slept well?' "

Robbie's nose twitched and he scrubbed it with one fairly clean wrist. "Good mornin' Mr. Walters . . . It seems we're in . . . we're for . . . we're for fine . . ." Robbie went beet red in the face and burst forth with a shocking phrase that no child of his years should know.

She was taken aback, not so much by the words, but by the fact that he knew them. What had his short life been like that he was already so lost to innocence?

She hid her shock and only gave him a measuring look. "Not bad," she said grudgingly. "A bit limited in scope, but not bad."

"What d'you mean, *limited*?"

"Gutter speech is only vulgar. A truly accomplished curser should know more than simple crudity."

"You're funnin' me, ain't you? You don't curse. You're a lady!"

"Yes, but I am an educated lady. Therefore, I am able to curse a blue streak and never let on."

"Huh. 'D like to see that one."

She leaned back and cut loose with a string of words that would have her stoned in any respectable Russian village. As the syllables rolled from her tongue, Robbie's eyes widened and his lips formed an O of helpless admiration. When she was finished, he gulped once.

"Cor. That were *beau'iful*." He sighed deeply, obviously

moved by her virtuosity. Then he stuck a finger in his ear and twisted it contemplatively. "Would you teach me a bit o' that?"

"If you wish. What do you say to a trade? One phrase of perfectly obscene Russian for one phrase of perfectly pronounced King's English?"

He pondered that for a moment, but apparently couldn't deny that it was to his profit. He nodded once, then spit on his palm and held it out. "'S deal."

Oh, no. So soon? Phillipa firmly suppressed a shudder and even managed a droplet of saliva for her own palm. She gave Robbie's a good hard shake. "Deal." It was worth it to see the respect dawning in his wary eyes.

She could always wash her hand later.

With a great deal of soap.

The afternoon's shopping expedition began well enough. When Phillipa took Robbie to a bookseller on Portobello Road in search of a slate and a hornbook, Robbie seemed awed by the sheer number of books that stood on shelves all the way to the high ceiling.

The owner had a very nice globe on his own desk that he was persuaded to part with, and she was directed to a stationers' where she bought paper and pencils and ink. If nothing else, the schoolroom would look useful, even if she hadn't a clue what she was doing.

The shadows were beginning to slant as they made their laden way back toward the house. Robbie was starting to lag, and quite frankly, to whine. He'd been a stoic little lout for most of the day, but now he was hungry. So was she, and she struggled for patience against the weight of her parcels and the emptiness in her stomach.

If she were herself in her old life, she'd have had a footman with her to keep her safe and to carry her shopping. Even to carry Robbie if necessary. Even at that, every fellow she met would likely attempt to assist her.

As it was, she was expected to not only manage her own

burdens, but to open doors for every lady who so much as twitched her skirt in Phillipa's direction. It seemed the masculine prerogatives weren't entirely enjoyable.

"I want my tea." Robbie's voice had taken on the unpleasant quality of rusting metal hinges.

"I want your tea too," Phillipa snapped. "So keep up, Robbie, or I'll gobble it all before you make it home."

She trudged on, her feet slipping in her too-large boots until she was sure the flesh of her heels was bubbled with blisters. She ought to hail a cabbie again, but found herself unable to part with the penny fare. There was no way to know how long her current prosperity would last.

They passed the entrance to a street at a right angle to the one they were on. It looked as though this street were just awakening when all the others were going to rest for the day.

Restaurants, she thought, as the smell of cooking food wafted her way and almost made her knees buckle. There were no gilded windows or signs that she could see. Private clubs, then, which only made the smells the more tempting for being forbidden.

It was too much for her. Hiking her parcels higher, she turned to speak over her shoulder. "Master Robbie, perhaps we should secure a hired carriage for the rest of our—"

Robbie was nowhere to be seen. Not behind her, not before her, not resting on the curb. Even burdened as she was, her panic spurred her to a run. She dashed back the way they had come for several blocks.

There was no sign of him. She asked stranger after stranger, but no one had seen a small boy carrying a very large globe. She returned to the crossing where she'd lost him, then hesitated. She was positive that he hadn't gone before her.

The scent of beef and gravy snared her attention. Robbie was as hungry as herself. Could he have possibly thought that anyone from one of these exclusive clubs would feed a slightly grimy boy of ten?

She trotted the length of the street calling his name. There was no sign of his sturdy little figure toting the globe.

"He's a smart lad," she told herself, though true panic

was welling up. She should never have snapped at him so. Oh, how could she have thought she could do this when she knew nothing of children? She was a failure as a tutor already and she'd been on the job for less than a day.

"He's been around London longer than you have," she muttered to herself. Keeping her gaze low and shooting glances into every alleyway and under every cart, she turned and made her way down the street once more.

She even ducked down to see into a stack of empty crates in the side alley of one of the establishments. Nothing. She stood, turning—

The impact of a large male body knocked her flat.

Papers slipped from their wrapping and fluttered down onto the sooty cobbles and her precious slate shattered on the stones.

It was too much. "Bloody Roman cat-gutting *hell*!" She bounced to her feet, ready to take her worry and fear out on the first person she saw.

Before her stood James Cunnington, charmingly disheveled from their impact and staring at her with lips pursed. He'd come up behind her silently once more.

This habit of his was beginning to wear a bit thin.

"I hope you don't let Robbie hear you talking like that, Phillip."

"Oh! No—no, of course not." Not a lie. She only cursed in Russian for Robbie. "Robbie! He's gone! I've looked everywhere, but there's not a trace—"

"He's fine. He just stopped at my club for a bite to eat. He's a great favorite of the cook there. I think Kurt still hopes to win him from me entirely, but Robbie's a lad who likes to keep his options open."

That made no sense to her whatever. Still, she was so relieved she didn't much care. A last piece of paper fluttered down to her feet. She bent to retrieve her parcels and received a resounding swat on her backside.

"Ow!" She whirled and glared at her assailant.

James rolled his eyes. "Don't be such a girl, Flip. Your arse is dirty."

"Oh. Right." Her arse was on fire, that's what it was. What big hands he had! The tingle she felt was entirely because of the blow, of course. What else could it be from?

James helped her gather the rest of her supplies into an untidy pile in her arms. Of course, he didn't offer to carry it for her, she grumbled to herself as she followed him. Why should he? After all, she was only a *girl* when she reacted to a clout.

She followed James to a set of unobtrusive double doors set into a rather Gothic façade. "This is where our miscreant fled to." He nodded at the stout young doorman and entered the club.

She followed, trying not to betray her wide-eyed curiosity. Women were never allowed into the hallowed halls of masculine retreats like this!

She was a tad disappointed to find that the place resembled nothing more than a rather tawdry billiards room. There was a small stage at one end of the room but the curtains were closed.

There were no customers as yet, but a few boys moved through the room, readying it for the night. The smell of something wondrous and decadent wafted from a pair of swinging doors in the back wall. Phillipa's stomach made its approval evident.

"Sorry." She grimaced. "We missed our tea."

"Of course you're hungry." James laughed. "You're still growing yourself."

She stared at him in surprise. "Growing?"

He held up his hands as if to fend off a glare. "Sorry, sorry, my mistake. You're a man, through and through. You just forgot to let your beard in on the secret."

She slapped a hand to her face. She hadn't thought about the fact that by this time of day even the most clean-shaven of men had a shadowy growth in evidence.

He thought her a boy, too young to shave . . .

James clapped her on the back. "Don't be so sensitive. You'll be as hairy as Kurt someday, mark my words."

As she was introduced to Kurt a moment later, Phillipa had

time to wonder about that statement. She'd never in her life seen anyone as hairy as Kurt. Or as large. Or as frightening.

Yet the kitchen felt warm and familiar, with the herbs hanging from the beams and the large pots bubbling with savory mysteries. She was reminded of when her mother had been well enough to indulge her love of cooking—warm memories indeed. So, when the intimidating Kurt handed her a plate full of beef and leeks that slopped to the brim with gravy, Phillipa promptly decided that he was her favorite person on earth.

She carried her plate of aromatic treasure to the heavy worktable that currently held Robbie and a mostly empty plate of his own. She flicked him across the top of his skull with her fingertips as she sat on the bench beside him. "Scared me to death, you know."

He shrugged apologetically but didn't answer due to the fact that his mouth was comically stuffed. Then he made a manful effort to swallow and leaned close. "Birds aren't allowed, you see," he whispered. "'S the rules."

"Oh, of course. And you always follow the rules, do you?"

He smirked. She tilted her head at him. It wouldn't do for him to discover how he amused her sometimes. Or how he exhausted her. "Run off on me again and I'll teach you to sew."

His eyes widened, but he put on a show of bravado. "Don't scare me. Tailors sew. Tailoring's good work."

She smiled mean. "I'm talking about embroidery, me lad. Needlework. *Doilies*."

He finally quailed. "I won't run again."

"Your word as a gentleman?"

He looked at her sideways, as if he suspected mockery. Poor little in-between Robbie. Not sure which world he would belong to in the end. She raised a brow. "I'm waiting."

"All right, then. My word as a gentleman," he grumbled.

She nodded her satisfaction. "That's all I ask." She tucked into her food, grateful yet again for her masculine disguise. Men were allowed to truly enjoy their food, not simply to pick daintily at it as if too sensitive for such common fare.

She decided that—carrying one's own parcels aside—men had all the goods.

Chapter Six

James snagged a roll for himself and left his two lads to their meal. He hadn't meant to spend so much time at the club when he had an important appointment with a certain lady. Still, since he was here . . .

Passing through the public part of the club, he entered the hidden doorway and made his way to the code room.

"Tell me you've got something for me."

Fisher shrugged woefully. "I'm trying, James, but you know I get new documents every day from France. With only one code-breaker left—" The man paled. "Sorry. I didn't mean . . ."

James held up one hand. "Don't apologize. Please don't."

"It's just that I'm not even supposed to be doing this. I was still apprenticing when Upkirk died. And until Weatherby comes back, if he ever recovers . . ." Fisher shrugged again. "What about on your end? Has anyone ever appeared at the Post Office to pick them up?"

James grimaced. "We don't have a great deal to go on. They are addressed to 'Mr. Amor, General Delivery, London.' Yet all your copies sit there still."

Fisher sniffed. "Mr. Amor."

James nodded. Considering the torrid contents of each and every letter, the pun had long ago lost any humor for them.

"Thank you, Fish." James had that one last unpleasant errand to run, then it would be time to get Phillip and Robbie home. Funny that going home didn't seem like so much of a chore today.

"You're welcome," Fisher called out as James left. "And don't call me Fish."

James didn't smile this time. He never felt like smiling when he was on his way to see Lady Winchell.

When Robbie and Phillipa had finished their enormous meal, Kurt picked up their plates with an approving grunt at the pristine condition of the thick china.

Phillipa fought back a belch and smiled up at the scarred giant. He seemed slightly familiar to her suddenly. Yet surely she would clearly remember such a face. Then again, she had seen so many people, in so many places. Sometimes the images in her memory tended to blur. In any event, he was a marvelous cook. "That was a lovely roast. It tasted just like my mother's. Did you use a snippet of dill in the gravy?"

Kurt stared down at her for a long moment, then blinked and nodded shortly. Phillipa made a mental note—apparently men did not discuss recipes.

Robbie grabbed her hand and pulled her to the door of the kitchen. "C'mon, I want to show you the club."

A rumble came from Kurt in the far end of the kitchen. Robbie looked back at him. "I know, sir."

Phillipa only stared from one to the other. That had been speech? She'd thought it was the big man's stomach.

She was as curious about the club as Robbie was eager to show it to her. To think, she was a woman in a gentleman's club!

The largest room seemed to be the front gaming room, with its gleaming woodwork and the green-felted playing tables. At the far end of the L-shaped room was a raised dais, curtained like a stage in red velvet. Robbie saw her interest.

"There's entertainment," he said importantly. "Like dancers with snakes and such."

"Goodness," Phillipa muttered. "How exotic." She wagered the dancer wouldn't be wearing much more than the snake would. "I certainly hope you're not speaking from personal experience."

While what she saw—the stage, the gaming tables, the smoking room which apparently doubled as a drinking room to judge by the liquor bottles lining one mirrored wall—did not seem too terribly depraved, neither did the club seem entirely respectable somehow.

She'd always pictured gentlemen's clubs being staid places where men read the newssheet and discussed politics in an atmosphere of tobacco smoke and male camaraderie. James's club seemed a bit more . . . wicked.

"Keep a close watch on James Cunnington."

Mr. Cunnington continued to show new facets daily.

Phillipa saw a hall leading back into the building. "What is down there?"

Robbie shrugged and toyed with a cork he'd found in the smoking room. "Nothin' much. Manager's office, storerooms—wait, don't go down there!"

Phillipa was already striding down the hall. Most terraced buildings were much deeper than they were wide. This one seemed very nearly square. She was struck by a powerful certainty that there was more to the Liar's Club than met the eye.

The hallway ended with access only to two doors. One was nicely carved and oiled. The office. The other was plainer, blending into the wood-paneled walls. The storeroom.

She put a hand to the latch of the storeroom. It moved easily. Poking her head within, she was greeted by standing ranks of broom, swab mop, pail and brush. There were shelves of folded linen, tablecloths, and such. There were jars of this and bins of that, mostly items for cleaning and maintaining furniture and floor.

Nothing odd at all. Phillipa backed from the room and closed the storeroom carefully, not letting the latch make a sound. Then she turned—

To find herself facing an older man with grizzled hair and a sincerely ugly waistcoat, watching her from the doorway of the office. She froze, her mouth half open to explain herself, but she couldn't think of a bloody thing to say.

The man folded his arms and raised a salt-and-pepper eyebrow. "Now why do you suppose a bloke—who isn't even a member of this very private club, mind you—why do you suppose he would be pokin' his nose into the broom closet?"

Robbie came up. "'E's my tutor, Mr. Jackham. 'Is name is Phillip Walters."

"*His* name, Robbie. Mind the *h*," Phillipa muttered automatically. Another reminder. Must teach Robbie the proper method of performing introductions.

Her thoughts swirled with such unimportant details while the man before her continued to gaze at her in unbroken suspicion. She'd been caught in the very act of snooping. What could she do, claim a broom fixation?

"So you work for James Cunnington, do you?" Jackham looked her up and down with eyes that she feared might see too much. "Had some hard times, have you? Lookin' for a kind master to take care of you?"

He moved closer to Phillipa, until she had to look up into his colorless eyes. "James Cunnington is the best man I know. The best man you'll ever know, I don't doubt. A man with friends, if you take my meaning."

He leaned close, putting his mouth close to Phillipa's ear. "There's something wrong about you. I can't place it, but I know I don't like you one bit."

Jackham stepped back and smiled, but it didn't reach his eyes. "Now, Robbie, why don't you take your new tutor up front where he belongs? There's nothing back here but the mops and my accounts."

Phillipa escaped gladly, Robbie on her heels. She felt cold and a little sick, with her stomach sloshing her meal about. But why was she so alarmed? A man who had every right to scold her for snooping had said he didn't like her. There was nothing so frightening in that.

"Who was that man?" she asked Robbie.

"Jackham runs the place, mostly. He was a great thief once, the best."

Taken aback, Phillipa added that item to her stock of information. James Cunnington, consorting with thieves. She could learn a lot from hanging about this club.

Still, she was happy when Robbie was ready to leave. There was something very strange about this club. As they walked from the front door, Phillipa saw a small alleyway leading down the side. Impulsively, she turned into it.

The way led to the rear of the building and around the back, where it narrowed until Phillipa could almost stretch out her arms to touch the high brick walls. It was a very long alley—much longer than one would have thought upon seeing the interior of the club.

Unless one had only seen *half* of the interior of the club.

Chapter Seven

As James approached the room of the old palace that served as a cell for Lady Lavinia Winchell, he saw the Prime Minister himself departing from the other end of the hall. "My lord!" he called, and rushed to catch up to Lord Liverpool.

The small spare man was accompanied by two others, one a guard, the other his secretary. As James caught up with the three, he saw Lord Liverpool raise a disapproving brow.

"Your dignity, man," his lordship said with mild reproof, except that reproof from the most powerful man in England was never mild.

James halted his headlong rush, but his mind was too filled with questions to care for his dignity. "My lord, have you been to see Lady Winchell?"

Liverpool pursed his lips and twitched a brow toward the men accompanying him. Then he stepped to one side, indicating that James should attend him. When he spoke, his voice was low. "Since you seem so eager for the knowledge, yes, I have just come from a talk with her ladyship."

"Did she say anything? Did you learn anything new?"

Liverpool waited, merely gazing at James. Catching himself, James bobbed his head. "I beg your pardon, my lord. I wish only to know if she has given any evidence that may be used to convict her."

Liverpool shook his head, a short, brisk movement. "She would hardly do that, I fear. No, she is too mindful of her danger. She still maintains that she had no intention of shooting me and that she was only reacting to your rejection of her."

James's shoulder burned where he had taken the bullet meant for this great man. His heart burned where he kept the memories of the men that Lavinia had killed. "We must break her, my lord! She is a traitor and a cold-blooded killer!"

"So you say, and so I believe, but if a beautiful woman of rank goes before judge and jury, do you think they will not be swayed by tears and pretty pleas? As long as we have no evidence and no real witnesses, we have no case but that of adultery against her husband, and he will not pursue such charges. Lord Winchell is once again besotted with his young and lovely wife."

"Not to mention his public reputation," James said bitterly. "I can find evidence. I know it. Our code-breaker is even now combing Lady Winchell's outgoing and incoming post for clues."

Liverpool regarded him coolly. "You have had many weeks to present your case, Cunnington. I cannot continue to ignore Lord Winchell's appeals to release his wife. More lords of Parliament are voicing their disapproval as well."

Liverpool's secretary made a reminding noise. Liverpool nodded to the man, then turned back to James. "Without concrete evidence or witnesses, I cannot continue to hold her."

The thought of Lavinia returning unscathed to her life of privilege and wanton pursuits made James feel ill. "But what of my sister's testimony? Lavinia confessed all in her presence!"

"Due to her connection with the Liar's Club, Lady Raines can no more afford scrutiny than you yourself, Cunnington. Your identity has been saved by Lady Winchell's very refusal to admit to the charges. She cannot expose you without revealing her own treason. You know quite well that the secrecy of the Liar's Club takes precedence over punishing the machinations of one woman."

"*Machinations?* Our men died, sir!"

"Indeed. As they would have gladly done rather than reveal the club to the world, would they not?" Liverpool fixed James with a cool gaze which reminded him that the Prime Minister would not hesitate to sacrifice him. Liverpool's own protégé Nathaniel Stonewell, Lord Reardon, had been thrown to the wolves of public disgrace in order to conceal a royal indiscretion, despite the man's deep and abiding loyalty—or perhaps because of it. After all, Nathaniel Stonewell was a member of the Royal Four, a secret and exclusive cadre of lords who served as advisors and shapers of the monarchy. The Four also occasionally acted as the hand that directed the weapon that was the Liar's Club—which only served to prove that Lord Liverpool would quite readily sacrifice a minor player such as James Cunnington should the need arise.

As if he needed such a reminder.

Before he could speak, Liverpool went on. "I therefore must call a halt to the investigation." He held up one hand against James's immediate protests. "I give you ten days, Cunnington. Find me evidence. Find me a witness." For the first time a trace of warmth entered Liverpool's gaze.

"I know I owe you my life, Cunnington. So I give you this time, and I give you a bit of advice. Vengeance is unproductive. It reeks of looking backward. One must move ever forward, or one will mire in the past."

James watched the Prime Minister go back to his staff. Helpless rage rushed through him.

Ten days. He turned to Lavinia's door, his purpose renewed.

Lavinia Winchell's cell was the most luxurious one James had ever seen, all supplied by the smitten Lord Winchell. Brocaded hangings protected the massive bedstead from any possible draft, and a fire roared in the spotless fireplace. A pretty young chambermaid assigned by royal order answered Lavinia's every need, and the room was littered with books, embroidery, and other ladylike ways to occupy one's time.

It seemed no lord in the entire government wanted to take responsibility for mistreating a lady—much less hanging one—not even the Prince Regent himself.

James could hardly blame any of them, for hadn't he sold his own soul for Lavinia's charms once upon a time?

Lavinia herself looked much the same as ever. When one thought of blond perfection, one thought of Lavinia. Graceful and willowy, she now had an imprisonment pallor that only added to her angelic fragility.

"James! My love, you've come to me once more!" She leapt prettily to her feet and ran forward as if to embrace him. James didn't move, nor did he take his hard gaze from the wide blue eyes that first appealed, then grew attractively wet with unshed tears.

"You've not forgiven me after all." Lavinia's shoulders slumped, but the posture only called attention to her gracefully bowed neck.

She was so beautiful that she had once made James's male instincts vibrate like a plucked harp string. It was too bad Lady Winchell's perfect body held the blackened soul of a venomous snake.

"Enough theatrics, Vinnie." James walked past her to seat himself in the chair by the fire, ignoring her penitent pose and all good manners in order to warm his chilled soul at the coals.

"Save your lies for someone who gives a damn, Vinnie. I'm not interested in the story of mad passion you've concocted for the court. We both know that bullet was aimed at the Prime Minister, not me. It is only through the intervention of my sister that I was able to get there in time to take it for him."

"Agatha!" For a split second, Lavinia's features twisted into a grimace of pure hatred. Then she covered her face with her hands and made pitiful weeping sounds. "Your sister hates me because she feared I'd take you away from her!"

The avidly curious maid finally saw fit to leave the room. Lavinia's sniffling stopped abruptly. She leaned back onto her chaise, laughing.

"The silly twit's gone to report to that fat idiot you call your prince. We have a few moments' privacy, if you'd like to take your frustrations out on my body." She inspected her nails. "I've nothing better to do."

James couldn't imagine touching her. Why would she think he'd want to? Yet Lavinia could easily manipulate the situation to present James as the villain in this piece for trespassing upon Lord Winchell's marital property as he had. "So you could cry rape? The poor misled wife, now the target of the evil seducer's revenge?"

Irritation crossed her expression, then she shrugged. "I simply thought you'd like to make love once more, the way we used to."

"We had sex, Lavinia. Hot, sinful, sweaty sex. That is, until you had me kidnapped and tortured. No more sex then. Not that I would have been very enthusiastic, what with being drugged and beaten on a daily basis."

She glanced away as if bored. "I had nothing to do with that."

He laughed. "No, of course not. You simply happened to stumble across me tied in that stinking ship once a week to protest your love."

"You never saw me there." Her voice was mocking and cold. "You testified yourself that you have no memory of seeing my face."

Frustration ground against fury in James's stomach. Drugged as he had been, most of his capture had been spent in a hallucinatory state. There had been strange lights and odd sounds and, of course, regular visitations from his own personal viper from hell.

"No, I do not remember your face. Only your voice railing at me again and again, pushing me always for names and information. Your voice and perhaps a glimpse of your cold and vicious soul."

She snorted. "So spiritual, James. You were a tad more

earthy back when you used to beg me to use my mouth on you."

She turned and moved sinuously toward him. The cool calculation was gone and a mask of lust had taken its place. James felt the impact of her sexuality as if through a shield. Memories washed through his mind to make his stomach clench.

When she reached a hand to stroke his chest, he caught her wrist in a hard grasp.

"Don't," he said coldly. "I just put on a clean shirt."

The insult struck her, finally breaking through her many layers of masks to reveal her true face. She snarled at him with acid in her blue eyes and raised her other hand to claw his face.

James pushed her away with ease then. She stumbled and caught herself on the chair back. Her expression was one of pure loathing and her beauty was quite gone.

Lavinia's fingers tightened on the upholstered chair until James heard threads pop beneath her nails. "You'll be back," she hissed. "You cannot stay away from me and you know it. I am everything you want in a woman. I am *everything*."

James managed not to shudder until he was on the far side of the guarded door.

The bloody hell of it was that Lavinia was quite right. He could not stay away from her. He needed her, but not precisely in the way she thought.

She alone held the truth behind his own betrayal of the Liars. She alone could help him absolve his guilt and pain. Until he could prove her guilt and send her to the gallows like the murderer she was, he would continue to go back to her.

Stopping for a moment in the empty hallway, he took a deep breath and ran a hand through his hair. Relaxing his shoulders by force of will, he felt the shield that he'd raised against her come down brick by brick.

He could still smell her scent on his palm where he'd grasped her wrist. Once, that soft musky fragrance had driven him wild. She'd known it well—had applied it in places most women wouldn't think of scenting.

He had not been able to get enough of her wild, wicked perfumed body. Often, he'd gone home exhausted and weak-kneed from hours in her bed, only to catch a whiff of her on his clothes and harden instantly once more.

Now the residual echoes of that lust made him feel sick. James swallowed back his revulsion, fully aware that as much as his disgust was directed at Lavinia, thrice that amount was directed at his own male susceptibility.

It was time to go home.

That evening, Phillipa found herself putting Robbie to bed, although she was fairly sure it wasn't a tutor's job to do so. Yet if not her, then who?

Certainly not Mr. Cunnington.

"He's goin' out again." Robbie's face was entirely expressionless. The very portrait of accustomed loneliness. "He's always goin' out."

Phillipa didn't know what to say. Robbie's guardian seemed fond enough of the boy, although she hadn't been about long enough to form an opinion on the subject.

Time for a change of subject. "Well you're not going out anytime soon, Master Robert," she said, shaking her finger at him. "Not after that jaunt you went on today."

His little face paled. "You goin' to cane me, then?"

Cane him? For dropping in on Mr. Cunnington's club for his tea? Good lord, where had this child been?

Still, she couldn't let him think he could perform that sort of exploit every day. Propping both fists on her hips, she looked down at him disapprovingly.

"You, me lad, are about to experience the patented Walters tickle revenge." She made her fingers into claws in the air.

Robbie jumped up to run, a giggle already bubbling through his mock fear. Phillipa snapped him up just before he made it to the door. He must not have been trying very hard, for he'd surely learned more speed than that in his years on the streets.

She swung him yelping into the air and brought him

down onto the rug before the fire, her fingers raking his bony little sides.

Robbie screeched, his rusty laughter another reminder to Phillipa of his short hard life before she'd met him. She bent to her task with all the more vigor at that thought. Robbie had missed most of his childhood, but this she could give him.

Grinning, she almost let him catch a breath before she began anew. "Robbie the Rebel, are you? Robbie the Great Know-it-all, are you? You look more like Robbie Twitter-on-the-rug, if you ask me!"

Time to go in for the kill. The volume of Robbie's screeches rose to full riot level. She heard another sound beyond it, but she didn't identify it as the thumping of running feet in the hall until the door of the schoolroom crashed open.

"What the bloody hell are you doing to him?"

Before Phillipa could turn around, she was lifted by the scruff of her neck and dragged from Robbie.

She found herself dangling from James Cunnington's grip, gagging on her cravat—which was apparently auditioning for the role as her brand-new Adam's apple.

Then her gaze sharpened on James and her eyes bulged further. It was probably a good thing she couldn't speak, for the man was more than a little naked. In fact, he was bare but for a towel around his neck and a pair of short drawers that clung to his bath-damp skin like paint.

He was revealed to her eyes in all his powerful beauty. His wide brawny chest looked like a wall of muscle from this angle, marred only by a star-shaped scar on his shoulder that appeared fairly recent. Her gaze traveled down, over his rippled belly, to the dark trail of hair that led the eye below the sagging waist of his drawers.

Drawers which did nothing to hide the muscular thighs framing what could only be *It*.

Great Greek gods. The faint stirrings of curiosity and attraction that she'd felt over the last two days had apparently been only warnings. Suddenly, she was swept by such a tide of arousal that her mouth went dry and her toes clenched within her boots.

She desired him. The realization sent fresh strength into her struggles.

She wanted him, when she couldn't bear to speak her own name in solitude for fear of discovery. When she couldn't allow her body so much as a moment of freedom from its bindings and trappings.

With more strength than she'd known she had, Phillipa twisted herself from James's grip and staggered out of his reach.

"Phil were just ticklin' me, Jamie." Robbie grinned. "Just like any lad."

James laughed, obviously realizing his mistake, and gave her an apologetic grin. Phillipa forced a sickly chuckle to hide her appalling new awareness.

She lusted for a man who thought she was a man.

What a fix.

Chapter Eight

After Mr. Cunnington—*James*—had laughingly apologized and had left to finish dressing his rather astonishing body, it took Phillipa quite a while to calm a giddy Robbie.

"Did ye see him?" Robbie asked again and again in an awed tone. "Came runnin' in here to rescue *me*! Did ye see him?"

"Yes, I saw him," she answered with a smile each time. Indeed, she had seen a great deal of Mr. James Cunnington of the hewn thighs and the ridged midriff. "Most impressive."

Most impressive indeed.

She was still having a bit of trouble catching her own breath. Not only was Mr. Cunnington exceedingly attractive, she found herself charmed by his defense of Robbie. Was there anything as appealing in a strong man as the habit of protecting those weaker than himself?

Add to that the ability to laugh at his own mistake . . . now that was charming indeed.

She ought to discuss with him what she'd learned today. Although she had promised Robbie not to reveal the depth of his illiteracy, she doubted that Mr. Cunnington was ignorant of it. After all, he'd said as much himself.

Denny was in the hallway when Phillipa left Robbie's

room. With a series of offended "humphs" he directed her to find Mr. Cunnington in the front parlor downstairs.

Reminded of Mr. Cunnington's warning about Denny, Phillipa apologized for the mess in the breakfast room and earned herself a slightly mollified nod. And another "humph."

The door to the front parlor stood slightly open. Phillipa was about to knock lightly when she heard Mr. Cunnington speaking to someone within.

"Are you sure we're not being too obvious, arriving in the same carriage?"

Phillipa held still, only turning her head to hear a little better.

A voice answered Mr. Cunnington, one deeper and more measured. "It doesn't pay to be too obviously reclusive either, I've found. You saved Lord Liverpool's life practically at my feet that day. I doubt anyone will think twice about my accompanying you."

Phillipa's eyes widened. Lord Liverpool, the Prime Minister of England? How utterly *fascinating*. So did that mean Mr. Cunnington was on the side of good?

His voice came again. "Liverpool has nothing to thank me for. Neither does the Prince Regent."

Hmm. Perhaps not. Her curiosity burned hot and she cursed herself fluently in an obscure Arabic tongue even as she stepped a bit closer to the crack in the door. She could almost hear Papa now. "Ever the curious cat," he'd say. "Best look out for your tail."

"And everyone knows I'm simply his lordship's shadow," chimed in another, younger voice. Not James, but with a teasing note in it like James's voice sometimes had. "The faithful little heir, trotting about behind him with my nose up—"

"Spare us all that particular image, Collis, I beg of you," interrupted the voice that must be "his lordship." "And behave tonight. I'd rather not have to drag you from some sotted wife's décolletage at the end of the evening."

"It's not my fault," protested the young man, Collis. "They do so enjoy comforting the wounded soldier."

"I shall wound you anew if you start another brawl with a jealous courtier. Prince George finds it amusing at the moment, but I shouldn't press him if I were you."

"Ah, but Prinny understands passion. Just last week he was telling me a tale about Lady Br—"

Out of sheer panic, Phillipa's hand raised itself and tapped on the door. She would not eavesdrop about a private conversation held with the *Prince*! That was probably treasonous under some law or another.

At Mr. Cunnington's invitation she cleared her throat and stepped into the room, then halted as she took in the array of finely attired masculinity before her.

Oh, *Lord.*

Tall, taller, and tallest.

What a good thing she wasn't actually male, for she'd likely take a leap into the Thames from a case of sheer inadequacy . . .

The two men standing with James were rather similar to each other, obviously related. Brothers? Cousins, perhaps. They were dressed in perfectly fitted and frankly dazzling court finery that made them into veritable princes themselves.

And James . . .

Gone was the rumpled farmer. In his place stood a gentleman, polished and flawlessly groomed. His deep blue satin frock coat was sculpted to his broad shoulders to show his manly build to perfection. His pristine knee breeches were snug about his muscled thighs and . . . other areas.

The glittering gold embroidery festooning the outfit should have feminized it, but on such a fine male animal it only imparted grandeur and a sort of military embellishment.

He looks like a king. A warrior-king with gentle eyes.

Her knees went suddenly quite weak.

Again.

James must have noted only surprise on her face, for he

grinned at her a bit sheepishly and tugged at his satin waistcoat.

"Rather blinding, wouldn't you say?" He almost ran a hand through his perfectly groomed hair, then stopped. "I've been requested to appear before the Prince Regent with all due pomp and circumstance."

The younger stranger grinned. "Yes. I'm Pomp. He's Circumstance," he added, cocking a thumb over his shoulder at the other man.

James slid his gaze sideways, his lips twitching. "He's Collis actually. Don't mind him." He beckoned Phillipa into the room. "Let me introduce you to Circum—his lordship."

Phillipa entered willingly enough, only to stop in alarm when James draped one arm over her shoulders to guide her across the room.

Knee-buckling awareness swept her anew. His arm was heavy and warm. She was pressed to James's side by the weight of it and could feel the warmth from his large hard body seeping into hers. He'd held her this way once before . . .

His square hand dangled over her shoulder less than an inch from her tightly bound breast. There were layers of linen between, so she must have imagined that she felt the heat of his open palm on her tightening nipple.

Her throat went dry. Her belly shivered, sending tremors lightly through her midriff . . . and lower still. She felt a single deep involuntary spasm from her own flesh—

She stepped forward hurriedly, her panic taking her from James's side in a move that she was vaguely aware might be considered rude. She bowed to the sophisticated man before her, nearly blind to his consequence, so stewed was she in surprise at her own betraying body.

James stepped up. "Dalton, may I present Mr. Phillip Walters? He has taken over Robbie's education and is doing remarkably well with the boy. In other words, he hasn't quit yet." James turned to Phillipa. "Flip, this is Dalton Montmorency, Lord Etheridge. My . . . friend."

Phillipa bowed again, but Lord Etheridge held out one

lordly hand for her to shake. Bother. She hoped he wasn't
going to begin the battle of the grip.

His lordship's handshake was firm but tempered, thankfully, and his expression benign, even pleased. "So you're
taming the monkey, are you? Any hope for him?"

Phillipa removed her hand before the man could notice
that she didn't have any knuckles to speak of. "Yes, he's
working very hard. In only a day he's learned several of his
letters and how to write his name."

One dark brow went up, making Phillipa wonder what
she had said. Those silver eyes made her uncomfortable, as
if he could see things with them . . . things such as lies.

"I see," he said. "I shall look forward to seeing more mir-
acles from you, young Phillip."

Oh. Not good. Phillipa smiled sickly and nodded, back-
ing away. "Well, you gentlemen obviously have somewhere
to be. I'll . . . take myself off to the schoolroom. Tomorrow's
lesson, you know . . . I can speak to Mr. Cunnington later
about the bills."

She was almost to the door. Two more steps and—

Collis tilted his head at her. "James, you really should let
Phillip out now and then. The poor bloke's pale as death."

James peered at her. Phillipa tried mightily to be less
pale. "You're right, Col. He is a bit wan."

"Too bad you can't bring him along tonight. An evening at
court would liven him up. Might be good for his career, come
to think of it. Meet some people, hear about positions—"

James's eyes widened. "No!" He sent Collis a quelling
glare. "Phillip works for me." He turned back to Phillipa.

One more step. The safety of the hallway beckoned. No
perceptive lords, no teasing friends, no disturbing physical
responses to her employer.

"Have you any good rags, Flip? I've been snared into accompanying the Trapp girls and their mother to a ball in a
few days and I need another bloke. Collis won't help me
out."

Collis nodded. "I refuse on the grounds that it might mat-
rimony me."

"Come on, Flip. I'll buy you a new suit if you'll come along. The girls are twins. And pretty . . . sort of."

Phillipa gazed from one man to the other. Why were they doing this to her?

A ball?

Twins?

She was supposed to be a man, she reminded herself. A young, penniless man, in desperate need of connections and influence . . . who would be expected to jump at the chance to improve his situation through an advantageous marriage.

She felt the door at her back. "Yes . . . very well. If I can get the proper attire in time—"

James grinned in relief. "Capital. I'll get my brother-in-law's valet over here tomorrow and we'll get you suited up for battle."

Phillipa nodded again, forced a smile and a bow, and escaped into the hall, nearly running for her life.

Battle?

Later that evening as he sat in the darkness of his carriage after dropping Dalton and Collis off at Etheridge House, James ran his hand through his hair, instantly disarranging Denny's careful work. No matter. He wasn't going anywhere but home.

It wasn't terribly late. A fellow bent on self-distraction might find any number of lively companions and barely legal activities to indulge in until dawn. As evidenced by his reaction to the woman in the park, he was sorely in need of some relief.

It had been so long since he'd held someone in his arms. He missed the feel of a woman's skin, the silken stroke of her hair upon his flesh.

Dear God, what hair she'd had, that mystery woman. Long and deeply red, if the dim lamplight had shown the truth. She'd smelled good as well. Unperfumed and clean, with only her own distinctly female scent to tease his senses.

Of course, he was so deprived he'd likely have been

stirred by a piece of garden statuary. Lavinia was proof that he couldn't trust his instincts in this matter.

No, expiation was the only route. Work and more work, until his tormented sleep became dreamless, until justice might make slight and inconsequential amends to the men who had died because of him . . .

James snorted at his own melodrama. He was tired to the bone and less than rational at the moment. In a perfect example of governmental hypocrisy he'd been called to court to receive another award for his "sacrifice." The very deed that had officially never happened.

The new medal weighed heavily on his chest, like a brick over his heart making it rather difficult to breathe. James held it up by the ribbon and examined the golden disc in the intermittent light from the street lamps shining into the half-open carriage.

The side which faced the world held a relief of George's profile, or at least the profile from a few years ago. There were decidedly more chins on the version he had recently left at the palace.

He flipped the medal to the other side, the one he was expected to wear against his heart. Raised arches of acanthus leaves surrounded his own name, and the large deeply engraved words "Virtutis Honor."

James let the medal drop. Courageous Honor. Oh, yes, to be precise he had taken a bullet in the shoulder that had been meant for the Prime Minister. Not so much an act of courage as it had been his duty to undo what he had wrought with his affair with Lavinia.

He rotated his shoulder, feeling the pull of damaged muscle and tendon. Small price to pay for his stupidity. Never enough for letting his libido lead him into the clutches of a beautiful French spy who had played him like a pennywhistle while he sang out the names of his comrades.

She'd plied him with drugs she'd called aphrodisiacs—drugs that he'd taken willingly, even eagerly, mind you—and when he'd lain spent and gasping in her bed, she had led him to speak of things he ought to have died rather than revealed.

He didn't remember revealing anything, not even after she'd given up any pretense of love for him and had him captured and beaten, imprisoning him on a ramshackle boat a short way off the English coastline. He'd believed that he had successfully resisted, even in his drugged fog. Yet the resulting deaths proved that belief false.

He did remember escaping, however. He recalled the long, nearly impossible swim to shore and the dragging journey on foot and by charitable cart-driver back into London and to his sister's house.

And nothing could ever wipe from his memory the moment when Simon Raines had told him how many of the Liars had died. Nothing could wipe out the fact that even now, his best friend and fellow liar, Ren Porter, lay silent and unresponsive in a bed in a private house here in London, as did the last codemaster, Weatherby, both with the finest of nurses and very little hope of recovery.

All of them attacked once they were revealed to Lavinia and her cohorts.

Revealed by him. The hero.

Virtutis Honor.

His stomach hurt.

Chapter Nine

Not terribly far away, in a less fashionable but still very respectable part of town, lay two men in a darkened room.

The nurse Mrs. Neely shadowed her candle with one hand when she entered, despite the fact that neither of her charges were likely to complain of being disturbed by it. Still, she was careful in every way. This was the best position she had ever had. She would not jeopardize it.

Mrs. Neely had worked in a few hospitals and private sanitariums in her time, but never had she been treated with as much respect and generosity as she was given by Mr. Cunnington and his friends. Most nurses were considered only slightly better than drudges and many were. It was one place to go for a servant who could not keep a job with a quality house staff.

But Mrs. Neely's father had been a physician, though never a wealthy one, and had imparted to her his own vocation to heal the sick. When she'd originally been hired to care for these two poor gentlemen, she'd taken one look at them both and lost her heart.

Not romantically, Lord no, not at her age. But never had a patient needed her the way these two did. She fed them, bathed them with the help of a footman, combed their hair and shaved them, read to them and talked to them day in and day out.

Those were her orders and she never neglected them. She'd even taken it upon herself to read up on the subject of such deep loss of consciousness. There was some speculation that routine exercising of the limbs kept them from atrophy, and with the permission of Mr. Cunnington, she'd begun such a program at once.

Her reward had been to see a bit more color in the cheeks of her young man, as she called him. His name was Lawrence but she'd been told to call him Ren in the hopes that he might more likely answer to it.

She drifted to Ren's bedside and let the tiniest glow fall on him. Yes, he looked much better now. The terrible bruising and swellings on his face and head had gone down significantly in the last six weeks, and the scars would fade somewhat in time. So young and handsome with that curly hair of his. So badly beaten . . .

She turned to step to the other bed. Poor Mr. Weatherby. He rather reminded her of her own beloved Frederick, God rest his soul.

Angus Weatherby had been found on the cobbles below his own bedroom window, four stories above. Not a mark on him except where he'd landed on his head on the old stones of the street.

She'd been told to call him Angus, but she simply couldn't refer to a gentleman of her own age in such a familiar fashion. So she called him Mr. Weatherby, and sir, and sometimes even held his hand and reminded him of all the odd and wonderful times they had seen in England over the last fifty years, and invited him to come along with her to see a few more.

But he never responded, her fine silver-haired gentleman friend, and she was beginning to lose hope for him. His face had sunken and grayed, and every day it seemed he breathed a little more shallowly and lost a little more ground.

A tear came to her eye as she bent to lay a forbidden kiss

on Mr. Weatherby's brow. The Lord might forgive an old woman her fancies, she supposed.

With her vision blurred by her fond grief, and her candle still carefully shadowed, Mrs. Neely might also be forgiven for missing a tiny, momentous event. Atop the sheet on the other bed lay a slack and open hand, one whose fingers had not moved of their owner's will for many weeks.

But as Mrs. Neely mourned what might have been, there came a hint of the future for her other patient as two fingers of that hand jerked in a small stuttering movement, as if to catch her attention.

She missed that call, but all was well. She would catch the next one.

Phillipa paced restlessly in her room. By all rights she ought to be catching up on all her many months of sleeping ill, but she was far too disturbed to undress for bed.

She had a problem.

Why couldn't James Cunnington have been either obviously evil, with his nature evident in a ratlike face and manner, or else benignly elderly, with angelic blue eyes and white hair? Why did he have to be so—so—

Abruptly, she sat in the chair by her fire and covered her face with her hands. So manly. So broad and warm and inappropriately unbearably delicious. Never in her sheltered existence had she felt such a response to a man. It was all she could do to breathe in his presence.

Sighing, she flopped back in her chair and stretched her legs toward the fire. So lovely, to allow her body such freedom as a man. She could flop, and stretch, and most probably *scratch* without reprisal. A lady could do none of those things.

A lady must not touch her face or person, or adjust her clothing in the presence of others. A lady must never let her spine touch the back cushions. Heavens, what were they for then?

Still, a lady had some recourse, subtle as it was. A lady knew the language of the fan and could spell out her attraction with the tiniest of gestures. A lady could flutter her lashes just a bit, or lean ever so slightly forward, or stroll and pose to flirtatiously show her figure to advantage.

But Phillipa could not flirt with Mr. Cunnington. Nor when he affected her as he had a number of times today, could she allow her attraction to show.

She was not a gentleman. Yet if truth be told, she was no longer a lady either. Should it ever be revealed that she had dressed like a man, had lived unchaperoned with a man—heavens, had seen him nearly naked—she would be branded a hussy and a whore.

Small price to pay for her father's life. Of course, she could have become a whore in fact, weeks ago. A woman could not walk the streets of that section of Cheapside and not gather a few suggestions from the rough and common men she passed. She'd been offered money, liquor, narcotics, even protection.

There was a difference, wasn't there, in being labeled a whore and actually being one? She'd done her best to protect her honor and her personal virtue, yet she had lied and she was in fact living in a most scandalous situation.

Well, reputation or no, she knew who she was. She idly reached for her braid to twist it in contemplation. Finding nothing of course, she let her hand drop.

At least, she used to know who she was.

"*Merde*," she muttered to the coals. "*Merde, merde, merde.*"

She must remember why she had come here. Her father knew James Cunnington in some respect. If she could only discover how, then she would know what to do.

Her mission was clearly to investigate . . . but where to begin?

She thought about this fine but austere house. Mr. Cunnington obviously spent most of his time in his study, surrounded by that clutter of books and papers. Papers that might very well tell her what she needed to know.

Phillipa stood abruptly and walked to the door of her bed-chamber. There would be no better time than the present. With the master out until late, Denny had retired hours ago. Robbie was fast asleep.

Her hand on the knob, Phillipa took a deep breath and swallowed, trying to ignore the trembling in her stomach.

As she stepped into the darkened hallway, she had to admit that a certain amount of her disquiet was due to excitement. After all her years of living in near seclusion with her father, it seemed she had a taste for adventure after all.

When James arrived home to the darkened house at midnight, the last thing he expected to see in his study was Phillip sprawled upon the floor in front of James's own desk, his hands in his hair and his brow furrowed as he studied something before him.

"Doing a bit of light reading, Mr. Walters?" James was careful to keep his tone easy. He had every intention of getting some answers for this intrusion, but it might yet prove to be more innocent than it seemed.

Phillip sat up quickly, barely catching the book before it tumbled from its perch on his stomach. "Oh! Mr. Cunnington." The fellow scrambled about, trying to set the study in some kind of order.

James let his gaze travel over what used to be a lovely ordered disorder. Now it was a true disorder. Opened books lay on every surface, papers lay spread across the carpet. James knelt to pick one up. Last month's bill from the butcher?

He raised an enquiring gaze to Phillip.

Phillip sat back on his heels and stammered nervously. "I was searching for a bit of paper."

James waited. Phillip swallowed. "I—I had an idea that I could make a—a primer for Robbie."

"Could you not purchase one?" James knew very well one could. He'd bought one for Stubbs.

"Not—not one that spoke of things he'd recognize."

Phillip wet his lips, seeming so nervous that James almost felt sorry for him. "The ones I found were too—too exotic. I think Robbie might need something . . . something a bit closer to home. M-markets instead of maharajahs."

James blinked. "Carts instead of castles?" It was a brilliant idea. The very thing for city-bred Robbie.

Phillip nodded quickly, seeming frankly relieved. "Only I cannot draw a cart. Or a cat. I was looking for things to copy . . ." He waved a hand at the mess.

"Among my personal accounts?"

"No—my apologies, sir. I was searching for a bit of paper to practice on, but I—I cannot even draw a straight line."

"I can." The words were out before James even realized it. "I'm no Sir Thorogood, but I can sketch basic things."

Phillip looked up, surprise in his narrow face. For the first time, James noticed how green Phillip's eyes were. The fellow would be quite a lady-killer, once he finished growing.

He had quite a way to go yet, but James did think the fellow looked a bit better already after a few good meals. And here Phillip was, up late, working hard to find a way to teach the unteachable Robbie. That showed sincere dedication.

He'd done a good thing when he'd brought those two together, James decided. The thought sat comfortably on his beleaguered soul. A good thing, small as it was, that perhaps lessened the sum total of his sins.

"I'll help you if you like," James said.

Phillip stood and nervously began to gather the paper and books together. "Do you think we'll find twenty-six items?"

"In London? Not difficult. P is for Piss?" James grinned. "For the Thames is surely full of it."

It was a mild joke, only slightly off-color. There was no reason for Phillip to stare at him in that startled manner.

"Oh, come on, Flip. Don't be such a girl. A bloke can say '*piss*,' can't he?"

"Of course a bloke can say 'p—piss.' "

James rolled his eyes in friendly disgust. Phillip looked as though he were about to wash his own mouth out with soap. James watched him as he bent to pick up another book.

Squatting quickly, James moved to help him gather up the mess.

Phillipa jumped as James's thigh bumped her own. She was still shaking from the shock of his arrival. She'd thought he'd stay out much later, seemingly being a wealthy fellow with nothing better to do with his time.

Thank heavens she'd come up with that lie about a primer for Robbie . . . although now that she thought about it, it was a perfect solution to Robbie's reluctance to read.

Moreover, Mr. Cunnington had believed it. Tension and a tremor of guilt made her stomach shiver. He was very trusting, this man who might be good or evil . . .

He reached across her vision for another book, then dumped the lot in her arms. The back of his hand brushed her breast as he did so and she lost her grip on the pile she held.

Books tumbled between them once more. James laughed and shook his head at her.

"Damn, Flip. How many thumbs do you have?"

"S—sorry." Phillipa bent to gather them again. James laid a hand on her shoulder. It was heavy and warm. Warm enough to ignite her inappropriate lust once more.

"Flip, look at me."

His deep voice was gentle. She looked up into his brown eyes, clutching the books to her chest.

James squeezed her shoulder. "Flip, I know you aren't quite what you claim."

Phillipa's heart stopped quite still. She'd been found out already.

James continued, his gaze kind. "I know you're not really a tutor. I know you're not as old as you claim. And I know you've been hungry, probably for quite a while."

He didn't know. Her secret was safe for now. Then the kindness of his words made it through her relief and she felt the burn of tears behind her eyes. She looked down quickly and began tidying the books she held.

"You don't have to be afraid of me, Flip," James continued. "I don't give a whit that you lied, because in the most important way, you told the truth. You *can* help Robbie, perhaps more than anyone else who has tried. You've experienced some things in your life, I imagine. Things that will help you reach a boy who never had a chance to find out what he was capable of."

She raised her face to gaze at him somberly. Who was this man? He seemed so warm, so open, yet somehow he never quite showed himself to her. Every time she might have learned something significant about him, he had deflected her with a jest, or a light half-answer, or changed the subject altogether.

He might be someone she could trust. He might even be able to help her, but how could she be sure?

No. Until she knew more about him, she could not risk it.

James's chuckle turned her musings aside. "Lord, Flip. The look on your face. What are you thinking now?"

"I'm thinking that Robbie was lucky that you found him."

"Oh, he found us."

"Us?"

James removed his hand and stood, unbuttoning his fine court frock coat as he did so. "Pour me a whisky, will you, while I go change? Then we shall see if we can think of something that begins with *P*."

Phillipa watched him move across the room. Gone again. Still, it was for the best—before she threw herself on his mercy and his broad hard chest and wept out her troubles into his shirtfront.

Odd, however, that she missed him when he left the room.

Chapter Ten

Dear God, would the man never leave? Phillipa let her forehead fall down on the last page of their nearly finished primer in exhausted frustration. "Z must be for Zebra, James. It's the only word we've got."

"What about Z is for Zephyr?"

Phillipa gritted her teeth. "Oh, lovely. *That's* tangible," she said. "Robbie," she called to the boy playing on the floor behind them. He'd been granted the day off from his lessons, only to discover a rain too heavy to allow tree-climbing in the garden. Phillipa had ordered him to create blood and havoc on the carpet instead. Robbie had gleefully obliged. "Do you know what a zephyr is?"

"No." Robbie didn't look up from his prized collection of painted lead soldiers. From the look of things, he was about to squash Napoleon forever.

Phillipa raised her head to send James a triumphant look.

He snorted. "Robbie," he said, "do you know what a zebra is?"

"No."

Phillipa let her head fall back down. They'd worked most of the night and all morning and she was beyond tired. Worse still, she was hungry.

Working with James had been difficult and full of stimulating opinionated debate. She'd had to stand her ground against his forcefulness with a strength she hadn't known she had. But she had come to think of this book as the key to teaching Robbie and none of James's flights of creative fancy were going to spoil it.

Yet somehow the entire project had been more fun than she'd ever had in her life. They had twenty-five pages of alphabet illustrated with some very serviceable drawings produced by James. All that remained now was Z.

"Zip, zap, zup," she muttered. Then she yawned into the desk blotter. James's chuckle rumbled through the room. She looked up at him blearily.

He smiled at her. "Who would have thought Z would be harder than X?"

"Ah, but you were brilliant. I never would have thought of X is for Rex, which is on every coin of the realm."

He gave a playful bow. "Thank you, my good man. But let us not forget the mind behind Q is for Quarrel—one of which can be seen every half-block in London."

She propped her chin on her fist and grinned. "I never knew I had it in me."

His brown eyes twinkled back at her. He had a wonderful smile, she mused in suddenly contented weariness. Open and warm and playful. She liked working with him, liked playing with him as well.

James looked down at the weary young fellow behind his desk and shook his head. Sometimes Phillip seemed to go off into such daydreams. Still, they had been up quite late together.

He snapped his fingers before Phillip's eyes. "You need some rest, man. You're drifting."

Phillip blinked and sat up straight. "No, not yet. I want to finish this. We only need one more letter."

"Z is for Zap," muttered Robbie behind them. "Saw the bell tower of St. Mary-le-Bow hit by lightning once. Zap!" He knocked down a soldier with a darting fingertip. "Zap! Zap!"

James blinked. "I do believe Napoleon's troops have run into a bit of a storm."

Phillip was grinning again. He reached for the last page and wrote quickly. "Zap! Why not? It's our book. We can use Zap if we like!"

Bending over Phillip and the book, James quickly sketched out a rather nice zigzagged shape beside Phillip's writing—a lightning bolt. They both tilted their heads to admire the finished product.

"Yes, it is *our* book." Smiling as well, James reached out to tousle Phillip's hair and was surprised when he flinched away.

Phillip blushed and sent him a half-shrug. "Sorry," he muttered.

Odd. Still, young men were notoriously sensitive about such things. James reminded himself of the delicacy of youthful masculine pride. It wouldn't do to treat Phillip like Robbie.

Instead, he ought to treat him as he would Collis or Stubbs. A respected equal. And he did respect Phillip. The fellow was smart and quick, obviously a real survivor.

James pursed his lips, thinking. Just the sort of young fellow the club needed, in fact. An educated apprentice, one without family ties, young enough to train up properly? James would have to fight the other Liars off with a sword. If only James could get Phillip to shed that girlish sensitivity of his.

A loud growl echoed through the room. Robbie looked up in surprise. James laughed out loud. "Gentlemen, I think there's a bear loose in this house."

Phillip let out an embarrassed snort. "That was my stomach, I admit it."

"Go. Off to the kitchens with the both of you. Tell Cook that I ordered an early dinner all around. I'll take a tray in here. Time to get some of *my* work done." He grinned at Phillip to take the sting from his words.

Robbie clambered up willingly enough and Phillip walked the boy to the door of the study. Then he stopped and looked back to where James had now seated himself behind the desk. "Thank you, sir. This will truly help Robbie, I think."

"You're very welcome, Sir Flip," James teased.

But Phillip wasn't teasing. His green eyes were deadly serious. James was taken aback by the emotion he thought he saw there.

"It meant a great deal to me, sir." Then Phillip turned and left with a curious stately dignity that somehow sat well on those thin shoulders.

James shook his head. "You are a very odd duck, Mr. Phillip Walters," he murmured to the empty study. "I wonder who you really are?"

Later as James strode through the door of the club, he considered his options. There were only two men currently with the Liars who had worked with Rupert Atwater. One was Simon, former spymaster and now James's own brother-in-law.

Although James was very fond of his former superior and new family member, he'd rather not consult Simon just yet, for Simon and Dalton were close as well. James didn't want Dalton to catch on to this not-so-terribly-official mission.

Kurt, on the other hand . . .

Kurt wouldn't breathe a word unless specifically questioned by Dalton—not so much out of any sense of loyalty to James as out of a general disinclination to human speech.

As usual, Kurt could be found reigning over his princely domain. Pots bubbled on the massive stove and the smell of baking filled the air. The kitchen would have felt positively homey had it not been occupied by one of the most dangerous men in the civilized world.

The giant assassin was chopping, James was pleased to see. Aside from the fact that watching Kurt use a knife for any purpose was like watching an artist at work, this also meant that after a rousing session of cutting things into tiny little bits, Kurt would likely be feeling positively mellow— for Kurt.

James entered with respectful silence and made his way carefully to the rough table at the far end of the kitchen. He parked one buttock on the tabletop and waited patiently for Kurt to complete the dismemberment of several plucked birds.

Most people made themselves scarce when Kurt worked his magic with the deadly flying knives, but James was fascinated. True, there was one moment when even James had to shut his eyes . . .

The sound of steel bisecting bone slowed, then stopped altogether. James risked opening one eye to see Kurt tossing his—er, bird remains—into a pan and then wiping his hands thoroughly with a piece of toweling. Kurt then abruptly tossed the bloodstained towel in James's direction.

James only had a moment to consider—catch or dodge? He decided to catch and found himself the lucky recipient of an approving grunt from Kurt, who then turned away to delicately sprinkle herb trimmings onto the pan of birds. There would never be a better time to question him.

Trying to hide the fact that he was holding the grisly towel with two fingers, James approached the large block where Kurt was working. "That looks . . . delicious." Actually it did, although James thought he might head on back to the house for his supper. Not that he was squeamish or anything.

Kurt did not answer, nor had James truly expected him to. He surreptitiously dropped the towel back over the gory area of the chopping block and breathed in relief. "So, Kurt, I was wondering if you could help me out with a bit of club history."

Not a word, but James did earn a noncommittal glance from beneath two bushy brows. He decided to consider that as encouragement and went on. "Some years ago there was a cryptologist named Atwater. Do you recall him?"

Kurt grunted. "Skinny bloke. Pretty wife. She were a right good cook."

James was startled by such loquacity. Goodness, Kurt must have fond memories indeed. "Yes, that would be Isabella. She was Spanish, I believe?"

Kurt paused in his work, his gaze gone positively dreamy. "She could do things with oranges."

Since Kurt only cared about two things—cooking and killing—James fervently hoped that he was referring to recipes using citrus.

"And the little girl, do you remember her as well?"

Kurt returned to his spicing. "Fifi."

Excellent. "Her name was Fifi?" It was always best to be specific with Kurt. "Was that a pet name, short for something else?"

Kurt shrugged. It was rather like watching the earth shift. "'Er mum called 'er Fifi."

Fifi Atwater. Well, it was a place to start. "What did Fifi look like?"

Kurt sent James a contemptuous flicker of the eyes. "A girl." Then he paused once more. "Red."

Red? Red dress, red lips, red—

A lance of solid ice went through James's gut. "*Red hair?*"

"Bright. Like a new penny."

Red hair was unusual, memorable . . . and exceptionally difficult to hide. So, his red-haired captive had been something more than a chance encounter. His suspicions about Atwater's disposition of his daughter had been at least partially correct. The girl was in London.

And if he was not mistaken, *she'd* been spying on *him.*

James felt the excitement of the hunt run through him. He clapped Kurt on the shoulder. "Thank you, Kurt. You've been an enormous help."

Kurt turned his cold gaze down to where James's hand rested on one massive shoulder. Then he looked at James without a word.

James jerked his hand back. "Ah. Sorry. Er, good then. Thank you." He backed away slowly, as if from an uncaged beast. "Right. Looks like a lovely meal!"

He made his escape even as a bestial growl rose to echo through the steamy kitchen. Oh, yes. Definitely home for supper tonight.

· · ·

The valet that Mr. Cunnington had sent for to fit Phillipa's new dinner suit greeted Phillipa warmly, then smilingly ushered Denny from the room.

Then the small immaculately attired Mr. Button turned on her fiercely. "Who are you, young woman, and what do you mean by this charade?"

Phillipa blinked, too shocked to feel fear yet. "Goodness, that didn't take you long."

Mr. Button rolled his eyes. "Please. I've dressed more lads as women and more women as lads in the theatre than a cat has whiskers."

He walked around her. "Your chest is full, but your waist is narrow. Your hips aren't terribly wide, but there is no hiding the set of your legs." He came round before her again and chucked her under the chin to raise her face to his gaze. "Eyes large, lips full, nose ridiculously tiny—dear me, is Mr. Cunnington blind?"

He stood back, shaking his head. "You'll be very pretty once you've had a few weeks of this fine living. I can tell you've been close to starvation. Pale . . . shadows under the eyes, the cheekbones . . ."

Abruptly his anger seemed gone. He stepped back to seat himself on the sofa. "You're no spy, are you, child? Just a hungry girl, looking for a safe home."

Phillipa was too taken aback to speak. She had expected Mr. Button to alert the house to her identity, not to pat the cushion beside him on the sofa and bend a sympathetic ear.

Much bemused, she sat carefully next to him. "How can you know so much about me? Who are you?"

"I am personal valet to Sir Simon Raines, if you must know. And I have *extensive* experience in spotting liars." He chuckled to himself. "Sorry, my little joke. So, tell me everything."

There didn't seem to be much point in hiding her history any longer, so Phillipa obliged his curiosity—withholding her true surname, of course, and the fact that Napoleon's men were involved. In all honesty, she didn't know if there was any point to keeping her story quiet . . . except for a niggling instinct that there was indeed something suspicious about James Cunnington.

So she told Mr. Button that her father was dead. Her very real grief at saying those words out loud resulting in making her quite convincing, despite the fact that she deeply hoped it was a lie. She told him that she'd come to London hoping for the protection of her father's old friend, but that the friend was dead. She told him about Mrs. Farquart, and Bessie's trunk, and Robbie's reaction to her at the interview.

"Ah, yes, our Rob's a quick one," chuckled Button, as he insisted she call him. "He'll be quite the man someday, if he manages to live long enough."

He then proceeded to tell her a number of tales of Robbie's escapades. Phillipa didn't stop him, for she learned more about her charge in five minutes than she had in the past three days.

Finally something he told her made her laugh, and he stopped, his eyes twinkling merrily.

"You and I shall be fast friends, I can tell. Now convince me why I shouldn't go to Mr. Cunnington at once with your story. He would help you, you know."

"No. Please . . . I haven't told you quite everything. There are some things I need to find out first. I think someone wants to hurt me . . . and James is so secretive sometimes . . . and then he can be so very kind . . ."

"Aha." Button, who had seemed frankly puzzled, now nodded wisely. "You've taken a fancy to our James, then."

"N—no!" Phillipa stood quickly. "I mean, I'm sure he's a wonderful fellow but—I mean, I *can't*—" She hadn't done any such thing! Absolutely not.

"Phillipa dear, you aren't making sense."

"I know—only please, Button, please don't say anything!"

He regarded her steadily for a moment, this small prim man who quite possibly held her very life in his hands.

"Will you vow to me at this moment that you have no motive here other than to stay hidden and safe?"

She nodded quickly. Those really were her motives . . . mostly. "That's all I ask for, I swear to you. And I can help Robbie learn, I know I can. It doesn't make up for the lie, I know, but it's all I can offer."

Button sighed. "I shouldn't do this. Milady will be very angry if she finds out."

"Milady?"

"My Lady Raines. My employer and Mr. Cunnington's sister."

Phillipa nodded. "Ah, yes. Agatha. James told me."

Button shook his finger at her. "Don't be so familiar, miss. It's 'Lady Raines' from you until Milady says otherwise." He looked frustrated. "Although she probably will," he grumbled. "No respect for her own consequence, I tell you. Friend to the Prince Regent himself, but she'd get right down and shear the sheep herself if we let her."

Sheep? This day was becoming so strange. Phillipa rubbed at her eyes. "Do I want to know about the sheep?"

"What's to know? Silly beasts, no more wit than a bucket." He stood, holding out a hand to bring her to her feet. A little thing, but it was rather charming to be treated like a lady for a brief moment. Then Button reached into his pocket and removed a numbered tape.

"I fear I am about to take unspeakable liberties," he said conversationally. "Hold out your arms and stand feet apart, if you please." He then proceeded to measure parts of her that had never been measured before. They were both blushing by the time he was done, although Button's flush lacked the sheer volcanic glow of Phillipa's.

"Goodness," she said breathlessly when he stood. "*That* was embarrassing."

Button cleared his throat. "Quite. Still, better me than another."

He tucked his tape away and bowed over her hand. "I take my leave of you now, Miss Walters. Your dinner suit will be ready by tomorrow night for your evening out." He turned to go, then spun about with a puckish grin. "One more thing, child." He chuckled. "When you dance with young Miss Trapp—"

"Yes?"

"Pray, do not forget to lead."

Chapter Eleven

James rapped on the ceiling of his carriage. When his driver flipped open the small speaking hatch, rain began to dribble in. "Take me home," he ordered.

There weren't too many Liars of Atwater's generation still living. Liars rarely did live long, by the nature of the business. Still, Atwater's code-breaking crew of years gone by wouldn't normally have faced too many personal dangers.

The files gave a few names of code-breakers that might remember Atwater. Unfortunately, all the ones that James had been familiar with were dead. Some of them had been working right up until the recent attacks, but they were all gone now.

Even Weatherby wasn't likely to wake. The nurse that James had hired for his two ill friends had recently reported that Weatherby was declining.

Most of the others had all died within weeks of each other by apparent accident, except for Upkirk. A fall, cleaning a pistol, sudden failure of the heart . . . Upkirk had been most obviously murdered, beaten and thrown into the Thames.

Upkirk would have been the most useful as well. James recalled that Atwater and Upkirk had been close comrades of old. If anyone knew where Atwater's daughter had ended up, it would have been Upkirk.

Of course, Upkirk had died before Atwater had been separated from his daughter . . .

But Atwater couldn't have known that fact. Even the best communications took weeks under the current wartime conditions. As far as Atwater could have known, Upkirk was alive and well in his house on—

James pounded his fist on the ceiling again. "I've changed my mind. We're going to Cheapside High Street."

Upkirk's house was shuttered and dark, but it wasn't the one James was truly interested in anyway. He began with the house directly to the left of Upkirk's. He ordered the driver to park several houses down, while he took a moment to change his persona. He slicked his hair back with a bit of water, changed his snowy linen cravat for a less distinguished striped one that he tied in a precise and unimaginative knot, and donned a pair of spectacles filled with plain glass that all the Liars were fond of using as an appearance distracter. That, along with a rather myopic blink, transformed him into a fussy, detail-mad clerk on an errand for his solicitor employer.

"Pardon me, but I'm in need of information about a young lady who might have come seeking your neighbor, Mr. Upkirk."

There was no luck at the first house. The inhabitants were not disinclined to help, but truly had no recollection of a lady asking for Upkirk.

The house on the other side bore more fruit.

The lady of the house had spoken to her at length. "Oh, yes, I remember her perfectly."

James smiled a tight superior smirk. "Excellent."

The lady nodded emphatically. "Perhaps a fortnight ago . . . no, longer. A month. Perhaps two?"

James's smile became a bit fixed. Oh, no. Not one of those. Some people were simply not inclined to recall details. This was going to require some patience.

An hour and two pots of tea later, James hadn't managed

to get much that was useful out of the lady although he had been treated to a long list of her ailments and contradictory political opinions.

"Well, I believe her name was quite long. Yes, very long. Desdemona? Wilhelmina? No, it was Philomena, I'm positive. At least . . . I believe so . . ."

Philomena could certainly be shortened to Fifi. In fact, anyone who didn't shorten such an unpleasant name ought to be shot. Philomena Atwater.

"Do you remember anything else about her? Do you know where she might have gone next or anything that might help me find her?"

The lady drank another sip of bloody tea. James forced himself to breathe slowly and deeply. He lifted his cup to sip primly from the paper-thin china. He was beginning to get a stiff neck from his own starched posture.

"Well, she did have very shabby clothing on. And so pale and thin. I don't mean to speak ill, but the girl obviously didn't have a farthing to her name." The woman sniffed disapprovingly.

And I'll wager you spared her none of yours, thought James. He dipped his head in prudish agreement.

"She seemed quite low after I told her about poor Mr. Upkirk. She seemed as though she had nowhere else to go. Really, she wasn't good company at all."

The lady had yet to mention red hair. How could the mystery girl be Fifi Atwater if she didn't have red hair?

Finally, James came right out with it.

"Did this young lady have bright coppery hair, or hair any shade of red?"

The lady blinked at his abruptness. "Well, yes, of course she did. Didn't I say that very thing?"

James strangled his impatience. Then he shot it. Sadly, that did no good. It still writhed within him.

"Ah, yes, my mistake. Thank you so much for all your help. No, not another drop, I really couldn't. So pleasant to have our little chat, dear-me-look-at-the-time."

He made good his escape and stepped out into a misting

rain. London weather. Neverending wet, making the cobbles slimy beneath one's feet and the soot run down the exterior walls and fall in a rain of black droplets on one's shoulders. Briefly James longed for the clean green hills of Lancashire.

Until he remembered the harvest. Apples here, apples there, apples bloody everywhere . . .

He hopped jauntily back into his carriage, suddenly well pleased with himself and life in general. He was young, alive, and in London, the greatest city upon the earth. So, apparently, was the pleasantly squirming armful that James was becoming more and more sure was Fifi Atwater.

And he was right behind her.

Phillipa combed back her cropped hair with the tortoiseshell comb with which Denny had grudgingly supplied her. Denny had been no help at all, having apparently decided that "Phillip's" appearance would not reflect directly on the household. The possessive butler had been impossible since the night she and Mr. Cunnington had worked on the primer. The suit that Button had sent over for her had been brushed and pressed to a fine point and her shoes, also on loan from Button, had been blackened and shined.

Button had taken care to fit her waistcoat perfectly and had reinforced the front of it to lie flat upon her bound breasts. The shoulders of the coat had been subtly padded to give her some prominence, and the trousers were cut just a tad on the loose side to hide the curve of her bottom.

She looked the very picture of a well-turned-out young fellow, if she did say so herself.

Blast it.

For a moment her shoulders slumped. How long would she be forced to keep up this façade? A month? A year? Forever? She had painted herself into quite the inescapable corner. If she revealed herself, her reputation would never recover. For that matter, if she revealed herself, there might be worse things in store than shame.

No, she must maintain her identity until the danger from

Napoleon was past. Despite the French retreat back over the Pyrenees, he was still a power on the Continent, and she was still a target. And how was she to reach Papa, when he had surely been taken along with the French Emperor to Paris? She refused to consider that Papa was not a living captive. He *was* alive, no doubt as worried about her as she was about him.

That reminded her to check Papa's bag. She'd pulled out the lowest drawer of her small bureau and had carefully hidden the small soft satchel within. The papers and book inside took up very little room and the drawer only required a little extra push to seat itself in place. Still, to be safe, she didn't use it, keeping her few things in the upper drawers instead.

It was safe and untouched. Denny didn't seem inclined to interfere too much with her bedchamber, a small insult that she accepted gratefully. For luck, she traced the symbol on the cover. The Greek letter Phi.

Papa had called her that in affectionate moments. Her vision went to mist. A tap came on her door, quick and hurried and rather low on the carved wood. She swiped at her eyes, then replaced the drawer smoothly and straightened. "Come in, Robbie."

The door opened slightly and Robbie's blue eyes peered through the crack. "All dressed?"

"Yes, sir." Phillipa smiled and gave a girlish spin, as if her skirts were floating out and her hair was tossing. "How do I look?"

Robbie's eyes widened in alarm and he glanced worriedly over his shoulder. Then he stepped hurriedly into the room and closed the door behind him. "Don't *do* that!"

He was truly upset. Phillipa frowned at him. "Robbie, I know why *I* don't want to get caught, but why don't *you* want me to get caught?"

Robbie looked away and fidgeted, digging one toe into the carpet. "Dunno."

Phillipa knelt in front of the boy and tipped his chin up with one finger. To her surprise, he didn't flinch the way he usually did when touched.

"Rob? Can it be that you're a little fond of me?"

He growled something and rolled his eyes, but the quick flicker of his blue gaze told her the truth. She settled back on her heels regardless of the crease in her trousers. "Well, I don't have any manly pride to preserve, so I'll tell you. I'm very fond of you too. More than fond. If I have any family in this world, then you would be in it, if you wanted to be."

"You could be, if you was to shackle up with James."

Phillipa blinked and withdrew slightly. "Shackle up? Do you mean *marry* him?"

"You could do it. I bet you don't look half-bad in a dress, even with your hair all ruined."

"Thank you," she responded automatically, her voice faint. *Marry James?* What fantasies had Robbie manufactured in that sly little head of his?

"I about gave up on havin' a mum, till you came along. But I decided you'll do." He tilted his head to look at her speculatively. "You're passing old, but I might even get a brother out o' the deal."

Phillipa forced her mind from its shock. "Robbie, I can't—I don't know how to explain this to you. I am not going to marry Mr. Cunnington. He is most certainly not going to marry *me*! For pity's sake, he thinks I'm a man!"

"But he likes you. And you already live here. If you asked him, he'd likely let you marry him."

Phillipa closed her eyes. How to get this across to a child who clearly had no idea how the adult system worked? "Robbie, when a woman wants to marry a man, she does not ask him. She must wait for him to ask her. But I don't want Mr. Cunnington to ask me."

Robbie blinked at her. "Are you one of those ladies what don't like men? Is that why you wear the trousers, then?"

Goodness, how could Robbie know about a concept that she herself was less than fully aware of? Of course, she'd heard of such ladies, and in some societies, they lived openly, albeit quietly . . .

She shook her head. Robbie was spinning her about again. "I'm sure I'm not one of those ladies, Robbie. I might marry someday, for I am not in fact all that terribly old. But Mr. Cunnington is far too—" *Mysterious. Delicious. Unattainable.* "He is far too important to be interested in some-one like me," she said firmly. "Nor am I interested in him."

Liar.

Robbie seemed less than convinced, but he shrugged. "If you say so." He turned to leave. Then he turned back. "When you're dancin' with Miss Trapp—"

"I know, I know. Don't forget to lead."

He grinned as he left her room. For a moment she could see the handsome man he would someday be shining behind his pointed little features. Mr. Robert Cunnington, master of the vast Appleby estate . . .

It quite boggled the mind. Although she doubted he would ever be able to completely quell his climbing ambitions.

"Little snot will likely be one of those moneyed dilet-tantes who climbs mountains with a packtrain and porters," she muttered. She smiled at the thought, but her smile faded as she recalled Robbie's assumptions. Actually, it was not Robbie's idea that disturbed her as much as it had been the way her heart had leapt at the concept.

Of course, she had no intention of marrying Mr. Cun-nington. She wasn't at all in love, and she'd sworn she'd never marry without love. Her parents' passion for each other had shown her how a true marriage of the spirit could be, and she'd settle for nothing less for herself. She had no such tender feelings for James Cunnington.

Yet he was entirely male. The broad size of him triggered a female animal response in her that no pale ascetic young man ever had. It was as though when she was in the circle of the heat radiating from his wide, hard body, she could only feel, hear, and see him, no other.

A spell. That's what it was. When he was in the room, she fell under his spell. That was a very satisfying answer to her confusion except for one thing.

She didn't believe in magic.

•   •   •

In his room, James tugged at his cravat. Denny slapped his hand away and straightened it.

"You'd look a proper sight, goin' out with your cravat all sideways," Denny muttered. "Won't let me press it again neither. You'd go out in your drawers, you would. I've a standin' to maintain, sir!"

James laughed. "You've spent too much time with Button, Denny. If you want to be a top-drawer valet, I'm afraid you're in the wrong household."

A tap came at the bedchamber door. It was Phillip, looking dapper in his new clothes. "Flip! Quickly, get Denny off me. I'm nigh unto suffocating from his attentions!"

Phillip didn't smile at James's teasing, although the sally did turn Denny's attention away at last.

"Mr. Walters!" Denny walked once around the young tutor, nodding grudgingly. "I see you've not that sorry 'abit o' runnin' your hand through your 'air. And you've pressed that shirt to a fine edge, you 'ave."

Denny took Phillip by the shoulders and marched him to stand before James. "There, sir. That's what a true gentleman looks like."

Phillip choked at that and turned an appalling shade of red. James shook his head. "He may look fine, Denny, but the poor fellow can't breathe with his cravat up to his ears like that."

Phillip stepped slightly away from Denny's improving hands. "It's the clothes, I fear. Anyone would look—er, manly after being in Button's hands."

"Humph." Denny fussed with James's cravat once more. "Button, Button, Button. You'd think he was the only valet in the entire cl—"

"Denny!" James cut in. "Ah, would you mind keeping an eye on Robbie tonight? Agatha was going to take him but she's been feeling a bit low lately."

"Milady? Oh, dear." Denny looked sincerely worried. "Oh, not Milady!" Denny breathed in his usual pessimistic fashion. "It'll be the influenza for sure. Has she called for the physician yet? Not that it'll do any good—"

Denny made for the hall, spinning woe as he went.

Phillip turned to watch him go, then turned back. "Perhaps we ought not to go tonight, if your sister is so very ill."

James grinned. "Nice try. Fortunately for your social calendar, my sister is quite well. Or at least I expect she will be, in about eight months' time."

Phillip's eyes widened. "Is she—?"

James nodded as he turned to look at himself critically in the glass. "So says Sarah Cook, according to the butler Pearson, and confirmed by Button."

"Oh, dear. How . . . forthcoming of Milady."

There was an odd expression in Phillip's eyes, almost . . . envy? "What's to do, Flip? Hankering after a little wedded bliss of your own?"

Phillip actually jumped. "What?"

"Well, if you're serious about settling down, it's fortunate we're escorting the Trapp girls. Never have I seen two young ladies more determined to step into the traces in my life."

Phillip flinched and James grinned at the horrified expression on his face.

"I d-don't want to step into *anything*."

James laughed out loud. "Then don't walk behind the horses, man."

He put one hand on Phillip's shoulder in a comradely fashion. Phillip tensed under his touch. Ah, yes. He'd forgotten about that prickly young pride.

"Shall we get on then? We're to pick up the young ladies shortly. Not that they'll be ready, of course. I foresee at least three quarters of an hour spent in the front parlor, sharing an uncomfortable settee and conversation with Mr. Trapp."

Phillip blinked at that but said nothing. Funny, he hadn't said much of anything since the two of them had completed the primer. Had he frightened the younger man? The more he thought about it, the more sure he became.

In the carriage, he decided to reassure Phillip. "See here,

Flip . . . I hope you'll tell me if you need anything, anything at all. I don't want you to think I'll be angry with you."

Phillip tugged nervously at his cuffs. "No. I don't need anything."

"Hmm. Listen, Phillip . . . do you trust me?"

Phillip turned. James could just see a gleam of green in the dim light. "I suppose so. Why?"

"Because I want you to do something for me."

"Yes?"

"I want you to try very hard to . . . well . . . how shall I put this? Be more . . . masculine."

There was a short silence. "You don't think I'm masculine?"

Phillip sounded absolutely appalled. James grimaced. "I'm not saying this well. What I mean is, if you were to want to be more so, I could help you. Teach you some things, you see."

There was a low gurgle from the other side of the carriage. Damn, he'd offended the fellow. "I know it isn't your fault, Flip."

"No, I should say it isn't."

"I mean, you might not have had a manly example to follow."

There was a pause. James waited it out, knowing he was treading on delicate ground.

"True. I can honestly say I have never followed a manly example."

James smiled in relief. "Well, then. We can start tomorrow."

Another pause. "Start what?"

"Why, to toughen you up a bit, that's what. I'll make a real man out of you, wait and see."

"Oh. That's very . . . kind of you." Phillip's voice sounded oddly muffled.

"If you like, we can start tonight. Take this ball, for instance. There's likely to be a smoking room of some sort, and a gaming room, and real drinks, not just tepid lemonade."

"That sounds entertaining, I suppose. Masculine."

"Precisely. You need to spend more time surrounded by grown men, Flip. And I'm here to make sure you do."

"How can I ever thank you?"

"Don't fret," James said expansively. "I'm happy to help."

Chapter Twelve

In the darkness of the other side of the carriage, Phillipa sat frozen in a state of sheer horror. He was going to make a man out of her? How? Would there be excessive amounts of perspiration involved?

Would she be expected to make unseemly noises and perhaps—God forbid—*spit*?

Oh, this was dreadful indeed.

The infinite and horrible possibilities continued to run through her mind until the carriage pulled up before a lovely house on an expensive square. Glad to think of something, *anything,* else, Phillipa was about to comment upon the attractive garden in the center of the square when she realized that she was only likely to inspire Mr. Cunnington to further efforts of manly transformation.

Right, then. No floral conversation. What did men speak of? Politics? She knew little of the war effort, despite her personal involvement.

She didn't think her view of the lamentable housekeeping habits of French soldiers would be of much interest, nor did she wish to invite curiosity into her past.

She considered the matter as they entered the house.

The Trapps' front parlor was quite comfortable, and a

good thing too. Just as James had predicted, it was nearly a full hour before the Misses Trapp descended to greet their escorts.

Bitty and Kitty seemed very nice girls, if a bit young. With a start, Phillipa realized that she was scarcely two years older than the twins. When had she become so seasoned?

In that tiny cell off the fireplace, she decided. In those hours she crouched in the silence, waiting for rescue that never came.

"You seem quite lost in thought, Mr. Walters. Are you such a serious-minded fellow, then?" one of the twins asked.

Phillipa reminded herself to bow. "I do apologize, Miss Trapp." The girl had been introduced as Miss Trapp, so she must be the eldest by a very short while. The other girl, Miss Kitty Trapp, looked sharply at Phillipa.

"Pray, how did you know you spoke to Bitty?"

James looked back and forth between the twins. "That's true. How did you know? I can tell the difference, but I've known them for some time. Still, I admit they do confound me occasionally."

Phillipa blinked. "Why, they look very little alike to me."

Miss Kitty Trapp slapped her on the arm with her fan teasingly. "Nothing like? Go on, admit it. 'Twas naught but a lucky guess, wasn't it?"

Phillipa wondered if she'd done something wrong. Should she pretend confusion? Whyever for? "Of course I see a resemblance, but there are many differences between you. Miss Kitty Trapp is slightly taller than Miss Trapp. Miss Trapp's hair is a shade lighter, while Miss Kitty Trapp's eyes are a deeper shade of blue."

Mr. Cunnington stared at her for a long moment while the girls complimented Phillipa effusively on her observational skills. Apparently they were quite taken with the idea of differing appearances. Why then did they wear identical dresses and hairstyles?

"You've won our true affection, Mr. Walters," gushed Bitty, as she insisted that Phillipa call her—when her mama was not present, of course—and wound her arm through Phillipa's in a familiar way.

Kitty wound her arm through Phillipa's other arm, apparently in the spirit of sisterly competition. "We'll not part with you for anything," said Kitty. "It is a rare fellow who can tell us apart even after great acquaintance."

"Indeed, Phillip," James added, "your powers of observation are quite impressive. How gratifying it is to see you fulfill my faith in you. Pray, continue to reveal other such skills for my edification."

Warmth went through Phillip at such praise, although she wasn't sure what James meant by that. Why was he looking at her so speculatively? She did not have time to ponder the matter long, for the girls virtually dragged her to the carriage, vying for her attention all the while.

It seemed she was courting now.

The ball was like any other ball, but for the urgency and frustration that kept James on edge. He'd buttonholed every influential gentleman in the room to try to win their support, but it had gained him little. Liverpool was right. No one wanted to charge Lady Winchell in this case.

James wasn't surprised to see Collis Tremayne wander into the ball a few hours into the evening. Collis protested wildly against social engagements on principle, but James suspected that Collis eventually needed distraction from his own thoughts. With his left arm nearly useless after his term as a soldier in His Majesty's service, the heir to the Etheridge title felt quite useless on the whole. His uncle had recruited him into training with the Liar's Club recently, but James knew that Collis still wasn't entirely sure about the prospect. How could a one-armed man serve the Crown effectively?

James rubbed his own healing shoulder in sympathy. What would have happened to him if he'd been as permanently disabled as Collis had?

Perish the thought. His gunshot wound was healing at

last and he'd completely recovered from his experience with starvation. He would be back on full duty very soon.

Collis approached James after a few minutes of meeting and greeting and took up his post on the other side of James holding up the wall.

"Ho there, Cunnington."

James nodded amiably. "Tremayne."

Collis looked around the ballroom. "Where's Phillip? Did he weasel out and leave you with the Trapp-me-now twins?"

James took a long swallow of bland lemonade. "No. He's here."

Collis grinned. "Hiding out, is he? Can't say as I blame him. Have you ever seen such a crop of avid young ladies? I believe we're going to have to import blokes from America to take up the marital slack."

James grinned slowly. "I don't think we'll be pestered much tonight."

Collis raised a brow. "Why not?"

James jerked his head toward a multicolored knot of silk and lace gowns on the far side of the ballroom. "They're all over there."

Collis studied the group. A line developed between his brows. "What's all that about? There must be twenty girls in that crowd. What are they up to?"

James grimaced. "What they are up to is . . . Phillip."

Collis exhaled a skeptical laugh. "Your skinny little tutor, the beau of the ball? I don't believe a word of it."

James shrugged. "Come along then. I'll prove it to you. He's probably due for rescue by now, anyway."

The two approached the circle of fawning women. It wasn't easy to spot Phillip until they were quite close, for the fellow was little taller than his admiring throng.

As Collis and James drew near, they heard Phillip speaking quite calmly, without any apparent need for rescue.

"Yes, Miss Tate, I quite agree. The high waist is doomed to fall soon. An economical young lady might think to have a bit of extra fabric left at the waist when she orders her gowns, as to let it down when fashion dictates."

This suggestion was met with many admiring murmurs of agreement, which then hushed immediately as Phillip opened his mouth once more. "But I think you can calmly put your faith into the purchase of a few good bonnets. One can always change the trim, can one not?"

Kitty Trapp pressed forward from the group to tuck her arm boldly through Phillip's. Bitty immediately followed suit.

Collis leaned to mutter in James's ear. "Looks like they're staking territory. Twins, for pity's sake. It's a shame there isn't more of the fellow to go around."

James nodded. "I'm taking him everywhere. I've never been so free of pursuit." All the better to wage pursuits of his own.

Collis elbowed him. "Wait a moment there! This was my idea! I should get a chance to take him along to my social engagements as well."

James pursed his lips. "True. You may have him on Tuesdays. I rarely go out on Tuesdays."

"Excellent." Then Collis caught on. "Just a moment! No one goes out on Tuesdays!"

James grinned and patted Collis on the shoulder. "Quite right. Good of you not to insist. Phillip should spend time with Robbie on Tuesdays."

"Blast," muttered Collis cheerfully. "Ah, well, I'll simply tag along with the two of you from now on."

James shrugged. "Fine with me." He pondered the crowd for a moment. Was there any point in remaining in the ballroom?

"Come along, Col. Let's see if there's anyone I need to speak to in the gaming room."

Collis nodded. "What about him?" He cocked his head toward Phillip.

James shrugged. "I'll take him into the gaming room another time. Tonight I'm too busy enjoying the respite from the predatory lassies of London."

Collis grinned. "I'm with you."

Phillipa happened to look up just in time to see James's back disappearing into the crowd. Had he been looking for her? She hoped he wasn't impatient with her. The Trapp sisters hadn't let her loose for a moment.

However, she could not deny she was having a certain amount of fun. It seemed that when a man uttered a proclamation about fashion, his views were taken much more seriously than another woman's. She alone had single-handedly banished puce from the wardrobe of no less than twenty girls tonight.

She wished she could declare "figure improvers" dead as well, but she didn't think a gentleman would expound on the new fad in underthings in the company of young ladies. Pity that, for she had seen more than one girl have a dizzy spell from a tight corset tonight. The things were a menace—unhealthy and ridiculous.

Therefore most likely invented by a man.

Still, enough was enough. She was being torn in two like a wishbone by the competitive maneuverings of the Trapp twins and the ballroom was becoming uncomfortably stuffy.

It took several moments of apologies and reassurances before the girls let her go. Phillipa looked about her, but could see no sign of James and Collis. In fact, there were very few gentlemen in evidence at all. How odd. She was sure there had been more about earlier. Had there been some sort of masculine secret signal to desert the ballroom?

Still, all the better. The more time before her first "Ways and Means of Manliness" lesson, the better. For now, she would have a lemonade and hide behind a potted palm until she caught her breath.

Quite comfortable in her hiding place, she dawdled there. Finally unobserved, she was able to gaze wistfully at the confections of lace and organza worn by the other girls. She'd never owned anything so pretty. Not that Papa had deprived her, of course. There had simply never been a need for her to own such a gown.

Anyway, wouldn't she look a fright with her hair mangled as it was? She was still as thin as a stick as well, although she was feeling much better after four days of good meals. Sighing to herself, she indulged in one more moment of cheerful envy before she tired of herself.

The evening was growing late. She had a view of the ballroom, but there was still no sign of James. What should she do?

It occurred to her that he might have left her. After all, she wasn't his escort. Men likely left each other to their own devices all the time. As a man, she herself could leave anytime she desired.

What a charming thought. Simply make her regrets and leave, with no escort, no footmen, no chaperone. She sighed in wonder. How free men were!

She had just about decided to make her own escape when her hiding place was invaded by two young men who looked over their shoulders as they ducked under the palm. Phillipa stepped about the other side of the giant pot before she could be spotted. No more men tonight, thank you.

She tugged her waistcoat straight and was about to make her way to take leave of her host when she heard a fragment of whispered conversation.

"—once I get her onto the balcony, count to fifty, then fetch Mrs. Wint."

"Why that old windbag? She'd gossip the ear off an elephant!"

"Precisely my goal. It cannot be anyone who could be trusted to keep quiet out of kindness to the girl's family. I need to be interrupted by someone who will ruin her if she does not wed me posthaste."

"I don't know about this, Tuttle. Are you sure you want to marry *her*? What if she ends up looking just like her mother?"

"What do I care what she looks like? Her inheritance will get the creditors off my back for a long while, and her papa will always be good for a hit as well." There came a low snicker. "Everything I always wanted in a woman."

"But Tuttle, don't they have highly placed friends?"

"All the more reason they'll want a quick and quiet marriage, then. Just do as you're told, Merrick, and stop trying to think. You've no talent for it."

The young men ducked from beneath the fronds to make their way across the ballroom and were immediately lost in the crush.

Hot red rage filled Phillipa as she realized what the two were planning. A very public compromising to force some young woman to wed out of shame and to hand her inheritance over to that indebted snake! Phillipa wished she could thrash the fellows herself, but she must remember that she was not a man after all. She could only try to stop them. But how?

Phillipa rounded the giant pot to dart across the ballroom without a care for her own unseemly haste.

Bloody hell. Where was James? This fellow Tuttle was a bruiser. Phillipa could not stop him on her own.

A glint of blond hair caught Phillipa's eye across the ballroom. Kitty.

Phillipa sidestepped dancers until she reached Kitty's side. "Kitty! Do you know a fellow by the name of Tuttle?"

"Do you mean John Tuttle? If you're looking for John, all you need to do is look for Bitty. They just went for a turn around the floor." Kitty waved vaguely to her right.

Oh, no. Not Bitty.

Phillipa grabbed Kitty's hand and towed the surprised girl along as she ran after Tuttle and Bitty. There was no sign of the couple in the ballroom. Abruptly, Phillipa changed direction.

The balcony.

Chapter Thirteen

Phillipa towed Kitty down the short hall to the sitting room. She'd been given a tour of the balcony and its adjoining rooms by the giggling daughter of the house earlier. The small room was dark.

Kitty cleared her throat. "Phillip? My sister isn't—"

Phillipa kept her grip on Kitty and led her to the balcony doors. She opened the door to see Bitty struggling in the arms of a large young man. Fabric tore harshly.

"John, please! You are hurting me! Please, stop!" There was real fear in Bitty's voice.

Phillipa heard the latch rattle on the other door. Oh, no! It was Merrick with his witness!

"It is a rare fellow who can tell us apart even after great acquaintance." Instantly, Phillipa threw wide her own door, flung Kitty out to stumble across the stone balcony, then snatched Bitty from the arms of the astonished John and pushed her back into the darkened sitting room. "Shh!" she urged the sobbing girl, then shut the door on her.

She turned back to observe a very interesting tableau. John stood in the rectangle of golden light coming from the ballroom, staring openmouthed at a composed and perfectly groomed version of the girl he had been ravaging a moment before. In the open doorway stood the gullible Merrick, along with a stout and disapproving dowager.

The woman sniffed. "John Tuttle, what are you doing out here alone with that girl?"

Uh-oh. Phillipa stepped forward and bowed deeply. "But they are not alone at all!" John jerked in surprise and blinked at Phillipa's sudden appearance. Phillipa ignored him. "Ah, you must be the divine Mrs. Wint. I have heard so much about you that I begged my good friends here to make introduction for me. Did Merrick not tell you of my deep admiration?"

Mrs. Wint melted on the spot. "Why, if it isn't Mr. Walters! I've heard nothing but wonderful things about you this evening. I've been most eager to meet you as well. But why out here on this chilly terrace?"

"Oh, but Miss Trapp was most overcome by the excitement of the evening and I thought a bit of air would do her good. John was simply aiding us." Phillipa stepped closer and gave Mrs. Wint a rueful smile. "You know how silly these young ladies can be. And now I fear I must escort her home and miss my opportunity to have the pleasure of your company." She bowed again, rising to see the flattered gleam in the older woman's eyes.

Mrs. Wint smiled, her sour face transformed by the besotted expression now upon it.

Phillipa managed to get the woman back into the ballroom and to shut the door on the four of them at last. Merrick seemed confused, but John Tuttle was darkly furious. He advanced on Phillipa.

"You ruined everything, you bloody little ponce!"

Phillipa faced him squarely, too angry to fear anything at the moment. "You swine. Have you any concept of what a forced marriage would mean to Bitty? Have you no care that you would ruin the rest of her life, taking any chance of her future happiness for your own selfish gain?"

"Stupid chit wants to get married, everybody knows it. What do you care, anyway?"

Phillipa shook her head. "There's no use explaining anything to you, is there? You've no thought past your own childish desires." She shook her head with disgust. "Get out of here. I've done with you both."

Kitty stepped forward. "Oh, but I am not."

Merrick stepped back in alarm, and Phillipa didn't blame him one bit. Kitty was pale with fury, her eyes snapping and her entire frame aquiver.

"You have no idea who you are dealing with, John Tuttle. The Trapp girls need bear no ill actions without reaction."

"What can you do?" Tuttle snarled. "There's no man you can tell without ruining your sister and yourself."

Kitty smiled slowly, a feral little showing of teeth that made Phillipa blink. "Who says I'm going to tell a man? Think you that men are the only ones with power in London? Have you not heard of Lady Etheridge, my own dear aunt? And what of Lady Raines, confidante of the Prince Regent himself?"

Tuttle's bravado was wearing a bit thin, Phillipa noticed. Could that be a sheen of sweat upon his brow? She stood back, satisfied to watch Kitty flay the fellow in her sister's defense.

"You'll be watched, John Tuttle," Kitty said. "Every ball, every musicale, every drive in the park. We'll be watching you . . . and we won't ever stop."

"Dear me," murmured Phillipa. "I say, Tuttle, have you considered a tour of the West Indies? I hear the weather is sublime."

Merrick fumbled for his friend's sleeve. "John, come. You don't want to anger them further."

"Anger who?"

"*Them.* The women." Merrick's voice broke. Phillipa realized the fellow was not quite as thick as he appeared.

Tuttle swallowed as he apparently began to realize precisely what he was up against. Kitty nodded. "All the women, John. The ladies, the daughters, the aunties . . . the *sisters.* Don't ever scotch with sisters, Mr. Tuttle. You are not equipped to suffer our wrath."

"I'll get you, Kitty Trapp. See if I don't—"

"Oh, do shut up, Tuttle," said Phillipa, rolling her eyes. "Get thee gone while you still can. I'll hold her back as long as I am able," she added lazily.

Merrick succeeded in pulling Tuttle back into the ballroom. The moment the door shut on the two young men, Phillipa and Kitty turned as one to dash through the other doors to Bitty's aid.

Bitty sat curled into the corner of the velvet sofa, crying softly in the dark. There was a coal or two left in the grate, enough for Phillipa to light one of the candles on the mantel. She stirred the remaining coals to add a bit of warmth to the room, for Bitty was visibly trembling.

The girl was a sorry sight indeed. Kitty knelt immediately to wrap her arms about her twin, pulling her close to rock her gently and stroke her hair. "Bitty, we're here now. All is well, darling. All is well."

Phillipa stood back, allowing Kitty to offer her sister the comfort she needed. The woman within her longed to give comfort as well, but she knew it would not be the same coming from a gentleman, fond of him as one might be.

Not that Kitty wasn't doing a marvelous job on her own. Phillipa had been wrong to mistake the girls' competitive bickering for lack of feeling. It was plain now that the bond between the two was deep and strong.

Pity the fellow who mistreated one of the sisters Trapp.

James finally took his leave of the gaming room after having exhausted every avenue of persuasion, along with most of his purse. A fine evening had been had by all the others, with the ladies apparently quite diverted for hours by their new playmate, Phillip.

Despite his frustration, however, he'd had a brilliant idea as the other men had held a rousing debate on sporting subjects. There was a place in London devoted to the very practice that James meant to set Phillip upon. Pugilism. Gentleman Jackson's gymnasium was devoted to the manly art of bare-knuckle fisticuffs.

Phillip was going to love it. Furthermore, it was precisely what he himself needed. All his hot-and-bother over the redhead was simply a sign of his general frustration. A bit of sweat and violence would take care of it, no doubt.

He collared two young men about Phillip's age as he left the smoking room. "Ho there. Have you seen Phillip Walters about anywhere? Thin bloke, brown hair?"

One of the fellows turned a curious shade of purple, the other an even more inexplicable shade of white. They mumbled a hurried negative and moved away in a profound hurry.

How peculiar. James watched them go, unease beginning to stir in his gut. Peculiar was never good in his experience. A lady approached him, a heavily wigged dowager who beamed at him with such approval that James nearly looked behind himself to see the object of her affection.

No luck. She was aiming for him all right. He smiled and bowed as she came even with him.

She tittered and held out a much bejeweled hand. "I do hope you'll forgive my boldness, Mr. Cunnington, but I had to tell you of the very favorable impression your young Mr. Walters has made upon us all this evening."

James managed to bow again over the lady's hand. "I thank you for your kind words, Mrs.—"

"Wint, dear. Mrs. Adolphus Wint."

Wint? As in, "Don't get caught by the Chill Wint"? The frightening matron who single-handedly held London society in fear of her malicious tongue? Good Lord. Phillip had managed to charm even this stout social warrior? The fellow showed no end of talents.

Frankly, James was beginning to think Phillip was too good to be true. In his experience, no one was that extraordinary without dastardly flaws to match.

"I can take no credit for your praise, Mrs. Wint, but I can say that I am most pleased to have brought Phillip to the attention of such discerning society as yourself." James glanced up to see the satisfaction on the lady's face. Excellent. Now to get away.

Fortunately, she gave him the out herself. "I do think

young Mr. Walters may need your assistance now, Mr. Cunnington. It seems the young lady he is escorting is overcome by the excitement of the evening."

"Ah?" Kitty Trapp, overcome? James couldn't imagine Kitty overcome by anything not bearing claws and teeth. Again . . . peculiar. "Perhaps I might prevail upon you to point me in the direction you last saw Mr. Walters?"

The lady waved her fan toward the balcony doors on the near side of the ballroom. James made his escape.

The balcony proved to be quite empty. Could Phillip have taken Kitty down into the gardens? That feeling of unease twined through him again.

There was only one reason to take a girl into the gardens and Phillip had already proven to be uncommonly appealing to the female population. Could he be so lacking in honor as to use that charm for ill?

Abruptly, James realized that he knew very little about Phillip. The fellow seemed harmless enough, even a bit of a milksop. Yet there was that element of mystery . . .

He turned to lean over the balustrade and call into the garden. "Phillip?" James's voice carried nicely into the night. "Phillip, are you out there?"

A tiny click sounded behind him. Before he could turn, he felt a hand come down on his shoulder. James spun, breaking the opponent's grip even as he brought his fist back—

Phillip flinched away from him, throwing his hands up in defense. "Goodness, James! Whatever are you planning on doing with that?"

James let his breath out in a burst of relieved laughter. "Why are you sneaking around out here? Where's Kitty?"

Phillip only stared at him for a moment. "Shouldn't you be asking, where's Bitty?"

Damn. He'd forgotten all about Bitty, so involved he'd been in his mission. "Where is Bitty, then?"

Phillip folded his arms and glared at James. He looked positively angry. James looked past the younger man to the open doorway he'd not noticed before. Kitty Trapp—at least he was fairly sure it was Kitty—stood with her arms crossed as well, glaring at him with equal animosity.

"Where have you been?" Her voice was deadly grim. Oh, yes, Kitty was angry all right. In fact, James thought he'd never seen her so angry.

What was going on here? If both Phillip and Kitty were angry, then—

"Oh, God. Tell me that Bitty's all right."

Kitty stepped back from the doorway. James followed her into the dim sitting room. One candle was lit on the mantel and by its light, James could see a tearful Bitty huddling on the sofa as if she were trying to be very small indeed.

He went to his knee in front of the girl. She sniffled once, but wouldn't look at him. Her hair hung tangled around her face and the bodice of her dress was ripped nearly in half. Even by the dim candlelight, James could see the bruises on her pale arms that marked rough handling indeed.

Fury blazed through him. He stood and turned roughly on Phillip. "What have you done to her?"

Phillip stepped back in reaction and to James's astonishment let forth a startled laugh. "I?"

Kitty Trapp stepped between them. "James Cunnington, when your sister Agatha gets through with you, you'll wish you'd never been born!"

"What?" This made no sense. "What did I do? Phillip—"

"Phillip not only rescued Bitty from that bounder, but he saved her reputation as well. Even Mama needn't find out. You, on the other hand, were nowhere to be found. You were Bitty's escort this evening. How could you let this happen?"

James flinched from the accusation in her voice. Bitty's sniffling broke through the confrontation. James returned to her side, offering her his handkerchief. Too little, too late.

"Are you—did he—?"

Bitty shook her head. "No. Phillip came in time. But I was so frightened."

"Who was it?"

Kitty opened her mouth, but Phillip stopped her. The

younger man turned to James. "What would you do about it if you knew?"

James felt rage twist within him. "Call him out. Have him arrested. A public flogging."

"That would make you feel better, would it?"

"Decidedly."

"How very nice for you. And what about Bitty? Would having her reputation ruined make her feel better?"

James opened his mouth but stopped. Phillip was quite right. Unfair as it might be, the one who was most stained by such things was always the lady. "So we do nothing?"

Phillip's jaw worked slowly. "I should very much like to beat him to a quivering pulp." He looked down at his quite obviously delicate hands. "I can't."

"God, no! If the bloke is such an animal, you wouldn't stand a chance!"

Phillip's lips twisted. "I thank you for your faith in me." However, he didn't seem truly offended.

James took Bitty's hand in his and pondered it. He turned to her. "Bitty, you are my friend and tonight you are my responsibility. What do you want me to do?"

Bitty dabbed at her nose with the handkerchief. "Well, the quivering-pulp part did sound nice . . ."

"That can be arranged."

She narrowed her eyes at him. "No. If we tell you who, then you'll do something honorable and annoying and everything will get much worse."

James sighed. "This is probably true."

Kitty came to sit on her sister's other side. "Well, then, we shall continue with our first plan."

James frowned. This did not sound promising. "What was that?"

Phillip grinned. "Oh, nothing you need to worry about, James. Only . . . don't ever make Kitty angry."

James decided that he was better off not knowing. "Only promise me that you will be very careful, Kitty. I wouldn't want this to happen to you."

Bitty shook her head. "Not Kitty. She'd never allow herself to be charmed to a deserted balcony. Why, she even carries a knife!"

James blinked at that and turned to look at plump pretty Kitty Trapp. She smiled sweetly back at him, blinking her lashes demurely. In a movement too quick to catch, she produced a narrow silver blade.

Appalled, James recognized a classic move from the repertoire of the inimitable Kurt. "How did you learn that?"

Kitty dimpled and the knife disappeared as quickly as it had come. "Auntie Clara. She gave us both one for our birthday, but Bitty said it wasn't ladylike." Her smile disappeared. "Oh, Bitty, I didn't mean—"

Bitty raised her chin. "No, you're quite right. One must always strive to be a lady, but I see now that one cannot always depend upon a man to be a gentleman."

"One most definitely cannot," Phillip agreed. "Now, we must get the girls home, James. Mrs. Trapp is still in the ballroom. She's likely mad to know where we've all gone off to. Distract her for a few moments. I'll find our cloaks. Kitty, you have your sister neatened up enough to pass by your mother. I'll get you two to the carriage and we'll have Bitty well covered up before your mother joins us. Bitty has taken a chill. Kitty, you'll volunteer to put her to bed and wait on her for a few days."

Kitty nodded and even Bitty straightened under such call to action. Phillip turned to James. "Give me ten minutes, then bring Mrs. Trapp along."

James nodded and accompanied Phillip from the room. As the smaller fellow strode away, it occurred to James that he had just been ordered about by a bloke he could toss with one hand. He shook his head and gave a short laugh. Never let it be said that Phillip lacked the ability to command!

As James made his way through the thinning crowd to find Mrs. Trapp, he recounted Kitty's story to himself. Phillip had acted quickly and decisively on unfamiliar territory to divert a very unpleasant fate for a girl he barely knew. Clever, quick, and honorable to boot. James was going to have to lengthen that list he was making of Phillip's qualifying traits.

As far as James could see, Phillip was a Liar born.

Tomorrow would begin his training, whether he knew it or not.

Chapter Fourteen

It was far too early in the morning for surprises. "What is this place?" Phillipa looked about her, fighting off a yawn. They had been out quite late last night with Kitty and Bitty and she would have dearly loved a little lie-in. Breakfast might have been nice, but as she detected the pervading odor of sweat in this otherwise fine hall, she thought twice.

"You're going to love this, Flip."

Phillipa didn't feel any too sure. James grinned. "Robbie's going to be entirely plagued off when he finds out where we've been. He can't get enough of Gentleman Jackson's sports hall."

Phillipa turned her head, looking this way and that. At that moment, a number of men left a side room and entered the main gymnasium. James raised a hand to greet one of them. "Hello, Bertie. Going up against himself today?"

One of the men turned in response, then approached. Beside James, Phillipa choked. James gave her a startled glance but she only looked away in a fluster.

Bertie stuck out a hand as he came near and gave James's a good wringing. "Haven't seen you lately, Cunnington. How's the shoulder?"

"I'm nearly in top form, Bert. This will be my first day back in the ring for a long while."

Phillipa was in a panic. The man Bertie was virtually naked, as were all the others now emerging from the side room. They wore only abbreviated drawers that ended above the knee, drawers that did as little to conceal their bodies as James's had done the night she'd disturbed his bath.

When Bertie reached to shake *her* hand, she stepped over the edge of panic into hysteria. Stifling a maniacal giggle, she shook the man's hand as firmly as she could, staring all the while at a point somewhere near his left ear. She nearly yelped when James clapped her on the shoulder.

"Shall we change?"

"Yes, please," she answered, before she realized that he wasn't talking about their location. She balked at the door leading to the changing room and peeped around the corner.

Men. Short men, tall men, skinny men, fat men. Men with pale shiny skin and men with skin darkened by the sun. Men with drawers on and—it must be said—men without. Her ears began to pound in shock as one fellow stripped his drawers off in one graceful bend, providing her with an astounding view of his hairy buttocks.

Eeep. She screwed her eyes shut, but it was too late. Those buttocks would live forever in her memory. Yanking her head back through the portal, she whirled to press her back to the wall next to the door.

Hell was a place full of naked smelly men, where a woman who lied had to spend eternity staring at the chandelier.

"I'll-wait-out-here-if-it's-all-the-same-to-you," she blurted.

She heard James snort. "Good Lord, Flip. You can't box in a shirt and trousers."

She shook her head frantically, although she didn't know what a box had to do with anything. "I'll be fine. No problem."

He sighed gustily. She felt his breath on her cheek and her gut twisted. She was disappointing him again, she knew. But how could she possibly explain?

"All right, Flip. But will you at least promise to try the ring?"

Anything, just don't make me go in there! "Absolutely. I will definitely try the ring."

"Very well. I'll be but a moment."

She felt him pass her but remained where she was, desperately trying to scrub that final image from her mind's eye.

No good. It was to be hairy buttocks forever. Damn, if she had to preserve someone's naked arse in her memory, why couldn't it have been James's?

She stayed out of the way of the other men and stared with great interest at the soaring architecture of the gymnasium hall. Majestic arches met overhead, supported by lovely Ionic columns that pierced the echoing chamber at regular intervals.

"Ready, Flip?"

Now don't let on that you're all atwitter over a bit too much skin. She took a breath and turned to face him.

And almost swallowed her tongue. His bare torso gleamed before her eyes, sculpted into rigidly defined muscles and sinews. The scar on his shoulder was like a medal adorning his heroic chest. He was wrapping the knuckles of one hand with a linen strip and she found herself fascinated by the tension in his bicep as it rolled and twisted.

Great Greek gods. How could she have forgotten how splendid he was? Or how his splendor turned her knees to porridge and her female parts to melted wax?

An attendant came to wrap the second strip around James's other hand. After pounding his fists together for a moment as if to adjust the fit, James gave Phillipa a challenging grin.

"Watch carefully now. If you work hard, you might be as good as me someday." Then he swung himself up onto the platform and climbed through the ropes. Another half-dressed fellow stepped up at James's invitation, but Phillipa had eyes for James alone. The high clerestory windows poured the pearly morning light down on his honed body, highlighting and shadowing his muscular form in a breath-taking way. At least, James took *her* breath away.

Then the other man hit him. Hard.

Phillipa cried out in protest and surprise, a high sound that was unmistakably feminine. Fortunately, the blow caused the other men who watched to break out in encouraging cries of their own. Her exclamation went unnoticed in the general bellowing.

She bit her lip, determined not to make another sound as she watched a most appalling display of masculine rivalry. Blow after blow rained on James, although she must admit that he gave as good as hc got.

He didn't seem to be coming to any actual harm in his ridiculous game, so Phillipa gradually relaxed enough to feel the pull of attraction once more.

Pull? It was a bloody force of nature. As the session progressed she watched James perspire, turning his body into sculpted bronze. Yet he was liquid metal as well, as his skin rippled over the flex and pull of taut muscle.

So graceful. So powerful.

She wanted to touch him. She wanted to run her hands up his bulging biceps to his broad shoulders, then bring her fingers to her lips to taste the salt on his gleaming skin. His hair dampened and clung to his forehead and neck in an unrestrained mane. He was like a great golden beast. He lunged and parried with his opponent, his brown eyes gone black and intent on his prey . . .

She wanted to be his prey. She ached to have that intensity directed at her. *Want me. Pursue me.*

Capture me.

Quite unaware of herself, she licked her lips and watched him with eyes wide and thighs pressed tightly together.

James ducked aside from his sparring partner's next blow in a graceful movement. Nicely done, if he did say so himself. He chanced a look out of the ring to see if Phillip had seen that one. The fellow had a lot of catching up to do in the manly arts—

Phillip was not only watching, he was *intent*. Excellent. James grinned and laid a nice uppercut to his opponent's chin. Then he had to laugh inwardly at himself. He ought to be more concerned with improving Phillip than impressing him.

Still, the fellow's avid attention was good to see. It seemed he had finally managed to snare Phillip's interest in something more than books and food. After all, everyone needed a bit of diversion, didn't they?

Time for Phillip's turn. James backed off a few dancing steps, raising his taped fists in the gesture for "halt." It wouldn't do to be too tired to give Phillip a good lesson.

He beckoned to one of the attendants, who brought forward another set of tapes. Phillip looked down when the fellow approached him, then backed away, hands up.

"No—"

"Now, Flip, you're going back on your word?" James leaned on the ropes. "Not an hour ago you promised to give it a try."

James had to laugh at the panic on Phillip's face.

"I've never struck anyone in my life," he protested.

James nodded agreeably. "Then I'd say it's past time."

The attendant was busy divesting Phillip of his frock coat. When the man reached for the buttons of Phillip's waistcoat, the young tutor stepped back out of range. "This is sufficient, thank you."

One of the men watching snorted. "Does the little bloke want his hat on too?"

James waved the fellow to silence and climbed through the ropes to jump down lightly at Phillip's side. He leaned in close. "Come now, Flip. You don't want to look the rabbit in front of this lot, do you?"

Phillip swallowed. "I don't care a whit for their opinion . . . but I did give you my word." His bony chin went up. "I can only promise to try, James."

James almost reached out to ruffle that mousy mop. Then he recalled Phillip's prickly pride and settled for clapping him on the shoulder. Phillip staggered a bit but scared up a wavering smile. Somewhat reluctantly, he held out his hands to be taped.

A few moments later, James stood across from him on the canvas. Phillip stood primly, feet together, fists held up and forward as if he were milking a cow.

Hoots sounded from the gallery. James shook his head at them all and moved around behind Phillip. Kneeling, he clapped one hand between Phillip's rigid knees to part them.

"Here. Stand feet apart for balance. Step forward with the left." Phillip didn't move. "Phillip?"

Phillipa was absolutely frozen in shock at the sensation of James's hand between her thighs. At his insistent shove, she managed to breathe and, yes, step forward with one foot.

"Other left, laddie," shouted one of the wags.

Phillipa switched feet hurriedly, feeling her blush climb to full purple. Then she felt James straighten and move his body close behind hers. He wrapped his arms around her to take her fists in his hands.

Weak with confusion and trembling desire, she allowed him to turn her wrists and to advance her left hand forward while drawing back her right. He gave the left fist a squeeze.

"Guard," he said softly. His breath warmed her ear and sent hot shivers down her neck.

He pulled the other fist back nearly to her shoulder. Then he extended both their right hands forward, forcing her body to twist as his chest pressed to her back until her arm extended to its full length.

"Straight Right."

His body was warm and damp from his exertions. She could feel his heat through the heavy waistcoat and shirt she wore. She could smell him—the scent of recently bathed man after a bit of healthy exercise. His scent was stirring and male, waking yet another sense of hers to be dominated by his presence.

He drew her arms back to the beginning position, then brought her left fist around in a curve to strike empty air.

"Left Hook."

His groin brushed her buttocks as they twisted and she found herself fighting the urge to grind gently against him there . . . to press back against the length of him, to rest her head back on his broad shoulder as he wrapped both hot hands around her tightening breasts—

"Flip? Are you going to faint or something?"

She started, bolts of chill disorientation making her quiver. "Zap," she muttered.

James was back across from her, staring at her through his raised fists. "Are you ready? Or do you need to sit down?"

Phillipa shook her head. "Might as well be done with it."

James shook his head. "That's no way to think. You seemed interested enough before. As if you couldn't wait to tussle."

She was unable to repress a surprised snort of guilty laughter at that. "Indeed," she affirmed shakily. Then taking a breath, she raised her fists in the stance he had shown her.

"En garde," she challenged gamely.

James grinned and she found herself most distracted by the way the corners of his eyes crinkled and the way his dimples flashed so—

He punched her in the shoulder.

"Ow!"

"Get your guard up."

She stared at him blankly. "Parry," he explained. "Block me with your left."

She tried, batting his light blows away, but enough got through that tears began to lurk behind her determinedly dry eyes. It *hurt* and she was getting bloody tired of it!

Facing Phillip, James balanced lightly on the balls of his feet. He tapped Flip again and again, easily slipping past the younger fellow's awkward defense.

"Hit me, Flip."

Phillip only ducked away from James's dancing fists. The men watching began to shout encouragement. James was glad to hear it, for Phillip needed all the confidence he could get.

Trying to get him to lighten his fierce tension, James teased him. "Come now, Flip. Take a swing. If you land one on me, I'll let you out of the ring."

Phillip only tightened his shoulders and kept his head tucked behind his own raised fists. The two circled, James easily, Phillip clumsily, while the spectators called out all the while.

"Come on, Phillip. Haven't you ever wanted to hit anyone? Well, now you can do it and get away with it scot-free. Set yourself loose, man."

Phillip stopped dead still and James caught a look at his face. The fellow had gone a deep humiliated red and his lips were pressed tightly together.

James halted and lowered his fists. "Ah, Flip, I'm sor—"

Phillip's fist lashed out in a perfect left hook, smashing into James's jaw. James felt his own teeth clench his tongue and staggered, more startled than struck. The blow had been technically perfect but not terribly heavy. Still, best to make good show of it. The one thing Phillip needed more than strength was confidence.

So James let his stagger grow into a spinning fall and landed flat on his back on the canvas. He lay there a moment, exploring his injured mouth with his swelling tongue.

He heard Phillip gasp and nearly shook his head at the girlish sound. Then he recalled that he was supposed to be knocked out and lay still, waiting.

He really should teach the fellow to grunt.

He felt Phillip land on his knees beside him. "James? Are you all right? Did I hurt you? Oh, James, I'm so sorry. You said to think of a time when I wanted to hit someone and I was thinking of that swine last night and I—oh, James, please wake up!"

What, no triumphant crowing? No grandstanding? No sportsmanlike faint praise for the downed opponent? James cracked open one eye to see Phillip kneeling over him, his narrow face flushed and tragically worried.

"Fwip?" Damn his swelling tongue. "Are you *cwying*?"

Phillip shook his head vehemently, then spoiled the denial by wiping one wrist across his eyes. For the first time, James noticed the appalled silence from the previously loud and cheerful gallery. Bloody hell.

He sat up and took Phillip's upper arm in a firm grip. "Pull yourself together, man," he hissed. "Or you'll never be able to hold your head up in this place again!"

"What? What did I do now?"

James sighed. There was no point in blaming Phillip. He should have realized that pugilism wasn't the place to begin. It was too bad, for the fellow had a naturally perfect swing . . .

Phillip sniffled. James couldn't bear it. He jumped up and pulled Phillip through the ropes to drag him off to the changing room. Once there, he sat him on a bench and straddled it to face him.

James sighed. "Phillip, what am I going to do with you?"

"Why must you do anything at all? Why can I not simply go on the way I am?"

"But haven't you any ambition, man? Haven't you thought that perhaps you'd like to be more than a tutor? Don't you ever long for adventure?" He looked away, disappointed. "Perhaps you're simply not the adventurous sort."

Phillipa was abruptly angry. In addition to her escape from Spain and near starvation, she'd been forced to wear ridiculous, uncomfortable clothing, dance with girls, carry her own parcels, and open her own bloody doors.

She'd been quite proud of the way she'd risen to such unfamiliar challenges. Yet here was James, discounting her ability to deal with adversity?

She glanced up to see James staring at her. With difficulty, she curbed her anger. "The difference between adventure and danger, James, is one's willingness to partake."

James held up a hand. "My apologies, Phillip. I simply thought—" He broke off to shake his head. "Never you mind. Perhaps we'll speak of it someday." He stood. "Well done, by the by. You've a fine left hook."

Phillipa sat up straighter and grinned up at him. "Too bloody right I do."

James's brown eyes shone pride at her. The changing

room swiftly became far too warm. A bit breathless at the joy that went through her at his admiration, Phillipa forced herself to look away, even if that meant endangering her peace of mind with further hairy male parts.

A sudden disturbance from the doorway thankfully drew James's attention from her before she embarrassed herself by climbing into his lap. A burly man had entered the changing room, swearing.

"The unbelievable bastard! He's out there right now, as if he has the right to come and go as he pleases!"

"Who?"

The big man snorted with disgust. "Lord Treason!"

Phillipa noticed James stiffen at her side. He stood as if to speak to the angry fellow, then simply brushed rudely past him as he left the changing room. Phillipa followed quickly. That was not somewhere she wanted to be left alone!

In the main hall, knots of men stood talking in low voices and glaring at a fair-haired man who was strapping his fists without the help of any of the trainers. The fellow was tall and well-designed and not at all hairy.

He was also quite the most attractive man she had ever seen, his classic features bringing to mind a work of art. Phillipa moved close enough to James to whisper, "Who is that?"

She saw James clench his jaw. "Nathaniel Stonewell, Lord Reardon."

"Why did that man call him Lord Treason?"

James gave a short laugh. "Don't you read the newssheets?"

"Oh . . . *that* Lord Treason? The one who is the last living member of the Flower Knights?"

James sent her a dark glance. "The Knights of the Lily, the Fleur de Lis. Napoleon's spies."

How fascinating. "He's a spy?" Lord Reardon certainly looked as though he could charm the secrets out of anyone, especially if that anyone was a woman. Or simply breathing.

James's reply was cool. "So they say."

Surprised by that response when everyone else in the

room was getting decidedly hot, Phillipa looked up at James in time to catch him giving the fair-haired man a tiny nod of acknowledgment. She blinked. Did James consort with Lord Treason? Surely not!

Yet there was no denying that small greeting. Nor was there any denying the slight flicker of Lord Reardon's gaze in response. Of course, no one else noticed, but Phillipa had spent far too much time analyzing James's features of late. She knew his every expression, and the one on his face right now held traces of sympathy.

Sympathy for a publicly notorious traitor.

Chapter Fifteen

James entered the sickroom a few steps behind Mrs. Neely. It seemed the very air in this darkened room reeked of reproach.

"Here he is, sir." Mrs. Neely pulled a bit of lace from within her sleeve to dab at her eyes. "I'm afraid Mr. Weatherby is leaving us even now."

James forced himself to step closer, to stare into the face of his guilt. Weatherby looked nigh unto death already, his skin gray and his breath so shallow his chest scarcely rose at all. Old Weatherby had been a fine Liar, a man full of vinegary humor and a nearly unearthly ability to spot and unravel even the most difficult codes.

When James had first entered the Liars, Weatherby had petitioned to have him as apprentice, likely on the basis of his father's work. What a blow it must have been to learn that young James had little of Jeremy Cunnington's skill with mathematics and even less interest.

Yet Weatherby had been a friend and a comrade, and now he lay on the threshold of death itself. James lowered himself to carefully sit on the edge of the bed. Taking one of Weatherby's dry papery hands in his own, James closed his eyes.

My life for yours.

He wasn't sure how long he sat thus, but finally Mrs. Neely placed one hand on his shoulder. "He's gone, sir."

Of course he was. They were all gone, one by one, all but Ren.

James tenderly folded Angus's hands upon his still chest. "Peace, old fellow. This road is done now," he whispered. Then he rose and forced himself to cross the room.

Ren Porter had been more than comrade. Had indeed been nearly a brother. As the best covert operative the Liars had had, he and James had run many a mission together. They'd been like boys out of school, taking pleasure in their lack of responsibilities and the freedom provided by their work. What more could a man want, truly, than worthy work that left one free to live a life of adventure and heart-pounding excitement?

"The difference between adventure and danger is one's willingness to partake."

Phillip was quite correct. And Ren Porter and James Cunnington had been more than willing to partake.

At least Ren was not so far gone as Weatherby. James tried to hope, he truly did, but in the end he turned away from the occupant in the bed, unable to look upon him for a moment longer.

"Lavinia will pay," he whispered as he stood there with his back to his friend. "She *shall* be brought down, and I shall be the one to do it."

Phillipa had very diffidently asked Denny for a hot bath and had received a warm bath and a plethora of "humphs." Still it was a mercy to lower her aching body into the warm water and relax her guard for a moment.

Her bedchamber door was locked and a chair pressed beneath the latch for good measure. She was going to be a girl for an hour and heaven help the miserable oaf who interrupted her luxury!

"Well, Papa," she murmured to the ripples on the surface of her bath. "I've had an interesting day."

She leaned her head back and slid farther beneath the surface. Her knees rose above the water level, chilling quickly in the air.

This tub was only a small wooden one that she had helped Denny carry from a storage room behind the kitchen. There was a fine tub in the master's dressing room, she'd been coolly informed, that was not for the likes of tutors, no matter how favored they were.

Phillipa chuckled at that memory. If being favored meant having the master pound one into next week, then she was favored indeed. As she scrubbed her skin, she marveled at the fact that although she still felt every one of James's light blows, he had left no mark upon her easily bruised skin. He truly had been careful, though it had not seemed so at the time.

She slid farther under, feeling the pressure and warmth of the water in her ears as she wet her hair. There was another advantage of the male existence. Short, simple-to-care-for hair. Still, she would trade all that ease to be endowed with her own hair—her own gender, for that matter!

"Silk," she muttered when she came up for air. "Silver brushes. Lavender bath scent." She peered at her now shriveled fingers. Her hands had suffered the most from her new life. "Lotion!"

Her wistful reverie was shattered by a hearty knock on her door. "The master wants ye, on the spot!" Denny's voice was gleeful. He knew no tutor would refuse a direct summons from the master of the house.

Phillipa cleared her throat and assumed her Phillip voice. "Tell the master I'll be but a moment."

Denny made his customary noise. "Best make that a quick moment. He's in a black mood this night."

"I'll give you black mood," Phillipa grumbled. Nonetheless, she stood and let the water stream from her body as she rubbed at her hair with a piece of toweling. She quickly dried the rest of herself and made for the clothes she hadn't meant to don again until the morning. Hopping on one foot, she shoved one damp leg into her trousers, forsaking drawers for the sake of speed. What did it matter, when she'd be back upstairs shortly, preparing for bed?

The shirt, quickly, then her old heavy waistcoat—so much coarser than the perfectly fitted ones that had been delivered from Button today. A short note had come as well.

I've taken the liberty of billing Mr. Cunnington for certain items of clothing for you. If anyone wants to know, tell them it was by Milady's order (which it would be if she knew of your situation!).

Still, the old waistcoat from Bessie's husband would do for an hour. She fumbled with the cravat, cursing all the while in several languages. Her boots she pulled over bare feet. Bother the frock coat, shirtsleeves was good enough.

Finally, disheveled and with her hair withstanding any effort to tame it now that it had dried on end while she dressed, she dashed down the long hallway and trotted down the stairs.

"On the spot," she breathed as she stood panting before the study door. She knocked. A deep mumble answered her, a single word. "Enter."

She took a deep breath and stepped into the room. For the first time it occurred to her that something of importance might be afoot. Suddenly less resentful and more alarmed, she advanced into the darkened room.

A fire blazed on the hearth—the only light in the room. Where was Mr. Cunnington? Then she saw the booted feet stretched before the high-backed chair pulled in front of the fireplace.

"You wanted to see me, sir?"

A muffled grunt came from the chair. "Sir Flip? No, not especially. Why?"

Denny. He'd known how badly she'd wanted that bath. Phillipa ground her teeth. Yet another petty deed, rebuke for threatening the fellow's little fiefdom. "Denny, you and I are due for a bit of a chat," she muttered.

"What's that, Flip?" Mr. Cunnington's voice sounded the tiniest bit slurred.

Phillipa stepped forward to see him lounging deep in his chair with his hand wrapped about a well-drained snifter. For the first time Phillipa noticed the nearly empty decanter at his elbow. Goodness, was Mr. Cunnington *drunk*?

"I believe Denny may have made a mistake, sir."

"Very well, then. You can go."

Phillipa nodded and almost turned away. "Is there something amiss, sir?"

He rolled his head on the back of the chair to turn back to the fire. "Only my honor bleeding on the carpet. Nothing amiss at all."

His voice was hollow, drained of the life and warmth that usually infused it. Phillipa felt dark sadness and pain emanating from him like cold from a chunk of ice.

Since their first encounter, in the park, she had been very aware of her attraction to his body. For the first time she realized that she actually liked him. He was amusing and generous, and obviously intelligent.

At the same time there seemed to hover in the background of his powerful personality a sort of wounded vulnerability. She only occasionally caught a glimpse of haunted shadow in those open brown eyes, a brief flash that was always quickly banished by his resolute good humor.

There was pain in him. She knew his parents were gone, and that he had no current attachment to any lady in town, but his sister was obviously much beloved by him, and he seemed to have strong companions in the men that frequented his club.

It wasn't loneliness, then. Or at least, that wasn't the primary cause of his darkness.

No, there was something else lurking behind that warm and easygoing façade. Something that kept him in a state of restlessness, that stole his days and most of his nights, that kept him from letting his guard down with Robbie.

If she didn't know better, she'd wonder if he wasn't run-

ning from something the way she had run from Napoleon's
men. She had the feeling that he didn't dare hold still too
long lest it not be safe.

"Well, I—I'd best leave you to your—your evening, sir.
Good night."

"Good night, Flip." His voice was almost wistful.

The splinter of loneliness in his voice held her quite still.
She should do something. He needed something . . . but
what?

"If I might, sir—"

"What is it, Flip?"

"May I ask what you meant by the bleeding of your
honor?"

"Someone died."

"Ah." She took another step toward him. "People do, I
know."

He cracked an eyelid open. "Is that supposed to be profound?"

She shrugged. "No. Simply true."

He let his head fall back against the chair back. "People
die, you say. And do people die at your hands, Phillip?"

She crossed into the circle of light from the fireplace.
"Perhaps. One never knows how one's choices affect the
world at large."

He snorted. "You are a philosopher. The old pebble-
causing-ripples axiom." He set his glass down on the side
table with exaggerated care. "If you are a pebble, then I am
a bullet. A somewhat more direct route to death for old
Weatherby."

Phillipa sat on the footstool opposite James and regarded
him silently for a moment. "Did you pull the trigger?" she
asked quietly.

"The real one or the metaphorical one?"

"The only one."

He sighed. "No, I did not personally pull the trigger."

"So you might grieve, by any rights. But have you earned
the right to guilt? Or is this simply a self-indulgent mo-

ment?" These were the words she ought to have said to her father, long ago.

He sat up. "Self-indulgent? How can you say that?"

She nodded toward his drink. "Are you drinking for someone else? Or for yourself? In my experience, spirits are more apt to soothe the drinker's pain than another's. I see you sitting here, drinking in the dark, and I must wonder . . . who is this moment for? For the one who died? Or for yourself?"

He stared at her for a moment, bemused fury gathering in his scowl. Unease began a tinny chime within her. She had taken a great chance being so frank. Yet she could not bear to see another man sink into the wallow of mistaken guilt. If someone had ever said those blunt words to her father, she might not be where she was today.

Alone.

Her isolation cut her deeply. How she would love to talk to him of her journey, of its desperation and then of her disappointment and despair once she had reached London.

He had said he knew what it was to be hungry. She believed him. He would listen if she told of her past. He would listen, and sympathize and perhaps even help her.

Or possibly . . . not. It was the "not" that would forever hold her tongue.

James snorted a reluctant laugh. Then he shook his head quickly, as if to dislodge his unfortunate train of thought.

"You are entirely correct, Phillip. I was indulging in a moment of dramatic self-flagellation. Silly of me, when there is so much to do."

She only nodded carefully, watching him. He seemed to have risen out of his personal quagmire, and now only stared thoughtfully into the fire. She stood to leave him in privacy.

"*Sit.*"

Chapter Sixteen

Young Mr. Walters froze as if James's command had prompted a spark of rebellion within him. Still, he was the employer. And he was weary of battling an inner darkness in the arena of night. He only wished a bit of distraction.

Phillip sat.

"We might speak of something else, if you like," he ventured.

"Let us speak of you, then, my young friend."

"There is little enough to know of me," Phillip assured him.

James could barely see the young tutor through the dimness and his own blurred vision. "You've done something interesting with your hair. Is there a new fashion that I'm not aware of?"

Phillip tried to pat down the upstanding bits of hair, then gave up, shrugging. "I was bathing."

"Again? Good Lord, Phillip, you bathe as much as a girl. Not that I mind, of course. Soap is a wonderful thing. I do hope you'll introduce Robbie to it sometime."

"I prefer—I've found that ladies prefer a man who has close acquaintance with his tub."

"I see. In your vast experience and all." James chuckled and rolled his head loosely on his neck. He didn't know if the brandy was finally taking effect or if Phillip's presence was lightening the darkness of his mood, but either way he was grateful. The black funks he'd been prone to since his capture both mystified and alarmed him. He'd heard of men grappling demons of mood and temper after serving in some particularly bloody battle, but he'd never learned of how they made those demons go away again.

Of course, there was always the example of one's friends. Simon had his Agatha. Dalton had his Clara. "Have you ever been in love, Phillip?"

Phillip turned his gaze to the fire. "I don't know, sir."

James nodded. "I know precisely what you mean by that. According to my sister, that tells us that we have most definitely *not* been in love. She's in love with the man who was once my best friend."

"Sir Raines? And are you not friends now?"

"We are . . . but he is hers now, in a way that I'm not sure I understand. And Lord Etheridge has married recently, and he is absolutely mad for his wife . . ."

"And you are wondering when it shall be your turn."

James turned to look at Phillip. "No. Perhaps once I might have, but no longer. Now I have another purpose, one that does not involve acquiring a lady of my own." He waved a hand in the general direction of the upstairs. "Hence Robbie. Heir by post express, as it were."

"You adopted him to be your heir? Not your son?"

James shrugged. "I fail to see your distinction."

Phillip looked down at his hands. "And the lady you will never seek? Did you have someone in mind, before you decided to pursue your other purpose?"

"Oh, yes. I had her all picked out. Beautiful, accomplished, entertaining, and witty. Elegant figure, pretty eyes, and of course, absolutely mad about me. All a man could want, really."

"Ah." Phillip said nothing more for a moment. "What ever happened to her? Did she marry another?"

"I've no idea. I never did actually meet her, you see."

A small bark of laughter escaped Phillip at that and

James grinned. "Come on, Flip. Tell me about your fantasy match."

Phillip cleared his throat. "Ah . . . well. You know, some-one nice."

"Surely you require more than mere respiration, Flip. What about her figure? Fat, thin, curvaceous? What sort do you dream about?"

"Well . . . the dreamy sort, I suppose. What about you? What sort of woman do you dream about? Or don't you dream of women anymore?"

James sat up slightly from his slouch, affronted. "Of course I dream of women! What do you think I am, a tea leaf?"

"N-no, of course not. Definitely not." Phillip seemed quite emphatic about it. James relaxed once more.

"Bloody right I dream about women! I've the best damn fantasy woman you could possibly imagine!" That came out a bit on the emphatic side as well. James wondered if he might just be a bit too drunk.

"Who do you dream of, then?"

Poor Phillip. So young, so curious. James remembered those confusing years well. Manhood was a trial when one could think of nothing but making love, yet could do nothing about it. He probably ought not to stir him up on the sub-ject—not that a fellow of that age likely needed any help. If he was anywhere near as randy as James had been at sixteen, there was no hope for his mental state anyway.

Thank heavens he'd gotten his own urges under control. Why, he hadn't thought of his flame-haired quarry in days. Well, one day, at any rate. Too bad that his new self-control had come far, far too late.

"So what is your fancy?"

James rolled his glass upon his forehead, but the crystal was warm from being too close to the fire and did nothing to cool him. "Fancy?"

"This dream woman of yours?"

James poured another brandy and handed it over to Phillip. "Here. You've some catching up to do."

Phillip took it from him gingerly. He sniffed it and wrinkled his nose. "It smells like varnish and roses."

James laughed. "That it does. But it tastes like nectar."

Phillip looked encouraged and took a deep draught—and came out sputtering it all over his waistcoat. "Bah!" He glared at James, who was snorting softly into his own refilled glass. "Why didn't you warn me?"

"Oh, come on, Flip. It's traditional to laugh at a bloke's first go. Besides, now you've numbed your tongue enough to enjoy it."

"Not to mention blinded my vision enough to render you safe from retaliation," Phillip muttered, but he took another tiny sip. His brows rose comically. "Oh! It is better now!" He tipped the glass back again. "Much better!"

"Whoa! Slow down, soldier. You'll gain yourself nothing but a crashing head in the morning." James leaned back once more and raised his glass in a toast. "Welcome to the drinking classes, Sir Flip."

Phillip smiled and raised his glass in return. "I'm glad to be here, my liege."

James was startled by the relaxed and mischievous quality of that smile. He'd certainly never seen that particular expression on Flip before. The poor tutor always seemed so tightly wound, as if constantly afraid to betray himself in some way.

"What were you saying?" Phillip slid from his perch to the floor, stretching his feet toward the fire and leaning back upon the footstool.

James watched this liquid movement with amusement. Flip was obviously in the bantamweight class. "Did you have any dinner, Flip?"

"No," came the slurred reply. "Why do you ask?"

"Oh, no reason." Much too late now.

"Remind me to supply you with plenty of headache powders on your night table."

Phillip turned and leaned one elbow on the footstool to prop his head on one fist. From the look of him, it was less pose and more architectural support. He looked ready to slither to the carpet entirely.

The younger man shook his head pityingly at James. "You are so obvious."

"What?"

"You always change the subject when you want to hide."

"Nonsense. I do no such thing." Well, perhaps he did. He should warn young Phillip of the pitfalls of manhood, but there were some things he truly didn't want Phillip to know. To be frank, it was good to feel there was someone who wasn't thinking ill of him every time they looked at him. Someone who saw him just as he was.

"You must be on your guard, Flip. Women can be delightful creatures, but you must be careful. Do not trust them. A woman's power is in her flesh. She can twist a man's mind around until he is her willing plaything. When a woman smiles at you, touches you, you see, you'll do anything for her. You'll tell her anything she wants to know."

He leaned forward to emphasize his point with a gesture toward Phillip's breeches. "When what lives in a bloke's trousers swells, it takes all the blood from his brain. Doesn't leave him much to think better of it with." He sat back, satisfied.

"Ah. Yet you still have not answered the question, have you?"

James grunted. "Persistent bloke. Very well then, I've a preference for the exotic and I've always cherished the notion of a harem dancer of my own. A woman who talks with her body and never says a word. A hot-eyed creature who wears nothing but veils and a come-hither look in her eyes . . ."

James's voice faded to a mumble. "But I'll never seek her out. Because that's when a man is at his weakest . . . when such a fantasy comes . . . true." He was drifting off into a drunken slumber.

Phillipa, however, had come alert. She knew a little something about Arabia, probably more than James, for she had spent a year there while her father attempted to track down a particular shaman who was known to heal with his hands.

That had been close to the end, when modern medicine had failed and even quackery had been exhausted. There was nothing left but the spiritualists. Phillipa had been nearly fifteen at the time. Her body had awakened and changed and her mind had taken paths most alien to childhood. Her burgeoning figure had been the source of both embarrassment and fascination, but her mother had been far too absorbed in her last chance for life to take note of Phillipa's unease and curiosity.

Restless and nearly jumping out of her skin, Phillipa had left the stuffy tent one evening when her mother had fallen into a listless sleep. She wasn't supposed to go about alone, but the Bedouin camp looked deserted and the air outside seemed to cool her disordered thoughts.

After several minutes of not seeing a soul, she felt secure in leaving the vicinity of their guest tent and wandering out onto the sands. She was careful to keep the tent in sight, of course, but the desert night called to her. Above her the stars astonished her with their density and clarity, above even what she had seen from the ships during their journeys. It was as if a pitcher of diamonds had been spilled across the sky.

Her worries, her loneliness, and her never-lessening grief seemed to fade before such magnificence. What did any of it matter to those stars? Perhaps some would have felt diminished, but Phillipa felt liberated by the realization that her existence was merely a passing thought when compared to such eternal splendor.

Then she had heard the music.

Still feeling unburdened by her relative insignificance, she lightly ran along the crest of the shifting dune to spy down upon a circle of men gathered around the fire. The flames were smoky and from her vantage point atop the dune, Phillipa caught the sharp scent of burning herbs.

One man sat with a drum between his knees, his fingers moving too quickly to follow. The thrumming made her heart beat erratically until it surrendered to the brush of fingertips across the tight drumheads. Surrendered its rhythm.

An eerie pipe air teased the beat, intensifying it even as it threatened to drown it out. Tension mounted as the out-landish music swept the senses and riveted the attention. Then she heard the bells softly jingling, as if tiny spirits were ringing miniature chimes.

The jingling counterpoint to the pipe and drum, rhythm as she'd never heard rhythm before.

Her blood was rocketing through her veins. Her heart was helplessly timing itself to the pulse of the music.

Then the dancer came.

For a moment young Phillipa was convinced the creature before her was magical, for she had appeared from behind a pall of smoke and rhythm as if conjured.

She was lush of body, with ebony hair that rippled to the backs of her knees. She was nearly naked in her barbaric glory, wearing little but strung coins and veils.

Phillipa had thought that nothing could have been more thrilling than the mere sight of this exotic being . . .

Until she began to dance. The supple bend of tawny limbs bare in the firelight . . . the undulation of that shock-ingly bare torso . . . the flash of bare feet and thighs from be-neath the veil . . . all had sent Phillipa's mind reeling with confusion.

That woman wore her bare skin the way a woman of Phillipa's world would wear a superior and expensive gown—with confidence and just a touch of boastfulness.

This so jarred against everything that Phillipa had ever been taught or had absorbed about womanhood that she could not take her appalled and fascinated gaze from the dancer. The woman before her looked as free as Phillipa had felt beneath the stars. She looked brave and powerful and anything but lost.

A new awareness began to creep over fifteen-year-old Phillipa. She was a woman now as well. She had limbs and torso and breasts. What if all she had ever learned was wrong? What if this body was not meant to be hidden, to be covered, to be ashamed of . . .

What if she could be like the dancer, free and bold and full of power?

She had lain there upon the dune for hours, a tiny figure in proper white muslin made glimmering in the starlight, lost in contemplation of the woman she might someday become.

The next day, the Atwaters had left the Bedouin encampment. Phillipa never knew if her parents had somehow learned of her midnight jaunt or if they had simply given up hope of a cure from the desert mystic.

Either way, it had served to be the last attempt for Isabella Atwater. She had begged her husband to take her back to Spain, to the village of her birth and what little family remained to her there. So her father had bowed to the will of his beloved and stifled his own desperation to keep her with him.

Phillipa came to the present slowly as she sprawled before the fire in James's study. Her senses were dulled and floating. If she was not mistaken, Mr. Cunnington had gotten her quite thoroughly drunk. Although the drifting sensation was interesting, she decided that she wasn't much fond of the swirling within her stomach and the faint prescience of a piercing headache.

Her memory of that influential moment in her own young womanhood seemed pitifully laughable now. Here she was, not only the antithesis of a free and sensual harem dancer, but hardly even female at all anymore!

She heard her own throaty laugh as if from a distance. James stirred in his slumping repose in the chair. His hair was mussed and fell down upon his forehead and his face was relaxed from some constant subtle tension that she hadn't noticed until it disappeared.

His long hard body was stretched quite unselfconsciously before her and she realized that for once she could look her fill. She rose to her knees and planted her elbows on the arm of his chair to steady herself when the room decided to take a bit of a spin.

Curiosity hummed within her and, surprisingly, she felt very much like indulging it at last. She had seen men from many lands and many walks of life, but never had she seen a man who fascinated her as James Cunnington did.

She leaned toward him to stare into his face, close enough to detect the brandy on his breath and the sandalwood on his skin. She shut her eyes for a moment and breathed deeply. Brandy and sandalwood and *James*.

Opening her eyes, she gazed at the structure of his face. The firelight bronzed the strong cheekbone and jaw, and shadowed that dent just below his full bottom lip. Stubble darkened his cheeks, giving him a dangerous air even in sleep. Her fingertips itched to feel that manly roughness. Then, with great serenity, she noticed her hand reaching toward him.

"Why, thank you, I do believe I will," she whispered to herself.

Chapter Seventeen

The prickly skin of his jaw felt new to her questing fingertips. What odd creatures men were. Each day, they scraped
the beard from their chins even though by nightfall it returned. Not that she minded, of course. She much preferred
clean-shaven to bearded.

Besides, it would be a crime against women everywhere
to hide James Cunnington's sculpted mouth from view. His
fascinating lips were bracketed by the dented dimples that
remained as shadows of themselves in repose.

Her fingers, all of their own accord of course, drifted to
trace the contours of those lips. He twitched slightly under
her exploration and she froze. He inhaled deeply and his lips
parted ever so slightly as he did.

Well, *that* was virtually an invitation, wasn't it? Phillipa
felt herself leaning forward and went along with her body,
deciding that it was a wonderful idea.

His lips were firm and dry beneath her feather-light kiss.
She backed away, waiting . . . for what, she did not know.
For him to turn into a frog? He remained still, as deeply
asleep as ever.

Her body leaned forward again. Oh, they were having another go, were they? Phillipa's mind was quite agreeable.

This time she kept her lips to his, softly adjusting the slant until the fit seemed perfect and as natural as breathing. Still, it was a bit dry. Her tongue flicked out to wet her own lips quickly. Somewhere between accidentally and inevitably, it darted between his as well.

The taste of him was startling and interesting. Oh, yes, that was interest she was feeling, all the way to the toes that suddenly curled within her boots.

She withdrew an inch or two and swallowed hard. She'd stolen a kiss, the first of her life. She was a very, very bad person, there was no doubt about it. Absolutely criminal.

Hard muscle filled her palm and she looked down to see that one of her hands had slipped down from the chair arm to brace itself on one powerful thigh.

It was like gripping cloth-wrapped iron. No wonder James thought Phillip soft! With fascination, her fingers kneaded lightly, but there was no give whatsoever beneath her touch.

Her mouth went entirely dry. He was so large and muscled. So different from herself. The contrast was deeply exciting. She felt as if she could climb directly into his lap and sit as lightly upon him as a butterfly.

The urge to board him faded, however. One couldn't examine someone as well if one was sitting on him. And she wanted to learn more about this fascinating male creature.

Much more.

Her muddled mind found nothing at all wrong with this expedition of discovery. Indeed, it made perfect sense. Moreover, who knew if this opportunity would ever come again? Her drunken logic decided the matter. Phillipa lowered her other hand to spread her fingers across James's other thigh. Delightful. As hard and burly as the first.

Truly, this was an excellent plan.

Slowly she stood to step between his outstretched booted legs. Lowering herself to kneel in the intimate space provided between his knees, she studied him from this vantage point. The man simply went on and on, the way one wished good dreams would do.

From her position, she became newly aware of the breadth of his chest and shoulders. He filled the chair, one arm even draping off into the air as if the chair would hold no more large delicious man.

Slowly she slid her palms up the tops of his thighs. From so close, she could see the ridges of muscle beneath the fawn breeches as well as feel the hardness of them. Her fingers spread to absorb the sheer rigidity of his flesh, she moved her hands higher, then higher still—

Something shifted beneath her hand. She pulled her hands away swiftly and checked his face. No, he slept on, fully lost in brandy-laced sleep. What had moved, then?

She lightly pressed her palm back to the spot. Again, there was a shifting beneath her touch. Something was growing . . . hardening?

Oh! She knew what that was. For although the statues displayed in English houses were thoroughly fig-leafed, the ones proudly decorating Greece and Rome were not. Some were quite detailed, in fact.

It.

His male part grew beneath her hand. She had accidentally awakened it. She let her fingers trace the outline of the shape pressing upward beneath the cloth. Yes, it was indeed similar to those found on statues, although she didn't recall the marble ones being quite so prominent.

In fact, *It* was still growing. She could feel it swelling further under her stroking hand. It grew on and on, until she dimly registered a sense of danger. There was something happening—

Suddenly, *It* bucked and pulsed beneath her hand. Goodness, had she *broken* it somehow?

The thought shattered the drunken spell of permissiveness she'd been under. She snatched her hand back and hurriedly scrambled from between James's knees. God, she was completely mad! What if he'd woken? What if he'd caught her tantalizing herself with his body?

The brandy still swirling in her mind and her stomach, Phillipa panicked. She ran from the study and up the stairs, not stopping until :he had shut her own bedchamber door firmly between herself and her scandalous moment of temptation.

Thank God, James had slept through the entire affair!

James was having a lovely dream.

A dancer whirled about him, her body undulating to exotic music. She was veiled but she spoke to him with her eyes and her body.

Come.

She put her hands on him, sliding hot palms up his thighs to trace his erection with questing fingers. She wanted him, he could feel it. Her hunger penetrated his skin, mingling with his own aching need.

It had been so long—hot hands stroked and stroked— months since he'd been touched with such longing.

He'd never been touched with such love.

She danced away suddenly, out of his reach. He tried to catch her but his arms were lead, his feet mud. With all his will he tried to catch her. She was fleet and full of sultry laughter. He was slow and full of aching need. Yet he gained on her, running her to ground like a hungry predator. She turned to mock him once more and he caught her to him. He carried her to the soft park lawn with the weight of his body. They landed without the slightest jar.

She squirmed beneath him, suddenly delightfully naked— as was he. She was hot and slippery with wanting. She wrapped her limbs about him, her arms about his neck, her long legs about his hips. She sang out as he took her. His pace was hungry and rapid, yet again languid and slow. He filled her with his flesh. She filled him with her giving warmth. They coupled like animals on the ground, like carnal spirits on a cloud.

He was close to his peak when she slid from his grasp, fading from beneath him to appear once more out of his reach, dancing away from him.

She was gone, running away from him even as his desire

reached its lonely peak, her long flaming hair trailing behind her.

With a start, James opened his eyes. He was in his study, slumped in his chair. Alone.

The coals were burned to ash. The decanter was empty. Phillip had been here, but had likely gone to bed long ago. There was no point in spending what remained of the night in a chair. James stood, only to look down at himself in surprise.

Good God, he hadn't done that in years. Not since he was a randy lad. How embarrassing.

It seemed celibacy was going to be more difficult than he'd imagined.

The next morning, Phillipa woke with an aching head and a profound sense that she had done something terrible the night before.

Then she remembered. "Oh, *no.*" She pulled the covers over her head in a fruitless effort to hide from what she'd done.

"Bloody brandy," she muttered, her face flaming so hot she could feel her ears burning. Why, oh, *why* had it occurred to her to do such a thing? Bad enough to touch a man so intimately. Much worse yet to steal those caresses like a bloody pickpocket!

The only comfort in the affair was that James was entirely ignorant of her behavior. She could live with her own new knowledge—at least once her blush faded enough to leave her bedchamber. What she could never live with would be the embarrassment of anyone knowing how low she'd sunk in her first encounter with the demon drink.

Oh, do dry up, said an impatient voice in her mind. *So you fondled the master? What of it? Wasn't it intriguing?*

The covers fell from her face as she considered the question. Heavens, yes, most intriguing. She could still feel his body under her hands—could still feel the heat of him sinking into her palms.

Could still taste the brandy on his lips.

She was blushing again, but not from humiliation this time.

Bloody hell, she was in trouble now.

She managed to stop thinking about James's hard body long enough to dress her own. The rest of the clothing had come from Button today. She now had a very dashing wardrobe. She suspected it was a far nicer one than most homeless tutors sported.

She tied her cravat almost without thought and pulled on her waistcoat without the slightest fumbling of the wrong-sided buttons.

She discovered that James had already left for the day when she tentatively entered the breakfast room. There was only Robbie, contentedly stuffing himself on bacon and eggs.

He looked up at her with a certain amount of defiance. "I'm goin' to read that book today."

She smiled. "If you do, you'll have the afternoon to do as you please." And she'd have some time to think. Not that it would change the fact that she was a shameless—

"Play soldiers!" Robbie crowed. In his excitement, a bit of egg flew from his fork to bounce across the table, leaving an oily trail on the linen tablecloth.

He looked up at her guiltily. "Denny will be right pissed."

Phillipa nodded, though she could hardly scold him when she herself had managed to send her eggs clear to the chandelier.

She picked up her plate. "Switch with me, quickly, before Denny comes back in."

Robbie's blue eyes were fountains of gratitude as he scrambled to take her place at the table. Phillipa sat down in the chair he had vacated, covering a sigh at the thought that she was doomed to be in Denny's bad graces forever.

Later, in the schoolroom, Robbie repaid her by getting every letter right in the homemade primer. "Z is for Zap!" he shouted at the end as he slapped the book shut. "Time for soldiers!" He ran for the study with Phillipa following more slowly.

She was astonished at the speed with which Robbie had learned his letters. It seemed the boy was even brighter than they had all thought.

She had mixed feelings about returning to the scene of her crime, but the warm sunlit study bore little resemblance to the dim and sultry setting of last night. Robbie poured his soldiers from their box and promptly set about trouncing Napoleon yet again. Apparently, one could never do enough in the cause of the Crown.

Phillipa attempted to spend her time constructively, expanding her knowledge with one of the many excellent books on the shelves, but she found her mind wandering to most distressing places. Such as—were all men as hard in body as James? And hadn't *It* swelled to a most astonishing size? And, yes, inevitably . . . what really had happened to *It* last night?

Slowly she raised the book to cover the flaming blush on her face. It remained up for at least an hour.

When she had indulged her scandalous thoughts quite long enough and had managed to beat back the scalding redness in her cheeks, Phillipa stood to put away the most excellent book that she hadn't read a word of.

She tried to step around Robbie's game of soldiers on the carpet. Little lead men were scattered everywhere. Apparently it had been a long and bloody battle. She missed her appointed step by an inch. Robbie's gasp echoed against the book-lined walls. "You smashed my foot soldier!"

She looked down at him holding the crumpled fellow in his palm. "So sorry. Might he be repairable?"

Robbie tried to reshape the little fellow but the soldier remained rather quadrupedal. "He looks like he's crawlin'. Soldiers march, they don't crawl."

"Not necessarily." Phillipa smiled, thinking of the adventures set down in her father's journal. "A spy might crawl, to avoid being seen."

"A spy! That's the ticket!" Robbie bent to place his man to skulk on the edges of the enemy encampment, behind a tent made of one of Denny's fine linen table napkins. Then he looked up at Phillipa as if struck by a thought. "What d'you know of spyin'? You're a girl."

"A little louder, please, Master Robert. I don't think Cook heard you." Phillipa sat beside her student, more in an effort to keep his piping vocal level low than out of sympathy for his neck. "And why wouldn't a woman know as much of spying as a certain little boy?"

"Huh. I know all about spies."

Phillipa raised a brow. "You do?"

Robbie shrugged carelessly. How curious, that he had made that statement without an ounce of young male bravado. He had said it as if it were simple fact. *"The sky is blue. The grass is green. I know all about spies."*

Something tingled in the back of Phillipa's mind. James . . . this house . . . his club . . . his friends . . . and always, her father's warning. *"Keep a close watch on James Cunnington."*

So many puzzles. Perhaps Robbie held the key.

Despite the sudden intensity tightening her shoulders, she affected a pose of bored indifference, propping her elbow on her knee and her chin on her fist. "I doubt it. You're no more than eight or nine years of age. 'Tisn't likely that a spy would teach you anything."

The war game was forgotten in the midst of a gigantic explosion of cannon. Robbie sat up with affront on his thin little face. "Why not? I'm as good as any man in Wellington's army. James said so."

Phillipa toyed with a cavalry soldier. "How do they make these tiny horses look so real? Oh, don't worry yourself, Robbie. Someday you'll be old enough to be a real spy. Many years from now, of course."

Her disbelief was hurting Robbie's feelings, she could see it on his face. Guilt twisted in her belly. She had fallen so far she would manipulate an innocent child to meet her ends.

Even worse, she was good at it.

She put the soldier down and smiled at Robbie. "Let us change the subject. I'm feeling peckish. Think we might be able to scout the kitchen and spy out a bit of teacake?"

But Robbie, stubborn little survivor that he was, would hear none of it. "I *do* know about spying. I'll prove it to you!"

He stood to look about the room. Phillipa followed his gaze about the warm and cluttered study. James's presence was everywhere in these books and furnishings, which was likely why Robbie loved to be here so much.

"Aha!" Robbie leapt into action. He scrambled through his own carefully placed battle scene to James's desk, where he took the top sheet from a stack of writing paper. He turned to wave it triumphantly at Phillipa.

"I can show you the last thing written here."

Phillipa stood, more carefully than Robbie had. No more four-legged soldiers, thank you. "Rob, there's no need. Come, let's have at that teacake."

But even food would not pry Robbie from his purpose. He turned to the fireplace, which sat dully glowing from the morning's fire. The day was not too cold, so Phillipa had let the coals burn away.

Robbie knelt just before the grate.

"What are you doing? Don't burn yourself!"

He only cast her a disdainful glance and bent to reach to the side of the fire. Phillipa came to kneel beside him, worried. "What are you after? Take your hand from there—"

He pulled back his hand rather quickly, his fingers covered in soot. "Look," he said. He laid the paper on the hearthstone, then lightly brushed the tips of his blackened fingers across the page.

Lines began to appear as if by magic, rising from the grimy paper as dark embossing. Phillipa peered closer, enormously intrigued. "But that's writing! What a marvelous trick! Where did you learn that?"

"Simon showed me—"

When he halted, Phillipa looked up to see his mouth shut most decidedly. Simon, hmm? Might that be the same Simon who was married to James's sister, Agatha?

Robbie bent to his work once more and soon the page was entirely begrimed. There wasn't a great deal on it, merely a paragraph at the top of the sheet.

Robbie handed it to her. "You read it."

Phillipa turned her head this way and that, but no matter how she read it, she could make nothing out.

"It's nonsense," she said in disappointment.

Robbie snickered. "It's wrongwise. That's the back of the paper. You have to read it in a mirror."

"Really." Phillipa carried the paper gingerly by the corners to the mirror hanging above a small side table. She held the paper high, squinting at it in the reflection. Her first thought was that it was most definitely James's handwriting, the same as in the primer they had made together.

Her second thought was that this paper was none of her business and the girl she once was would have put it right down without reading it.

She read it most carefully.

". . . and there remains the fact that Atwater has systematically fed critical information to the enemy from our own coded dispatches. I feel there is no recourse but that of Elimination."

Robbie's voice seemed to come from a far distance. "What does it say?"

Phillipa's numbed fingers let the sooty paper slip away to float to the floor. She stared at her own reflection in the mirror but saw nothing but that one word.

"Elimination."

James Cunnington was a spy.

A spy who wanted Papa dead.

James came home that evening to find Robbie sprawled sleeping on the carpet in the study. Not alarming in itself, for the boy had often ended his days so before the coming of Phillip Walters.

But that had changed now, hadn't it? The young tutor had taken on every aspect of Robbie's care, ensuring his bath and appropriate bedtime was maintained on a daily basis. And Robbie took to such structure like a fish to water. Poor little rat was absolutely pining for someone to give a damn.

This made James think of his own inexplicable lack of ability in managing Robbie. He'd thought it would be simple enough. Adopt a street child. Feed him, clothe him, educate him, give him a house to live in.

No less than he himself had grown up with.

And no more, said a tiny voice in his mind.

Yet, what more was there? He didn't shout at Robbie, didn't beat him, didn't touch him at all, for that matter. It was all as it should be.

Phillip does more.

Well, Phillip was paid well for it, wasn't he? Still, James set down his hat and gloves, then knelt by the prone Robbie. There was dirt on the boy's hands and a smudge on his face.

The clock in the hall chimed twelve times. It was past late. Where was Phillip?

James reached out to shake Robbie's shoulder. "Wake up, Rob." There was no response. The child slept so deeply that only the regular huffs of breath gave credence to the presence of life.

James gave him another small shake. Still nothing. The small bones under his hand felt as delicate as a bird's. The boy needed some flesh. What did children need to eat? All James could remember from his own childhood was apples.

And milk. Tall frothing glasses of milk at the table, stolen swigs from the pitcher kept chilled in the springhouse.

Well, that was simple enough. There were any number of dairies set up on the outskirts of the city, and milk wagons were seen with regularity. Likely his cook already received cream and butter from one of them. He'd just have the order increased, then.

The nutrition issue might be solved, but there still remained the fact that Robbie was not in his bed, nor were Phillip or Denny anywhere to be seen.

"No help for it, then." James pulled off his frock coat and laid it over a chair. Then he bent to wrap his arms gingerly around Robbie and lift him up.

So light. Robbie awake seemed to take up so much

bloody room, it was surprising to realize how small and spare he truly was.

Not to mention limp. The boy almost slithered right out of James's grip. Grunting, James tossed his burden a little higher to rest on his chest and shoulder, then made his way upstairs.

Robbie's bedchamber was cool and dark, but not so cold that he needed to bring up more coals tonight. James balanced Robbie with one arm and reached to pull down the counterpane and linens. He laid his small grubby heir on the pristine sheets without a worry about Denny's reaction. Serve the bloke right for leaving Robbie to sleep on the floor like a dog.

The warmth of his anger at Phillip and Denny shook James. There was no real harm done after all. It was only that he'd gotten used to Robbie's life having order and rhythm, even in just the few days since Phillip's arrival.

He pulled the covers high around Robbie's ears and awkwardly tucked them in beneath the feather mattress once more. He straightened to regard his heir, a small mop of black hair showing on the pale linen of the pillow. He looked entirely small in his large bed. James hadn't thought to order a child's bed for the lad. He'd simply assigned him one of the many already furnished rooms in the house. He'd never actually come in the room since, he realized.

The large tester was somewhat imposing in the room, not that there were very many other furnishings to compete. As a matter of fact, the room looked bloody barren in the dim glow coming through the door from the lighted hall.

What had his own room been like as a boy? Fully chaotic, as far as he could recall. From his bats and balls to a collection of birds' nests that he had deemed inexplicably valuable, the chamber had been packed with the debris of country boyhood.

This room held nothing that signified boyhood. The dignified tomes on the shelf would not likely be read for years, if ever. The gleaming bureau boasted only a man-sized hairbrush, probably very lightly used.

The chamber looked stolid and permanent, while its inhabitant seemed temporary, as if Robbie were merely a not terribly welcome guest, soon to disappear once more.

As he gazed back down upon the sleeping boy, he spotted something peeking out from beneath the pillow. He reached to carefully draw it out. It was the primer he and Phillip had made, lovingly wrapped in a bit of linen.

Denny was going to be looking for that table napkin, James thought absently. Then he flipped through the small book. Someone, Phillip probably, had punched the pages and tied them together with an oddly feminine bit of ribbon.

The book already looked well used, although carefully so. One page in particular seemed to be a favorite, by the creasing of the tied spine.

Z is for Zap.

James smiled, reminded of Phillip's frustration that day. He carefully rewrapped the book and tucked it beneath the pillow once more. Perhaps there was a bit of Robbie in the room. A bit of all of them, in fact.

James left, shutting the door quietly behind him, though likely he could have run through the house slamming every door without disturbing Robbie's dead-to-the-world slumber one little bit.

Grinning at the thought, James went to find his missing tutor.

Chapter Eighteen

Phillip's room was not too far from Robbie's, just a few doors down from James's own master chamber. There'd been no reason to put Phillip up with Denny in the servants' quarters on the third floor, when it made much more sense to keep him near Robbie.

James tapped on the door but received no answer. He entered to find the room dark but for the last glow of coals in the grate. The room was almost stiflingly warm.

"Phillip?" He waited but there was no response. He turned to leave. Where else might Phillip be?

Then a quiet voice hailed him from the sitting area by the fire. "Here, sir."

James approached the fireplace to see Phillip huddled in the large chair that every bedchamber featured. There wasn't much to see but mussed hair and extreme pallor. Phillip was curled up as if he were cold, which was impossible in this overheated room. "Good God, man. You look bloody awful."

"Yes, sir."

"Are you well? Should I call a physician for you?"

"No, sir." Phillip's voice was hoarse. "I've only had a bit of bad news."

"In the post?"

"Ah . . . a letter, yes."

James well knew the black news that could come in the post. "Did something happen?"

"No, sir. It was something I learned . . . but I'd rather not say, if it is all the same to you."

"Is there anything I can do to help?"

Phillip turned to look at him for the first time. James was shocked to see red-rimmed eyes and blotched skin. He pulled up another chair to sit where he could meet Phillip's eyes.

"Sir . . . James . . ." Phillip shook his head abruptly. "No, I know of nothing that can be done. Nothing that I am capable of, at any rate."

James regarded him for a moment. He didn't want Phillip to hurt. The empathy he felt was quite surprising. Yet this was Flip, his wry young companion who always had some compassionate good sense to offer, vastly wiser than his apparent years. Flip, whose humor drove away the blackest of James's moods and whose genial manner had made this sober address into a home. Indeed, companion might not be strong enough a word for what Phillip was becoming to him.

Family.

But, of course, that was not truly so. Phillip Walters was simply a valuable employee, an asset to the household. James was bound to offer what he could in comfort by his responsibility as master of this house. That was all.

"If you will not allow me to help you, at least allow me to give you some advice. You are a very intelligent fellow, quick and resourceful. You are capable of a great deal. Whatever it is that must be done, you *can* find it within yourself to do it."

There came a small bark of hoarse laughter. Startled, James blinked. "What amuses you?"

"Oh, sir, I am not amused. I am only terribly confused. Your support is most appreciated, but I think I'd prefer to be alone at this time." Phillip took a breath and wiped a wrist across his eyes. "If it is all the same to you."

James nodded, reluctant to press further. Phillip was such

an odd prickly fellow sometimes. Still, Phillip was sitting straighter already, his eyes now dry, James noticed with satisfaction. Perhaps he'd managed to help in some way.

When James turned to go, leaving Phillipa sitting in the dark, he unknowingly left a coal of burning rage in her heart.

As the door closed after him, Phillipa leapt to her feet, unable to keep still for the volcanic ire within her. How could he gaze into her eyes with such warm concern, when at the same time he was plotting to kill her father? What sort of monster could appear to be so kind when death was all he knew?

Phillipa paced, fighting back more of the hot tears of rage that she had been crying these last hours. No more of that, by God! She would save that anger, save it and use it to stop that evil man from his plotting.

She rubbed at her face. Let there be no more girlish displays. She was fighting for her father's life now, and her own. Her pacing stopped short at the thought.

Her own life. Dear God, what would such a diabolical man do if he learned her real identity? There was no doubt in her mind that he would order her eliminated as well.

"Eliminated"! The very word reverberated with the man's cold heart and moral void. "I'll stop you, James Cunnington, fear not."

But how? She had sat here all evening, torn between fleeing this house and the danger she herself was in, and staying in place to find some way to help her father.

She would not flee again, she'd decided. Regardless of the risk to herself, she would never again hide away in some hole when there was a chance she could save Papa.

Evening had become full night as she'd tossed out ideas both ridiculous and impossible, but as yet she had come up with no way to do what was necessary. Now she made herself sit, forcing her manic feelings to calm. How could she help Papa? She didn't even know where he was.

But James knew.

How obvious. After all, one could not eliminate someone unless one knew where that someone was. James was likely part of the whole affair. Somehow Papa had been helping the British cause from Spain and James and his evil crew had learned of it. The soldiers had come to take Papa away and had destroyed Phillipa's quiet world.

James had ruined her very life.

She fought down her storming emotions as they threatened to rise anew. Bad enough that James had done all of this, but terrible things were being done on both sides. It was war, after all.

But she had *liked* him. Admired him. Even—and here she began to feel a bit sick—*wanted* him! Her stomach roiled at the thought, and at the memory of the way his nearness affected her.

She glared at the floor and tried to think. What could one woman do against a clan of spies?

"You are capable of a great deal."

Again bitter laughter rose up at James's words. She was capable of starving to death in a Cheapside hovel. She was capable of putting herself into a situation that made her survival a matter of limited engagement. She apparently had no power at all, other than the power to flee from the cookpot into the coals.

"A woman's power is in her flesh. She can twist a man's mind around until he is her willing plaything." James's voice was quite real in her mind. She could even hear the bitter undertone, the cynical rasp that gave an edge of truth to such an outrageous statement.

Phillipa's hands went to her face, then to her breasts, bound flat as they were. The flesh was there, if hidden. Could she—could she *seduce* the information out of James Cunnington?

A vengeful, rebellious part of her heart leapt at the idea. *Yes.* Make him want you. Trick him. Make him pay for making you want him.

Still, a part of her—perhaps the respectable girl she once had been—quailed at the thought. What was she becoming, that she could think of such a thing? Her character was changing, becoming something quite nearly unrecognizable. She'd always been so quiet, so compliant!

How convenient for your parents, the new rebel within her said snidely. They had their grand passion, their abiding romance. And you. *You were the perfect daughter, able to adapt to any world, able to nurse and tend and care for them.*

Yet what was wrong with that? Mama had needed nursing. Papa had needed tending. And if she had never had so much as a single suitor to call her own, well, what of it? Family came first. She had learned that lesson well.

What about you? When were you to come first? Did anyone ever ask you, even once? What did you need?

A choice, came the answer, almost against her will. I needed a choice.

She shook both voices from her mind. There would have been no point in insisting on a choice. Likely she would have devoted herself to care for Rupert and Isabella, in any case.

Perhaps, someday after Papa had been returned to her and James Cunnington was nothing but an acrid memory, perhaps then she might make a different choice for the remainder of her future.

Perhaps.

For now, she needed to think of a way to discover what James Cunnington knew of the whereabouts of Rupert Atwater.

Before either she or her father were *Eliminated*.

A flash of memory came to her—a file that she hadn't seen again in the study—and James, entering something from that file into a small leather-bound book.

The book he carried with him wherever he went.

If she were a spy, she wouldn't leave anything lying about in her study. If she were a spy and she wished to keep some information available, she'd keep notes in something small enough to disappear into a pocket.

Something like a small leather-bound book.

Several hours later, when the night watch called an obscene hour, Phillipa stood outside James Cunnington's chamber door while desperation warred with trepidation. This had seemed like such a wonderful idea in her room.

She'd never seen the book anywhere but in James's inner coat pocket. On James himself. But a man changed coats, did he not? And where did a man change his coat?

In his chamber.

Phillipa laid her hand gently on the latch. Part of her mind was chanting, *Be unlocked, be unlocked.* Another part of her mind was praying, *Be locked, be locked.* Sneaking into a gentleman's bedchamber in the middle of the night was definitely on a young lady's list of "don'ts." The power of her own training nearly sent Phillipa scampering back to her own room.

After all, perhaps she'd read the note wrong. It had been backwards. She may have misinterpreted it—

The door opened beneath her hand. The panicky little voice in her mind stopped. She was in.

She had a candle, but it was yet unlit. She'd planned to ease a spark from the coals of James's bedchamber hearth, but then she saw that it wasn't necessary. His window was thrown wide, letting the cool damp air of night course through the chamber and letting the nearly full moon lay down its brilliance over James's naked body on the bed.

Phillipa closed her eyes for a moment, then opened them once more.

Oh, *merde.*

There was a naked god lying sprawled before her, one arm and leg wrapped about the bundled bed-linens as if he were hugging a lover. Naked back, naked limbs, and oh yes, naked buttocks. Gorgeous, muscular, delightfully un-hairy naked buttocks.

What she wouldn't do to be those bed-linens.

You are here to discover where this foul beast is imprisoning your father.

Perhaps he wasn't foul. He certainly didn't look foul at the moment. He looked completely delicious.

He consorts with Lord Treason.

True, and there was no argument that Lord Reardon was rather delicious as well. But James might yet be different. Was different. He laughed, he teased, he protected Robbie—

He lies. He plots. He recommends things like Elimination.

She wanted him to be good. Wouldn't it be wonderful if he were good?

Then find the book. Prove him out, one way or the other.

Find the book.

She tore her gaze from those divinely sculpted buttocks to focus on the rest of the chamber. His clothing was hung in a large, fine wardrobe, with other things kept in a chest of drawers and a press. She searched them all as well as she was able with her hands trembling with anxiety and her eyes aching in the shadowy darkness of the room's perimeter.

Only the bed was well lit by the moon. One could almost imagine it as a sign, if one was inclined to believe in signs. A signal that she was not supposed to be creeping about the shadows, but should be rolling around in those bed-linens.

If only he were good.

Finally, she was forced to declare defeat. She'd searched every pocket she could feel in the darkness. She'd even run her hands through his knitted drawers, feeling the heat in her face despite the chill in the room.

Wherever the little notebook was, it wasn't in this room unless it was under James's pillow. Phillipa chewed her lip. She'd be a fool to risk it.

She took a step toward the bed. He was sleeping so soundly, doubtless because he'd gone to bed so very late. Late to bed, early to rise. The man seemed to need little sleep. She took another step. The floorboard creaked beneath her stocking foot.

James twitched. Then stretched. Then rolled over, leaving the clump of bed-linens behind.

Oh, *merde!*

Phillipa snapped her eyes shut and turned to flee the room. At the threshold she stopped. She hadn't found the book. It was somewhere in this room, she knew it was. But so was a naked man who would be dangerously angry to find the tutor sneaking about his bedchamber, even if said naked man was innocent of any crime.

Retreat. Regroup. Return another day.

Where had those words come from? Ah, yes. Papa's journal. Abruptly, Phillipa felt the cold certainty of her duty wash over her. This pointless attraction she felt to James Cunnington meant nothing, not when her father's life was at stake.

Phillipa left James's room, carefully letting the latch fall back into place. She would retreat and regroup.

Then she would return to ferret out the darkest secrets of this spy.

The next morning, James was partaking of a quick midday meal, impatient to get back to his quest after a tedious morning of tending to the affairs of his estate. All his instructions for the harvest had been sent off by express to Lancashire and James was more than ready to leave the house.

Today his mission was to question a number of landlords and landladies of some of the cheaper boardinghouses in the district where Upkirk had lived. If his instinct that Miss Philomena Atwater would not have settled far afield were accurate, then he ought to be able to track down one spying red-haired woman by evening.

All in all, he couldn't wait to get started. Atwater's daughter meant code keys, and code keys meant finally decrypting Lavinia's letters. With any luck, he'd have Liverpool's proof in his hands within days.

The door opened and Robbie wandered in, his face cloudy.

James was surprised. "What, lessons over so soon? Where's Phillip?"

Robbie shrugged. "In his room, I s'pose. He let me go early. Said he was feelin' a bit low."

James set down his fork and sat forward in his chair, leaning his elbows on the table. "Low, eh? Well, don't fret. He told me he got a bit of bad news in the post yesterday. I'm sure he'll be right and proper by supper."

Robbie shrugged again. Ah, yes, the universal noncommittal gesture of the young male of the species. James recalled wearing out his own shoulders in his day.

"I am on my way out, I'm afraid."

Robbie sat in the chair across from James, slumping back against the cushion, obviously deep in the doldrums. James fought back impatience. There was much to be done. "I'll only be about for a few more minutes."

Abruptly, Robbie slid to his feet and stood. "Wait here!" He galloped off, rumpling the hall carpet with the force of his exit.

James decided to take advantage of what little peace Robbie's venture would bring him and picked up his fork once more. Just a few bites, then he'd be through the door and well away. He'd only managed a few swallows before he looked up to see a breathless Robbie before him and the homemade primer at the ready.

"I'm goin' to read to you!"

James found himself intrigued. "Reading already? But you've only had Phillip for five days."

"I'm a right smart bloke. Miss—ter Walters says so."

James opened his mouth to put Robbie off once more, but found himself locked in the hopeful gaze of those blue eyes. He shrugged, giving in to the inevitable.

Two chairs were pulled close together in the study and soon Robbie was working his way through the primer.

"B is for Bird."

James looked down at Robbie skeptically. "How do you know it says *'bird'*? Are you merely looking at the picture?"

The drawing was of a plucked and hung bird hanging upside down from a butcher's window. Robbie shook his head. "No, honest. It's a bloody good picture, o' course."

"Thank you," James said dryly.

"But see here? B-I-R-D. I know the letters." He pondered the page for a moment. "Seems to me B is for Butcher too."

James was astonished. He was no judge of such things,

but that seemed an excellent rate of learning. It seemed Phillip's instincts about the primer had been quite correct.

Robbie shifted in his chair, obviously uncomfortable in the outsized furniture. James looked about them. "Would you like to sit on that footstool? Then your feet could touch the floor."

Robbie shrugged. James looked away. *Good-God-give-me-patience.* He took a deep breath. "Rob, is there somewhere else you might be more comfortable sitting?"

Robbie nodded, not looking at James. "Phillip lets me sit in the same chair with 'im."

"Oh." James blinked. "How . . . informal."

Obviously, Robbie took that for agreement. In a flash of bony knees and elbows, he had wedged himself alongside James in the big chair. He propped the book up on his knees and turned the page.

"C is for Cat on the Coal Bin."

James sat, listening to Robbie read. The boy's sticky little body gave out a great deal of heat. Holding a child so close was something that James had had little opportunity to do in his life, and to be entirely honest, little desire to as well.

He shifted in the chair. Robbie snuggled closer in response. As he listened with half his mind, James found himself trying to remember if he'd ever snuggled in a chair with his father. His mother? He had some vague memories of her arm about him while he read something to her. Perhaps snuggling was a mother's job, then.

But Robbie had no one but James. Not a proper mother, nor even a proper father. Just a houseful of men and one small boy.

He'd thought that adopting Robbie would keep him from the necessity of complicating his life with a wife and children. It had seemed quite obvious and simple at the time. Need an heir? Find a likely boy.

Well, perhaps once Robbie caught up on his education a bit more, he could be sent off to school. Many boys left home to live at school, it was almost national tradition. Then things could go back to normal. Of course, it would be bloody quiet around here.

And James would have to find a new position for Phillip, unless he followed through on his recruitment plans. Actually, the idea pleased James considerably. The young man had become his friend, one that James would be loath to lose. Besides, with Phillip's potential, there was so much more the fellow could do with that fine mind and that resourceful manner.

Perhaps a few years and several inches of growth would liberate Phillip from his fainthearted ways. James congratulated himself. A capital plan, all around.

Robbie reached the last page. "Z is for Zap. Z-A-P."

"Very well, then. Off you go." James moved to stand, leaving Robbie to sink into the large chair alone. He glanced at the clock. There was still time to check in at the club before he began his round of the boardinghouses. He glanced at Robbie as he straightened his waistcoat.

Robbie's eyes were deep blue pools of anticipation. James blinked. What was the boy waiting for? "Go on, lad. Look Phillip up. I imagine he's feeling better after a rest."

Robbie slid to land on his feet on the floor, never taking his waiting gaze from James. Bloody hell, he'd listened to the book, hadn't he?

The anticipation in the child's eyes began to fade, replaced—as usual—by disappointment. James felt almost resentful at the feeling of failure that engulfed him. "Good God, lad, give me some clue! What the hell am I supposed to say to you?"

Robbie looked away and shrugged. James passed an impatient hand over his face. "Very well. What does Phillip do after you read?"

"He says, 'Well done,' or sometimes, 'Good lad.' "

James let his breath out in a huff of laughter. "Is that all?" He waved a hand at Robbie. "Fine. Well done, Robbie. Good lad."

Slowly Robbie's face screwed up into a most appalling expression. "Don't lie!" He flung the primer to the floor. "Stupid book! I don't want it. I don't want to read anymore!"

James felt his jaw drop. "Robbie, what—"

Robbie turned to flee the room. At the door he stopped to send James a scathing look over one skinny shoulder. "It's a lie if you don't mean it!" He ducked out, almost barreling into Phillip, who skipped back a step to let the boy pass.

Then the tutor leaned one shoulder on the frame of the open doorway and shook his head at James. "That might have been better done."

"How? I don't even know what I did."

Phillip sighed wearily and entered to plop himself down in one of the chairs. "It isn't what you did, it's what you didn't do, you self-absorbed fool."

Startled by Phillip's frankly insulting manner, James took a second look at the younger man. Dark shadows ringed his eyes and his skin had an unhealthy pallor. "Bloody hell, Flip. You look like death."

"Thank you, I'm sure. At least I'm not a stupendous ass, unlike some people in this room."

"Ass? Now see here, Phillip—"

Phillip sprang to face him. "Now see here, James! I just watched you crush a little boy's heart in one careless wave of your hand! I know you haven't the least idea how to be a father, but that doesn't give you the right to be cruel!"

"How was I cruel? I didn't beat him. I didn't even berate him. All I did was listen to him read the alphabet and tell him to seek you out. Where the hell have you been, by the way?"

"*Don't* change the subject, James! You were cruel when you didn't think to give Robbie the slightest bit of praise. Have you any idea how hard he has worked in the last few days? He's overcome years of ignorance in a matter of hours. And you don't even know why, do you?"

"So he's quick-minded. I knew that."

"Well, he doesn't know that. And he won't unless he hears it from *you,* you colossal idiot! We learn who we are by the praise and criticism of those around us. But not you. You would likely praise a dog before you'd pass a kind word on your own child!"

Phillip's face had reddened and his green eyes were

bright with disdain and anger. "Good lord, James! He's dying for praise and attention from you, just as you had from your own father!"

"I didn't." The words were jerked from James before he realized it.

Phillip stopped in mid-rant. "What did you say?"

James took a step backward and shook his head. "I don't know why I said that. What nonsense."

Phillip came closer, peering into James's face with astonishment. "You really don't know what I'm talking about, do you?"

James blinked. "Well, I'm assuming you mean for me to pat Robbie on the head and say 'Good boy' whenever he performs a trick," he said bitterly. "Should I feed him a biscuit as well?"

Phillip only stared at him for a moment, then shook his head as if clearing his thoughts. He gestured to one of the two chairs that remained from the reading session. "James, please sit down."

James sat, without making a snide comment about being invited to sit in his own bloody chairs. Still, a man could only be pushed so far. "Phillip, about your behavior—"

"I'm not done presenting you with my behavior. You may certainly chastise me later, but for now you must listen." Phillip sat in the other chair and leaned forward intently. "You are a father now, James. You must understand what it is you have taken on. Robbie is not a hound, that you might provide a bowl of food and a bit of training and expect a good result. If you do not give Robbie what he needs—what he has been lacking all the years of his life—if you do not give it to him soon, it will be too late for him. He will be so full of rage and disappointment that I cannot foretell what sad end he will come to."

James opened his mouth to speak, but Phillip put one hand on his arm. This was startling in itself, for Phillip had never voluntarily touched him before—had in fact shied away. Yet it seemed such a natural, unconscious gesture. The surprise of it made James forget how he'd planned to deny Phillip's words.

"Please, simply listen," Phillip went on. "There is still hope for Robbie. I know little of children, but I know what my father's love and approval meant to me. For so long, he was the sun in my sky. My mood and opinions rose and set with him. He was my hero, James. As you are Robbie's hero."

Phillip took a breath. "Do you realize that he knows very little about you? And what he does know, he learned from your sister. Do you never pass a conversation with him? You have taken on a son, do you understand? Not simply another member of the household, not simply an heir. A *son.*"

Phillip's intensity rang through the room. As much as James would have liked to dismiss the tutor's insights out of hand, he had himself seen what Phillip could do with Robbie. Phillip might very well be on to something.

And he wanted to understand, truly he did. But even as the new concept of himself as a father began to shimmer in the back of his consciousness with a light of its own, there came a brisk knock on the open door and Denny strode importantly into the room.

"Mr. Tremayne has arrived to accompany you to your club, sir."

Chapter Nineteen

Phillipa waited, scarcely breathing, for James to respond to her words. But the interruption had cost her the game. He only nodded at Denny and stood.

"Thank you, Denny. Tell him I'll be out directly." He walked from the study without looking at her.

Her cause lost in the bustle of donning hat and coat, Phillipa sagged back into her chair, nearly ready to weep. She'd thought, just for a moment, that there might have been some saving of James. When she'd earlier witnessed his cold carelessness of Robbie's feelings, she'd thought him truly foul.

Then, when she'd seen the glimpse of lonely boy in his eyes when she'd compared him to his own father, she had remembered his various and real kindnesses to her and others.

There was good in him. And who knew, if not for the war and its inherent politics and plays of power, he might never have taken the road to treason. He might have stayed on the path drawn for him, raising his apples and sheep in the Lancashire countryside.

So she'd hoped, in those few minutes when he'd really seemed to be listening to her, that she could still confide in him. That he would yet be revealed as someone she could trust, that she could explain her love for her father and her need to bring him home safely. That she could still remain James's friend, and not be forced to become his enemy.

Denny came back to the door of the study to give her a disdainful sniff and an arch look. He had obviously heard some portion of her argument with James and just as obviously disapproved of Phillipa's cheek in disrespecting the master.

"I'm shutting up this room. Mr. Cunnington will not be returning to his study this evening and he has requested me to lock the door."

The loss Phillipa had been feeling crystallized once more into anger. James was shutting her out, shutting Robbie out. Running again.

She stood and smiled widely at Denny. "Of course he did." That was what one did, with an enemy on the premises. She strode away from Denny and up the stairs. Robbie was likely still in an injured fury. She ought to hurry before the schoolroom saw true damage.

She had tried to raise a flag of peace. She had been rebuffed. As it had meant from time before time . . .

This meant war.

James climbed into the carriage that stood at his walk, nodding with friendly courtesy to Etheridge's driver, who looked decidedly odd out of his usual livery.

No identifiable livery, no emblem on the doors of the nondescript carriage, shades pulled tight despite the clear weather—

"Is this the infamous invisible carriage from your uncle's days as Sir Thorogood?" James settled in across from Collis and grinned. "I'd have thought there would be puce velvet cushions at least."

Collis grimaced. "Himself decided that I'm not being careful enough in my travels to and from the club."

James shook his head. "Dalton had to learn that lesson the hard way. Remember how many times he was attacked while portraying Sir Thorogood? I'm sure he's simply trying to preserve your worthless hide."

"Hah. He simply hates seeing me get ahead with the ladies using the lordly conveyance. Not that all that black lacquer and polished brass ever got him rogered!"

Surprised, James laughed out loud. "I don't think the mighty Lord Etheridge ever lacked for company. Not before he married Clara, at any rate."

"You'd be surprised. Bloke was a bloody monk. I used to think he belonged to some mysterious order of knighthood. You know, one of those 'I shall save my sacred energies for my holy mission' factions."

James smiled but looked away. Best not go down that road. Collis was still unaware that Dalton Montmorency *had* belonged to a sort of secret order of lords. The Royal Four was the most select and exclusive of clubs, a hand-picked group who secretly advised the Prime Minister and the Crown—four brilliant, principled men with such a depth of honor and commitment to England that no amount of power and promises could sway their faith. They even abandoned names and rank within their secret circle. The Fox, the Falcon, the Lion, and of course, the Cobra, the seat that had been held by the current Prime Minister Lord Liverpool, and briefly by Dalton Montmorency before he had stepped down to take a more active role as leader of the Liar's Club.

A secret knighthood indeed.

Time to change the subject. "So tell me how your training goes."

It was Collis's turn to look away. "Slowly. But then, having only one usable arm makes everything take twice as long."

"Is there any improvement?" James hadn't asked the question in a long while, for he knew Collis hated to answer it. The answer was always the same.

"None to speak of. The muscles are a bit stronger according to Kurt, but I still can't feel the hilt of a dagger in my hand, much less use it to defend myself." Collis's face was dark. "Most of the time I just bloody drop it," he added disgustedly.

"Not all of Liar training is in defense."

Collis shrugged. "Oh, I do well enough in the other subjects, although I do find myself rather nonplussed at the fact that I am sitting exams with housemaids and rat catchers."

"Snob."

"Ooh, listen to the mighty apple farmer! You'd bloody well be a snob, too, if you were being passed up by an illiterate chambermaid!"

Aha. The root of the problem was revealed. Lady Etheridge had once befriended a canny little housemaid named Rose. When Dalton had searched for Clara and found Rose, he'd taken her from her servitude to a noxious lord and installed her as the first woman ever to be recruited by the Liar's Club.

"She scored higher than you again, didn't she?"

"Bloody right she did! And I studied that time!"

James nodded. "I'm sure. But Rose has a lifetime of education to make up for. She is very determined."

"She's bloody obsessed, is what she is."

"That might not be overstating the case, but what of it? Obsession can be a handy thing in an operative."

Collis only grumbled something unintelligible, then changed the subject. "You looked like a thundercloud when you left your house. What happened?"

James shifted restlessly. "Phillip thinks I don't pay enough attention to Robbie. He thinks I don't treat him like a son." James toyed with his hat. "He was rather heated on the subject."

Collis nodded sagely. "Seen it before." He cocked a thumb over his shoulder in the general direction of James's house. "That bloke needs a good rogering."

"Now, Collis, you know how I feel on that subject—"

"Hah! The whole world knows how you feel on that subject. Look at your household! It's even more of a bloody monastery than Etheridge House. All you've got is Denny and that bristling sea cook of yours. And now Robbie and Phillip. Are you planning on starting your own brotherhood?"

James shrugged. The fact that he hadn't dared challenge his own decision to avoid women with so much as a housemaid within reach didn't say much for his proposed self-control, but it was nonetheless true. "I simply don't want to think about women if I can avoid it. Not any of it. Not the swish of skirts, or the way they smell, or how they hum when they work—I thought it best to stay focused on my goals."

"Well, you may have donned a cleric's collar, but I'll wager Phillip hasn't. Why don't you let me bring him along to Mrs. Blythe's ball in a few days? He can have a taste of fun, no strings attached. Every bit of lace in the demimonde will be there. One of them is sure to make a man of him." He toyed idly with his cravat. "I could use a bit of time on the mount myself. The bored wives at court are making my life bloody miserable. All tease and no bite." Then he grinned. "Well, a few of them bite."

James snorted at Collis's indelicate confidence. "Such a gentleman, Col." Still, perhaps a bit of manly satisfaction would boost Phillip's ego and confidence. Make a man out of him, as Collis had said. And if it would get Phillip out of that strange mood he'd been in lately, all the better.

"Very well, then. We'll take him along."

Collis blinked. "We? Are you coming as well, Father James?"

James held up a hand to halt further teasing. "Only to keep a close eye on him. Knowing you, he'd end up singing naked in a tree in Hyde Park."

Collis shook a finger at him. "No one ever proved that was me."

James laughed at his friend's mock outrage and settled back into his cushions, more relaxed than he'd been in days. Yes, a night out was the very thing for Phillip. Then perhaps he would stop looking at James as if he'd failed somehow and things could go back to the smooth and even.

That would be very pleasant indeed.

•   •   •

Since her employer meant to stay out late and her charge was in no mood for schooling, Phillipa declared the day a holiday and proposed a walk in the park.

"*He* wasn't even listenin'," muttered Robbie in response.

"Well, *he* has gone out and I'm in the mood for an ice. If you don't wish to come along, that is your prerogative. Too bad. It's difficult to find ice vendors once summer is gone. Who knows when you'll taste your next—what was your favorite again?"

Robbie gave her knowing look. "You know I like the red ones."

"Ah, of course. Who knows when you'll taste your next raspberry ice?"

Robbie heaved a great sigh and stood as if it pained him. "Bloody interfering bird," he muttered. "Don't know when to leave a man alone."

"No, I never did catch on to that one," Phillipa replied cheerfully. "Simply didn't take, I suppose."

Robbie sighed heavily, the adult act almost humorous in such a small person. "Go on, why don't you? Leave me."

Phillipa bit her lip as she gazed down at the top of his dark head. In a way, she had left him already. She'd been so absorbed in her anger and helplessness that she had shut Robbie from her, abandoning him to James's awkward heartlessness. She knelt to tip his chin up and gaze into his woeful blue eyes.

"No," she said with quiet intensity. No matter her issue with James, she would not abandon Robbie again. Ever. "We go together, or not at all. I pledge this to you."

Robbie blinked at her vehemence, then nodded. "Cor. When you wants an ice, you really wants an ice."

Phillipa laughed, shaking away her fervor as they left the schoolroom for their outing. "Never get between a girl and her sweets, Robbie. Every man should remember that."

•   •   •

When they reached the district in Cheapside near Upkirk's, James tossed Collis a red waistcoat.

The younger man blinked. "Did you cosh a Bow Street Runner for this? I hear they hold them closer than gold."

James pulled on his own, then donned the coarser jacket kept for such occasions. "It's good cover. When people see the red vest, they don't look any further. I find out more interesting bits this way. No one crosses Bow Street if they can help it."

Collis donned his and the jacket that James had asked him to bring along. "I always wanted to be a Bow Street Runner when I was a lad."

James twitched his lips. "Is that so? I always wanted to be a spy."

Collis and James hit good fortune with the fourth boardinghouse they investigated. They entered the shabby building under the pall of a gray sky which threatened rain, which should have made the indoors seem rather cozy and warm.

The place was full damp, and James suspected it would be so on the sunniest of days, for the old house was shaded on all sides by higher structures. Wilted and straggling weeds were the only adornment on the outside of the plain stone structure, if one discounted years of accumulated soot and bird droppings.

Within, there was an overwhelming smell of wood rot and boiled cabbage, and other things still less pleasant. The landlady, Mrs. Farquart, a spare woman with the face of an unfriendly hatchet, affirmed that a red-haired young woman had indeed stayed there.

"She were here for two months or so. First she was right smart about the rent, but then she got later and later. Said she were lookin' for work, but I don't think she ever found none. Why, what'd she steal from you?"

The woman's tone broke through James's excitement. He exchanged a look with Collis. "Have you proof of her thievery?"

The woman sniffed. "I should say so! She took the war

pay of a young widow, stole forty pounds right from the poor child's trunk!"

"May we speak to this widow?"

Mrs. Farquart shook her head. "Done kilt herself. Lost her mind, she did. Lost her man, lost her fortune, lost her mind. And that faithless red-haired witch stealing from her all along. Bessie should have let me keep it safe for her." She flicked gimlet eyes this way and that. James wouldn't have trusted her with a broken copper, much less forty pounds.

"So this woman is no longer with you?"

"Run her out, I did! She came to pay me with that filthy money. That's when I knew she'd taken it!"

"What name was she using?"

Mrs. Farquart stopped then, quite suddenly. Her expression became craftier, if that was possible. "You want her bad, don't you?" She rubbed four fingers into her other palm. Collis rolled his eyes at the not-so-subtle signal. James quietly stepped on Collis's foot and smiled at the woman.

"I can certainly guarantee you some recompense for your trouble."

"Her name was Watts." She halted, dismayed surprise upon her face as she desperately tried to remember. "Penelope?"

"Are you asking me?"

"Watts, yes. Penelope Watts. That's what I told the other bloke."

James froze. "What other bloke?"

She shrugged. "The bloke what was in here this morning again."

"Did you get his name?"

"Didn't give me one."

"Can you describe him?"

The woman blinked at his urgent tone. "A *bloke* is all. Had a limp."

Useless. James struggled against his own edginess. "So you claim this Penelope Watts—whose name you're unsure of—with red hair stole forty pounds from a fellow boarder, then paid you in full. Whereupon you threw her out?"

Mrs. Farquart shifted her eyes and bobbed her head. "Yes. That's it. Five days ago."

"Have you any notion where she may have gone next?"

Obviously seeing her chances of "recompense" slipping away, the woman shrugged bitterly. "She said she found work."

"A thief who works?" inquired Collis. "How remarkable."

James stepped down harder on Collis's foot and nodded to the landlady. "I thank you, madam, for your kind attention."

He turned smartly and strode out, Collis on his heels. The air may have been damp and redolent of soot and the Thames, but James breathed deeply, his lungs needing cleansing after their turn in that dank house.

Collis rubbed his hands. "Gah! I shan't be able to touch cabbage for months! Still, we did learn something useful. We're hot on her trail now." His smile faded when James turned on him with a grim lack of expression.

"We have no trail. She has forty pounds. She has the means to run full to the Americas if it takes her fancy. A broke red-haired woman we could find. A woman with resources . . ." He climbed into the waiting carriage. "Our search just expanded beyond our means."

Collis climbed in after him. "Are you sure? Wouldn't she stay in London if this is where her father sent her?"

James cocked his head as he considered that notion. "Yes. Still, it will be a long slog to track her, even if we limit ourselves to London." He sighed and leaned back into the cushions. "Five days. We missed her by five bloody days."

Chapter Twenty

The carriage was rounding the park when Collis sat up abruptly. "Look, there's Phillip now."

James leaned to peer beneath the half-open shade to see Phillip strolling down the walk with Robbie, who was fast demolishing a paper dish of ice. As he watched, Phillip looked down at Robbie and laughed, then stopped to pull out his handkerchief and give the boy's face a much-needed swipe.

Collis leaned forward. "James, old man, I think we need to get Phillip off to Mrs. Blythe immediately."

"What do you mean?" James continued to watch Phillip and Robbie. The boy certainly seemed happier and more comfortable with his tutor than with James.

"He's acting more like a governess than a tutor. Or did your tutor wipe your chin for you?"

James didn't have an opportunity to reply to this, for Collis leaned through the small window to call for the driver to stop. Then he opened the door before the footman could jump down and stepped halfway down. "Phillip! Rob!"

Collis's bellow traveled halfway across the park with ease, scattering flocks of pigeons and causing irritated glances from one and all. James shaded his face with one hand and slunk down into the tufted seat. So much for the invisible carriage.

Robbie arrived first and scrambled aboard, sticky hands and all. He turned excited eyes to James. "Did you come looking for us? Where are we going?" He seemed to have no memory of his earlier anger. James found himself grateful for that at least, for when Phillip quietly stepped into the carriage, one could have chilled champagne with the glare James received.

Collis grinned. "No more work today, James. I want to take Rob here to visit Clara. She was asking about him at breakfast, complaining that she hasn't seen him in days." He smirked at James. "Then you can tell Phillip about our plans for him."

James shot Collis a quelling glare but agreed. Robbie was nearly as mad for Clara as he was for James's sister Agatha. Both women were putty in the hands of the Blue-eyed Bandit, as Collis had dubbed him. As James was fond of Clara as well, there seemed no reason not to give Robbie the chance for some maternal companionship, especially following Collis's crack about starting up his own monastery.

Unfortunately, that left James and Phillip together in an uncomfortable silence once Collis and Robbie climbed from the carriage.

As they shut the carriage door, Phillipa heard Robbie's voice. "Aren't you supposed to call her Aunt Clara, if she's married to your uncle Dalton now?"

She heard Collis laugh. "Not bloody likely, when she's younger than me and twice as pretty! She'd clout me for sure if I tried it . . ."

As they drove away, the rattling of the wheels on the cobbles drowned out everything happening outside the carriage, making the space inside seem even more confining and intimate.

Phillipa shifted uncomfortably. She and James had left matters entirely unresolved earlier this afternoon. Would he act as though nothing had been said?

By all rights, he ought to sack her. She was only a sort of

trumped-up servant. Yet if apology was required of her, she wasn't sure it wouldn't stick in her throat and choke her, despite the need to stay where she was.

Finally, she could stand the silence no longer. "What did Mr. Tremayne mean, about your having plans for me?"

James leaned forward, fidgeting with his hat. "Now, Phillip, don't take this ill, but—"

Dual-edged panic lanced through her. "I apologize," she blurted, surprising herself. "I overstepped. It won't happen again."

He blinked. "Ah . . . very well then. Thank you." He looked down at his hat, turning it round by the brim. "I think I know why you've had the blue devils . . . or at least, I think I know of something that will help."

Phillipa sat very still. He couldn't know, she was sure of it. Yet what was he talking about?

James shook his head quickly. "I'll just come out with it, shall I?"

Phillipa tilted her head at him, completely mystified. "Please do."

"When a bloke gets to a certain age, there are needs— well, he can be very distractible and . . . and overly impassioned. You understand that, do you not?"

Phillipa nodded, entirely at sea.

"Right. And so, being a gentleman, this bloke can't very well go to a lady, now can he?"

Guessing between two possible responses, Phillipa shook her head gravely.

"Now, needing another sort entirely . . . well then, Collis and I are taking you to a demimonde ball. If that's all right with you."

Phillipa found herself nodding automatically, though her mind was blank with confusion and surprise.

James looked massively relieved. "Good. I'm glad we understand each other." He sat back on the cushions, obviously much pleased with himself. "We go tomorrow night."

Opening her mouth to ask him what the bloody hell he was getting at, Phillipa halted abruptly. *Demimonde?* As in courtesans and mistresses? She took a breath and held up one finger to ask him for an explanation, when the answer suddenly came to her.

Needs? James thought Phillip needed a *prostitute*?

"Ah, James?"

He looked up at her expectantly, but she had no idea what to say. Tell him that Phillip didn't want to? Was that what a young man would do? Somehow she rather doubted it.

"Yes, Flip?"

"Perhaps you could tell me—" Phillipa folded her hands in her lap and stared down at her fingers, wholly embarrassed. "What precisely is involved in attending a demimonde ball?" Heavens, her mental image was something resembling a country dance, performed stark naked.

"Oh, you'll not be required to wear a costume, if that's what you're asking. Many of the . . . ah, ladies wear fanciful getups, and anyone who doesn't want to be identified may wear a mask. If you wish it, I'm sure Button could find something for you." James set his hat on the seat beside him and stretched his arms over his head. "Mrs. Blythe runs one of the more reputable houses in London. She avoids trading in the darker vices. Her ladies are healthy and willing, since they are paid better than most."

Phillipa frowned. "Do you—I mean, do the gentlemen pay them?"

"No, not directly. Mrs. Blythe's system is quite ingenious. There is a fee to enter the ball, which I shall gladly foot for you. Then of everything within—food, drink, favors—one may indulge as one wishes." James smiled at her encouragingly. "There's no need to feel intimidated, Flip. It's all very welcoming and relaxed. Simply an opportunity to fulfill one's fantasies, you might say."

Fantasies. Phillipa suddenly recalled the fantasy he had confided in her a few nights past. His perfect dream—a harem dancer. Memories of the Bedouin dancer flickered across her mind then. The dancer's sensuality . . . her power . . .

"A woman's power is in her flesh. She can twist a man's mind around until he is her willing plaything."

Phillipa sat very still as vengeful excitement coursed through her. She had wondered how she was to help her father—how she was to divine James's plans. Now she knew.

James carried that little book on his person every waking hour, but hid it while he slept. So when was a man undressed, yet not sleeping?

He had given her the weapon with his own hand. All she needed now was a costume.

Button entered the parlor of Sir Raines's fine house where Phillipa had been installed by a very impressive-looking butler. The little valet stood for a moment with his hands outstretched. "Phillipa! My dear, you look simply dashing! Your own mother wouldn't know you." He twisted a finger in the air. "Give me spin, will you?"

Phillipa turned obediently. When she faced him again, there was a very smug glint in his eye.

"I must say, dear girl, that you may just be my finest work. And what a challenge! The perfect cut to fool the eye, the proper fabrics to make you seem taller, oh, and those waistcoat fronts nearly sent me into fits!" He put his fists on his hips and nodded briskly. "Yes, I am a genius."

Despite the tension within her, Phillipa could not help a small smile. Then she became serious once more. "Button, I need your help. I need a costume. James and Mr. Tremayne are sponsoring Phillip to a demimonde ball."

"Ah, an Elegant Madness! How delightful." Button beamed and rubbed his hands together. "What shall we make of you now? There's a bolt of scarlet silk I've had my eye on, 'twould make a perfect Spanish bullfighter's cape—"

"No, Button." She took his hands in hers. "A *lady's* costume."

Button's eyes widened. "But why? When we've gone to such troubles to make a man out of you?"

Goodness, everyone wanted to make a man out of her. The situation was beginning to play hell with her feminine confidence. Phillipa shook her head. "But I need to be a woman, just for one night. In disguise."

Suspicion crossed Button's puckish face. Phillipa looked away. She hated lying to this kind little man, but there was no help for it. Turning away, she did her best to portray a shy young girl. Not easy in breeches and boots.

"It's only . . . well, do you recall when you asked me if I fancied James?" She couldn't bear to meet his eyes. *Remember Papa.* Taking a deep breath, she turned to Button. "I want to meet James as a woman . . . just once. I need to know . . . that is . . ." *Do it! Lie!* "I love him," she said in a rush. "I need to know if it is possible he might love me."

Her breathless delivery only seemed to make her more convincing, for the suspicion was swept from Button's eyes by a delighted twinkle. "My dear, I'm so happy for you! And for James as well, as soon he falls for you! And he will." He winked. "I'm never wrong about these things."

Then he apparently thought of something. "You do realize that if you approach him at this particular ball, in costume, he'll think you . . ."

"A demirep? Yes." There was no need to falsify the blush that followed. She was most definitely demolishing any last traces of good reputation she may have owned. "There is a price but it is all in the finest of causes." That, at least, was unvarnished truth.

"Well, if you're sure?"

She nodded. Button clapped both hands with glee. "Good. What shall we make of you? A Greek goddess? An Egyptian queen?"

"No," Phillipa said firmly. "I will be James's harem dancer."

The following evening, the ballroom of Mrs. Blythe's "house" was draped in a fantasy of rainbow silk. Lengths of it draped round columns and cornices, creating small rooms of counterfeit intimacy within the teeming crowd. White India doves fluttered freely from upper-level balcony to balcony, although James had to wonder if the accumulated smoke from the various pipes full of narcotics would cause any of them to fall to the floor by the end of the evening.

He looked down to where a few of the guests were already on the floor, sprawled giggling or sleeping against the walls and in the corners. Narcotics, food, and wine lay in abundant supply on every available surface. As if that weren't enough, any guest who stood still for long would eventually be approached by a masked and scantily clad young woman—or young man—offering to provide any needed sustenance.

Yet with all of the above, sex reigned supreme in this house of sin. Sex for sale, sex for trade, sex for free. In his younger, wilder days, James would have loved every minute of this madness.

He hoped Phillip was having a good time.

The pressure of the ticking clock built within him, until he thought he might explode. Of the ten days he had been given by Liverpool, six had passed. There was no red-haired woman, no code key, and no evidence against Lavinia.

He ought not to be here. He ought to be—

There was nothing left to try, nothing that he could think of, and he had racked his brain for days.

Seeing another serving girl coming his way with a tray of delights, James ducked behind a swath of silk to avoid her. At least this time it wasn't a bloke. Apparently someone had taken note of his solitude and had decided that he simply hadn't met the right gender yet. It had taken him half an hour to shed that young man off his trail.

The girl with the tray passed and James stepped from his concealment. That had been a close one. Perhaps it was time he gathered Phillip up and made their way ho—

A swath of Turkish-blue silk rippled across his vision and he turned his head just in time to catch a glimpse of gossamer veils and golden filigree. He blinked, then shook his head. Did he hear tiny bells? The smoke was getting to him.

If he didn't know better, he would have thought his harem fantasy girl had just come to life.

Then a great caped brute wearing Viking horns stepped to one side and James saw her again. She stood just beneath the central chandelier of the ballroom. The light behind her diaphanous costume made it quite clear that she was wearing little else but silken veils wrapped intriguingly about her slim form and dangling from a golden belt that showed a fascinating bit of taut belly.

She turned her head in his direction briefly and he saw that her hair as well as the lower half of her face was covered with yet another veil. Yet her long pale arms were bare and so were her feet.

The crowd swelled between James and the woman like the incoming tide. He moved forward, pushing rudely and apologizing profusely until he stood beneath the central chandelier himself.

She was gone.

He wanted to run through the room until he spotted her again but he stopped himself. She was probably some man's prized mistress—the territory of a fellow who would not take kindly to a poaching outsider.

Besides, a mistress was the last thing James wanted. No women, no distractions—

There she was again, standing facing him not twenty paces away. She was looking directly at him, her eyes dark and alluring over her veil. James's mouth went entirely dry.

She took one graceful step toward him, then another. With every swaying movement of her hips, the veils hanging from her low-slung golden belt parted to show mesmerizing glimpses of calf . . . knee . . . thigh . . .

As she approached, he could see that her dark eyes were lined exotically with kohl, her black lashes thick and sooty on her pale cheeks. Her gaze had flickered demurely downward as she drew nearer, until she stood just outside arm's reach before him.

Then her gaze rose as if in challenge and he found himself breathless at the impact of her captivating gaze. Her eyes seemed the exact color of the blue-green silks she wore, but that was not possible, was it?

Her gaze ran over him slowly, like a touch that began at his lips and stroked over him to his knees and up again. Her darkly etched brows rose in an expression of teasing approval.

The effect was startling, stunning him with the power of his own rising desire. His body tingled and his trousers tightened.

She almost slipped away as he stood frankly gawking. She turned in a cloud of silk and spicy scent and walked away from him. He heard bells once more.

Damn, he should have spoken to her, should have taken her hand, gotten her name—

She paused in her catlike exit to turn her head. Over her shoulder, she gave him a long glance, then blinked one darkened lid in a slow, inviting wink. *Follow,* that look commanded.

He followed.

Chapter Twenty-one

The mysterious woman led James through the crowd and out to the terrace doors. All the double doors stood open to the gardens, doubtless to freshen the stifling smoky air within the ballroom. Yet there were surprisingly few souls out of doors.

James supposed there was no reason to hide away at one of Blythe's hedonistic events. There were no rules to break in secret or otherwise. He and his dream enchantress had the gardens nearly to themselves.

She danced lightly across the stone terrace and down the steps to the garden path. James had to proceed at a brisk pace to keep her in sight. As she wandered she reached a long delicate arm out to stroke the occasional late-blooming flower. It was as if her pale hand caressed the night.

The light breeze of the evening caressed her in return, teasing her veils from her skin, teasing James with glimpses of her flesh that grew more difficult to see as he followed her exotically scented path through the overgrown ivy trellis that covered the walkways for many yards.

Then she disappeared through a silvery portal. James followed her to emerge in a moonlit clearing that was clearly the center of Blythe's "pleasure" garden.

Sexually explicit statuary graced various nooks and bowers along the skirts of the clearing, but James spared them no more than a glance. The exotic work of art that danced before him was all the revelation his narrowly focused mind could bear at the moment.

Away from the loud and lewd entertainments of the ball, James became aware that the girl was humming along with the chiming of her bells. She danced her way around the fountain that centered the garden, coming back his way with a delightful amount of supple swaying.

The tune she hummed was strange and as exotic as herself, yet it perfectly suited her sinuous movements. Those movements became more exaggerated as she came to dance before him.

He stepped forward. She spun away, casting him a scolding glance over her shoulder as she went. He reached a hand to her. "Stop, please. I—"

She fled him completely, dancing to the far side of the fountain. He could hear her low unsettling tune but he could no longer see her.

Defeated, he shook his head and laughed helplessly. "Very well then. You win. I'll stay still."

She immediately emerged from concealment to whirl back to her previous place before him. Breathless from his brief glimpse of supple bare bottom when she turned, James had no problem staying put. She truly wore nothing beneath the veils. Lord, it was all he could do to swallow!

And where the hell was she keeping the bells?

Still humming that song that brought to mind Bedouin tents and sunlit sands, she danced before him. She moved in ways he had not known a woman could move, her taut belly rippling in a mesmerizing movement that made him think of both hot aching sex and dark feminine mystery.

The tune seemed to creep under his skin, until his pounding heartbeat began to keep perfect time. His lust rose until he was as hard as he'd ever been in his life. He ached to touch her, to taste her, to own her.

Then she removed the first veil.

•   •   •

Phillipa held her breath as she unwrapped the first veil from around her breasts and shoulder. She flung it high, whirling out from beneath it and watching James watch the fluttering silk float to the ground in the sudden silence.

His gaze glued to the scrap of veil on the grass, James's expression was priceless. If she'd not been so frankly terrified she might have laughed. Well, she had certainly gained his masculine attention!

She set her hips to quivering just the tiniest bit and was rewarded by the silvery chime of her bells. James's gaze flew to her once more. His eyes were black in the moonlight and his jaw clenched rhythmically.

His hunger was almost palpable in the air between them. Phillipa felt her own desire rise in response to his raptor gaze. She fought it back. That was *not* her purpose tonight.

But he was still wearing far too many clothes.

She began the song once more, increasing the pace to a wild tempo. Before he could react, she whirled in close enough to kiss him, but then merely tugged sharply at his cravat and danced away once more.

He was quick, she had to give him that. Immediately, his hands flew to his cravat to untie the intricate knot. As she danced just out of his reach, he tossed the length of snowy linen to drape across her own discarded veil.

Then his gaze rose to hers in hungry challenge. She swayed closer and reached for his hand. She almost hesitated then. So far he had not touched her, had not done more than gaze at her with those hungry eyes. She was reluctant to allow this first caress. Even knowing what she knew, there was a part of her that ached for his hands on her skin.

He raised his hand to hers slowly, as if he, too, placed importance on this first link of physical rapport.

She slowly wrapped her slim fingers around his strong ones. His hand was warm and hard, rough and callused in places, yet he allowed it to sit lightly in her grasp as if he feared to frighten her away with a sudden movement. Lastly, but perhaps most charming to her own insecurities, it ever so slightly shook in hers.

He was as dreadfully unsure as she was herself. And she now held his hand in hers. She alone owned his hunger, she alone danced for him in this silent erotic moment in time.

Slowly she drew his hand to her throat and allowed the back of his knuckles to drag slowly, sensually down between her still covered breasts, across her dance-dampened belly, down to meet the gold links of the belt that rode just beneath her navel.

His breath was harsh on her face, causing the veil that covered her hair to shift between them. He half-raised his other hand to move it back once more but halted at her tiniest movement away. She raised her gaze to his. His face was hard and intent, even through the veil that separated them. So close that she might take his mouth on hers with only a step . . .

Remember your purpose.

Never looking down, she gently wrapped his willing fingers around one of the veils dangling from the side of her belt. She leaned into him. His lips parted in expectation. She closed his grip on the silk—

And danced away again, leaving the veil behind, fluttering from his clenched fingers.

This time it took less than a minute for him to discard his next item of clothing. His frock coat flew through the air in a dark blur to cover his cravat. She rewarded him with a swift twirl, feeling her silks shift and move to reveal teasing glimpses of her skin.

She played this game with him until he stood shirtless and barefoot in the moonlight. She was nearly out of veils herself. Only one silk dangled before her and one dangled behind. One scrap of nearly invisible blue-green wrapped from a single shoulder was all that hid her breasts from his avid gaze.

And it was her turn.

Chapter Twenty-two

Breathless and frozen in the moment, Phillipa and James stood no more than a foot apart in the moonlight. She could almost feel the heat from his skin on hers. He was so beautiful, so sculpted . . . so hard. Her gaze ran over him, touching upon his broad chest, his rippled belly, his bulging trousers.

She knew what to do with It this time. Button had told her as delicately as he could. She hadn't had the heart to tell him that she had no intention of making love with James, but only wished to drive him senseless with lust.

Up until this moment, that had seemed like such a good idea.

Looking at him now, so male and hungry in the moon's glow, she was feeling rather female and hungry herself. Her purpose began to fade behind the diamond-cut angles of his body. He was manly and beautiful and he wanted her.

When he reached to wrap two hot hands about her bare waist and tumbled her to the ground, she discovered what hunger truly was.

He covered her with his body, pressing a knee between hers. Wrapped in his arms, feeling his mouth on her neck, her shoulder, her breasts—

He pulled away the veil she wore angled across her torso

to cover her breasts with his hard, searching hands. He was pressed to her, skin on skin. His mouth—he used lips, tongue, teeth on her flesh as if she were a feast.

His mouth covered her nipple.

Heaven.

Hot, wet, torturous heaven.

She fought to keep her mind from floating away on the wave of his lust—of her lust. She must remember, once he was past the point of reason, she must search him—

His hand slipped between her thighs, seeking her center through the silk veil. Her mind went stark blank as his fingers found her cleft. He pressed the silk down onto her wetness and stirred her with a gentle but implacable touch.

She clung mindlessly to him, her arms wrapped about his brawny shoulders, her fingertips digging into his muscles. Her head fell back, she didn't care a whit. There was nothing but that mindless, exquisite pleasure.

Please, don't let him stop. I would do anything—

Cold shock washed through her at her own thoughts. What was she doing, rolling about in the grass with her father's assassin? She struggled beneath him, trying to push his shoulders away with her hands. She pressed him back—

Pushing past the silk, he stroked a finger deep within her.

Silken, slippery *rapture.*

Her hands stilled on his shoulders, then tightened once more. She pulled him to her, nails digging deep as he thrust in again.

She couldn't breathe . . .

She couldn't think . . .

She couldn't do this.

Gathering up the last shreds of her disintegrating will, she shoved him from her to roll back on the grass. His sound of surprise was lost in her mad scramble to gain her feet.

"What—wait, come back!"

His husky, confused cry followed her as she fled the clearing, bare-breasted and unnerved. She ducked into the darkness beneath the oaks and ran, leaving James and his wicked breathtaking allure far behind.

• • •

When James returned to the ballroom—by the long route, for his erection refused to fade—he found Collis, bedraggled and blissfully weary, waiting for him in the aperture by the doors.

"Had a kip in the grass, did you?" Collis blearily waved his glass to indicate James's hair. "Still carrying a bit."

James brushed at his hair angrily. His shoulder ached like hell from rolling around on the ground, though he'd not felt a twinge at the time. "Nothing so relaxing as a nap, unfortunately. Have you seen a woman, a harem dancer in Turkish-blue veils?"

Collis shook his head regretfully. "Not since I caught a glimpse of you leaving with her an hour ago. Fantastic courtesan, I'll wager."

"I wouldn't know," James muttered bitterly. "Where's Phillip?"

"My footman found me a moment ago—said Phillip's passed out in the carriage." Collis wavered on his feet. "Capital idea, that. I think I'll join 'im."

James took a good look at Collis for the first time. His friend was fair to collapsing. He bolstered him on one side and they made their way from the hall.

"Met a charming girl in a housemaid uniform." Collis held up his finger and thumb not an inch apart. "*Little* scrap of lace and gabardine, it was." He rubbed his forehead. "Utterly charming. Unfortunately, she wasn't what I had in mind."

"Why, Collis, I never knew you had a yen for house-maids! Or have you got that Rose on your mind?"

Collis went absolutely ashen with horror. "Take that back! You know I think she's unbearable." He lurched at James. "Take it back this instant—"

The champagne sloshed and so did Collis, fortunately into an uncomplaining bush. James waited patiently, for he'd been known to douse the greenery a few times in his life.

When Collis returned, pale but a bit steadier, James only

led the way to their carriage waiting patiently in the stands. The Etheridge footman opened the door for them quite expressionlessly. Good man. Lack of expression was a handy trait in a servant.

After he virtually shoved Collis up and in, James climbed stiffly into the carriage to see Flip stretched out across one seat, and Collis, already snoring, stretched out across the other. James shook his head and stepped back out.

"Hawkins, it seems I'm up with you this evening." Wearily, James climbed to the upper seat. At least the cool air might do his aching groin some good. The condition that sultry dancer had left him in was probably going to require ice.

Women.

Unfortunately, the venom of his thoughts lacked strength when he put his hand in his pocket to toy with the silk veil he'd tucked within it.

Inside the carriage, a wide-awake Phillipa lay still as a stone and listened to Mr. Tremayne snore.

She'd gotten the idea of faking a drunken sleep when she'd made her way out to the carriage stands after donning Phillip's clothing in the garden gazebo where she'd left it. Although most of the coachmen seemed to have kept themselves in check, the carriages themselves were absolutely draped in groaning, snoring, vomiting male youth.

Collis being in matching condition she could not have hoped for. That meant she had the entire ride home to contemplate what a monumental ass she had been.

A silly, susceptible mad *fool.* She'd known what effect James had on her, yet she'd persisted in believing she could maintain the upper hand in such a confrontation.

You liked it very much.

Phillipa sat up and pulled her hat down over her eyes. She was in no mood to listen to conflicting inner voices battle out her emotions. She knew precisely what her problem was . . .

No matter his intentions toward her father, she still had a weakness for James.

Finally, they arrived in Ashton Square. Unwilling to allow a footman to sling her over his shoulder, Phillipa decided to "wake" when the carriage pulled up before the Cunnington house. She stood on the walk with James while he sent Collis off with a few encouraging words. He obviously mistook her silence for hangover, for he very sympathetically guided her into the house.

"I told Denny not to wait up. Come up to my room. I keep my secret cure for the drinking man up there."

"No, I—"

"I won't accept protest, Phillip. You have no idea what you are in for tomorrow. Go up, now." He was smiling, but she could see he would brook no refusal. He led her up the stairs and into his bedchamber.

The huge tester bed loomed in Phillipa's guilt-ridden vision like a banner declaiming her lack of character. *Traitor,* the bed jeered, *you want him still.*

Yes, she did. So she stood absolutely still in the center of the large, luxurious room and would not look at the bed where she so longed to tumble with James.

A wrinkled cravat landed at the carpet near her feet. Her eyes widened, but she did not raise her gaze in the slightest, not even when she heard shirt studs jingle as he dropped them into a crystal dish.

"Damn. Lost one," he muttered, obviously to himself, but she heard him. Should she tell him that she had found it snagged in her last remaining veil after she'd fled him?

Perhaps not.

He pulled off his boots and tossed them to the end of the bed. She stared at them. One lapped over the other as if embracing it. She shut her eyes. She was seeing lovers everywhere.

"Here you are." A glass was thrust before her nose. She took it automatically. Liquid swirled unappealingly in the glass. It looked as though someone had taken a fistful of garden dirt—leaves and insects and all—and slopped it into a glass of pond water.

It smelled much worse than that. She held it away from her, looking up at James for the first time. "No."

"Go on, Flip. It's a mess of herbs and such. There's nothing harmful to it. I have it made up for me by the housekeeper on my estate, Mrs. Bell. She raised me. She'd never poison me."

Turning away, he pulled his shirt over his head and tossed it on the pile of clothing as if she weren't even there. Then he stretched, twisting this way and that. Phillipa gulped when she saw the red marks on his shoulders from her blunted nails.

And his body—in candlelight it was even more beautiful than in moonlight, for his golden skin seemed to glow with animal health and fire. Mesmerized by the shadows rippling under his skin, she unthinkingly took a large sip of the remedy.

And spat it right out again, spewing it across the pristine counterpane of his enormous bed.

As she tried to inhale past her burning tongue and tried to see past her burning eyes, she heard James utter a soft expletive.

"Damn. Denny's going to be right pissed."

A perfect echo of Robbie's boyish fears. It was too much. Phillipa began to laugh completely against her will. Half weak-kneed protest, half sheer exhaustion, with perhaps a dash of leftover confusing arousal—she laughed until she couldn't talk.

She staggered to a dressing table and collapsed in the chair. Lowering her head to her arms folded on the tabletop, she laughed until there was nothing left in her.

When she was at last able to draw an unbroken breath, she realized that the room was very silent. She looked up into the mirror before her to see James leaning on one of the bedposts with his arms crossed over his bare chest.

"You laugh like a cat."

"Cats don't laugh."

"Neither did you, until now. Not really."

She inhaled deeply, now that she could again. "I'm sorry about the bed. It wasn't humorous at all. I've ruined it."

James shrugged. It did lovely things to his chest. She blinked, pulling her eyes away with difficulty. If he should catch her watching, he'd think her mad.

"I'll pay for it," she insisted, though she knew not with what. That lovely creation of velvet surely cost more than what remained of her quarter's advance. She looked down to avoid seeing the ruined bedcover and examined the objects on the dressing table with sudden interest.

There was a silver comb and a buttonhook and a sheet of paper with curling edges that appeared to be a political cartoon by the popular artist Sir Thorogood. She touched the cartoon with one finger to turn it upright. It slid to one side, off its supporting pile of ribbon and gold . . .

Medals.

Two enormous medals, the sort that were granted heroes of the highest order. The Prince Regent's profile gleamed from one of them. She blinked. James . . . a hero?

She traced a finger along the edge of one gold disc. It didn't shift under her touch. She turned surprised eyes to James. "It must be solid gold!"

He shrugged. "That's likely. Weighs a bloody ton." He rubbed at his chest as if he could still feel its weight.

She looked back down at the medals glowing like treasure amid the clutter of the dressing table. If James was a hero—a *British* hero—then why was he part of the plot against her father?

There was something here . . . something she didn't understand. It skittered through her mind while her consciousness trailed just behind, unable to grasp it. She turned to James. "Will you tell me about these?"

He looked away. One hand still pressed over his heart, almost as if he cradled some hurt. "Not long ago, there was a plot to assassinate the Prime Minister."

She remembered. It had happened just a few days before

her own arrival in town and everyone had been much abuzz with the details. "A woman fired a pistol. A lady."

His eyes darkened. "Yes. Some might call her that." He dropped his hands to his hips and contemplated the carpet. Unfortunately, this only pulled Phillipa's attention from his perfect chest to his perfect stomach. And that little trail of dark hair that led somewhere most—

"I was close enough to push Lord Liverpool aside and . . ." He indicated the starburst scar near his shoulder with a dip of his chin.

"You were *shot*?" Phillipa's jaw gaped. "That was *you*?"

He shot her a warning glance. "Don't make a racket over it, Flip. I didn't do anything all that grand. It's only that the Prince is fond of giving medals and—"

"You're a national hero."

She turned back to the table to hide her smile. She wanted to do so much more than smile. He wasn't on the wrong side. He was as brave and honorable as she ever could have dreamed. She wanted to jump and run into his arms and tumble him back onto that massive bed—

" . . . *Rupert Atwater must be Eliminated.*"

Oh, no. If James was a loyal Brit, then he must believe that her father was a traitor.

"*Atwater has systematically fed critical information to the enemy from our own coded dispatches.*"

No. Papa *wouldn't*! Nothing on earth could make him work for Napoleon!

Unless he thought Phillipa was in danger.

She knew it, for she knew her father. She knew the lengths to which he would go to keep a member of his family safe. Had she not seen it, when he'd nearly beggared them with the fruitless travels, the noxious remedies, the charlatans who said they could heal her mother?

Somehow, Napoleon must have convinced her father that his men had found her after all. If Rupert Atwater thought his daughter in the hands of the Mad Emperor, as he'd called him, then he would do whatever was necessary to fight for her life.

Even betray his own beloved England.

James cleared his throat behind her. She started, looking up to meet his curious gaze in the mirror.

"I believe there's smoke coming from your ears, Flip. Whatever are you thinking about so hard in my chamber in the last hours before dawn, when we both ought to be sleeping off our night of genteel debauchery?"

A reluctant laugh broke from her lips at his long-running speech. "Never subtle, are you, James?" She stood, wishing things were different, wishing she could tell him what she'd realized.

No. She could not reveal herself now. Now she must decide what to do about saving Papa on her own. She turned to James and gestured at the counterpane.

"Will you allow me to pay for that?"

"No." He grinned. "I'd rather watch Denny take it out on you."

Phillipa grimaced. "Thank you. So kind."

She walked to the door, feeling as if she were leaving behind the chance for something precious. Her hand was on the latch when James called out, "Did you have a good time tonight, Flip? Did you find someone you fancied?"

She nodded without turning. "Indeed I did." She left the room and shut the door behind her. She'd found someone she fancied.

And lost him again, all within a single night.

Chapter Twenty-three

Phillipa did not even try to sleep that night. Instead, she curled up on her small chair by the grate in her room and pondered the impossibility of James.

He was on the right side.

What an honor to befriend him, to see his strengths and weaknesses, to be his confidante. Had any woman ever had the fortune to know the unrestrained confidence of such a fine and principled man?

He was all that was admirable and good. He was generous and strong, intelligent and kind, rather heart-poundingly attractive and yet not at all vain—in fact, he was altogether wonderful . . .

"I am smitten," she whispered to herself in awed surprise. "I am in love with James Cunnington, gentleman farmer and British patriot. The man who wants to kill Papa."

She leaned her elbows on her knees, dangling her hands loosely at the wrist. Her eyes traced the design on the carpet without seeing a bit of it as her mind raced. "Oh, *merde.*"

Of course, she realized that now more than ever she must keep her identity from James. James was an honest man. Could he love a woman who had lied to him? And no simple "I feared for my life so I dressed as a man" lie, either. No, tonight she had dived to new depths with her harem dancer charade. She would be little better than a prostitute in his eyes, and men of James's station did not marry prostitutes.

The only thing that remained clear was that James was hunting Papa. And she was the only one who could try to prevent that. She was right where she'd originally planned to be when she'd journeyed to Mr. Upkirk's, in a house of the British intelligence service.

Where she had promptly managed to discredit herself—and likely Papa—in every way possible.

Oh, she was too clever for her own good. Such a tangled web she'd woven, only to catch herself.

But now, how could she stay where she was? If she remained with James, she would either suffer a broken heart or her own exposure. Not to mention leaving Robbie when he had just come to trust her. He'd been betrayed too many times in his short life. She feared that one more loss would destroy his capacity to trust forevermore.

The coals went gray, then white, then cold. Still Phillipa stared into them, waiting for answers that wouldn't come.

The next morning, James could scarcely concentrate on his mission for the questions filling his mind. Who was she? How could he find her?

And how could he be so selfish as to want to pursue her when he had so much to make up for? Angry at himself for such self-absorption when he had more important things to do, he tried to disparage the dancer in his mind. She was only a whore. Only a prostitute trolling for a new protector.

Yet no matter how he tried to deny his own captivation and longing, he could not resist keeping the turquoise veil in his pocket.

When he arrived at the club after escaping the house without breaking his fast, Stubbs was waiting for him. "I learned it all," he said eagerly, waving Robbie's primer.

Robbie had passed it on to Stubbs after extracting his promise to return it soon, and James had high hopes that

Flip's book of wonders could do for Stubbs what it had done for Robbie.

"I've work to do in Cryptography, but let's have a go at it this evening." He clapped Stubbs on the back, forcing a smile for the man.

"That's fine, sir. I'll learn it more while I watch the door." Tucking the battered primer into his liveried coat, Stubbs went to work quite happily.

James wished his other problems were so easily solved. "Maybe you'd better let Flip unravel them," he muttered to himself.

His own foul mood notwithstanding, James was glad he'd taken Flip to Blythe's ball. Whatever had been bothering the fellow seemed to be nigh resolved now. James had missed the cheerful atmosphere that Flip had brought to his home. He hoped he could eventually help the fellow become more adventurous.

What an asset to the club he'd be.

Thinking of Stubbs happily studying the primer, James amended that thought with a smile. What an asset to the club Phillip already was.

There was only one person Phillipa could take her confusion to.

Button poured her another cup of tea and handed her a dry handkerchief. "I still don't understand why you cannot simply tell him."

"I can't reveal myself now. It's too soon . . . or perhaps too late, I'm not sure. He can never know who I am or what I've done. Don't you see? He'll never be able to believe that I truly loved him while I duped him. And if he were to hate me . . . I think I would be quite destroyed by that."

Button shook his head. "It is a sad thing. Like one of the plays by the great Bard himself. Love lost between warring houses . . ." Button sniffed. "So you are going to leave us? Just like that, with no explanation?"

"If I leave now, James merely loses a tutor."

"And a friend, don't forget. He calls you friend."

"And a friend," she agreed quietly. "And I lose my last chance to know his love."

Button's silence changed, going from supportive to scheming in a heartbeat. She turned to him. "What? What are you thinking?"

"That perhaps . . . perhaps there might be one last chance for that."

"What do you mean?"

Button dried her eyes with his handkerchief, suddenly quite purposeful. "Dance for him, once more."

Chapter Twenty-four

James sat with Stubbs at a table in the Liar's common room, using Phillip's insightful primer and having the most success he had ever had with his apprentice.

"Oy, that's one I know!" For the first time, Stubbs was actually showing eagerness in the presence of the written word. "Let's see now . . . M is for Market, A is for Ash all alone, for Ale with a mate . . . no mate here . . . N is for Newgate . . . M . . . A . . . N . . ." Stubbs sat back with a glazed look of astonishment and looked up at James. With one finger he slowly pointed to the word. "That there says 'man.' "

James tilted his head to read the word. "Indeed," he said solemnly.

Stubbs bent over the words again. "Bloody 'ell. One minute it's just scratch on paper, next minute it says somethin' to you."

James didn't smile at Stubbs's wonder. How could he, when the man was so profoundly exalted? For the first time James caught a glimpse of the bare and limited world of the illiterate. Stubbs had never been swept away in a grand tale of adventure, or quickened by the discovery and attainment of just the knowledge and information one had been searching for.

Regretting every moment he had wasted with his impatience and lack of sensitivity, James leaned forward. "Stubbs, they all have something to say to you. Every word, every page, every book in the world has something to say to you. All you need to know is this"—he patted the primer—"and you'll never be without knowledge, or entertainment, or companions."

Stubbs stroked the primer possessively. *"Cor,"* he breathed. He looked up at James, his expression hungry. "I want to do another."

Now James did chuckle. "Very well, then, my ready student—"

Abruptly the door into the common room swung open and Rigg, one of the guards, stuck himself halfway into the room. "You lot have got to see the girl dancin' for the marks!"

James gave Rigg an irritated glance. "You know the Liars aren't supposed to frequent the front rooms."

"Don't worry, James. No one saw me. There ain't a mark out there what has a thought about anything but which one o' them veils is comin' off next!"

Veils.

Memory jolted through James. The touch of the silk, the moonlight, the soft and eerie Arabic tune she hummed as she bared herself for him—

He was out of his chair and past Rigg in an instant, only vaguely aware of Stubbs following close behind. Apparently even the miracle of education couldn't compare with disappearing veils.

Phillipa had removed three veils before she saw James enter at the back of the room. Thank heavens, for she wasn't sure how much more she could bare before these avid strangers. If nothing else, it was good to know she would never starve again, for coins were ringing to the stage at her feet with every flutter of her silk.

At least the young piper that Button had found to accompany her would benefit greatly this evening. She was not here for coin. This dance was for James and James alone.

He was closer now, slowly winding his way through the gaming tables. The games had halted abruptly when the curtain had opened on her, so abruptly that one man still held a handful of dice in midair while his chin hung halfway down his cravat. His tongue as well, which sent a shiver of distaste through her.

James. She must remember, she danced for James. The others watching her were no more than wooden figures, like the chairs and tables.

She spun for him, setting her silks to fluttering high, ignoring the catcalls of the others for the gleam that appeared in his intense dark eyes.

She locked her gaze with his. The others disappeared as she drew him. *Come. Come to me,* she called with her body. *Come, love me once more.*

He came, moving through the crowd that had surrounded the low stage, turning his body to make his way without ever taking his eyes from hers.

She loosened another veil, the last one she could spare before she exposed herself irrevocably before those strange and hungry eyes all around them. With a graceful motion, she signaled her piper to quicken the pace of the music even as she moved faster.

With all the power of the memory of his stroking passionate caresses crackling through her and across her damp skin, she undulated before James, close enough to touch if he reached out to her.

His hand moved, slowly and hesitantly, as if he were not even aware of his own motion. His fingers opened and reached—

She spun away, leaving that last veil dangling from his grasp. Turning, she dashed from the stage, past Button, who yanked mightily to close the curtain between her and her audience.

Hardly had the curtains met in a rippling rush before James found himself leaping to the stage and parting the draperies to follow his mystery dancer.

He could not believe it was her. Moreover, he could not believe that she had come to him here. What happy accident had caused their paths to cross just now when he was fair to losing his mind with obsessing about her?

He swept the velvet closed behind him and strode to the center of the stage. She was gone of course. But there was only one exit from this space and he knew it well. He brushed by Button on the short span of stairs leading to the back stage and followed her through a door that still swung from her abrupt passage.

She was just there in a narrow stretch of hallway lit only by one smoking tallow candle on a sconce. The yellow glow barely reached her as she stood facing him, her back to the small window at the end of the hall. Her veils glowed shimmering blue against the black night outside and her skin was tinted golden in the sputtering light.

She stood quite still, as if she had no purpose other than to wait for him to cross the distance between them. James stopped, distant alarms in his mind trying to be heard over the din of his sexual obsession. Who was she? Why was she here, of all places? A hired entertainer, a woman of the demimonde who displayed herself in veils and sinuous moves. Did she dance for everyone, then? For some reason he couldn't bear that thought.

"I thought you danced for me alone that night," he whispered.

Slowly, silently, her chin rose and fell. *Yes.*

"And tonight?"

Yes.

"And now?"

The corners of her eyes crinkled slightly. That mere sign

of a smile lightened James's heart. She was here for him and no other. That the others had seen her dance was of no consequence after all. She was *his* dream.

She began to hum. The exotic tune flowed down the hallway to him like a warm and scented desert breeze. Slowly, in perfect time with her rising and falling notes, her hips began to sway.

He heard bells.

Phillipa danced toward James, standing so straight and stiff there, as if he were bound tightly by her actions. He did not move, nor did he speak again. He only waited as if he were afraid to move for fear of waking from a dream.

So fine and strong, her James. So powerful in body and so wounded in spirit. She would heal him with her love if she could.

This time she would.

As she passed the single lighted sconce, she reached to the corner of the veil covering her face. James's eyes widened in obvious surprise. She wished she could show her face as he so obviously wanted her to.

As she detached the veil, she turned to the sconce and lifted the grimy glass chimney to blow out the candle in one smooth motion. The hallway went entirely black. Nothing remained but the lilting notes of the tune she hummed and the sound of James's breathing growing steadily harsher in the darkness.

She could sense his proximity so forcefully that she was able to stop her body from touching his with only an inch to spare. She raised both hands to cup his jaw softly and pull his face down to hers. He bent willingly enough, seemingly content to take her lead. She held him there, his lips so close to hers that she could feel his breath on her cheeks.

Their first real kiss.

She rose on tiptoe, finally letting the music fade away as she tentatively brought their lips together.

James quivered at the touch of soft lips on his. His hands clenched at his sides. He wanted to touch her again. He had to touch her again. He raised his hands to stroke the backs of his knuckles down both soft cheeks. Was she beautiful? Did he care? He was so mad for her damp and sinuous body that it scarcely mattered.

In a sudden movement he wrapped her slight body in his arms and pulled her tightly to him.

The only thing that mattered was that it was he who had brought her to this moment. He whom she had sought out, and he whom she kissed. His dream, alive and eager in his arms.

He deepened the kiss, almost coming undone at finally being allowed to possess some part of her. Her lips answered his for every pressure, every caressing, devouring movement. When he slipped his tongue ever so gently between her lips, she only answered him with the welcoming caress of her own.

The touch of her willing tongue against his sent his desire spiraling out of control. His mouth left hers to kiss a hot trail down her neck to her bare shoulders. His hands tore hungrily at her remaining veils, which came free from her golden belt and neckpiece. She made no objection, only urged him to further his exploration by taking one of his hands and moving it to cover one bared breast.

He tucked his face into her dampened neck in order to devote his every sense to the exploration of her silken flesh. The darkness wrapped about them both like a protective barrier from the world, the velvet bubble of dream.

Phillipa was naked but for the golden choker and the belt of coins. And her bells, a slender chain of chimes that dangled from the front of the belt, traveled between her thighs to ride the crevice of her bare bottom to fasten at the back of her belt once more.

Invisible, undeniable, they were meant to entice and intrigue, and inevitably . . . reward.

But for her barbaric golden adornment, she was completely naked in the arms of her fully dressed James. The contrast excited her immensely. She was his harem wife, his concubine, the object of his desire.

His hot hands on her body proved his passion, for he was

almost clumsy in his eagerness, when she knew him to normally not be clumsy at all. He was so endearingly, obviously available to her, so powerless to resist her that she was forced to stop the heady progress of his exploration in order to step away for a brief second.

She could not speak to him, though she longed to tell him of her heart. She could only try to communicate her desire by touch.

She tugged at the knot in his cravat. She felt his breath leave him in an exhalation of surprise.

"Here? In the hall?"

She pressed her fingertips to his lips and took his hand. Trailing her fingers on the wall, she found the plain narrow doorway to the small storeroom where she had changed into her costume earlier this evening, and where Button had presumably been hard at work while she danced.

She opened the door to find the room beyond every bit as dark as the hallway. Good, exactly as expected. It was a pity that she could not light a candle to see the results of Button's labors, for it was sure to be a sight to behold, but she could not risk James's getting a glimpse of her features below the veil.

And she did want to kiss him more. For hours . . .

Chapter Twenty-five

As Phillipa led James into the room, her bare toes encountered a soft mass. Yes, the pallet that Button had promised would take nearly the entire floor, wouldn't it? She turned and placed her palms upon James's waistcoat, turning her fingers under the lapels.

And tugged. With a yelp of surprise he fell with her to the pallet. With graceful ease he arched his body away so as not to fall directly on her, but to land at her side on the mounded piles of what felt like featherbeds. Phillipa sank deeply into the billowy stuff. Her body stretched at the sumptuousness even as her skin reacted to the sinful luxury of the velvet and silk beneath her.

"Where did you go, my dream?" James whispered from the right. Then a caressing hand found her naked rib cage. "You are a minx, are you not?" His deep warm voice teased in that special way he had, making her heart ache for him to know it was her.

She responded by reaching for him to pull his fully dressed body over her naked one. *"Cover me,"* she whispered in Arabic, breaking her solemn promise to herself that she would not speak. *"Wrap me in your power and make me yours."*

"So you can speak!" He maneuvered to lie between her thighs and took his weight from her by leaning on his elbows. She felt him press a softly ravenous kiss to the corner of her mouth. "Tell me your name," he pleaded as he stroked his fingertips down her neck to toy with the gold filigree about her throat.

"Amilah," she whispered back. *Dream.*

"My Amilah." His breath feathered across her lips. *Mine.*

She nodded, knowing he could feel the motion of her agreement. She was his, irrevocably. What they were about to do could not bind her to him any more than she was already, for she would forever bear him in her heart, no matter the nature of his feelings.

She brought her hands to caress his face and kissed him once more in the openmouthed way he had shown her. His mouth was so hot and male, their stroking of tongues so intimate and outrageous, that she could have kissed that mouth all night.

But for one thing. She wanted to kiss the rest of him as well.

She pushed him to his back. He laughed as he sank unresisting into the downy depths. She rolled on top of him, relishing even the cold bite of his waistcoat buttons on her skin. To writhe naked upon him as he lay fully clothed might be greatly diverting had she the time, but there was far more that she wished to accomplish tonight.

"I still hear the bells," he murmured. "Yet I am quite sure you are as bare as a winter elm. Have you bells in your—"

She kissed him quiet, unable to stop a muffled laugh against his lips. *"Be still,"* she whispered in Arabic. *"You shall find my chimes soon enough."* She began to untie his cravat. Discovering that she needed more leverage, she sat up to straddle his hips.

"Oh, Amilah," he groaned, pressing his groin into hers. "Have you any idea what you are doing to me?"

She pulled his cravat free and unbuttoned his waistcoat. His shirt studs were next. Finally she scrambled off him to pull him to a sitting position. He yanked his clothing off without her help at that point, obviously impatient to proceed.

She helped him with his boots and trousers until he was as naked as she. More so, for he wore no golden adornment.

How she wished she could see him.

"How I wish I could see you," he whispered. "But you will not allow it, even had I candles in every pocket."

She bent over him, trailing her hands over his skin. He shivered under her touch. *"I see you,"* she whispered. *"I see every strong and virile line of you. You are mine, my gentle warrior-king. You are my moon and my sands and I shall travel you so well this night that I might never forget an inch of your skin."*

James lay back upon the pallet, both mystified and exalted by the words she whispered on his flesh. She was his every dream, but she touched him as if he were her heart's desire. How could her caress be so laden with aching emotion? He must be imagining it, mistaking passion for love in his loneliness and lust.

No matter. He would accept this moment out of time, this interlude in the darkness, for he ached for her. He ached to be loved, even for one night.

And perhaps, this time, he could convince her not to disappear.

Her caressing hands found his erection and faltered in their motion. Then slowly, with a mind-altering delicacy of touch, she explored him with critical curiosity.

Phillipa was not prepared for what she found. This was not quite what she had expected from viewing statuary in Greece and scrolls in India. This rigid shaft of male flesh was *significant*. Almost appallingly so.

Yet so fascinating. The silken feel of his skin entranced her as she wrapped her fingers about him and instinctively slid them up and down. His warm hands came up to cover hers. "Amilah, I fear you shall disappoint us both if you continue."

She pulled her hands from beneath his reluctantly. He found them again in the darkness and replaced them. "Please. I want your caress—only not that particular motion."

Phillipa returned her attention to that fascinating rod of

male difference for a moment, then reluctantly left it. There was so much of him to know.

She passed her palms lightly up his muscled thighs, as they had figured prominently in many a fantasy since the night she'd touched him by the fire. And his chest, that brawny expanse of hard ridges and hollows that she had longed to explore since she had seen him fresh from his bath.

And that furrowed iron expanse of abdomen, which rippled so invitingly under her light trailing touch.

"Amilah, I must touch you. *Now*."

Phillipa smiled in the darkness. He was not a subtle man, her James.

His large hard hands came up to encircle her bare waist and she found herself on her back once more. She wrapped her arms about his neck and pulled him down for a deep and breathless kiss that left them both gasping.

"You are so passionate, Amilah. How I wish I knew if it was only for me that you pine."

Phillipa dragged her fingers through his hair as he kissed his way down her neck to that delicate spot where it became shoulder. The heat of his mouth there made her quiver within. *"I am only yours,"* she whispered, longing to spill her heart to him. *"I dance only for you. I dream only of you."*

His hot mouth moved down to her breasts. She started when he took one air-chilled nipple between his warm lips. The heat of him tingled through her as his teeth raked ever so gently across her tender flesh.

The other breast was covered by a hard and gentle palm, and he teased both nipples in time, one with tender bites and sucking, the other with soft plucking caresses. When he traded nipples she let her head fall back, awash in the tingling pleasure. Her thighs tried to tighten, to press together of their own volition, but she only succeeded in wrapping them snugly about his bare hips as he wedged himself between her open legs.

He was large and broad above her. Her hands explored his chest and shoulders, stroking through his waving hair, pressing slowly down his back as he kissed lower still upon her belly.

He found the jewel she had pasted in her navel with honey in the tradition of the Bedouin bride and sucked it free. "I wondered how you kept this in." She felt his chuckle against her lower body as he dropped it into his hand. "Finders, keepers," he whispered, and tucked it away somewhere she couldn't see. Then he made sure to remove any trace of the honey glue.

A thorough man, James Cunnington.

He kissed from one hipbone to the other, leaving a trail of hot, damp skin that quickly cooled to send shivers absolutely *everywhere*.

Then he stopped to fondle the golden belt that had once held a rather demure collection of scarves and now held nothing but very fond memories.

"I don't know how you keep this on when you move the way you do," he murmured. "Yet another delicious mystery for me to unravel. In time."

She felt a lancing ache of regret at his assumption of a future. It melded with her growing desire, adding a depth of poignancy to his every touch.

He kissed his way to the tops of her thighs, then stopped to press her legs wide with his palms. "I want to taste all of you," he murmured. "I'm afraid I won't be stopped."

She had no intention of stopping him, although she did not know why he thought she would object to more kisses—

He found the bells.

When his tongue slid past the thin gold chain to delve within her, Phillipa arched in ecstatic disbelief. He couldn't—*he wouldn't*—

Pleasure. More pleasure than she could have dreamed. The shivers grew to tremors, then grew to shudders of racking ecstasy as his nimble tongue slid within, up, around, flicking endlessly at the core of her sex, driving her helplessly onward.

She clutched at the puffing sides of her velvet prison,

mindlessly kneading the fabric in her searching hands. She was flying into the diamond-studded sky—

Phillipa shattered, pieces of her spinning off into the void. There was no Phillipa, there was only light, and pleasure and the flowing, growing tide of radiance that sprang from her center and shimmered to the tips of her fingers and toes.

James felt Amilah shuddering and pulsing beneath his caressing kiss and knew she was ready for him. He continued to taste her gently as she drifted back down to him, not stopping until the last pulsing spasms had slowed.

Now. Finally.

James rose to his hands and knees to crawl back up her body, dropping a kiss here and there as he went. He settled himself between her thighs, allowing his erection to press slightly into the slick folds of her.

"Are you ready for me?"

In response, she stroked her hands up his arms to dangle loosely around his neck. She said something breathless and exotic, and shifted her hips invitingly. Thank heaven, for he felt as though he might embarrass himself by bursting at the mere touch of her hot, wet center.

He drove himself in, parting her easily enough at first. Then, astonishingly, there was a barrier. Not a firm one, for he could feel it start to give way when he first pressed himself to it. Nonetheless, he backed off.

Virgin? He could not seem to grasp the meaning of the word. This mad, passionate, wild, and exotic flower of the fleshly world—virgin?

He must stop. He must think. There was something not right here. Something that his instincts had warned him of but he had been too lust-crazed to listen to.

God, she was so hot and tight around him. She wriggled a bit as he hesitated. A brief question in her outlandish tongue. Damn, he couldn't *think*!

Phillipa breathed a gutter word in Arabic. He had discovered her virginity. Would he leave her? There was such a thing as being too bloody honorable!

She didn't think she could bear his leaving her. This man, this strong, gentle, dark man was her destiny. He was the reason for her journey, the reason for her very birth.

Already she was thrumming inside at the feeling of his shaft beginning to spread her. If he stopped now, she would bloody well clout him one!

He began to withdraw from her. "Amilah, are you—"

"Not this time, my stallion," she muttered. Wrapping both calves about his buttocks, she drove him into her with all her strength. He gasped and bucked away, but the damage was done.

Ow. He was so large within her. She felt herself burning, stretching . . .

She kept him tightly captured by her thighs and forced herself to take deep slow breaths. This was no worse than boxing and she had faked her way through that well enough. She became aware that he was holding her, kissing her as he stroked her face.

"You should not have done that, darling," he whispered against her ear. "I did not want to cause you pain."

She wriggled experimentally beneath him. The burning ache was ebbing, though the fullness only seemed to be growing.

"Shh. Hold still a moment, my dream."

She could not. When she rotated her hips against him, pleasure burst through her once more. Oh, yes. She let her head fall back and ground herself into him again.

His breath left him in a rush that warmed her skin. He wanted more, she could feel it. His entire body was held rigid and his breathing quickened. He raised himself upon his elbows and gently bit the lobe of her ear.

"If you will release me from the iron grasp of your thighs, I might be able to give you more pleasure."

To make sure he didn't leave her, she pulled his head down for a kiss while she slid her legs from around him. He laughed hoarsely against her mouth.

"Amilah, I'm not going anywhere. Good God, do you really think I could?"

She eased her embrace, finally allowing him the freedom to move within her. He withdrew almost entirely, then slowly thrust into her once more.

She *ached*. Hot, pulsating pleasure burst through her. She reached for him, grasping his wide shoulders to keep from spinning off into the void of ecstasy once more. She didn't dare speak, even to urge him on, for she'd never be able to remember what language she was supposed to be using.

Another deep thrust. Another sweetly agonizing withdrawal.

Again.

He was within her, inside her, possessing her. She turned to liquid for him, easing his passage and increasing her own rippling pleasure. She wrapped her arms about him and locked her legs loosely about his waist, holding him in every way. She wanted nothing more than to be his conquered country, to submit to his invasion forever.

The pleasure that arced through her with each thrust began to increase until there was no end. The bursts of pleasure mounted, until she was climbing her way up once more.

Yes. More.

She clung to him, her mind going blank and primal.

More.

He gave her more. He took her higher, thrusting her through a shimmering lake of silvery rapture until she broke the surface in a great splash of radiance. She cried out, dimly aware of the sound but caring not. His lips found hers, covering her high song of ecstasy with a hot, openmouthed kiss.

She clung to him as she drifted down once more. Drawing rasping breaths as if she'd truly been submerged in a lake, she became aware that he had gone still within her and was holding her tightly in his arms, murmuring to her.

"Shh. Just breathe, darling. You'll be fine in a moment."

She didn't want to be fine. She wanted to go back there. Soon.

Or at least as soon as she caught her breath.

She wished she could tell him. *"I saw the stars,"* she

whispered breathlessly. *"Like a great swath of silver across the sky . . ."*

The power of that stunning moment notwithstanding, Phillipa knew something had been missing. She felt him flex within her, still large and still most interested.

Was there more?

Dear God, she didn't think she could survive more.

The darkness was folded about them, hiding them from the world, but also hiding them from each other. She wished she could see his face and read his eyes. She wished she could ask him why he remained rigid within her, and why he seemed to not have felt what she had felt.

She wished she could tell him that she loved him.

James could feel her relaxing. Good. He wanted her back with him. She had gone so high, and he doubted she'd ever flown before tonight.

Yet she was so passionate, so responsive. Her mystery deepened, but he did not want to ponder that now. She was still hot and tight around him and he wanted to take her anew.

He began to move again. She gasped slightly and he kissed away the small noise. She was not so sophisticated if she did not know what he was about.

Soon he would unravel her every knot, but not now. Now he was her lover, not her investigator. In this moment he was not a spy. He increased his pace, his gentle motions becoming more demanding, less controlled.

Phillipa reveled in his wildness.

"Fly with me," she urged softly.

They flew.

Chapter Twenty-six

Phillipa became aware of something smothering her and fought it off sleepily. Her fingers encountered something filmy and she opened her eyes, blinking at it in the dimness.

Oh, it was only the scarf from her headpiece, the one she wore in lieu of the long hair that dancers wore rippling down their backs. She flicked it away from her face and snuggled back down into the warmth of James's embrace.

The velvet was delicious against her naked skin, but not as perfectly satisfying as the feel of James's skin on hers. She lay there, mind not moving quickly yet, gazing sleepily above her at the curious tower of shelves. The storage room looked very different in the dimness. When she'd been wrapped in James's passion in the dark, it hadn't seemed nearly so mundane—

In the dark. Why wasn't it dark any longer?

She'd fallen asleep. Cold shock jolted the last sleep from her mind.

It was morning. Light from the window in the hallway must be shining in under the door. At any moment James could awake and see her here!

It didn't take long to ease her way out from under James's encircling arm, though it seemed like an hour. Every time he so much as paused in his breathing, her heart had stopped its beat.

Her body was somewhat sore from James's . . . ah, delightful incursion, and she was more than a bit sticky, but there'd be no opportunity to wash until later.

She dressed quickly in Phillip's gear, which was neatly tucked behind a bin, where she'd left it last night. Then she gathered up the bits of her Bedouin dancer's costume that lay about the tiny room. Those she stashed high on a shelf behind a box. She could fetch the costume later or ask Button to get it for her.

If she ever needed it again, which she doubted. Yet if Amilah must disappear entirely, she ought not to leave bits of herself about like a bread-crumb trail.

The light was growing clearer. She should get out as quickly as possible. She didn't think Phillip would cause any comment exiting the club, but still she hoped to get out unseen.

Her hand on the knob, she turned for one last look at her sleeping lover. He lay sprawled across the pallet of red velvet where they had lain together. His naked body was covered only by a flap of fabric he'd pulled across his groin. Sinewy legs stretched far, his feet trailing right off the pallet. One arm was flung up beside his head, the other still clutched the wad of bedding she'd used to fill her space.

He was holding her still.

No, not her. Amilah.

Abruptly, she hated the dancer she had created. She was no Bedouin goddess. She was only thin and ordinary Phillipa, who had not even her own hair to boast of. James had been seduced by his own imagination, not by any real charms she possessed. If he were to meet her as herself, he likely wouldn't take a second look.

Pain sliced through her. Why had she done this to herself?

She took a step to look down on him, sprawled there in his manly grace and power. He looked like a tawny sleeping predator. He would certainly become dangerous if he knew what she had done.

The light grew brighter. Something glinted in the rumpled velvet by his thigh. Phillipa bent, peering. The bells. Damn.

She should leave them. They didn't matter. But Amilah was supposed to disappear . . .

Kneeling, she bent to catch the delicate chain around one fingertip. She tugged gently and they slid slowly from their place to dangle from her hand, catching the light as they swung in the air.

"Flip?"

The morning huskiness of James's voice broke the silence of hours. Phillipa's gaze flew to his face to see him blinking at her in puzzlement. She opened her mouth, but what could she say?

"What are you doing here?"

That sent a faint breathless thought across her blank mind. "I'm—I'm looking for you. What are *you* doing here?"

James looked down at his nudity and made a rueful noise. "I seem to have spent the night in the backstage storage room."

Phillipa nodded soberly. "I see that." She took a chance and spun the chain between her fingers. "Do you really think this is quite your style?"

Seeing the bells, James sat up and reached for them. Reluctantly, Phillipa let them go. Bloody harem-dancing hell. She'd never get them back now.

Sitting quite unselfconsciously with his elbows on his spread knees, James toyed with the golden chain with an unreadable expression on his face.

"What are you thinking?" she asked. *Dear lord, I hope it's something good.*

James dangled the chain, making the bells chime. "I'm wondering . . ." He caught the bells up into his fist and made a long arm for his clothing, which Phillipa had tossed next to the bed when she'd been gathering up her own things. Quickly and efficiently, James checked every pocket.

With a sinking heart, Phillipa realized what he was hoping to find. Or rather, not find.

He thought Amilah was a traitor. He was searching for the book that such a creature would have undoubtedly stolen.

He found his small notebook and held it in his hand. "Odd," he murmured. "I simply don't understand."

Phillipa cleared her throat. "What do you not understand?" She wasn't at all sure she wanted to know.

James raised his gaze to hers. "There was a woman here last night. A dancer. She drew me in here and—well, let us simply say that she provided services."

Services. Phillipa felt ill.

"But she asked for no payment, and she took nothing from me." James stuffed his notebook back into his clothing and shook out his trousers. A small glimmering something flew out to ring onto the dusty floor near Phillipa's feet.

Her belly jewel. She knelt to retrieve it, but James was too quick for her. He snatched it up and stuffed it quickly into a pocket. "Sorry," he said a bit sheepishly, "That's personal."

"All right," Phillipa said faintly. First he labeled Amilah a schemer, then he saved away her jewel as if it were a real gemstone instead of colored glass.

"Perhaps she simply . . . liked you."

"Or perhaps she was after something a bit more important than money," James murmured, as if to himself. "Perhaps she was after information."

"Information about what?"

James blinked. For a moment, he'd forgotten Phillip was there. "Ah, sorry. I know I don't make sense." He regarded the younger man solemnly. "Do you recall when I warned you about a woman's wiles?"

Phillip seemed to go very still. "Yes, I recall."

James passed a hand over his face and gazed ruefully at the wad of gold chain in his fist. "What I didn't tell you was that I learned that lesson from personal experience. I can't reveal everything that happened, but—and this is in strictest confidence, my young friend—I had a lover once who betrayed me. She was everything beautiful and sensual and she had me completely in her thrall. So much so that I told her things I should have died before revealing. The consequences were profound. And most permanent."

He sighed and stole a glance at Phillip. The fellow was listening intently, apparently with every fiber of his young being. James waved the fistful of bells at him. "I swore unto God that I would *never* allow myself to be swayed by sex again!" He threw the chain across the tiny chamber to strike the closed door with an inharmonious jangle.

Phillip turned to watch the chain slide to the floor and lie there in a small glistening heap. He didn't turn back, but kept his face turned away for a moment. "Not every woman will be out to betray you, James."

James stood and began pulling on his clothes. Phillip remained discreetly turned away.

"You don't understand, Flip. The point is that I am no judge of that. I trusted Lav—my old lover. In the heat of the moment, I seem to be incapable of the least amount of sense. When I am on the path of sexual satisfaction, I am a most pathetic, telltale—"

"No!" Phillip was gazing at him now, his green eyes intense. "Never say it. You are a good man—a principled, heroic—"

"I am without honor!" James heard his own hoarse shout echo through the tiny room.

Phillip stood to face him. "This old lover tricked you. Used you. It could happen to anyone. You cannot blame yourself—"

James reached to grip one thin shoulder in his hand. "They *died,* do you understand? My friends died because of my lack of self-control!"

He turned away, pulling his shirt over his head, taking advantage of the privacy provided by the linen to swipe at his watering eyes. "I vowed that I would make amends. That I would avenge them, that I would devote my life to the cause they died for, and that *I would never touch a woman again!*"

He settled the linen on his shoulders and turned back to Phillip, who stood pale and wide-eyed, watching him. "And so, my young friend, you see me forsworn," he said quietly.

"My honor, so recently, painfully rebuilt, in a rubble at the feet of yet another lying, faithless female. And do you know the worst of it?" James laughed bitterly. "The worst of it is that I have no one to blame but myself."

"That man, the one you spoke of . . . was he one of your comrades that she killed?"

"One of several. There remains only one survivor, a fellow who was so badly beaten that he has never awakened once in the months since. He lies even now near death." James tugged on his waistcoat and knotted his cravat loosely about his throat.

"James, I . . . I want you to know . . . I wish last night had not happened, with your feelings being what they are."

James turned to look at Phillip. That was an odd way of putting it. Then, pulling on his frock coat, James gave a small bitter laugh. "Not nearly as much as I do, Flip. At least this time I doubt anything has died but my honor."

The first sensation Ren was aware of was pain. Hollow, echoing pain, like the hammering of a blacksmith heard from a distance. The gray existence in which he floated held no interest, so he felt himself drawn to that distant pounding.

Moments passed, or perhaps hours. No matter. There was no time in the gray place. No light, no darkness. No vigor. The hammering of the distant pain began to be felt as well as heard. Each blow was like a pinprick at first. Such sensation was wildly diverting after so many hours/years in the formless limbo.

Ren willed himself closer to the pain. The tiny prickles became small stabbing pains. Fascinating. And there was an ache in the place that used to be his gut. Hunger? He'd almost forgotten the name of it.

Without thought, he floated closer to the open doors of awareness. The stabbing pains increased. The ache in his belly expanded. There came new and unwelcome sensations—a tearing pain behind his eyes, a shocking tingle up and down his limbs.

No.

I want to go back.

He'd come too far. It was too late. He was pulled into the maelstrom of pain like a twig into raging floodwaters. He was tossed in riotous agony and battered with jolts of anguish.

Everything hurt. The press of bedding on his skin. The glaring, lancing rays on his eyes from a burning candle. The booming of someone's voice, whispering like a sharp-bladed saw upon his ears.

"—orter? Mr. Porter? Ren, can you hear me?"

Ren made a harsh sound that made his own head ache further. "L-light! No . . . *light!*"

The agonizing glare receded. He heard steps across the floor boom as if they impacted the inside of his head. More scraping rasping sounds of whispering.

"Contact Mr. Cunnington! Ren Porter is back with us once more!"

Ren Porter. My name is Ren Porter and I am back.

Agony wracked every fiber of his body. Shocklike jolts of misdelivered nerve response traveled up and down his damaged arms and legs. He quivered from the torturous pain, and each tiny shiver caused more misery to rake his flesh.

Ren Porter was back.

I wish I were dead.

Phillipa sat on the lowest step of the stairs of the club and dropped her face into her hands. Her chest felt physically torn, as if James's condemnation were rending her in two.

So this is what a broken heart feels like.

The worst of it was, she'd done it to herself. James hadn't hurt her as much as she'd hurt him. She'd ruined it all. In her stupidity, she'd done the unforgivable. She'd used his sexuality to manipulate him, something he could not forgive. Never had she loved James more, and never had she made it more impossible for him to love her.

Forgetting Phillip for a moment, even forgetting where

she was, she allowed the tears to well behind the darkness of her closed lids. She had truly lost him now.

Lost in her pain, she didn't interpret the click she heard until almost too late. Then her head snapped up from her folded arms. The door.

Someone was coming in from the street. Someone who likely belonged here, who might find it decidedly odd to see Phillip Walters crying on the stairs. With more speed than she'd known she possessed, Phillipa slid about and scrambled up the stairs to the upper floor, making the security of the hall above just as the front door opened to admit Collis Tremayne, followed by the doorman Stubbs.

Phillipa pressed close to the wall and sank down to her knees. As soon as they entered the club proper, she would make for the front door. She'd had enough of this place.

Mr. Tremayne handed Stubbs his hat and gloves. "Is James about?"

"Right here, Collis." James entered the foyer, tugging his cuffs into place. He looked wonderful to Phillipa . . . and very far away.

Collis Tremayne grinned. "I've got some news for you, concerning a certain Titian-haired lady."

Titian-haired? Red-haired, he meant. Phillipa went cold. Was he talking about her? The real her? She maneuvered to see better down the stairs. Collis was tilting his head significantly in the direction of Mr. Stubbs.

"Ah, Stubbs, if you would excuse us?" James waved a hand to indicate the stairs. "Shall we take this discussion out of the main room, Collis?"

Stubbs shook his head with disgust. "You gents and your ladybirds. How you get anything done is beyond me." The plump doorman returned to his post outside.

Only then did James react. Phillipa saw him grab Collis's sleeve before they'd even made it off the foyer carpet. "What have you got? Did you find her?"

"Hold on, man. Nothing so grand." Collis straightened his coat. "I thought about the hair, you see. Such distinctive locks on one so apparently determined to hide. I wondered if perhaps she'd try to dispose of such a distinctive feature. So I put word out in a few Cheapside pub rooms that I wanted to buy some red hair for a certain lady's fall. Last night I heard from a wigmaker in the area that said a young lady sold him her hair one week ago."

Oh, *merde*. Phillipa went cold inside.

"One week? That would make it the very day she left the boardinghouse." James rubbed his jaw. "She knew she was being followed. She was trying to break her trail by changing her hair."

"There's another thing, James. She didn't just bob her hair—she sold him all of it."

James looked up sharply. "That's not how it's done?"

Phillipa cringed at the black glint in his eyes. She shouldn't have sold her hair, she ought to have thrown it in the sewer. She'd thought herself so clever, so economical. Instead, she'd left a flaming trail for someone to follow her by.

For James to follow her by.

Collis had continued. "The wigmaker said not usually, which was why he remembered it so well. He didn't even pay her for the extra. She *wanted* it chopped off. He said she looked terrible after, like a skinny boy. Could she be wearing a wig herself now, do you think?"

James paced for a moment on the foyer rug, then turned sharply. "One week ago? Exactly?"

"Yes. Why?"

Phillipa could almost see the quicksilver chain of James's thoughts falling into place. When his jaw clenched and his face went white with rage, she knew he'd deduced correctly.

"Get upstairs and grab Fisher," James bit out. "I'll get a hired carriage."

Collis blinked, but turned toward the stairs once more. "Where are we going?"

James was already at the front door.

"My house."

Phillipa ran for her life. Only there was nowhere to run. The hall was not long, with only a handful of doors leading off on both sides. Doors that did not give way to her surreptitious twists of their latches.

She was at the closed end of the hall when the top of Collis Tremayne's dark head appeared coming up the stairs. Desperate but quite hopeless, she wiped futilely at her wet eyes and pressed her back to the wall, waiting to be found out.

The wall behind her gave way and she tumbled backward into nothing.

Phillipa sprawled awkwardly on a dusty carpet, banging her tailbone and clicking her teeth shut on her tongue. She blinked rapidly, only to see a pair of small scuffed shoes appear before her eyes.

Robbie grabbed her by the jacket collar and yanked her backward. "Get your legs in!" he hissed.

Phillipa obeyed automatically. Robbie pulled shut a panel before them, cutting off her view of the bowed head of Collis ascending the stairs, mercifully not yet looking forward.

Climbing to her knees, she rubbed her stinging palms together as she looked about her. She was in another hallway, mirror to the first, but shabbier and decidedly dustier. "What are you doing back here, Rob? What is this place?"

"Looking for you and James." Robbie had both hands on his hips, scowling at her. "And this is someplace you aren't supposed to see," he whispered, disgust in his tone. "Now you've done it."

"Done what?"

"Shh! Never mind. If I can get you out before Himself sees you, likely they won't kill you."

"Who are *they*? The spies?"

Horror crossed Robbie's features, and he grabbed her hand to begin towing her down the new hallway. "You didn't say that. I sure as hell didn't hear it."

"Don't curse in English," Phillipa reminded him absently. Her mind was working furiously. "James is a British spy. Therefore, so is Lord Etheridge." The people she had met over the last several days passed through her mind. "Collis Tremayne . . . Sir Raines . . . *Denny*?"

Robbie shook his head. "Not Denny." Then he clapped a hand over his mouth, since he'd as good as confirmed the others by omission.

"Well, it's good to know the future of England doesn't hang in Denny's hands," Phillipa murmured, fighting the wild hilarity that rose within her at the thought. She was panicking, sure enough.

They turned the corner of the hallway, passing a tiny window set high in the wall. The mirror counterpart to the hall behind the stage where she'd lured James. Pain flared. She suppressed it. Time to worry about her heart when her life wasn't in danger.

They ducked into a storeroom, much like the one she'd shared with James last night. This one had a window and Robbie ran to it, his hands deftly working at the latch. Phillipa felt a spark of hope, until she saw that it was covered on the outside by a heavy iron grille that was locked shut.

"I can't get out that way, Robbie—"

The window swung inward. With a flick of his wrist, Robbie opened the grille, somehow bypassing the old rusting lock and chain entirely. He raised one knee to the sill, then turned to hold out his hand. "Come on!"

Phillipa took a step back. "Robbie, get down from there at once. You'll fall!"

He rolled his eyes. "All the Liars come and go this way. It's their back door."

Phillipa stepped forward to peer down. Below was the grimy alley that ran behind the club. *Far* below. She glanced directly below to see only a narrow ledge beneath the window.

"Have you ever used this back door before, Robbie?"

"Well . . . no. But I done worse than this when I was climbin' for the chimneysweeps. This ain't dangerous! James even does it in the rain sometimes."

Phillipa shook her head. "Then James, I'm sorry to say, is a blooming idiot."

Sending her a look of trenchant disgust, Robbie climbed full onto the sill. "Don't be such a girl, Flip." Before she could stop him, he'd slid beyond her reach and out of sight.

"Robbie!" She lurched forward to peer down. The top of Robbie's head was just a few feet beneath her. He stood with both feet on the ledge, but by the look of dismay on his face, she knew that he hadn't realized how far down the ledge ran. She sagged with relief. "Robbie, hold very still. Slowly reach your hand up to me."

He shook his head stubbornly, despite his pallor. "You can't pull me up. I'm goin' down this way."

"Down how?" It was a straight drop to the ground as far as Phillipa could see.

"They jump over," Robbie explained, pointing across the narrow alley to the building on the other side, where Phillipa could see a much wider ledge and a rough iron ladder to the ground. She blinked. "And what, pray tell, is wrong with using the front door?"

"Spies don't like usin' the same route all the time. Throws off pursuers," Robbie defended stoutly. Then he swallowed hugely, as if he weren't any too wild for the idea of jumping across.

The alley was narrow, but not that narrow. A long-legged man like James might find the jump simple, but Robbie's legs suddenly seemed far too short to Phillipa.

"No, Robbie. Don't do it. I can lift you," she promised, although she was none too sure of it. She was leaning quite far down as it was. He was almost out of her reach. How would she leverage him higher? "Robbie, just hold still. I'll fetch James."

"But then he'll catch you for sure!"

"I don't care, darling. I love you. I don't want you to be hurt." He looked up to meet her eyes then, wonder in his gaze. Encouraged, Phillipa smiled and stretched toward him once more. "Come take my hand, Robbie. This is not for you. You don't have to be like James. He's a grown man. You're just a little boy."

It was the wrong thing to say, she knew it the moment the words left her mouth. His chin went pure Cunnington and he took his first step, sliding one foot along the ledge.

Fear turned Phillipa's blood to ice. "Robert James Cunnington, you don't move again, do you hear me!" She raised one knee to the sill. With shaking hands clinging to the window frame, she straddled the window, clinging to it with her thighs like a horse. Even stretching as far as her single-handed grip would allow her to dangle out, she couldn't reach him. "Please, darling, come back closer," she gasped. "Please take my hand!"

Gaining confidence as his small feet balanced easily on the ledge, Robbie only grinned back at her. "Follow me, Flip. If we go this way, we can shinny down the drainpipe."

Phillipa looked down the length of the ledge to see the pipe in question bracketed to the building. Heavy and black, it looked reassuringly sturdy despite the layers of rust. One very likely could shinny down it, if one could only make it all the way there without falling.

She shook her head. "Robbie, just come back."

"But it's easy! See?" Totally comfortable, a city boy quite in his element, Robbie danced farther down the ledge. He reached the drainpipe and stretched one hand out to take firm hold. "Watch me, Phillip. Watch—"

Beneath his grasp the old pipe crumbled into a handful of rust. Robbie teetered for a moment, his mouth open in surprise at the sudden lack of stability in the metal. Then he looked over at her in horror as the pipe pulled away from its rusted brackets above his head. His small figure cartwheeled through the air, hands outstretched in an impossible attempt to break his fall to the ground below.

Chapter Twenty-seven

A woman's scream tore the air, causing James to come to a startled halt as he stepped into the carriage he'd hailed. It was a terrible sound, full of dread. James turned his head, searching for the source. From the alley? He dashed into the narrow opening.

He rounded the corner of the alley before being slowed by the scattered rubbish. He ran farther into the dimness, leaping piled litter with the ease of long practice.

A familiar figure crouched in the alley, sobbing openly and struggling with a fresh pile of debris. Flip? James hurried forward. The figure turned. "He's hurt—he fell—oh, God, James!"

Oddly reddish curls tumbling over smooth forehead, tear-filled green eyes surrounded by spiky lashes—

Female. Despite his suspicions, cold shock swept through James as he staggered to a halt. *"Flip?"*

It was Flip. And yet it wasn't. James blinked, his perspective shifting oddly from past to present, then back again. The clothing, the mannerisms . . . and yet those eyes. How could he have been blind to the audacious beauty of those stunning eyes? Something dark twined within him—further warning.

Those eyes.

Then he saw the tiny figure lying so still beneath the length of iron drainpipe that Flip was trying desperately to move. "Robbie!"

James threw himself to his knees on the ground alongside Flip and heaved violently at the old iron. Urgency robbed his breath but thankfully only added to his strength. He pulled the heavy pipe from the boy and knelt carefully to touch his little round face. "Rob? Can you hear me, Robbie?"

No reply. So still. So white. The pain in his breast took James quite by surprise, even as he tenderly gathered up his heir. His boy.

His son.

James was scarcely aware of Flip hurrying alongside him as he made for the mouth of the alley. Collis had followed him partway and now stood openmouthed on the street.

"Robbie has fallen," James informed him tightly. "Fetch the physician." Then he looked down at the blotchy tear-streaked face of the woman he'd thought his friend. "And when you've done that," he said from between gritted teeth, "lock up this spy."

As James cradled Robbie gently against the motion of climbing the stairs to the upper rooms, his only thought was of getting aid for his son.

He'd deal with the deceitful bitch later.

The physician came. Dr. Westfall was the Prime Minister's own physician and a man of impeccable discretion. The Liars used him rarely, preferring to patch up their own if possible, but even Kurt had turned to a quivering mess at the sight of a wounded child.

James was waiting outside the door when Dr. Westfall emerged from Robbie's room. The only distraction he'd had while waiting most of the day had been the various and painful means of punishing the traitorous woman who had been contained in the room just next door to Robbie.

At least she had finally stopped pounding on the door and calling for help. Her pleas and protestations of innocence had begun to wear at James, even muffled as they were by the heavy oak door.

By the time Dr. Westfall left Robbie, all was quiet and James had been alone with his thoughts for far too long. Immediately, James moved to peer into the room.

Robbie lay very still, a small heap in the center of the man-sized bed. His continued lack of consciousness was testified to by the pristine condition of the counterpane. Never had the energetic Robbie slept so still. Carefully, James closed the door on the sight of his son, lying so vulnerable in the silent room.

The stout elderly physician stopped to mop his face with his handkerchief before turning to face James. "Your man stoked the fire a bit high in there. All to the good, however. Wouldn't want the little nipper to catch a chill as well."

James couldn't bear to be polite any longer. "How is he? Will he recover? He was so pale—"

Dr. Westfall held up one hand to halt James's urgency. "His arm is broken, as you know."

James did know, for Stubbs had aided the doctor in setting the bone. James had not been able to stand the thought, and even Stubbs had left the room a bit green.

"But has he yet waked?" *God, don't let him be like Ren.*

Dr. Westfall sighed. "No, not yet. But that could be from the laudanum we had to give him to relax the muscles so we could set the bone. It was a clean break, and other than the knot on his head, he seems uninjured." The doctor stuffed his handkerchief back into a pocket and hefted his bag. "My wife has held my breakfast and my lunch, young man. It would behoove neither of us to ask her to hold my dinner."

James stepped back, only now becoming aware that he had blocked the good doctor's path. He passed a hand over his face, trying to bring himself under control. "My apologies, sir. I've not been a father long." No more than a day.

Yet he could not now imagine his life without Robbie in it.

Dr. Westfall nodded as James showed him to the door. "Parents do take it the hardest. Mothers, usually, although I have seen a few fathers shaken as well. I'm glad to see you're one of those. The little lad will need you, when he wakes."

James nodded tightly. "I will be there for him." He would be. Forever.

Downstairs at the door of the club, Jackham approached James as Dr. Westfall boarded his carriage. "Cunnington, you had a message come, but I didn't want to disturb you." Jackham grinned. "But it is good news for you."

James felt impatient to go to Robbie. He'd been kept from the room for hours, thanks to an apparent new tendency to overreact. "What is this news?" he said absently.

Jackham put a hand on James's arm. "Ren Porter is awake."

James stopped and turned to Jackham with a disbelieving smile. "Truly? When did this happen?"

"This mornin'. The news came hours ago, but Himself wouldn't let anyone visit Ren, thinkin' the watchmen might take note of all of them in one place like that."

James nodded, appreciating Dalton's discretion. Wanted thieves would never congregate in that way outside of home ground. And the Liars made a ragtag bunch in any setting. Likely not the best guests for a convalescent. But someone should visit Ren to catch him up on matters.

Only a day ago, the news would have sent James on a scramble to Ren's side, more to beg forgiveness and to absolve himself of guilt than to greet a friend. James sneered at himself. His own self-absorption bid fair to sicken him.

Tonight, James had more pressing matters to attend to.

"Go in my place, would you, Jackham? Tell Ren I'll come to him tomorrow. In the meantime, keep the men from crowding him. You can take their greetings as well."

Jackham looked startled. James couldn't imagine why, since Jackham had known Ren for years. In fact, the three of them had spent many a night sharing tales of adventure over whisky and cigars—carefully edited, of course. It still astonished James how tales of thieving and tales of spying resembled each other. The difference lay in the goal, presumably.

Tonight James's goal was to tend his son and question a

certain lying spy who had turned his life and his family upside down.

Phillipa sat upon the bed in the small room in which she'd
been stored away. She was able to sit now only because she
had long ago exhausted any other action.

Pounding on the door had not gained her anything. Trying to wrest open the small window to cry for help had not
worked. Pacing restlessly had only exhausted her. Even
sleep upon the narrow bed would not come, not with her
desperate worry and guilt about Robbie twisting her gut.

She watched the day pass through the window until the
gray edge of darkness tinged the city. From the circle of
James's arms she had seen the sun rise in this place, and now
she saw it set. Alone.

A part of her wondered if she would ever see it rise again.
*"If I can get you out before Himself sees you, likely they
won't kill you."* Robbie had said that in complete seriousness. He would likely know better than she. In all their time
together, she'd never known Robbie to exaggerate.

Robbie. Phillipa rose, forced to pace once more in restless distress. Dear God, he'd been so still and pale. She
wrapped her arms about her chilled gut but could not warm
it. She ought to have snatched him from the sill of that window the moment he opened it.

She ought to have climbed right down on that treacherous
ledge and tossed his stubborn little body right back into the
club.

She ought never to have contacted James Cunnington in
the first place. All of this—Robbie's accident, James's bitterness, her own imminent danger, not to mention her broken heart—had begun the day she'd walked through the
doors of that house.

Now she was imprisoned here in this mysterious club.

The door finally opened. Phillipa blinked against the light
streaming in, for the room had grown full dark and she had
not been given a candle. A broad-shouldered figure moved

into the rectangle of light, casting Phillipa into shadow once more.

"Miss Atwater, I presume?"

Ren Porter would have gladly journeyed back into the darkness if he could. Unfortunately, God and Mrs. Neely wouldn't let him. The kindly nurse was so grateful for every move he made, every muscle he twitched. She praised him like a toddler for eating a spoonful of mush and wept when he sat up unaided in the bed.

The only way to banish the motherly woman was to feign sleep. So Ren did so, as much as possible. Still, the first day of awareness seemed to stretch into ten.

A familiar voice came from the dimness to rouse him from the weak half-slumber he was reduced to. Too much pain for real sleep, too much weariness for real acuity.

"There's a lot that's happened down at the club since you've been out."

Ren rolled his head to blink at the blurred figure standing beside his bed. It was still difficult to bring images into focus. Finally, the outlines that continuously shifted and wavered coalesced into clarity for a brief instant. Jackham. Ren let his head fall back onto the stabilizing safety of the pillow. The slightest thing made him dizzy.

Cursing the weakness and the pain was his primary entertainment today, but he was weary enough of it by now to welcome the raspy and familiar company of the club's manager. He reminded himself to keep up the façade of thieves' den even through his fog. "Hello, Jack."

Odd that it was Jackham who had come, however. Ren would have expected Simon or at least—

James.

Ren turned his head once more and opened his eyes to blink at Jackham. "Why isn't James here? He isn't . . . he isn't wounded, is he?"

Jackham snorted. "Not a bit of it. He's right as rain. Saw him myself, not an hour ago."

"Is he coming?"

Jackham cleared his throat, apparently uncomfortable. "Well, now you have to understand something, Ren. James is in a difficult position. Here you are, alive after all, and now he's got to face you down, knowing that he was the one to put you here."

Put him here? Cold began to twine through Ren's bruised gut. "I don't follow you, Jack."

Jackham heaved a sigh. "I'm sorry to be the one to tell you this, Ren, but the fact is that James sold you out to a rival outfit, you and some others. You should thank your stars you've still got enough brains to know your name. Most of the lads that James informed on are growin' grass these days. Why, Weatherby lay here for weeks right beside you, until he passed away a few days ago. We thought you were done in as well."

Ren's stomach had gone to ice, but he could only blink at Jackham as the man went on.

"Of course, James made up real sorry for the whole thing, and the new owner took him back on. I, for one, think he meant every word of that regret, but there's some . . ."

Ren swallowed, fighting to make sense of Jackham's report. "New owner?"

"You should know that Simon Raines was bought out. Seems he bargained himself a knighthood with all the money he made thievin', and when he decided to get married he sold the club to a real fancy gentleman by the name of Lord Etheridge. Now, his lordship seems a decent bloke, and he's a right good rooftop man, though I never heard tell of him on the streets afore he bought the club. But the lads have taken to him well enough."

Ren could not contend with James's betrayal. "So James can't face me now?"

Jackham reached out a consoling hand, but stopped before he touched Ren. "Don't be too hard on him now. He's had a real tough time of it. I know some of the lads are thinkin' he's gone straight now, what with being the hero that saved Lord Liverpool and getting gold medals from the Prince Regent and all—"

"Medals." The word was acid on Ren's unwieldy tongue. "They've given him medals."

Jackham blinked at him, worry plain in his eyes. "I know it don't look good, Ren. But I know he's still our James. It's only the responsibilities that are weighin' hard on him. He's practically runnin' the whole operation down at the club. No one gainsays James Cunnington, exceptin' me, I guess. But I just had to see how you fared, us bein' mates and all."

"He told you not to come."

"Not just me. Told all the blokes. Can't think why. Unless you can? Maybe it has somethin' to do with you gettin' attacked. Do you remember anything about that night?"

"I was working the . . . the dockside pubs." Keep the club's cover. The warning suddenly didn't seem to ring as deeply as it used to. "There was a fight, I wasn't part of it, but when I left the place someone motioned me to duck down the alley, away from the ruckus. I think . . . I think it was a woman." He screwed up his eyes against the throbbing behind them. "Perhaps. I don't know."

Jackham leaned back in his chair. "Well, likely it doesn't matter. Have you a thought to what you'll be doin' with yourself now? A thief who can't steal ain't much use to anyone, now is he? I should know."

Ren thought of Jackham's life of bone-deep pain from his fall, and how the man was old before his time, reduced to running numbers and counting pennies for the club. Revulsion shuddered through Ren at that, and more so at the following thought.

He himself might not be so lucky.

Jackham dusted at his hat. "Might be you should get out of London for a bit, once you're up and about." With a sigh and a habitual groan, he stood. "I know it still hurts me to see the heights I used to dance on, when I can hardly climb the steps."

Away. Emotions threatened to pull Ren apart at his badly

healed seams. "Perhaps . . . perhaps I will," he managed to choke out.

Ren felt sick from more than the pain wrestling with the laudanum. He had been sold out to the French by his best friend, and now James was a decorated hero while Ren lay crippled and discarded like a broken sword.

Bitterness welled within him, laced with a dark fury that Ren had never before experienced. He'd lost everything. His strength, his work, and like as not any real clarity in his sight.

The thought crossed his mind that Jackham could be lying, but why would he? Jackham knew nothing about the real purpose of the Liars, nothing about Ren's efforts to be recruited by French intelligence in order to expose their network in London.

No, Jackham was simply reporting what he had observed, oblivious to its larger significance to Ren.

Ren was dizzy with the bitterness of his own fury. His life was a ruin, his friends were dead—and James, the bloody traitor who had caused this damage, was a national hero.

Seeing that Ren was lost to conversation once more, Jackham quietly left the room. Once outside the door, he paused to press one palm to the paneled wood and to pass the other shaking hand over his face.

"I'm sorry, lad," he whispered. "But it's for the best. There's them that will want you too dead to tell tales, now that you've woken. Best you disappear and take your memories with you."

It wasn't much, but it was the least he could do.

Chapter Twenty-eight

"Miss Atwater, I presume?" James stood there, solid and rather menacing. Phillipa shivered at the cold tone of his voice and looked away. She hesitated, so long used to the safety of anonymity. But she owed this man the truth, after what she had done. "Phillipa Atwater."

Her gaze was down, locked on her entwined fingers, but she was aware that he had halted before her at those words. *Oh, Robbie, I'm so sorry—*

"The missing daughter of the traitorous Rupert Atwater."

Phillipa's head jerked up at that. "No more traitor than you!" she retorted. Instantly she saw her mistake, for the cool judgment in his eyes was erased by hot and angry loathing. She should have held still, should have waited until she was in a better position to defend Papa—

Her inward gibbering panic was stunned to silence by the impact of his fist on the paneled wall. She sat stiller than still, aware that something had just gone even more horribly wrong, but not sure what.

James rubbed his fist with the other hand and leaned his forehead on the paneled wall. He faced away from her, but Phillipa could hear his deep mutter. "Rupert Atwater. The biggest traitor in the history of the Liars and I let his daughter into the club. By God, I let her into my *house*."

Phillipa stepped forward. "How is Robbie? Please, tell me. I've been so worried."

"Robbie has a broken arm and has yet to wake from his concussion. Not that you would care."

Phillipa made a sound of protest. He whirled on her and she started backward. Then he was down on one knee before her, his hands planted on the cushions on either side of her, penning her in. He leaned his face close into hers, his once warm brown eyes gone black and shadowed.

"What did you tell them? How many have you betrayed? Was it only me?" His hands came up to clutch her shoulders in a hard grip. He didn't hurt her, not really, but there was no escaping him either.

"Who have you betrayed? *Tell me!*"

Phillipa could only shake her head frantically, gulping back her remorse in the face of his naked torment.

She leaned away from him, breaking the snare of his furious gaze. She could not escape the wall of his body but she would not allow him to sap her will. She was fighting for her life again, hers and quite possibly Papa's.

"I have betrayed no one. I am not a traitor. My father is not a traitor. There must be some explanation—"

She was interrupted by a bark of harsh laughter. "Explanation? For giving the French our codes? For creating codes for them that cannot be broken by us?" He leaned closer, until she could feel his breath on her cheek. "And what of you, *Phillip*? How do you explain your deception? How do you plan to explain away using a child to further your traitorous ends?"

His voice broke slightly. He turned his face away. "I hired you. I gave him into your care. What happened? Did he discover you raiding the back rooms? *Did you throw him from the window with your own hands?*"

"No!" She faced him at last. "James, I would never—I *couldn't* hurt Robbie! I love him like my own, like I—" *love you.* She bit back the words and took a shaking breath.

"James, I would never hurt you—him. Either of you." Raising her hands to his large ones encasing her shoulders, she gently wrapped her fingers around his to ease his shattering grip.

James found himself in the small hands of this strange creature. His mind continued to play tricks on him. Phillip—not Phillip—Phillip—until he thought he'd go mad from it.

He gazed into large green eyes that were reddened from hours of tears. Her cheeks were smooth as silk and softly rounded. Her chin was small, her jaw fine, her lips full and pink. She was undeniably a woman.

The extent of his own stupidity washed over him. He pulled his hands away and stood abruptly. "I am an ass," he muttered furiously. "Have I no judgment left at all?"

"Do not blame yourself, James. I worked very hard at being male." Her voice came from behind him, completely different from Phillip's husky accents. That at least gave him solace, for she'd masked the natural feminine music of her tones well.

"Indeed, you did. We were all quite—" James stopped, remembering Robbie's response to the new tutor. Robbie hadn't been fooled for a second. James turned to her. "Why did Robbie keep your secret from me? How did you sway him to betray me?"

"I don't know what you mean." She glanced away, her lashes lowering almost shyly over those amazing green eyes. He stepped forward, clearly menacing her but not caring. This evil creature had ruined his life and he was not about to take pity because of this newly charming manner.

"From nearly the first day, Robbie knew you were female. How did you persuade him to keep that secret? Dear God, I left him completely in your power! Did you abuse him into compliance?"

She jerked in obvious surprise, her horrified gaze meeting his once more. "Of course not! The only thing I did to him was to teach him to read!"

She had indeed. James didn't want to be reminded of the true help she had rendered Robbie, and indirectly, himself. And Stubbs—

He shook off that silent litany of her virtues. How she had amused herself gaining their confidence did not signify. The meat of the matter was that she had lied and betrayed them all, leaving the Liars vulnerable and Robbie lying unconscious in the next room.

"Answer the question."

She hesitated, then nodded. "All right. But you must not blame Robbie. He truly didn't mean to hide anything from you." She shrugged. "He simply has a great deal to learn about being a gentleman."

He nodded shortly. She continued. "I believe that Robbie's original intention was to use his knowledge as a sort of blackmail—for the student to control the teacher." A small smile flitted across her face.

James refused to be charmed. He only waited stonily.

"Then I believe he began to have . . . certain fancies of our being a sort of family." She glanced up at him warily then. "I didn't encourage this, you understand. It was only natural for him to wish to fill the void with the man and woman nearest him. I never pretended to be his mother and you—"

Never pretended to be his father. The unspoken words hung in the air between them. James did not bother to deny it.

"So Robbie knew."

She nodded. James continued to regard her with his jaw clenched, for there was no doubt in his mind that this particular charade had obtained aid from elsewhere as well.

"Who else?"

She focused her attention on her hands, quite simply and quietly refusing to betray her co-conspirator. She sat like a lady now, feet together, back straight as a rod, frock-coat-clad shoulders straight.

James stepped forward to take hold of a lapel of her coat. "Stand." She stood, giving him a single worried glance before looking down once more. He placed his hands on her shoulders and turned her in place. Every stitch of her clothing had been taken for the sole purpose of hiding her femininity.

"Button." The conspiracy went deeper than he'd imag-

ined. If there was one person who he would have vowed possessed undying loyalty, it was Button. The little valet quite unashamedly worshipped Agatha and by association, Simon.

She turned then, still standing quite close to him. He gazed down at her as she placed one pleading hand on his arm.

"Button didn't know anything but that I was a girl who needed help." She came a step closer in her urgency, until she stood within the circle of his embrace, should he care to embrace her. As if he would.

"He would never betray you. You must believe me."

"I wouldn't believe you if you told me the grass was green."

Her mouth quirked. "So says the Liar." She tilted her head at him. "So you're a spy. Like the Griffin?"

He flinched. "The Griffin is dead."

She gazed at him for a long moment. "Then I'm sorry for your loss. Just so you don't lay that at my door as well, I didn't kill him."

"No," murmured James, distracted by her nearness. "I did."

She was closer to him now than she had ever been. Her scent rose to him. Not that of flowery soap or eau de toilette, but simply woman.

Suddenly, James was back in the shadowed park, holding a soft and struggling redhead in his arms. Hot want flashed through him once more.

Apparently his night with Amilah hadn't completely taken the edge off his needs, not if he could feel desire for this sexless creature. He stepped back.

"Button and Robbie. Who else? Denny?"

She shook her head. "Not Denny."

"No, of course not. Denny likely couldn't see past the end of his own nose." His lips twisted cynically. "Much like myself."

"James, you must understand. I had to know whose side you were on before I revealed myself."

"And when you discovered that, you should have run for your life."

"I thought about it. Even planned on it. But you mistake me still. I am on your side. My father is as well."

"Ah, yes. The fabled *explanation.*" He assumed an indifferent pose, leaning one shoulder on the frame of the window. "Go on."

Phillipa swallowed. James had never seemed so large and intimidating before. She was beginning to see the other side of this man, the side that no doubt made him a spy and a hero. Drawing her desperation about her in lieu of any real courage, she raised her chin to look him in the eye.

"My father was taken from our home in Spain by force. He managed to hide me in time, but the French soldiers abducted him and ruined our home."

James nodded but said nothing. The light did not reach his eyes where he stood, but she could feel them like lances of black ice upon her.

"I made my way to London on my own, as he'd instructed me."

"To Upkirk's."

Phillipa blinked. "Yes, to Mr. Upkirk's. But he'd died in the meantime and I had no way to find any other of my father's old friends."

"And so on to Mrs. Farquart's boardinghouse."

A cold chill went down Phillipa's back. How could he know so much, unless—

"*You're* the one who has been following me?"

James grunted. "Yes, but too far behind to catch you. And much farther behind than another."

"There is another after me? Who?"

"You would know that better than I, I'd think."

She shook her head. "As far as I know, the only one who wants me is Napoleon."

"Really? Why is that?" James's voice was casual.

The tone snapped Phillipa's last thread of control. "One would assume he wants to use me to force my father's compliance, you dolt!" She threw out her hands. "Good God, no wonder England is losing the war, if you're any example of our secret weapons!"

One hard hand wrapped itself around one of her outflung wrists. She was pulled close as if she were nothing more than a toy, until she slammed against his hard frame. He leaned down until she could feel his breath on her ear.

"Don't anger me." His low rumble ran through her like a tremor. "You wouldn't like me thus."

She could tell he was being very frightening. Surely any other woman would be trembling in her stays at this moment. It simply wasn't working on her. When she was this close to him, she wanted him. All of him. Hot, naked, and angry, if that was how he wished it.

Her knees buckled and her palms grew damp. She wished he were thinking what she was thinking, about how they had touched and pleasured each other—

A thought ripped through Phillipa's heated daze. *He doesn't know it was me.* Last night, James had made love to Amilah, not Phillipa Atwater. And she could never, ever tell him otherwise, for he would never forgive her.

Suddenly, Phillipa hated Amilah more than ever. She herself would be treated as a spy and a traitor, while Amilah would live on in James's memory as a fantasy fulfilled.

"Damn," she muttered, and wrenched herself from his grasp, turning to pace the room as she pondered this new twist.

"What did you say?" The surprise in James's voice was obvious. Apparently, most people didn't become distracted and wander off when he was in the middle of intimidating them. A half-tearful giggle rose in Phillipa's throat. She was too late covering her mouth and it escaped to fly into the room like a hummingbird uncaged.

Oh, *merde*.

James's expression was priceless. He'd likely never had someone laugh in the face of his intimidation before either. The hysteria within Phillipa only rose the higher for it.

He stood with folded arms until she was finished. "I do believe you're mad," he said with complete seriousness.

She sighed. "I do believe you're right." He continued to gaze at her sternly. She smiled at him sadly. It made him scowl. What a wonder he was, all righteous patriot and restless adventurer in one.

How I love you, my warrior-king. She couldn't say it, as much as she longed to. He wouldn't believe, not now.

She continued to smile into his scowl. "Are you going to listen to me now?"

"No." Then he sighed. "I think I need to bring in clearer heads." He turned toward the door. "You'll be kept here as long as it takes, you realize. And don't try your wiles on the man guarding your door. Stubbs will be forewarned."

He left then, with an audible click of the lock to assure her of her captivity. Phillipa paid no mind, for she was looking down at her rumpled, grimy, trouser-and tweed-clad self in wonder. "Wiles?" she murmured. *"Wiles?"*

Phillipa was wearily contemplating sleeping in her shirt— for she had nothing but what she wore—when a diffident tap came upon her door. She turned to stare at it. Did someone think *she* had the power to open it?

"Yes?"

"Miss Atwater? May I beg a moment of your time?"

The extreme politeness of the request made Phillipa snort. "Oh, by all means."

The lock tumbled and the door opened to reveal a bookish young man adorned with spectacles and a painfully earnest manner. "I beg your pardon, Miss Atwater. I know this must be a tremendous imposition."

Phillipa flicked a glance left, then right. "Actually, I would call it a prison cell, but then, that is simply my opinion."

The fellow nodded in earnest agreement. "Too right. I couldn't agree more." He stood there in the open door, fidgeting with a small stack of documents in his hands. Finally, Phillipa lost patience. "Come in or go away. But if you come in, you must bring your own candle. Mine went out from a draft and I have no way to light it."

Actually, the candle had been left by James, and ironically, it had been his exit that had provided the draft that had extinguished it. The symbolism of it had given her many a droll moment in between.

Muttering apologetic noises and waving flustered gestures, the fellow bent over her candle with a small box in his hands. With a single quick motion, he created a flame from apparently nothing at all.

Phillipa was astounded. "Who are you people?" she asked, alarm beginning to twine through her once more. James she knew, or believed she knew. The rest—well, perhaps she ought not to relax just yet.

"I beg your pardon," the fellow said for what had to be the tenth time. "I must introduce myself, I fear. Oh, dear . . ."

Phillipa was quite exhausted by his blithering. She stood and offered her hand in a masculine manner. The man shook it automatically. "Hello, my name is Phillipa Atwater. What is yours, may I ask?"

He blinked at her. "Fish." Then he shook his head quickly. "No. It isn't. It's Fisher. Bartholomew Fisher."

"And what is it you've come to see me about, Mr. Bartholomew Fisher?" Phillipa asked wearily. "For I'm expecting royal guests soon and I must prepare the tea."

"What? Oh, a little jest. I see." He didn't look as though he saw at all, but Phillipa didn't hold it against him. Her humor was most uncertain when she was tired.

"Perhaps you could tell me—I mean to say, if you think it is at all possible that you might help—not that you would know the codes, I suppose—"

"Mr. Fisher, I fear you've confused me completely. What codes don't I know?"

"Your father's, of course. But you're a lady. You likely don't know them at all."

"But I do. A few of them."

Mr. Fisher rushed forward at that. "I've so wanted to meet you. Your father is a great influence on my work, you see. I mean, not that I'm a traitor, of course—oh, dear . . ."

"Mr. Fisher, it is my opinion my father is only helping Napoleon because he must believe that I am in danger, or possibly a prisoner of the French myself." Phillipa turned away. "Not that you will believe that, of course."

"Oh, but I do believe that!"

Phillipa turned back, startled. "You do? Why you, when I cannot convince James Cunnington of this?"

"Well, James may be a brilliant saboteur, but he's not a cryptographer, is he? I've been handling the decryption process for the last few months and it seems that the codes have been getting simpler all the time, as if someone on the other end is trying to help us decrypt them."

Phillipa smiled, hope blooming in her at last. "Yes! That is precisely what he would do!" She threw her arms around a very startled Mr. Fish and danced him about in a circle. "Do you know what this means! It's proof! He's alive!" She kissed Mr. Fisher on the cheek from the sheer welling of happiness within her. Papa was alive and she was finally going to be able to help bring him home.

The door opened. Phillipa looked up, still smiling and still with her arms around a further flustered and blushing Mr. Fisher.

James was glaring at them from the doorway, a nearly visible storm cloud gathering over his head.

Phillipa released her not-terribly-unwilling dance partner and wiggled her fingers at James. "Hello." Then she decided not to care that he was simply simmering with fury and smiled at him happily. "Papa is alive, James. And I can prove he isn't a traitor."

James's eyes narrowed. "Then you do have the code key."

Phillipa blinked, her smile fading slightly. "Key?"

Mr. Fisher stepped forward. "Do you have your father's notes? Perhaps a book, filled with notations?"

A book? "The journal!" She turned to Fisher. "Before he shut me in the hiding place, he gave me his journal to carry to Mr. Upkirk!"

"Ah!" Fisher beamed. "Wonderful! If it contains the key, then there will be no doubt of your father's loyalty! Will there, James?"

James didn't appear any too convinced. "Perhaps. If it indeed contains the key."

At James's grim expression Phillipa sobered. "Will that make you believe I am innocent?" She must not forget that this man, the very man whom she loved beyond the boundaries of her soul, had every intention of having her father killed.

Eliminated.

"We shall see." James watched the emotions flicker across that oddly unfamiliar pale face topped by untidy reddish-brown hair. His mind was quite resolved on one issue at least. She was as female as Venus, despite her garb and butchered locks. He'd felt it when he'd pulled her close earlier, and he felt it now, watching her watch him.

The flash of hot possessiveness he'd experienced when he'd seen Fisher awkwardly embracing her was not something he was going to be able to think rationally about anytime soon.

"Fisher, you're needed. The Gentleman is waiting." His voice was gruffer than he'd intended.

Fisher blinked and straightened his waistcoat, then gathered up the papers that had fallen to the floor. Then he smiled shyly at Phillipa and murmured words of encouragement. James flexed his jaw. The bloke was entirely besotted.

That hadn't taken her long at all.

About as innocent as a snake charmer, she was.

Chapter Twenty-nine

Dalton was waiting in the Cryptography room for them, still eerily elegant even at this late hour. He nodded to Fisher and indicated a chair. Then he turned to James.

"I understand that Robbie has not yet awakened."

"No," James replied shortly. "And I should like to return to his bedside as soon as possible, so let us get on with this."

Dalton raised a brow but offered no reproach at James's tone, though James knew he was being rude.

"Very well." Dalton seated himself, as did James. "We have a problem. Phillipa Atwater has broken no law, nor has she offered any harm to anyone. We don't even have proof of her giving any information to the French. In short, we have no reason to hold this woman prisoner."

James bolted to his feet. "Are you mad? She nearly killed Robbie!"

"James, Robbie has climbed every vertical surface in his path since the day he came to us. He was bound to fall eventually."

"And 'eventually' simply happened to occur in her care. Does that not twinge your suspicions at all?"

"Stubbs said that she claims that Robbie was showing her the back door and that she tried to stop him."

"Well, she obviously didn't try very hard."

Dalton shook his head. "James, you aren't thinking clearly. If she'd wanted to kill Robbie by throwing him from the window, would she have screamed and drawn your attention? Or would she have kept silent and let Robbie lie there indefinitely?"

"She climbed it herself, you realize." Fisher sat forward. "After Robbie fell, she had to jump over and climb down the ladder herself. With no one to show her the trick of it either."

James looked away. He well remembered his first go at the back door. Heaps of soft rubbish had been piled at the foot of the ladder, and he'd been encouraged by the laughter and helpful shouts of the other Liars.

And he'd still missed the handholds when he'd jumped across, landing arse-first in the rubbish. Twice.

"I don't give a damn if she bloody well flew down," James bit out. "She spied on me, infiltrated my home, and endangered my son. She is dangerous, I tell you. Even Button is not proof against her, and Button is nigh immune to every woman on earth but Agatha."

"I will deal with Button's part in this, James. That is, if you are pleased to allow that I am still spymaster of this club?"

The cool tone in Dalton's voice reminded James of why the man was known as the Gentleman. There was nothing more disquieting than Lord Etheridge at his lordliest.

"My apologies, my lord." Civil words, even if he had not been able to force a civil tone. What was happening to him, that he was so near the edge of his self-control?

Her.

She was happening to him, confusing him. How could he let his lust control his mind again, after all that had happened with Lavinia Winchell? The very near passage of his own redemption made him long for it all the more.

James sat, tamping down his swirling emotions. If he allowed the spymaster to see how very much involved he was in this issue, he would be pulled from the case immediately.

He wanted to see this case through. Oh, yes.

James managed to meet Dalton's gaze now with some small amount of calm. "You were saying?"

"I was saying that we have no evidence. Nor am I entirely convinced that there is any to find. With our manpower shortage, I don't see that we have the resources to pursue a case against Miss Atwater."

"But her father—"

Dalton held up a hand. "Her father is another story entirely. There is a great deal of evidence that Rupert Atwater is aiding Napoleon. Even Miss Atwater admits the possibility, does she not?"

James grunted. "She claims that her father is being coerced."

"You do not accept this possibility?"

"I do not. Atwater is a traitor. End of the matter."

Fisher made a protesting noise. Dalton silenced him with one raised digit, still regarding James very closely. James shifted, restless under the cool gaze. Dalton had learned well from Lord Liverpool. James wished he would take that most intimidating habit and use it on someone else.

Phillipa Atwater, for starts.

"So quick to judge, James? Is it possible that you are taking this matter a bit too personally?"

James hardened his jaw against a snarling retort and merely shook his head.

Fisher snorted. "Well, I for one don't know what grudge you hold against Miss Atwater. I was very impressed with my interview—"

"I'll wager you were," muttered James. *Hands off my suspect, you poacher.*

Fisher warily slid his chair a few inches from James, but continued. "She has volunteered her father's journal for my examination. She is quite convinced that she was sent to Upkirk expressly for the purpose of giving him the key to break her father's codes."

Dalton nodded. "You believe this journal to be Atwater's key, then."

Fisher nodded. "Indeed. And if so, then that proves her story, does it not?"

Dalton leaned back in his chair. "So it would seem. If we could then pass a coded message *to* Atwater of his daughter's safety, that would no doubt cause him to cease his cooperation."

"Exactly."

"But that will only alert him!" James could not restrain himself any longer. "I cannot believe you are considering this! You intend to collaborate with a traitor?"

"I'm considering it part of an investigation into a possible traitor, yes." Dalton rose. "I think you would do well to remember what it was like to be on the wrong end of that investigation, James. The practice may have an improving effect on your attitude. Now, it is past midnight and I am for home. I am releasing Miss Atwater from confinement, although I will ask her to remain as a guest of the club. We shall need her help with this, I should think. Give her something harmless to decode, see if she is accurate—test her without her knowledge."

James only nodded stiffly, but inwardly he felt as if he had received a body blow. After all that she had done, to him and to Robbie, she was free.

He rose and left the room without a word. Etiquette be damned, he was not about to spend another minute away from Robbie.

As he reentered the room where he had spent so many hours today, he wanted nothing more than to see Robbie sleeping sprawled and tangled in his bedding as of old. His heart sank as he saw that Robbie had not moved a hair while he had been meeting with Dalton and Fisher.

Sitting in the bedside chair, he brushed back a lock of heavy black hair from Robbie's forehead and began to speak. "The trees are enormous at Appleby, Rob. You've never seen such climbing. Why, I broke my arm falling out of one of those very trees when I was a lad . . ."

·   ·   ·

At the sound of whispered voices in her room, Phillipa swam from the depths of sleep most unwillingly. Bloody shark-infested *hell*. Wasn't it enough to be kept prisoner? Did she have to be woken so early after yet another night of little sleep?

After a moment she realized that the voices were female, and then she became aware that they were discussing her. Curious, she lay quite still and listened.

"Are they going to kill her, milady?"

Phillipa was *very* interested in the answer to that question herself. She forced herself to appear relaxed as she listened.

"If she is indeed working for the French, I hope so. She wormed her way into Jamie's *house*. She could have killed him as he slept, and Robbie as well!"

"Oh, Agatha, I hardly think she looks capable of murder," said a third voice. "She cannot be more than nineteen!"

"Clara, age has nothing to do with it. Why would she disguise herself if she had nothing to hide?"

"I don't know, Agatha." There was gentle laughter in the voice. "Why don't you tell me?"

The first voice spoke again, the one that seemed to slip in and out of proper speech as if the speaker were not quite born to it. "But milady, Milady is quite right!"

The woman called Agatha snorted. "Rose, I've lost track again. I do wish you'd address us by our given names. It would make things so much easier."

Rose drew an appalled breath. "Oh, but I *couldn't*!"

"Agatha, don't press her," said the woman called Clara. "She'll become more comfortable in time. Now, did you ever meet this girl when she was pretending to be Robbie's tutor?"

Pretending, my foot! Phillipa almost jumped up in protest right then. She had spent many grueling hours teaching Robbie, something these people seemed only too eager to forget.

Robbie. Fully awake now, she felt once more a shock of deepest worry.

If Clara was Lady Etheridge, as Phillipa recalled, and

Agatha was Lady Raines, then these women likely had the latest news of Robbie's condition. Opening her eyes, she blinked at them, not needing to feign sleepiness. "Hello," she offered, not sure of her reception after hearing Agatha's bloodthirsty words.

Three women met her gaze. One stepped forward with a smile. She was dark-haired, slender, and very elegantly dressed. "Good morning, Miss Atwater. I am Lady Etheridge, although I prefer to be addressed as Clara. You must forgive our barging in, but if we had not brought in your breakfast, I'm afraid it would have been left to Mr. Stubbs."

Suddenly remembering that she was nearly bare beneath her man's shirt, Phillipa drew the covers to her chest, mightily glad she had not woken to a male intrusion. "Thank you, Lady—Clara. Can you please tell me, how is Robbie? I've been half-mad with worry—"

One of the other two women made a disdainful noise. "Half-mad, perhaps . . ." The buxom brunette crossed plump arms and frankly glared at Phillipa.

Agatha, James's sister. Her opinion was likely colored by James's own response. Phillipa tried to appear most obliging, although being undressed in bed put her at a severe disadvantage against these stylish ladies. "I know what you must think, my lady, but I beg of you—" Quite unintentionally her voice broke as she remembered Robbie so small and still on the cobbles.

Clara moved to place an arm about Phillipa, casting Lady Raines an admonishing glance. "Robbie has the best care in London, do not worry. His arm is broken, but he seems unwounded otherwise."

"Seems?" Phillipa's chest tightened. "Has he—has he not yet woken?" The last word was squeezed from a throat tight with dismay.

Even Agatha seemed to relent at that. She uncrossed her arms to clasp her hands protectively over her own midriff. "Children are very resilient . . . at least, that is what Dr. Westfall tells me," she said softly. "He'll wake soon, I know it."

Phillipa closed her eyes. So careless. So bloody stupid. "I should have *forced* him to climb back in that window," she said.

That brought a laugh from an unexpected quarter. Phillipa, Clara, and Agatha looked up to see Rose clap a hand over her mouth, her wide eyes rueful. "Sorry, miss. But forcing young Master Rob to do something ain't—isn't an easy thing." The girl shrugged. Phillipa noticed that she was not dressed nearly as well as the two "miladies," although she looked very presentable. She was not a plump beauty like Agatha, nor an elegant sylph like Clara. In fact, she was rather ordinary but for a pair of large, heavily lashed hazel eyes.

Even Agatha had to agree with Rose. "No," she said with a sigh. "He's fair to becoming a Cunnington in truth."

Phillipa nodded. They were being very kind and she would not refute them.

"I'd like to see him, if it is permissible?"

"Oh, you may come and go as you please," Clara reassured her. "You are not a prisoner." Then she glanced up at Agatha, who shrugged.

"Jamie isn't likely to let you in to see his son."

Phillipa looked up at that. "Is that what James called Robbie? His son?"

Agatha blinked suspiciously. "Of course. Why wouldn't he?"

"Well, well," Phillipa murmured, looking down to hide a small smile. "Good on you, Mr. Cunnington."

Gazing down at herself, she picked at her shirt with two fingers. "I don't suppose there is any point to wearing this lot any longer." She sighed with longing at the very thought of girl clothes. "I don't suppose I've anything feminine to wear?"

Rose stepped forward, pulling a familiar rucksack from behind her back. "Mr. Fisher already took the book out. He said you wouldn't mind."

Phillipa gathered the grimy bag close for a moment, feeling Papa in every fold. Inside she found her one tatty dress, slightly the worse for being stuffed in a hole for more than a week. With mice, apparently. "Oh, ick."

"That won't do." Clara put a finger to her lips. "Well, you cannot wear one of mine. You're far too tall."

Agatha shook her head. "Nor mine. You're far too slender."

Phillipa smiled and cast a glance at the girl Rose. "And what of you, baby bear?"

Rose grinned at that, her smile transforming her face from ordinary to striking in a single beat. Phillipa blinked. Then the smile was gone and Rose was gazing at her soberly, as unremarkable as before.

"I don't think so, miss. You'd be too tall for anything I have, though I'd be glad to give it."

"Thank you. I suppose I might ask Button—" Phillipa looked up in alarm. "Oh, no! Button! He hasn't caught trouble for helping me, has he?"

Agatha raised a brow. "I'd like to see them try it. Button is in *my* army, not theirs. I merely allow them to borrow him on occasion."

Clara nodded. "Don't worry over Button, Miss Atwater. Even the Prince Regent takes a step back when Agatha puts her foot down."

Phillipa cast a single quick glance at Agatha's rather astounding assets, then looked away, repressing a short laugh. She wondered if Clara realized exactly how her comment had sounded. Apparently Phillipa was not the only one to have that irreverent thought, for she swore she heard a muffled giggle from the general direction of Rose.

Phillipa sent Rose a look of companionably repressed humor and was answered by another one of those smiles. Then she looked down at the sorry traveling dress in her hands and sighed. Well, she'd at least be decent in her trousers. Not that it mattered, for James was scarcely going to care.

Agatha and Rose left, declaring they were off to check on Robbie for her. Clara left her with a pat on the shoulder. "Eat your breakfast. I've a feeling Kurt outdid himself this morning."

After dressing and trying to tame her ragged hair with a damp brush, Phillipa lifted the dome that covered her meal.

Heaven. Nectar and ambrosia. On the platter lay a breakfast fit for a queen. And several of her ladies-in-waiting.

Phillipa ate heartily, for she'd not eaten at all yesterday. In addition, it seemed she'd quite lost the habit of nibbling in a ladylike manner. Looking down, she also noticed that her knees were most definitely spread. She clapped them together.

Oh, *merde*. She'd forgotten how to be a girl!

Chapter Thirty

All that afternoon in the code room James drove himself, Fisher, and Phillipa hard. At first, Phillipa had been given a few nonessential items to work on, until he was sure she could be trusted. Then James had insisted she begin on Lavinia's letters.

She obviously suspected that he still did not trust her. It was a sign of his desperation that he set her to this task at all.

Phillipa rubbed at her cheeks, then pressed her palms flat over her eyes as if to relieve them. "There is nothing here."

"There must be!"

Clearly losing patience, Phillipa drew her hands down to slap them onto the tabletop. "I may not be my father's equal, but I know enough to spot patterns. There are certain patterns in codes, certain repetitions, certain rhythms. Even if one cannot break the code, one can spot the fact that it is indeed coded."

She grabbed up a handful of the sheets to wave at him. "These love letters of Lady Winchell's are just that. Love letters—maudlin, boring, frankly pornographic, and did I mention boring? There is no code."

James ground his teeth. "There must be hidden meaning! Else why write so many, so often?"

"I don't know, James. Did you ever think perhaps she might be in *love*?" Exasperation was plain in her face. "However, I didn't say there was no hidden meaning."

James leaned forward eagerly. "Aha! Will it help us prove her guilt?"

Phillipa picked up a sheet covered in florid script and squinted at it. "That depends on what you think her guilty of. Personally, I find her guilty of being the filthiest woman I've ever come upon." Shaking her head, she handed the sheet to James. "Here, for instance. What is the meaning of that particular phrase, may I ask?" She pointed halfway down the page.

James read where she indicated, then looked away. "Haven't the faintest idea." He shoved the page beneath the others, hoping his face didn't look as hot as it felt. Phillipa's inquiry had involved a particularly diverting activity that even James had never encountered before Lavinia. It had been one of her favorites, and he had been a bemused but willing partner more than once.

His stomach churning as he remembered her wicked charms, James forced himself to think of Amilah. Compared to Lavinia, even a veil-clad dancer of the demimonde seemed a fresh and wholesome diversion.

He'd thought of Amilah often in the past two days. The mystery of her teased at his mind, never quite letting go. He'd likely never know what possessed a young woman to tease a strange man into a storeroom to gift him with her virginity. Had she seen him from afar and longed for him?

She'd more probably seen him as a willing and not too objectionable way to divest herself of her burdensome innocence . . . although wasn't that sort of innocence financially valuable to a courtesan?

The puzzle would have to remain unsolved, for he had much more pressing matters to attend to. He cleared his throat and wiped Amilah from his mind. No more dwelling on those eyes that so closely matched the Turkish blue of her veils—

"James!"

He jerked himself back to the present to see Phillipa glaring at him, eyes emerald green even when reddened. "Yes?"

She threw down the letter in her hand. "If I am forced to read this smut, the least you can do is to pay attention when I have a question."

"What was your question?"

"Why are you so interested in this woman's letters? What can you possibly gain by examining this rubbish?"

James looked down at the dozens of scattered sheets of Lavinia's particular brand of seductive poison. "Justice," he breathed.

"Justice? Or vengeance?"

James jerked his head up to glare at her. "What is the difference?"

She gazed at him somberly. "If you have to ask, you cannot understand."

James rolled his eyes. "Pray, spare us your profundities, Flip."

She visibly started. "*Flip.* You haven't called me that since—"

James scowled. "Do not fret. It shan't happen again."

She smiled, a hint of sadness in her eyes. "How unfortunate. I liked it very much."

"If it is pet names you are after, perhaps you ought to get out of those ridiculous trousers," James said scornfully. And her shirt, which, without the waistcoat, did little to hide the unbound curves of her breasts. Good God, where had she been hiding them all this time? "What sort of woman are you, to dress so brazenly?"

She blinked, but her smile was wry. "One who prefers not to smell of mouse," she replied.

"I think she looks most charming," Fisher broke in, offering a besotted bow.

Phillipa smiled back at the young cryptographer until James felt his ears begin to steam.

"Why, thank you, Mr. Fisher," she said.

"Oh." Fisher blushed. "You may call me Fish."

"Enough." James could scarcely speak for the tension in

his jaw. His best and last hope of proving Lavinia's guilt was worthless, his son lay wounded and unwaking, his friend was no friend at all—

"Poor James." Phillipa's voice was light, but not mocking. "What have I done to you now?"

He turned to see her gathering up Lavinia's letters while she watched him with rueful eyes. For the first time, he realized that she seemed far better fed and healthier than when he'd first encountered her.

What was it that Upkirk's neighbor had said? *"She seemed as though she had nowhere else to go."*

That was both of them, wasn't it? Nowhere else to go.

Phillipa carefully stacked and stored Lady Winchell's revolting letters, though she wanted nothing more than to burn them. To think that James had been returning to these awful, sickening things for months now as he searched for answers.

It wasn't so much that the letters were sexual that repelled Phillipa. She had recently discovered that she herself was a sexual creature and had no issue with that.

Lavinia Winchell's letters, on the other hand, were purposely intended to be deeply shocking, to arrest the attention and rivet the reader in an awful net of revolted fascination. By the very act of reading them, Phillipa felt as though she had willingly participated in a sort of obscene manipulation.

This terrible woman was the one who had seduced and betrayed James. Knowing that James had had a lover was one thing. Meeting that lover through these explicit and disquieting descriptions of sexual acts was quite another. Lavinia's hands had been on him. His body had been within hers. The things that they had likely done together—things that Phillipa had never dreamed of before today.

She was in agony. Yet she dared not show a single sign of it.

Worse still was that she could see that Lavinia was still at the center of James's thoughts. He was obsessed with the woman. True, he was obsessed with destroying her, not bedding her—but he was fixated nonetheless.

Was there even room in James's heart for another, no

matter that she loved him well? Phillipa watched as James paced the room, rubbing at his jaw with one hand. He was as blind to her as if she were still a man in his eyes. Even Amilah had only had his body, not his soul.

That bit of goods clearly yet belonged to Lady Winchell.

James finally fled the code room and Phillipa's presence. There was someone he needed to see and even though the encounter was bound to be painful, at least Ren Porter wasn't female. James had had quite enough of women for one week.

But the sickroom visits over the past six weeks were not enough to prepare James for the cold rage in his friend's eyes.

"Fancy you stopping by," Ren greeted James. He was sitting up in bed, seeming surprisingly well—yet the friend James had known for years would not meet his extended hand. "To what do I owe this honor?"

James stepped back under the force of the quiet fury in Ren's voice. "I came as soon as I could get away." He took a chair nearby. He hadn't expected a tearfully joyous reunion, but this was very odd.

Unless someone had told Ren of James's error. But who? The only one the club had sent to represent them was Jackham, and all that Jackham knew was that Ren had been jumped down by the docks. The club manager knew nearly nothing of the leak in the Liars, and even less of James's part in it.

"Who has been to see you?" James tried to keep the anger from his voice, but he'd wanted so badly to explain himself to Ren, for absolution perhaps, but definitely in the hopes that his old friend would understand. Now the bleakness in Ren's restless gaze spoke of more damage than mere words could undo.

"I've been reading the papers, or rather, my nurse has been reading them to me. Mrs. Neely was kind enough to save every newssheet from the time I was . . . asleep." Ren thumbed through the stack on his lap. "So kind of her, don't you think?"

Actually, it had been James's impulse to save the newssheets and he'd given Mrs. Neely the charge. Now, as he realized what Ren had been reading, he cursed his own stupidity. It would all be in there, every word of gossip and innuendo but unfortunately, few facts.

Agatha's public disgrace, her royal redemption, the shot fired in front of Parliament, James's medals. The entire mess, some of it slanted in decidedly unfavorable ways, from James's perspective.

"Medals," murmured Ren. "How proud you must be."

A handful of papers hit the wall opposite James, sending a flutter of pages to the carpet. On the top rested a drawing by an influential political cartoonist, the very one which had sentenced Nathaniel Stonewell to be forever known as Lord Treason.

James rubbed his face. "Ren, I—"

"Mrs. Neely read the wedding announcements to me just before you came. Did you know that my fiancée is now happily married to a solicitor from Brighton?"

James swallowed. He'd never thought about the girl Ren had been so mad for before his accident. She'd been informed of course, but no one had been given Ren's location for security reasons. James vaguely remembered his friend squiring about a pretty blonde before he'd gone covert. Ren had talked of little else for weeks but the girl.

Who had deserted the engagement posthaste, apparently.

"God, Ren. I'm sorry—"

"Are they nice medals, James? Shiny and bright? Do you polish them and keep them under your pillow?"

James stood. "Ren, please listen—"

"No!" Ren came off the pillows in a convulsion of rage. "I give you no hearing, no reprieve, Cunnington. You cost me everything! *Everything!*" He slumped back, apparently sapped by his outburst. "Leave me alone. You and all your fellow traitors . . ."

Shocked, James stepped forward. "Ren, the Liars had nothing to do with it—"

"*Get out!*" Ren was white and shaking, but his eyes burned dangerously.

James drew back, then turned to go. "I'll be back, Ren. When you're feeling more like yourself."

As he shut the sickroom door behind him, he heard another handful of newssheets strike the wood at his back.

Ren was a destroyed man, and James had done this to him. With Lavinia's help.

James felt no qualm interrupting the evening meal of the most powerful man in Britain. Lord Liverpool still had napkin in hand as he entered the parlor where James had been placed by the Prime Minister's exceptionally austere butler.

"Cunnington, you do realize the hour?"

"Yes, my lord." James bowed tightly, but could not sit. "I have come to beg more time."

"Ah." Liverpool tossed the napkin to a side table and clasped his hands behind his back. "The ten days have nearly passed and you have nothing on Lady Winchell."

"No, I have nothing." James looked away. "Her letters are useless, her lover has disappeared, and she is too cunning to allow any incriminating information to slip."

"Well, then." Liverpool nodded briskly. "We must release her at once."

"No! I have one more day!"

Liverpool sent James a quelling look. "Are you crying me nay, sir?" The words were mild but the tone could chill fire.

James swallowed back his alarm to carefully rephrase himself. "My apologies, my lord, but if I could only have more time. I can—"

"The point of the matter is, Cunnington, that you *cannot.*" Then Liverpool seemed to take pity on him. "One learns with maturity to choose one's battles wisely. If I should pursue this case against Lady Winchell with no evidence, I should lose the support of a number of very influential members of the House of Lords. They, very rightly I might add, dislike the idea that their ladies could be arrested and imprisoned without proven guilt of anything other than being overly emotional."

"But we know—"

James halted at Liverpool's uplifted hand. "Yes, Cunnington. *We* know. But they do not. I cannot operate this government well if it has been torn asunder over this issue, not when there are so many other more pressing issues at hand. My decision stands. The lady is released."

James seethed but said no more. What could he say? A part of him knew the Prime Minister was quite right in taking the larger, unemotional view—but that part was diminished and obscured by the great rushing fury that flowed through him along with every drop of blood in his body.

Consumed with his rage, James had only a dim memory of taking his leave of the Prime Minister and flinging himself into a seat in a hired carriage that he grimly directed back to the club.

Lavinia was free. The murdering, manipulative whore who had stolen his honor was free to return to her luxurious and indulgent life with all charges dropped.

Lavinia was free.

If only he could be.

Ren swung his feet to the floor and eased himself into a standing position, biting his lip against the agony that shot through his legs and back. Shattered, the nurse had told him of his right leg. Likely never be the same, having been broken in so many places.

His head exploded with pain at every beat of his heart. He ignored it. His pulse was loud in his own ears as he forced himself to walk. A large standing mirror had been pushed aside to make room for that other bed that lay so empty now. Ren caught a glimpse of himself in motion and peered closer, fighting his blurred vision for a better look.

His face was a horror. His hair was gone in great swaths where it had been shaven to stitch his scalp closed. What was left was matted and uneven. Thick red scars swam over his patched head like rivulets in sand. His face was swollen still, even after so long, but the worst was the scars. They traced over the right side of his face, one long slice carving right into the corner of his mouth.

Well, that explained his difficulty speaking. He'd once been called handsome and liked it. That would never happen again.

No matter. He turned away from the glass. He had more important things to think on. Moving carefully, he tried each limb for strength and ability. Coldly, he evaluated every ache and agony, allotting them no more than an instant of his attention.

Much of his weakness came from lack of activity, he decided. What could not be fixed with rest and food he chose to ignore. His sight might never truly return to normal—but there was little reading done while pursuing vengeance, was there?

He needed his mind sharp, but his body need only be functional. He no longer had any intention of living forever.

Only to live long enough to make things right.

Lady Raines and Lady Etheridge were arguing when Phillipa made her way from the code room to the common room on the secret side of the wall.

She was free to roam the club now, but not to leave. No matter. There was nowhere else where she could do so much for Papa.

The spies' den had always seemed oddly familiar to her, as if she knew what lay about every corner before she reached it. She'd been down into the kitchen this morning and seeing Kurt again had explained it all. When she'd thanked him for the extraordinary breakfast, he'd only mumbled, "Not as good as your mum's."

Only then had it had truly reached her that this frightening

giant had been a close friend of her mother's. It was as though
a candle were lighted in the depths of Phillipa's memories.

She'd been in this place, with these people, before. These
were her father's compatriots and her mother's dear friends.
Unlike Arieta where she had lived so quietly that she had
known few of the villagers, this place might be the closest
that Phillipa could ever truly call home.

Or at least, she might if James could ever accept her.

Now in any case, it seemed his sister had no objection to
her presence, for Agatha wasted no time drawing Phillipa
into the debate she held with Clara.

"I simply don't agree," Clara was saying. "Mr. Underkind
is not the artist that Sir Thorogood was."

Agatha shrugged. "Perhaps, but Mr. Underkind takes on
topics that I want changed myself. I didn't always agree with
Sir Thorogood's mission, not when innocents were affected,
like the wives and children of some of the men that were
lampooned."

Clara stared at her friend for a long moment, then turned
to Phillipa as if seeking her support.

"Tell me, Phillipa, you've lived in London for a number
of months, haven't you? Which cartoons do you prefer? Mr.
Underkind's or Sir Thorogood's?"

Phillipa couldn't imagine why the spymaster's wife cared
for her opinion either way, but she tried to answer anyway. "To
be honest, I like them equally. The drawings were perhaps better in Sir Thorogood's, but Mr. Underkind seems more compassionate somehow, at least compared to Sir Thorogood."

She pondered the comparison for a moment longer.
"Didn't I hear that Sir Thorogood was actually a woman? If
so, she must have been as sharp-tongued as a harpy. I pity
her poor husband, if she indeed has one—"

A snort came from behind her. The spymaster himself
stood in the doorway, snickering helplessly into one fist.
Phillipa stared at him. He'd seemed such a sober, dignified
gentleman before.

Clara stood and circled the table to stand before her husband, fists on her hips. "I'll show you sharp-tongued when I get you home, Dalton Montmorency!"

"Show me now." With a quick motion, he wrapped his wife's waist with one arm and pulled her close for a kiss that made Phillipa's ears buzz with fascinated embarrassment.

"Come along, Phillipa. When they get going, it takes a while for things to subside." Agatha led her from the room, but not before Phillipa looked back to see Clara's hand on her husband's buttock. It was a very nice buttock too, although not as nice as James's.

Agatha rolled her eyes. "And I thought Simon and I were shameless. We manage to confine our wrestling to our own four walls . . . mostly." The last word was said with such dreamy lasciviousness that Phillipa felt herself coloring all over again.

Agatha noticed. "Oh, dear, now I've gone and made it worse, haven't I?" Then she eyed Phillipa with a hint of her old suspicion. "Then again, you did live unchaperoned with my brother for many nights. Tell me, are your intentions toward James honorable?"

Perhaps it was the audacity of the question, or perhaps her mind was still on James's buttocks, but Phillipa's reply was short and immediate. "Not in the slightest."

That surprised a laugh from Agatha. "This should be interesting. My brother has been much too grim of late. What he has been through warrants it, to be sure. Still, I do believe I shall be your champion, my dear Phillipa. With me on your side, Jamie doesn't stand a chance."

"I'm honored," declared Phillipa dubiously. Then her mind cleared as she played back part of the conversation in the other room. "Is it my imagination, or is Lady Etheridge the woman who drew the Sir Thorogood cartoons?"

"Mm-hmm. She's very clever."

"Oh, dear. And she's envious of Mr. Underkind's success, I suppose. I hope I didn't hurt her feelings."

"I doubt it." Agatha continued serenely down the hall. Phillipa let her go, for in truth it was sometimes difficult to be around James's sister when they resembled each other so. Agatha's eyes were the same warm brown, and when she smiled, it only reminded Phillipa that James never smiled at her anymore.

Clara bustled up behind her then, none the worse for the interlude with her husband, although she was tucking a bit of tousled hair neatly away with one hand while she held a large box on one hip with the other. "Did we misplace Agatha? I'll fetch her back, for Button has just come with a lovely surprise for you."

"Button? Where is he?" Phillipa looked beyond Clara, but saw no one. "I must make my apologies for lying to him so."

Clara nodded. "I imagine you should, but now is not the time. Although Button is not directly under the authority of the club, I think Dalton has a few things to say to him."

"Oh, no. Button will never be able to forgive me."

"He already has, if this box holds what I think it does." She handed the dress box to Phillipa and dug into one pocket of her gown. "Now, this is from me. I sent to Beatrice Trapp for a solution to your hair and she sent me this." She held up an apothecary's bottle of deep brown glass. "This should remove most of the dye!"

Phillipa raised one hand to her hair. She'd resigned herself to the ragged condition, but she still missed the color that had defined her most of her life. "Shall I be a redhead again, do you think?"

Agatha approached them again. "Did it come then, Clara? Oh, and a dress!" She rubbed plump hands together with glee. "Jamie Cunnington, you're not going to know what hit you!"

Chapter Thirty-one

Hours later, Phillipa was feeling a bit as though she had indeed been hit by something. Perhaps three whirlwinds known as Clara, Agatha, and Rose.

Her hair had been shampooed until her scalp throbbed. The color had returned, almost as bright as before. Then Clara had cut and set it, using her artist's eye to shape it into a fluffy cap of curls. The end result was unusual but entirely feminine, especially after Rose had threaded a ribbon of turquoise silk through it all.

Phillipa stood before the mirror in her room, at long last clad in pretty underthings courtesy of the thoughtful Button, reacquainting herself with the girl she had once been.

"I don't know if I can do this," she said to the looking glass.

Clara looked up from where she was brushing out the pretty day gown of turquoise silk. "Do what, pray tell?"

"I don't know if I can be Phillipa again." Or even if she wished to be. Phillipa had been a child-woman, willing to be held back from the world, to obey and tend her parents and to put her own dreams aside. "I'm not that girl anymore."

She knew she made no sense, yet Agatha, Clara, and

Rose came to stand beside her, gazing at her in the mirror with complete understanding.

"Maybe you needn't be Phillipa again," ventured Rose.

"No." Clara smiled. "You could choose to be Phillipa anew."

Agatha nodded with satisfaction. "Yes, Clara, the very thing. Our intrepid Flip."

Phillipa anew. A woman who had learned, and loved, and grown beyond her girlish boundaries.

"Oh, yes," Phillipa breathed, her throat tight. "I think I can do that."

When James returned to the club that evening, his barely contained fury was compounded by a heavy layer of fresh guilt when he was told by Stubbs that Ren Porter had gone missing.

"His nurse said he just weren't there. He'd asked her to let him be and she did most of the day, but then she went to see if he was wanting his dinner. That's when she saw that he was gone, his things with him."

The few things that had been kept in Ren's room were the odd bits of clothing that had been left in his seldom-used room at the club. At some point, those had been sent to Mrs. Neely's house to await Ren's awakening.

"But how could he just get up and leave? Surely someone helped him."

"Mrs. Peel says he were mostly only weak and half-blinded. His legs healed up pretty well, considerin'."

James rubbed his face. His friend alone in London, feeble and near blind. He couldn't bear to think what might happen to Ren in his condition. "Alert everyone. They're to look for him at every opportunity. He might be right out of his mind—we simply don't know."

A tiny voice told him to check the Thames. Ren had been a fit and hardy bloke once, the sort that didn't take well to infirmity. James quashed that voice with every ounce of his will. No Liar would take that route, not while he had his brethren to turn to.

Please, Lord, not another life on my soul!

Even now, Ren's assassin was returning to her beautiful home, free to wreak more havoc and death. James turned from Stubbs, his fury threatening to spill over onto his apprentice. Blindly, he climbed the stairs to enter the secret door at the end of the hall.

As he paused there in the near darkness, he heard something that teased at his memory—

Phillipa had quite stunned poor Fish with her transformation back to a woman. When she'd entered the Cryptography room, the man had positively stammered in his surprise. He had then made himself scarce as soon as possible, supposedly to fetch some documents for her to give a try at decoding.

Phillipa watched him back from the room with a bemused smile. Perhaps she hadn't quite lost her looks after all.

While she awaited his return, she made an attempt to sort the awaiting decryption work into piles according to what she thought was needed. Numerical codes over there, alphabetical codes over here. While she worked, she hummed idly, for she didn't mind such puzzle-solving—though it certainly lacked the excitement of undercover work.

At the sound of a footfall in the doorway, she turned to greet Fish with a smile. "That was quick. I think I've made a dent—"

It was James, staring at her with a dark and painful fury in his eyes. *"Amilah."*

Oh, no. The tune she'd been humming had been the same Arabic song that Amilah had danced to. The breath left her lungs and she took an instinctive step back. Wetting her dry lips, she held up one hand. "James—"

Phillipa Atwater wore Turkish blue . . . and hummed Amilah's song.

James went cold—then hot. Volcanic rage welled up inside him. Amilah had been another lie. The one bright spark of these last hellish days, snuffed out by the sickening realization of his own foolishness.

This woman—this twisted wicked woman—had invaded his every moment. She had taken over his home as clever Phillip, had charmed his friends, his *son*, as vulnerable Phillipa, and had infested his very dreams as Amilah.

Phillip—Phillipa—Amilah. For the first time, he saw all the faces of this chameleon-esque female in one lying, betraying, beautiful face, gazing at him with wide emerald eyes that glinted with a hint of blue.

Self-loathing crested in him. So stupid, so bloody damned *thick*. Blinded by loneliness and desire, lost in his guilt—what a simple target he'd made. How she must be laughing now.

He could hear her in his mind. Laughing at him with that hot, devouring mouth—

In one swoop, he was upon her. With the force of a charging stallion, he pressed her backward several stumbling steps until her back was pressed to the wall. His hands gripped her shoulders painfully as he pressed her back.

"What is your game?" he hissed. "Why have you pursued me? What is it that you want of me? If you want a piece of my soul, you'll have to stand in line!"

Phillipa shook her head wildly. Her breath hitching from distress, she could hardly speak. "No—no game!" she denied.

James growled, pressing his body to hers crudely. "Then this? Is this what you wanted from me?" He released one shoulder to wrap his hand about her breast, kneading it and pulling at her nipple through the silk. "This I can give you, freely. It is what I do best, it seems."

Tears of regret and anger began to leak from Phillipa's eyes. She ignored them to tear his hand from her body with her free hand. "Stop! You don't want to do this, James!"

"No? Then perhaps I want to do *this*!" His mouth came down on hers, hard and punishing. He pulled her close with pitiless hands, ignoring her squirming and her muffled sounds of protest.

She realized that her struggles were only driving him farther down this unforgivable road. Instead, she gave in to her heart and kissed him back. Kissed him for all his pain and his fury—kissed him for all the damage she had done him, for all the damage Lavinia had done him. She kissed the man she knew he was beneath his anguish and ferocity, the man he had forgotten he could be.

His hands became less unforgiving, his grip on her more embrace than captivity. He kissed her now with need beneath his wildness and she answered that need with her own.

His mouth moved from her lips to her neck. "Oh, God," he murmured, "I need to—"

"Yes," she whispered as she let her head fall back. "Yes, please."

This time his hand surrounded her breast with tenderness and urgency and she leaned eagerly into his touch. This man was hers—at least for now, hers alone. She wanted his heat and his need. She needed him even as he needed her.

Hot blood swelled her nipples and sent rich tingles between her thighs. He pressed her to the wall again and this time she welcomed it, for it allowed him to press her close yet freed his hands to explore her ready flesh.

"Touch . . . yes . . . please!" Broken and senseless, her words seemed to inflame him nonetheless. He pulled her bodice down, trapping her arms in the short tight sleeves. She could scarcely care since it allowed his hot mouth access to her aching nipples. He bent to her, feeding on her, caressing her with his hands until the sweet torture bid fair to make her cry out with yearning.

In the fog of her overwhelmed senses, she became aware that he had slid both hands down her skirts to her ankles and was now sliding his wide palms up her calves. She could not say nay to him now, wisdom and clarity be banished to hell. When his hands slid between her knees to press outward, she willingly parted her legs for him until he knelt almost between her knees.

Her new skirts a wadded froth between them, she could not see him at all, only feel his progress up—up over her knees, his hands stroking up her thighs much the way her own had once stroked up his. Over the tops of her stockings now, skin to skin. She shuddered, letting her head fall back to lean limply against the wall.

Arms bound by her lowered sleeves, legs pressed wide by his shoulders, pinned to the wall by his touch . . . she had never felt so deliciously helpless in her life. With all her heart, she fell into his power, granting him an ownership of her body that she'd never imagined giving up to anyone.

She felt his mouth on her and started. Shock and thrill moved through her as one. Anyone might walk into the room. Bound as she was, there was naught she could do to stop him—and then she no longer wished to. Wet and warm delight flickered through her from his tongue. There was ecstasy in his lips and, yes, even in his teeth. The danger of discovery only spiced the moment. She had never known— oh, dear heaven, who could have known?

When her knees went weak, he supported her with broad hands on her bottom. When she cried out loud for more, he gave it to her. And when she shattered at his hands, he would not stop, but drove her upward yet again. She was helpless, bound, and nearly senseless, and he forced her to come apart for him again and again, until she could scarcely draw breath.

Only then did he take pity on her and pull away, kissing her thighs as he left. Even just the touch of his beard stubble on her skin made her quiver at this point. Then he emerged from the tent of her skirts to rise before her, though he still did not release her hips.

Pressing fully clothed against this woman who was bared to him was entirely erotic, but not enough for James. "Wrap your thighs about me," he whispered to her as he lifted her, and she lazily obeyed. He wanted her embrace, so he pressed her to the wall with his hips as he eased her arms free of the tiny sleeves trapping her elbows. At his urging she draped them limply about his neck.

She was liquid compliance in his urgent hands and he thanked God for it. To go one more minute without her meant the end of him, he would swear to it. Unfastening his trousers was the work of a moment, despite his profound erection and shaking hands.

She slid onto him like hot wet silk and he groaned into her neck. Her gasp blew over his ear like flame and he thrust deeper just to feel it again. As she roused now at his penetration, her thighs gripped him more firmly and her arms embraced him with urgent strength. No frail flower, this woman. She was supple and strong enough to match each of his deep thrusts with a rise and fall of her own.

The slide of her around him sent his mind sideways with pleasure. There was something he ought to remember, but he could not pull himself away from the feel, the scent, the heat of her.

She was generous with herself, offering her breasts to him even as she rode him hard. She kissed him with open hot mouth, making soft sweet shameless sounds that spun him further away from sanity. Her hands stroked through his hair, tugging sensuously at it, adding that tingle to the symphony that she wrought upon his senses.

"Come to me," she murmured into his mouth. "Come with me."

She began to gasp in rhythm with his thrusts and he followed her willingly into the rushing torrent of their orgasm. For one blinding moment they were one, she was his, and he was no longer alone.

For long sweet minutes they stayed there, her limbs wrapped about him, her back pressed to the wall. Finally, their breathing slowed and their hearts resumed the rhythm of sanity and logic.

They remembered who and where they were.

Phillipa stiffened as she remembered, her softly caressing fingertips going quite still on his neck. James froze as well, though he did not let her go. Tearing his mouth from hers, he let his head fall back to send a gusting exhalation to the ceiling.

"And there goes the last shred of honor I ever possessed," he said, his voice raw. "I don't suppose you can ever forgive me. Nor will I ever forgive myself."

He put her from him then, supporting her until she stood steady, but not looking at her at all. He turned away as if to leave, then stopped. "Can I ask—why? Why Phillip? Why Amilah? Why *me*?"

Phillipa eased her bodice up over chilled flesh, tugging her sleeves back up to her shoulders. "You know the purpose of Phillip," she whispered. "Amilah . . ."

He waited, still turned away. She was glad he was not looking at her, for she didn't know if she would have the courage to say it to his face.

"Amilah was because I fell in love with you."

He jerked then, as if that were the last thing he had expected to hear. He turned his head until she could see his profile, though he did not try to meet her eyes. "Flip, you don't love me. You do not even know me."

I know you. Phillipa slowly closed her empty hands into fists. He would not listen.

At that moment, Fisher returned, bringing with him the spymaster. Dalton greeted both James and her with equal ease, although Phillipa felt again that eerie sense that those silver eyes saw more than she knew. She found herself surreptitiously checking the lay of her gown and raising a nonchalant hand to her hair.

All was in order, if a bit wrinkled. If she was uncomfortably aware of James's essence within her, it was apparent to no one but herself.

One hoped.

Fisher began to show Dalton the progress of some item while she saw James edging toward the door. Dalton, however, didn't seem inclined to allow James his escape.

"James, I should think you'd want to see this."

James turned to join the two men, although Phillipa noticed that he did not meet anyone's gaze directly. At first

Phillipa was happy to be excluded from everyone's attention, but then when she recognized her father's journal in the piles under consideration, she moved to enter the discussion.

"The journal is not coded, Fisher," she informed him. "I have read it most closely, but I saw no patterns that would indicate coding."

Fisher mumbled to himself as he rearranged the stacks of messages. "Here is a pattern that has shown repeatedly in the intercepted letters and messages. But I have not been able to break it."

He handed a handful of these to Phillipa. On the surface they appeared to be no more than assorted personal letters, receipts, and written lists. She saw the pattern in the repetition of certain root words.

"Where did these come from?"

"Oh, we've scouts and couriers all over—"

"Fisher!" barked James in warning. "Mind yourself!"

Dalton was more polite, but quite as adamant. "It is not necessary for Miss Atwater to know the source of the information, Fisher. Please confine your eloquence to need-to-know limits."

So, Lord Etheridge did not entirely trust her or her father yet. The anxiety that had lain seething beneath the last few months rose to claw at her nerves again. If she could not find a way to prove Papa's innocence, these men would kill him and call it duty.

Fisher gulped and flushed, then made himself busy with his documents. James finally allowed himself to look fully at Phillipa. She was pale beneath her calm, and her eyes were wide as she gazed at the spymaster.

Dalton nodded at the quelled Fisher, and at James. "Cunnington, if you would kindly keep Mr. Fisher on topic while Miss Atwater is participating, I would much appreciate it. Notify me at once if there is any new information." With that he was gone. James supposed he was not the only one in the room who breathed a sigh of relief, though he was not well pleased to have been ordered to stay in Phillipa's presence.

Fisher cleared his throat, then scrubbed at his youthfully balding head. "It's numerical, I *know* it's numerical! I just can't discern the pattern. It's probably just a simple translation code . . . simple if you know the key."

He looked up at Phillipa with almost comical tragedy in his eyes. James folded his arms and leaned one buttock on the desk. Comical—if one didn't know how many had died and how many might still if Britain could not learn more of Napoleon's plans.

Phillipa wrapped her arms tightly about her waist. "I don't know that I can help you, Fisher. I am not a professional, merely a daughter who enjoyed the puzzles set by her father. I never knew of the journal until recently."

James flicked his gaze to her face, watching for those little signs that betokened a direct lie. Her expression was frustrated and weary, but clear of deceit.

Which might only mean that she was a very good liar. This he had already had personal experience with.

Fisher slapped his hand flat on the desk. "But there must be something in it! Else why would he take so much trouble to send it safely to Upkirk?"

Phillipa lifted the journal in her hands and traced the design embossed into the cover with her fingertips. "I rather think it was me he wanted sent safely to Upkirk," she said softly.

James watched her fingertips, entranced by their delicate motion despite himself. His skin still tingled from her delicate touch . . . the way that she explored him with feather-light caresses in the dark . . .

He felt heat within his collar and tugged at it with one finger. Damned third story was too bloody hot. He raised his gaze to find Phillipa watching him watch her. She smiled. It was not the triumphant smirk he expected, but a soft, hopeful curve of her full lips. Her tiny overture hit him in the raw.

He drew himself up. "So if what you say is true and your father only wished your safety, then he withheld information that might have helped Upkirk understand the codes that the

French are using." He sneered as her face paled. "Score one for my side."

Fisher made a small sound of protest, but Phillipa held up her hand. "No, Mr. Fisher. James has far more anger to dispense than that. I fear we shall all bear the brunt of it for some time."

She stood and, with a pitying look at James, crossed behind the desk to bend over Fisher's shoulder. James took it from them both and snapped the journal shut. "There's nothing here, Fish. Atwater never meant for us to crack his codes. I told you that all along. Napoleon owns his soul now."

"No!" Phillipa rounded the desk in a blink. "You've no call to accuse him! You barely even knew him!"

"I know the sort. The sort that cares more for money or glory than for loyalty. The sort that can be bought with a handful of shiny gold or a—"

"A woman?"

James flinched. Phillipa shook her head at him, her anger apparently gone. "Don't blame my father for your mistakes, James. He has made plenty of his own, I'm sure, but that one is all yours."

James slapped the book down on the desk, bracing one spread hand upon it to stand. He towered over her, quite dwarfing her, yet she held her ground to gaze levelly at him with clear green eyes. "Yes, James?"

He broke first, looking down and away from those eyes that knew him far too well. Bloody hell! If only he'd never confided in Phillip Walters! His gaze traveled to his own fingers, tracing the raised symbol on the front of the journal.

Phillipa must have been watching him, for she turned her head to peer down at it as well. "It is a Greek letter. Phi. Some call it—"

"The Divine Proportion," murmured James. In a blink he was back in his father's study in one of those rare moments of communication with the elder James Cunnington. He could still feel the wool of the carpet beneath his elbows as he lay on the floor with his chin propped on his hands, listening to his father combine mathematics, science, and philosophy in a rare garrulous moment.

" ' 'Tis proof of a holy plan, irrefutable scientific, mathematical proof! The key to the universe, from the spiral of a snail's shell to the patterns of the stars. The Golden Ratio! A scrap of mathematics that can tell you the proportion of things unimaginable!' " His father had drawn it for him, each stroke of the nib as slow and reverent as any sacred ritual. "Phi."

Phillipa's exclamation pulled him from his past. "Oh! You know of it? Not many do," she said.

James ran one finger along the symbol. "I'd little choice. My father was a mathematician, a rather prominent one. Unfortunately, I didn't inherit his scholarly talents."

"Bloody liar he is," grunted Fisher to Phillipa. "He could have been the greatest code-breaker since Atwater himself." He shot James a chastising look.

Phillipa blinked. " 'Keep a close watch on James Cunnington,' " she murmured so softly he could barely hear it. "He wanted you for an apprentice, didn't he?"

James nodded reluctantly. "Yes, I believe so. Simon agreed with me, however, and assigned me to the primary saboteur."

Fisher sniffed. "But, of course, he'd rather blow things up than face the challenge of cryptology."

"Imagine that," commiserated Phillipa.

Yet her eyes told a different story. They gleamed at James like emeralds before firelight and he saw a glimpse of what had enabled a sheltered young woman to cross three nations on her own and to brave the home of a possible enemy in disguise.

She was like him, attracted to the thrill and the challenge, and yes, even the fear. A moment passed between them that rang of the old camaraderie between himself and Phillip.

Then James blinked and she was simply a woman with short red curls and rather too much mouth. A woman who had lied to him with a cool professionalism that he had only ever seen in Lavinia Winchell. A woman he would never allow himself to touch again.

He tore his gaze away to look back down at the book. "Phi. Why would he have that put on the cover of his journal?"

"He spoke of it often, especially after my mother died. He swore that since it proved order and a purposeful hand in the universe, it also proved that she lived on in heaven and waited only to be reunited with him."

"Well, no one ever mentioned it to me!" Fisher said indignantly. "You'd think one of my old masters would have taken a moment to explain it. Unless they thought it too difficult for me to understand."

"Oh, no, Mr. Fisher. It's quite simple. It is a ratio that is found repeatedly in nature. In the petals of flowers, and even in the proportions of the human body. I can explain it like this." She reached for his pencil and a scrap of paper. "You begin with ought and one."

She quickly wrote a sequence of numbers upon it. *0,1,1,2,3,5,8.* "Now see? Each number in the series is simply the sum of the two numbers before. Further, the ratio—phi—of two consecutive numbers will always be one and six-tenths.

"I learned it as a child. After all, I am named for it!" She laughed. "Thank goodness, for the other option was Ruperta."

Named for it? Phi. James turned to look at her slowly. *"Phi. Phillipa,"* he breathed. *"You* are the key!"

Her startled gaze flew to meet his, then they both turned to look at Fisher, whose eyes widened.

"Phi!"

Chapter Thirty-two

In an instant they were all three on one side of the desk, scrabbling through the papers to find the almost cracked code. Feverishly, Fisher bent over the sheet while Phillipa murmured the ratio into his ear once more. Fisher tried it first one way, then another to no good result.

James fought down the suspense within him. If this wasn't the answer, then everything had been for naught. The French would win. Napoleon would win.

Lavinia would win.

Suddenly Fisher froze. Phillipa caught her breath. James opened his eyes to look down at the sheet that lay flat between Fisher's hands.

"Where is Phillipa? Is she with you? Upkirk, please reply."

"Sent again and again." Phillipa released her breath with a broken sigh that was half-sob. "Oh, Papa."

James sagged back, his heart pounding like a steeplechaser's. Atwater had been proven loyal after all. For all his apparent treachery, the man was innocent of evil and had been redeemed.

He raised his gaze to meet Phillipa's. Her eyes were shining and her face had that odd twisted look women got when they were trying very hard not to cry. James crossed behind Fisher to take her trembling hand and bow over it.

"My apologies, Miss Atwater. I find myself very pleasantly in the wrong. I wish you and your father the best." Then he straightened very stiffly and left the room to inform his spymaster.

While Mr. Fisher wrung her hand and congratulated her profusely—apparently for being the child of such a brilliant cryptologist—Phillipa watched James turn his back on her and leave the room.

She didn't know what she'd expected of him. Had she thought he would fling his arms about her in joy that they could finally be together?

That wasn't very likely, was it? Not with all that still lay between them. She sighed and smiled at Mr. Fisher. Her relief at Papa's redemption was great, but it didn't quite fill the bleeding James-shaped hole in her heart.

"You do not even know me."

Phillipa stayed where she was, still feeling him within her, still tasting him on her lips. *I know you better than you know yourself. I love you better as well.*

"Flip? My head hurts." The small mumbling voice pulled Phillipa from the dreamless void of deep sleep. "And Jamie's havin' a bad dream."

Robbie. Her thoughts were slow. She opened her eyes into flickering dimness. Hadn't she doused her candle? *Must wake. Robbie needs me.*

Then she remembered. She sat up straight in her bed. *"Robbie?"*

He stood before her in a too-large adult nightshirt, clutching a candlestick in one trembling fist.

"I don't feel good, Flip. Can I sleep with you? Jamie's makin' too much noise. It hurts my head."

She wanted to sweep him violently into her arms and squeeze him until he couldn't breathe. Instead, she pulled aside her covers to allow him to climb in. "I'm glad you're here. I was becoming quite cold."

After putting the candleholder on the night table, Robbie climbed onto the bed, supporting his splinted arm with care. "Guess I broke it, huh?" he said when he had settled in.

"Yes, love, it's broken." She kept her voice soft. "Does it hurt very much?"

"Lots. I think it needs trifle."

She chuckled, blinking back tears of relief. "I think that can be arranged."

"Good." He snuggled closer. "You're inside the club. Did you get caught?"

"I did indeed."

"Are they goin' to kill you?" The words were slurred, as if he fought sleep in his urgency to know.

"No, my darling. Not I nor my father. He's been proven innocent and so have I."

"That's good." He yawned. "Now, you can . . . marry . . . Jamie." He slipped back into sleep, a healthy snoring slumber full of twitches and tweaks. Phillipa lay there for several minutes, relishing his small knobby-kneed presence.

Then what Robbie had said came back to her. James was having a nightmare. Should she go wake him from it? He likely wouldn't thank her. Still, nightmares were hellish things, and if Agatha's stories were any indication, James's dreams would have a wealth of demons to call upon.

Finally she could bear her own indecision no longer. She would wake a dreaming hound from its nightmares, would she not?

She had no wrapper, and only her old nightgown from home to sleep in—the very one in which she had hidden behind the wall—so she gathered the counterpane from the bed. The room was warm enough for the light wool blanket that remained, so she need not worry for Robbie. Wrapped in the counterpane, she took the candle that Robbie had brought with him. It must have been the one left burning by his bedside all night, for the stub was nearly burned through and guttered halfheartedly.

The hallway was chill but Robbie's room was nearly a furnace. The candle scarcely pierced the darkness. She heard James before she saw him for he was indeed making noise.

He was sprawled on a cot near Robbie's bed, shirtless but still clad in his trousers. As she stepped closer, the dimming candle gleamed on his perspiring chest and shoulders. He tossed his head with a formless groan. She bent over him, reaching with one hand to smooth his sweat-soaked hair from his brow.

"James, wake now," she said softly. "It is only a dream."

James was trapped. Bound and helpless, starving—feeling his strength ebb even as his dread grew. Filth covered him and waves of heat engulfed him. The tiny cell in which he lay bound was too small for a tall man, too small for any man. It shrank steadily, until the walls threatened to choke the life from him.

Then a door opened, a door that had not been there before, yet he immediately knew what it meant for him. The beating began as if it had been in progress for hours—or perhaps years.

Agony.

There was only the black depths of pain and the sickening awareness of his own helplessness. He raged against that vulnerability, fought it with everything he had, everything he was.

Yet, to no avail.

She came. She wound about him like a serpent, her tongue flicking from her mouth to touch his lips, his chest, his privates. "I own you," she hissed. "You will always be my creature, and I shall always be your mistressssssss . . ."

Sick revulsion consumed him, twisting in his guts like a knife. Faces emerged from the dimness surrounding them, familiar faces. Weatherby. Upkirk. Ren Porter and the others. His comrades watched him with dark condemning gazes as she fondled him.

No! I am not her minion! I did not give you to her! I did not! His soul shouted the protest, but he could make no sound. The shadowed faces turned from him, abandoning him even from their scorn, leaving him all alone.

Alone with *her.*

Cool hands touched his face. He struggled against his bonds—they were gone. The dark cell was gone.

There was only Flip's worried face in the clean glow of the candle.

He must have startled her, for she pulled back with a jerk. "Are you awake now, James?"

Inhaling deeply, he nodded. Then he released his lungs in a long shuddering sigh. The nightmare was gone, at least for now. He managed a sickly smile.

"That—that was a kindness, thank you." He sat up on the cot, swinging his legs to the floor. She settled on her knees beside him, still holding the candle up to see his face. He took it from her to set it upon the table between the cot and Robbie's bed.

The dull glow shone only on rumpled sheets and a dented pillow. The bed was empty. "Robbie!"

Phillipa laid a hand on his bare arm. "Shh. He is in my room, sleeping normally." She smiled. "You woke him up. Isn't that wonderful?"

It was more than wonderful. It was worth a thousand such nightmares. James closed his eyes against the relief that burned behind them. "Is he—is he himself?"

"Entirely."

He laid a hand over hers and squeezed it, sharing his intense elation with perhaps the one person in the world who understood and equaled it. She returned the pressure without a word. They sat thus for a moment, their differences set aside in a moment of unity.

Finally she spoke. "Your dream—it must have been ghastly. You would not wake for so long."

He opened his eyes to gaze down into hers. "Not dream, I'm afraid. More like memory."

She turned her hand in his to lace her fingers through his. "Agatha told me you were a prisoner for months."

"Indeed."

She continued to regard him soberly. "Yet you recovered."

"Outwardly, at any rate." Perhaps it was the darkness and the eerie solitude . . . or perhaps it was the clear lack of judgment in her eyes, but he heard himself confessing his darkest fear. "I do not think I am entirely recovered . . . within."

"How so?"

"I am not who I was. I remember that man as if he were someone I knew well, but I am no longer him." He pulled his hand reluctantly from hers, but he could not bear to be touching her when her gaze became accusing.

"I fear I may be going mad." He'd said it, wrapped words about the dark shadow that stalked him. He'd made it finally real.

She laughed in his face.

He drew back, affronted. "I am deadly serious, Phillipa!"

She clapped a hand over her mouth and waved a finger at him. "Oh—oh, dear!" She drew a breath, obviously trying to control her great amusement.

James clenched his jaw. Honestly, she was as irritating as Aggie! Here he'd told her his deepest fear and what did he receive? A belly laugh!

She wiped her eyes. "I'm sorry, James. It was only that I expected you to say 'I'm ill' or 'I'm slowly bleeding to death inside' or something of that sort." She hiccuped a last giggle. "But *insanity*? That is the least of your worries, I should think."

"Why do you say that?"

"Because for one, you are the sanest person I have ever known. And for another, people who are truly mad believe with all their heart they are sane. That is *why* they are mad, after all."

"But the dreams—the black spells of mood? What could that be but the onset of madness?"

She shook her head. "I think you are very sad at the loss of your friends. I think you have not allowed yourself to grieve them. I know you have not allowed yourself forgiveness."

"How am I to forgive myself for betraying them? I killed them all!"

"No, you did not. French spies killed them. The same spies who kidnapped and tortured you for months on that boat." She glanced away. "I asked Agatha.

"At any rate, you did not give up your comrades. The information may have been stolen from you—in a sense, raped from your mind—but you are no more responsible for that than Robbie is for being an orphan." She moved closer to him, still on her knees, until she looked him full in the face. Her hands came up to cup his jaw so that he was forced to gaze into those clear and steady eyes.

"Grieve your comrades. Grieve your lost innocence. But you must set the blame aside. Stop looking back. You have so many who need you to look forward."

He shook his head, a quick motion of denial. "No I don't. I have made sure to keep myself free of attachments."

"No attachments? How can you think you have no attachments?" She drew her hands away, her eyes puzzled. "What about your sister? What about the Liars? What about Robbie, and Stubbs and even Denny? You are nothing but a walking talking bundle of attachments! We all are." She shook her head at him, as if he were being unnecessarily obtuse.

"How can you say you have no responsibilities? You've Appleby. And family. And God and country—"

"Enough!" James pressed his hands to his ears to shut out her voice. He felt the tangle of it all around him. No step could he take, no word could he speak, that did not somehow impact one or more strings of that tangle.

Fear swept him. How could he touch all these people and not hurt someone? How could he hold all those souls in his hand and not betray one or all of them somehow? He could not bear the pressure. It seemed to crush his heart, to steal the breath from his lungs . . .

"James."

Her voice, so low and sweet without its imposed gruffness, seemed to soothe the raw tumult in his mind. "James . . . don't forget—"

"Forget what?" His voice was gravelly in his own ears. His head was full of clamoring voices, voices that wanted too much, needed too much—

She was speaking softly and clearly. James took his hands from his ears to better hear the gentle soothing tones.

"The attachments—the burdens that you feel? It goes both ways. You have others who depend on you, yes. And you have others on whom to depend." She laughed, a small rueful sound. "You could not stand alone, even if you wished. You stand on their uplifting hands, as they stand on yours."

Hope brightened briefly within him. Was that so? Was the tangle not a trap, but a net? Was he held close as he held others close? Was he alone neither in his debts nor in his due?

He felt cool hands on his cheeks again and allowed her to tip his face up to meet her gaze. Those eyes . . . so beautiful and shining with life . . .

"Do you uplift me, Phillipa? Are you one of those who hold me high?"

She knelt before him and gazed into his eyes. "I didn't want to be. It is not my choice to be attached to you, James Cunnington. I only meant to stay a while, to find a way to help my father. I don't know what my future holds with the Liar's Club, or what Lord Etheridge will decide."

He took her hands in his and drew them from his cheeks. Looking down at her delicate fingers, a portion of his mind bothered to wonder how he could have been so blind to that delicacy for so long. Her fingers were cool so he warmed them, clasping their four hands together.

"James, about the lies I told you—"

"Phillipa, did you ever have any motive but loyalty and survival?"

"Ah, well. There were a few other moments in there."

"When?"

"In the storeroom. That was purely for selfish reasons."

He hesitated. "Because you fell in love with me?"

"Yes." Phillipa waited. James said nothing in return. No matter. She knew her own heart, and it was his alone.

He kissed her softly, as if in amends for his earlier harshness in the code room. She kissed him back. How could it be that her mouth fit his as though made for it? Of all the men in all the world?

Perhaps there was some order in the universe after all.

They drew apart finally. James tilted his forehead down to touch hers.

"Your hair." He fingered one curling lock in regret.

She reached to take his hand in hers. Gently she pulled it down and kissed his palm. "It will grow back."

He drew back and shook his head in wonder. "When I think of the things I said in front of you—" His eyes widened. "I took you boxing! I *struck* you!"

She smiled. "I struck you back. It was not my rear on the canvas, if you recall."

"Would you believe me if I told you I let you win?"

She scoffed. "Would you meet me in the ring again so I can prove you didn't?"

He chuckled, that rumbling sound she loved so dearly. "Do you know, I just might." He stood, lifting her easily in his embrace, and carried her to the bed. He paused, as if testing her agreement. Phillipa turned her head to kiss his shoulder in assent.

James put her down gently, easing himself down beside her. Then he rolled her effortlessly beneath him. "There, you see? You've lost."

Squirming beneath the heavy comfort of him, Phillipa twined her arms about his neck. "I dispute that call. *I've* won." She pulled him down for another kiss. Had any man ever tasted so delicious?

"I'm obsessed with your mouth," he whispered when he'd caught his breath. "There are so many things I want to do to it."

Phillipa laughed and trailed her own hands down over his rock-hard buttocks. "I know precisely what you mean."

They undressed each other slowly, stopping often for

deep kisses that stole their breath and gave voice to all the things they didn't know how to say.

This was no heated mating. This was a tender languid exploration. Phillipa felt like a newly discovered continent, the way that James traversed her hills and valleys with such attention.

At one point, his tongue swirled about her navel, then dipped inside.

"No treasure inside tonight, my brave voyager."

He chuckled into her stomach. "I do believe that this is now my favorite bit of female flesh. And to think, I used to be a leg fancier."

"If you go a bit further, you may find a couple of those as well," she hinted.

"Don't worry, Flip. I'll find them."

Her eyes burned at the name, once said with friendship, then anger, now murmured in all tenderness.

"Phillipa anew," she whispered to herself. Then aloud, "You've changed me, James. It is as though I am finally awake. No matter what happens now I can never go back to sleep again."

He rose on one elbow to gaze down at her, his eyes nearly black in the candlelight. "Is that a wrong thing?"

She shook her head as she stroked a hand up one thick and solid arm to a wide shoulder. "I've learned that it is not enough to merely survive the days. Not when there is so much more."

He only gazed at her. She had to laugh at herself. "Very well. Now is not the time for philosophy. You can go back to what you were doing."

"I have a better idea." His grin was pure wickedness. "Flip, have you ever ridden astride?"

Her toes curled at the thought. "Why, Mr. Cunnington, are you offering me your mount?"

With a deep laugh, he rolled onto his back and lifted her with ease. "Mount me, then," he whispered. "Ride me."

"*My stallion*," she whispered to him in Arabic. His face went hard with lust at her words. As did other things.

She threw one leg over and straddled him just above his knees.

"You missed," he said, his voice gravelly with desire.

Phillipa only wrapped both hands around his shaft. "No, I didn't." He groaned and moved beneath her, his hard thighs trying to shift her higher. She tightened her double grip on his erection. It swelled further in her grasp, until it darkened and thickened to an astonishing degree.

How had she ever accepted something of this size?

Yet she wanted it again. Her cleft was throbbing quite on its own now as she contemplated impaling herself on his great rod. *Oh, yes. What a marvelous idea.*

James reached for her but she only leaned away from his hands and squeezed her own more tightly. He dropped back to the pillows with a blissful moan. "Do with me what you will, then, you wicked creature. I am in your hands."

Phillipa didn't quite snicker, primarily because she was far too aroused for laughter. His shaft was beautiful in its rigid form, like a sculpture made solely for her enjoyment.

If only for tonight.

Slowly she rose to her knees and moved forward until the great ruby head nestled in her curls. She hesitated. Could she even accept him fully this way?

"Use me," he whispered. "Stroke yourself with me. It will help."

Phillipa braced one hand upon his massive chest and wrapped the other around the base of his shaft. Stroke? Where?

He took himself in hand for a moment to show her. Oh, *there.* Oh, *yes.* The blunt hardness of him swept across her sensitive spot, making her quiver at the sensation. Again. Her cleft became slicker with every sweep, and every sweep became more and more delightful. Beneath her, James moaned aloud. His fists clenched in the bed linens in his effort not to interfere.

"Oh God, Flip! Mount me now. Please!"

His hoarse cry melted the last of her resistance. With the next sweep, she aimed him deeper and sank quickly onto him.

Aching hot pleasure at the hardness of him within her. Sharp tight pressure at the size of him. It was a deadly mixture that threatened to steal her very thoughts. She rose upon him to ease the pressure. She sank upon him to increase the pleasure.

More.

Faster.

Oh dear God, she was going to die from it! She couldn't breathe, she couldn't speak, she could only rise and fall at her body's whim as James twisted and groaned beneath her. His big hot hands came up to grasp her hips. She planted both her own hands upon the rock stability of his chest and together they plunged her even faster.

Her breath was gone. Her mind was a blank. Her body was a white-hot ember.

Suddenly James thickened within her still more. Beneath her, he stiffened. His grip became fierce on her hips. The almost-pain was too much. She burst into flame as his shaft began to pulse within her.

Someone cried out, a high keening sound. Someone groaned deeply. She fell. It was a long, sweet slide down.

She landed sprawling on James's sweating chest, her trembling arms too feeble to support her any longer. Inside her, she felt him throbbing. It sent tiny shocks through her. She submitted to them weakly.

With a final gusting breath, James relaxed beneath her. One big hand came up to stroke the short damp curls from her face. "You've an excellent seat," he said faintly, his breath coming hard.

She laughed then, with the little strength left to her. Draped limp upon his chest, she laughed away every tiny voice that wanted to wonder what lay ahead.

She didn't care one whit for tomorrow. In the middle of the night, in this bed, with this man, there was only now.

Their skin cooled. Their breath returned. James shifted her to lie in the crook of his shoulder, her head still pillowed on his chest. She dozed to the great slow music of his heartbeat for a time.

James did not sleep. He stared at the dim ceiling until the candle sputtered, near its end. Then he stroked his hand across one silken freckled cheek. "Phillipa? Flip?"

She stretched sleepily. "Hmm?"

"Be attached to me. Stay. I—would miss you."

She lifted her head from his chest and considered him with sober intensity. "You would miss me? I don't know that our attachment is strong enough after all. To stay—feeling as I do about you—it would not do me well. Indeed, I think it would do me a great deal of ill."

"You are not making sense."

"And therein lies the problem, doesn't it?" She sighed. "You don't understand something that I cannot explain, for it defies explanation. Either one understands, or one does not. You do not. Therefore, I must go. I have obviously stayed too long already."

She sat up. He released her to watch her wrap the coverlet about her as she walked from the room. For a moment he pondered the meaning of her words.

She'd only meant that it was late, that she should not stay alone with him in this room.

Hadn't she?

Chapter Thirty-three

The next morning, James was cursing himself for a fool. He'd made Phillipa an offer last night, yet he'd not used the magical words that would have convinced her. Now he was pacing the hall outside her room, waiting for her to emerge.

Agatha approached him with a wrapped parcel in one hand and an apple in the other. Grinning mischievously, she offered it to him. "Want a bite? Mrs. Bell just sent a basket of them from Appleby."

James shuddered. "I wish you wouldn't do that, Aggie. You know the smell of those things puts me off my feed."

She took a large bite, grinning around her full cheeks as she chewed. "You don't know what you're missing, Jamie. So crisp and sweet—"

Phillipa's door opened. James turned toward it so swiftly that Phillipa stopped in surprise.

"Good morning, James, Agatha. Was—was there something you wanted?"

James slid a glance to his sister, hoping he could signal Agatha to leave them alone. Aggie's eyes narrowed as she looked from him to Phillipa. Then she swallowed her bite of apple and gave him a small evil smile.

"James and I have come to walk you down to breakfast, Flip."

"Oh. Yes, well, I'd be delighted." She motioned behind her. "Robbie is still sleeping, James. Would you like me to wake him?"

"No, but I—if I may?" She stepped aside to let him pass, but not so far that he couldn't catch a whiff of her scent as he entered the room. That scent had left traces on his pillow and his bedding, allowing him to wake surrounded by her, though he woke alone.

Robbie was sprawled with blessed awkwardness upon Phillipa's bed. The covers were a tangle and the lad was snoring with a will. James grinned and reached down to smooth back a mussed lock of black hair. Robbie stirred, then opened his eyes a slit. "G'way. 'M sleepin'."

"Indeed you are, son. Do try not to snore the plaster from the ceiling," James said with a soft laugh.

"Gumf." Robbie batted at the hand on his hair.

James let him sleep, pausing only to drop a kiss on his son's brow. Turning, he saw Phillipa and his sister watching him from the door. Agatha seemed very pleased indeed, but Phillipa appeared close to tears.

"What is it, Flip?"

She shook her head quickly. "It is only . . . very good to see the two of you together."

He smiled at her. "I could arrange for you to experience that sight for the rest of your days."

She blinked at him. "What do you mean?"

Agatha rolled her eyes at him and muttered something that sounded like "About bloody time, you silly sod." Then she stepped back through the open doorway, leaving James and Phillipa alone with the sleeping Robbie.

James stepped close enough to take Phillipa's hand. "Last night when I asked you to stay, I left out the most important part, didn't I?"

She bit her lip then. "Did you?"

He tilted his head at her. "That's why you refused, isn't it?"

She blinked a few times rapidly, then nodded. Raising her

brilliant green gaze to his, she reached to stroke one finger across his jaw. "I wasn't sure of what you wanted, I suppose. Will you tell me now?"

Tell her? Suddenly, James had the distinct feeling that they were talking about two different things altogether. "I came to you this morning to beg your hand in marriage."

She slowly dropped her hand. "I see," she said, seeming entirely unsurprised. "Why?"

"Why? Because of last night and yesterday, and when you danced for me, of course! We have become lovers. I am a gentleman and you are a lady. After such intimacy, there is no option for us but marriage!"

"Ah." She withdrew her hand from his. "No, thank you very much."

"No?"

"No." She turned to leave the room. James caught her hand to stop her.

"But convention merits—"

"Convention go hang!" She pulled her hand away more violently this time. "I am but twenty years, James. Marriage is for life. Would you condemn me to threescore years of existence with someone who cares not a whit for me?"

"How can you say that? Of course I care for you!"

Phillipa went very still, yet her heart began to race. "You do?" Could she have been wrong about his feelings? Did he love her after all?

"And Robbie cares for you." He smiled at her. That boyish grin on such a manly visage nearly melted her heart as it always did. "You have attachments, Miss Atwater, whether you like them or no."

Perhaps . . . perhaps she asked too much, too soon. Perhaps if she wed him, he could grow to love her as she did him. Phillipa stepped closer to him, feeling the warm solid pull of his presence. Perhaps she could teach him to love—

"James!" Stubbs came trotting into the room from the hall, waving a paper and crowing. "We got 'im! That bloke Lady Winchell's been writin' to finally picked up them letters! Feebles is on the gimpy bugger's trail right this minute!"

Without hesitation, James dropped her hand to take the message from Stubbs. His eyes lit with unholy glee as he read it. Phillipa stepped back, unable to bear to stand too close to the flame of his obsession as it roared high.

"We've got you now, you lying bitch." James's voice went ugly with hatred.

Though she knew he referred to Lavinia, Phillipa still felt the burn of his venom. He had such passion for this woman, such a need. Phillipa had once heard that there was a fine line between love and hate and now she saw the truth with her own eyes.

James left her standing there without so much as a farewell, his plea for her hand gone to ash in the fire of his fixation. Phillipa watched him hurry down the hall with Stubbs, heads together.

"Is he goin' out again?"

The small voice came from the bed. Phillipa turned to see a pair of dear blue eyes peeping from the mess of bedding. "Yes, I'm afraid so."

Robbie blinked. "I thought . . ."

"As did I, darling." She sighed. "As did I."

Her heart ached from the loss of that short-lived fancy. She'd been a fool to think for one moment that James Cunnington could ever love her more than he hated Lavinia Winchell.

After soothing Robbie back into a healing sleep, Phillipa made her way to the kitchen, though she'd lost the will to break her fast. Agatha waited within, chatting with Kurt. Or rather, chatting at Kurt—who merely loomed and interposed the occasional grunt.

But then, Kurt was very fond of Agatha.

Upon seeing Phillipa, Agatha hopped to her feet expectantly. "Well?"

Phillipa blinked. "I don't know what you wish me to say, Agatha. James has left with Mr. Stubbs to pursue his case against Lady Winchell."

Agatha gaped, then narrowed her eyes. "He *botched* it! I knew he'd make a muck of it, I just knew it!"

Phillipa felt obliged to defend James, she knew not why. "If you're referring to his proposal, he didn't botch it. He was very polite."

Agatha clapped a hand to her mouth. "Oh, no! Not *polite!*" Her ire crumpled into sympathy. "Phillipa, I'm so sorry."

Stiffening, Phillipa lifted her chin. "Nonsense. I was the one to refuse him."

"Well, of course you were! Quite rightly too. And to think he ran off to play mouse to Lavinia's cat again."

"Do you know that of Lady Winchell?"

"I should say so. The woman is stark staring mad, if you ask me. Especially when it comes to James. Why, she was jealous enough to want to kill me, when she thought I was his mistress, not sister."

Agatha bustled around the table and past Phillipa. "I must talk to Clara! She'll know what to do about that brother of mine."

As the door swung shut on Agatha's curvaceous figure, Phillipa distinctly heard "*Polite!* Oh, Jamie, you silly sod!"

But her words about Lavinia Winchell were the ones to remain in Phillipa's mind.

Stark, staring mad . . . especially when it comes to James.

How mad was Lady Winchell? Mad enough to let something slip when faced with her worst nightmare?

James and Stubbs followed Feebles's trail across half of London during the next few hours. When they arrived at whatever pub from which Feebles had sent his last message by street-child courier, they'd find another from him leading them the next step in the chase. This sort of urban tag had worked for them many times before, allowing close pursuit and much-needed backup of the tracker.

But then the chase fizzled when they arrived at a seedy

taproom in the worst district of Cheapside to find Feebles himself there, morosely nursing his ale.

"Lost 'im."

James lowered himself heavily to the bench beside the small ragged man. Feebles was the best, small and fast and nearly invisible. The operative who could lose Feebles was a professional indeed.

"Damn." Cursing seemed worthless. There were no words to release the burden of rage within him. "Do you think he was actually heading into this district?"

Feebles shrugged. "Maybe he was, maybe he wasn't. Led me a merry chase, he did. Wound me up like a bloody mechanical monkey." He peered into his ale. "Might be time for the Feebles to hang it up, James."

"Not likely, old sod." James roused himself enough to clap Feebles on the back, though it raised a small cloud of dust. "We've a confirmation of his existence, and we have a description. Get yourself down to Lady Clara and have her draw the bastard for us."

Feebles looked as though he were about to cry. "Didn't see his face, not a bit. His cap was pulled low and his collar was up. All I can tell you is he was a regular-sized bloke with a limp."

James clenched his fists until he heard the wood of the table creak. "Hell."

Pulling himself back from the brink of rage, James stood and flipped a coin to the publican for Feebles's ale. The three men went back outside to the bright day, though their quarry was as much shadow as ever.

"There'll come another chance, James," Stubbs said. "Don't despair now—"

"You!" The shout came from across the grimy street. James raised his gaze to see Mrs. Farquart—who truly did not suffer the light of day well at all—striding toward them, bony legs kicking her dark skirts high. "I thought it was you! Did you find her?"

James blinked. Now that he thought about it, he and the

other two Liars were indeed standing near the woman's boardinghouse. How curious. "Well, ah—"

Mrs. Farquart narrowed her eyes suspiciously. "You did find her, didn't you? Where's that money she took?"

James regarded the woman for a long moment. "Who makes this claim of theft? You or the dead woman's family?"

"Ha! Think you can trap me, do you? That money will go to them that needs it the most, that's a fact. Now where is she? Where's that money?"

Though James found the woman distasteful beyond belief, he could not deny that the creature truly believed Phillipa guilty of stealing a grieving widow's fortune.

"I'm . . . still looking into the matter. You will be notified if anything is found." With that, he turned away from her and all the mistrust and ire that came with her.

Phillipa had his trust. He believed in her wholeheartedly. He only wished he had as much faith in his own ability to judge.

Chapter Thirty-four

According to Agatha's description, Lady Winchell was a woman who had the lot. Beauty. Wealth. A doting husband.

There was no way for the Liars to break Lavinia's advantage, no currency with which to negotiate with her. They had nothing she wanted.

But Phillipa did. She had the one thing in this world that Lavinia Winchell desired. The one thing that the traitorous woman couldn't have.

Phillipa had James Cunnington, at least in body. His heart and soul were apparently up for grabs.

This time, Phillipa didn't intend to lose.

Not too surprisingly, Phillipa found that Lord Winchell's house was fine indeed, as evidenced by ... well, everything. Exclusive square, fine architecture, supremely arrogant butler—

"I do not have a calling card, I fear."

"Then Lady Winchell is Not At Home." The exquisitely carved door began to close.

"Wait!" What would gain her entrance? "Tell Lady Winchell that—that James Cunnington's fiancée is here to see her."

The butler hesitated. Surely the man knew of James

From what she had heard and read herself, the scandal had been momentous indeed. He eyed the people passing on the street nervously. Did he think someone from a newssheet was lurking about?

The door opened wider. "If you'll please come this way?"

She was settled into a lovely parlor, filled with treasures and bright with candles. Yet Phillipa was certain this was not even the finest room this house had to offer.

The door opened. Phillipa turned to face the enemy.

The woman who entered wasn't simply beautiful—she was spellbinding. Her skin was porcelain fair and her hair was true gold—which only made her rosy lips and blue eyes more riveting. Phillipa was stunned wordless for a long moment at such perfection of face and form—until she saw the gleam of snide satisfaction in the woman's eyes.

Sorry that she had given this creature such pleasure with her reaction, Phillipa affected a pose of polite indifference with all her will.

The smug gleam faded. *Good.*

Lady Winchell did not come forward, nor did she extend her hand. "Who are you and what do you want? Why did you lie to my man?"

Phillipa regarded her serenely. "Why would you assume it is a lie?"

Lavinia lowered her lids suggestively. "James Cunnington will never marry, not while I live in his dreams."

Phillipa laughed. "Dreams? More like nightmares."

"You know nothing of his dreams. You are a poseur, come to fish for information. Were you sent by one of those hideous newssheets?"

"I know his dreams. I know everything about him. He is my love."

"He is not!"

"Do you wish proof? I could tell you any number of things. He drinks brandy. He loves to box. He is a superior dancer, an excellent athlete, and a lover of great stamina."

"Foolish girl. Anyone could know that, or guess."

"Well, then. Shall I mention his fancy for harem dancers?"

Lavinia jerked at that. "No such thing. I would know that."

"One would think he would have mentioned it. Still, he never actually *loved* you—"

"He did—he *does* love me, you fool! Look at me! How could he not?"

"Perhaps he desired the surface . . . once. But surely this is not the first time someone has informed you that your heart is as black as tar? A man of James's nature would find that most unattractive, I'm sure."

Rage contorted Lavinia's face. Reaching out one long elegant arm, she snatched something lovely and no doubt priceless from a side table as if preparing to fling it viciously across the room at Phillipa.

Sidestepping easily—for ducking was second nature by now—Phillipa continued to taunt Lavinia. "Pray, don't take it so to heart. Once we're married, we'll be sure to call on you often."

"You're lying!" Lavinia's voice was harsh and her features twisted by her rage. "There is no woman in James's life but me! I know it!"

"Yet here I am. Already mother to his adopted son, friend and confidante of his sister—"

That reference seemed to send Lavinia's ire to new heights. *"Agatha!"*

"Oh, do you know her well?" Phillipa circled, keeping out of range of projectiles. "Such a dear friend. I feel like a member of the family already. When I marry James—"

"No! You lie! The thief would have told me if James had—" Abruptly, Lavinia ceased her tirade. By the worry that flashed swiftly across her face, Phillipa surmised that the woman had just said something she shouldn't have.

"The thief? Who is he, Lavinia? How would he know the intimate details of James's life?"

Still heaving giant breaths, Lavinia visibly attempted to pull herself together. "I . . . do not know what you speak of."

"Well, whoever your informant is, he has lied to you. I have known James well for quite some time . . . very well."

Lavinia snarled, but Phillipa could see the woman was now on her guard. She would get no more from this source today. Without bothering to make a single polite noise, Phillipa turned and left.

If only she could be sure that she hadn't just made things much worse.

Though the night had grown late, James sat reading by Robbie's bedside. The book was one of his favorites, *Robinson Crusoe*. Daniel Defoe might not be everyone's cup of tea, but nary a single Liar failed to enjoy the man's work.

After all, the imaginative founder of the Liar's Club understood the human need for adventure very well indeed. A Crown spy in the days of King William, he was the first to utilize the skills of street thieves and pickpockets for national security.

Yet Defoe's words, usually so absorbing, only lay lifeless before James's eyes tonight, dull print on paper. He felt the familiar blackness descending after the disaster of losing Lavinia's lover today.

Spending the evening with Robbie had helped. Sapped of his usual energy by the ache in his head, the lad had been a good listener to James's stories of his boyhood. The only uncomfortable moment was when Robbie had asked James about his own father.

"When you was sick, did your da sit with you too?"

James almost laughed. "Far from it, I'm afraid. The servants cared for me, and Aggie, when she was older." He gazed at the candle flame, remembering. "I think my father liked me best when I was not at home. I think he was proud of me, in his way—as long as he wasn't required to disrupt his work."

Robbie had gazed at him for a long moment. Then he reached an unusually clean paw to pat James on the arm. "Don't worry. I'll sit with you when you're sick."

Carefully, James did not smile at Robbie's gravity. In fact, he felt an ache deep in his throat at the words. "Thank you, son. It will be a mighty help."

Robbie's eyes had glowed at being addressed so. He hadn't spoken again, but only settled down to listen as James read to him. Several pages later, James had looked up from the book to see Robbie sound asleep, small fists by his chin.

Something peeked from one of those curled hands. James pulled the small lead soldier from his son's slackened grip. The toy was crumpled and bent as if it had been stepped on. The poor foot soldier looked as though he were crawling.

James had carefully placed it on the night table. He well remembered how a bit of rubbish could find a place among boyish treasures. This broken thing must have some significance for Robbie and James respected that.

Now, with the silence of the empty club about them and even the distant street noise abated by the lateness of the hour, James felt as though he and Robbie and the little lead soldier were quite alone in the world.

Which was nonsense of course, for Phillipa slept in the next room. She had not spoken to him again today, but quite frankly James was relieved by her distant manner. He had yet to resolve that tiny niggling voice that reminded him of his severe lack of judgment on previous occasions.

What did he know of her really? She was a consummate actress, a gifted teacher, and a skilled liar. She could take on any role, from young man to exotic seductress, and be entirely convincing.

Might it not be true, then, that she was acting even now? Could the entire club be falling under the spell of her chameleon charms? The Liars were heroes all, no matter their backgrounds. And what better way to seduce a band of heroes than to appear to require rescue?

A poor and friendless girl, who wanted only to prove her kidnapped father's innocence and save his life. It was tempting to believe it, for it would mean that no barrier stood between them. He could have his harem dancer and his friend. He could have what every man dreamed of—a brave and lovely partner who suited him like the lost piece to his own puzzle.

It would be so easy to believe. He wanted very badly to believe.

That alone was enough to cause him doubt.

The club had gone quiet long ago. Phillipa pressed her ear to her chamber door to listen. Nothing. Earlier, she had been able to hear the faint rumble of James's voice from the room next door, but that had long faded away.

It must be well past midnight by now. Phillipa eased her door open. The hall was dark and still. Taking her candle and the small box of wonderful new matches that Fisher had given her, she moved through her doorway, silent as a wisp of fog.

The carpeted hall made her careful steps soundless and one hand trailing on the far wall kept her oriented in the proper direction. At the end of this hall lay the secret door, although it was not nearly so well concealed from this direction.

She managed the catch after a moment of fumbling, but she had no confidence in her ability to do it from the public side. Taking a small piece of wood from her pocket, she wedged it in the frame in order to keep the door from closing completely.

Now she stood on the more luxurious carpet, in a hall that smelled of wax and lemon oil, not dust and elderly woolen runner.

To her left would be the broom closet. To the right would be her destination. Jackham's office. Jackham, who limped. The "gimpy bugger."

"He was a great thief once." Robbie's words had not come back to her until this evening and even then she'd not known if she was correct. James had known Jackham for many years. They were friends.

Would James even listen to her suspicions about Jackham? Especially when the hint came from Lavinia? And if she was wrong, would he ever forgive her for accusing his friend?

She came here tonight to search for something, anything, that might substantiate such an accusation.

Surprisingly, Jackham's office was not locked. Startled by the ease with which she entered, Phillipa hesitated. Then she shook her head at herself. She was seeing moon shadows, for there was no one about. She let herself in and lit her candle.

The office was spare and manly. A fine desk was balanced by an elderly sofa that looked uncomfortably sprung. Stacks of ledgers teased at her mind. Might she find some sort of embezzlement recorded within those pages?

Still, that would likely be a petty offense in the eyes of the Liars. The only thing this motley mix of patriots and criminals would find unforgivable would be the selling of their own to the enemy.

That act would not be recorded in a ledger book.

Yet where would such evidence be kept? A professional thief would be wary of all the usual hiding places—the safe box, the false bottom drawer, the loose floorboard. Phillipa crossed to the sofa to take a seat on the edge of the cushion. From her vantage point she could see the entire room.

What would she use to hide the truth from experienced spies? Perhaps another false panel in one of the walls? The Liars were all too familiar with that mechanism. A loose stone in the hearth? She moved to the cold grate to examine the marble closely. All was securely mortared in place.

Discouraged, she returned to her perch on the sofa. She felt a spring dig into her buttock through her trousers. Shifting position, she wondered grumpily why someone would hang on to such a disreputable piece of furniture. Surely the club could afford to replace Jackham's ghastly old—

Sofa. Phillipa jumped to her feet to regard the piece with suspicion. Why, indeed?

She punched at the cushions with enthusiasm, yanking away those of the seat to the floor. Kneading them carefully revealed nothing to her touch. She didn't want to risk slicing into them until she had examined other possibilities. Wrapping her hands around the arm of the sofa, she pulled it away from the wall.

The back was faded and the upholstery dusty, but the tacks looked entirely whole. Phillipa knelt behind the sofa to slide her hands across every inch, feeling for anything that might signify a secret.

As her hands neared the bottom corner of the upholstered back, she felt a crackle beneath her fingers. "Horsehair does not crackle thus, Mr. Jackham," she muttered as she ran her hands lower. Something that had been slid beneath the fabric must have an entry point somewhere—

Underneath and out of sight, her fingertips encountered a loose thread. "Ah, yes." She reached further and discovered several more. Then she found it. A slit in the damask, as straight as a razor's cut. Only the dangling threads had alerted her.

The sofa was raised on turned legs of undistinguished wood. She rolled onto her back and stuck her head under in order to see the hole. The slit was large enough to slip her entire hand into. She did so, feeling upward for that promising crackle.

Beneath the sofa abounded rolls of dust. "Mr. Stubbs, you've been neglecting your duties," she murmured, fighting back a sneeze.

"I'll be sure to tell him for you," rasped a voice from above her. "For I doubt you'll be seeing him again."

Bloody thieving-traitor hell. She ought to have realized that the reason Jackham's office had been unlocked was that Jackham was still in the club.

Chapter Thirty-five

Phillipa's room was empty. Her bed stood untouched with her nightgown laid carefully across the pillow and her only two dresses hung from the pegs on the wall. James stood in the middle of the silent room, too stunned even to curse.

He'd come to talk to her—in all honesty, to touch her, talk to her. He had found only this. She was abroad in the middle of the night, dressed as Phillip, for some hidden reason of her own.

He tested his emotions. He felt no suspicion. No doubt.

Only worry.

He went back out into the hall. His candle guttered in a draft. When he shielded it automatically with one hand, it cast a shadow down the hall toward the hidden door to the outer club. In that shadow shone a narrow but unmistakable line of candlelight from the other side.

Upon investigating, he discovered the door propped open very slightly. On the public side, Jackham's office was open and lit from within.

James entered carefully, but there was no one there. What he did find were obvious signs of struggle. Ledgers were knocked from the desk. The sofa was out of place and the cushions were scattered.

He knelt to retrieve a toppled candlestick from the floor before the flame had the opportunity to ignite the entire club. The candlestick was the dented one from Phillipa's room— on its side, the small puddle of wax beneath it was still warm. The scuffle had not been long ago.

James walked around the back of the sofa, pondering what it all meant. Why pulled *out,* into the room? A fight in the room might possibly push it askew, or to one side, but it was obvious the piece had been pulled out apurpose.

Dark apprehension twined through him. Phillipa had been here, he had no doubt. What had she been doing? Where was she now?

As his gaze traveled downward, James spotted a small white triangle protruding from beneath the sofa. Sofas did not ordinarily come stuffed with paper.

He bent to retrieve it carefully, feeling beneath as he pulled. Several sheets came with it. James went to his knees to investigate further and found more items stuffed within. Pulling them out, he moved to the desk to look them over by the light of the two candles.

One was a message, threatening and vicious. "Remember, thief, who they will blame!" Another, cajoling. "You thought the payment generous when you gave me the first list of names."

More of the same, many of them. And all, even when read in shaking hands by the light of guttering candles, un-mistakably in the florid and looping script from the hand of Lady Lavinia Winchell. The same hand that had written the other letters, the twisted sexual messages that James now began to suspect had been meant expressly for him.

And at the bottom of the stack of evidence now in James's hands lay a confession. *"If you are reading this, Simon, I am likely dead. Being as how Lady Winchell probably killed me, I hereby make full confession so I can take the evil bitch along with me to hell."*

It went on to tell a tale of betrayal and regret that made James's chest burn with mingled revulsion and sympathy.

Jackham. The limping man.

He had known deep down that something was not right within Jackham. Simon had rescued the man from his life on the streets and had given him a position of responsibility within his club, yet had never taken Jackham into the inner circle.

For that matter, neither had James. He'd been more than willing to consider Phillip as a recruit, but he had always been careful to keep his cover intact around Jackham.

Jackham.

For a moment, James sat quite still, too stunned by the implications to react.

It was not I who betrayed the Liars.

James nearly dropped the documents, so great was the weight that rose from him. *I betrayed no one.* And with that, the veil of darkness and guilt rose from his vision. He saw it all so clearly.

That was why Lavinia had imprisoned him on that boat. Because she *couldn't* break him.

How had she bought Jackham? Was it the man's lifelong weakness for diamonds?

All the while James had searched for evidence, or a single witness, there Jackham had stood, watching him. Slow fury twined through him. Then he remembered.

Phillipa.

With horror, he realized what she had been doing in Jackham's office in the dark of night. She'd known somehow, had cleverly discerned what the most experienced Liars had been blind to and she had been searching for evidence.

Why hadn't she simply come to him? Why hadn't she come forward with her suspicions—

Because he would never have believed her and she'd known it. Pain knotted in James's chest. His mistrust had sent her into danger.

And now Jackham had Phillipa.

• • •

Standing before the club, James dug in his pockets for coins. "Take this to Etheridge House." The boy nodded and ran off down the street, one fist clutching the message, the other wrapped tightly around the money. His feet made bird-wing sounds on the cobbles in the predawn quiet. James watched him run. He was a trustworthy lad used often as a messenger for the Liars, one of the many invisible street children of this district.

It wouldn't take long for Dalton to respond, or for Clara to come to care for Robbie. Still, James could scarcely bear the anxiety within him. Phillipa was in danger and he had no idea where to look for her.

Except that he knew—all roads led back to Lavinia.

Should he go to Lavinia's now? Lavinia had been cunning enough to keep him imprisoned on a fishing boat. Surely she wouldn't slip now and confine Phillipa in her own home, would she?

Damn it, was he a spy or wasn't he? Sudden certainty filled him, washing away the confusion and self-doubt of months. The brash anticipation and objectivity that had marked his past missions filled him once more.

He nearly laughed out loud at the sheer relief of it.

Hello, Griffin. You've been missed.

He had decided to take a chance on invading Lavinia's house when another child ran up to him.

"Got a message for someone at this club, sir."

The boy was breathless and weary. Absently, James dug for more coins as the boy gasped out the message. " 'The limping man is headed west. The Scarlet Hart. The carrot-top is with him.' "

Feebles.

"Thank you, God," breathed James. Then he sat the boy down on the steps of the club. "A gentleman and a lady will be coming shortly. Tell them what you told me and you'll get a full quid."

The child nodded and sat willingly. James eyed him. He didn't know this lad. "The lady is *very* generous. Be sure to stay for her." He hoped that would be enough to keep the boy, for he could bear to sit still no longer himself. Liar protocol required that he wait for reinforcements, but he couldn't.

With a last admonishment to the boy, James was off, hailing down the first hired carriage he saw. He should be close behind Feebles.

If only Feebles didn't lose Jackham again.

Phillipa felt quite lost, for she didn't know London well enough to recognize precisely where Jackham had brought her. They stood in an empty house in what had appeared to be a shabbily genteel area of town. Jackham held her by one arm, as he had all the way here. He might seem infirm with that limp of his, but there was nothing wrong with the strength in his hands.

The other hand held a pistol, which had been more or less aimed at her brain since she'd looked up to see him standing over her in the club. Had it been an hour past? More?

The danger she was in made it very hard to determine the passage of time, and the house had no clock.

Nor any furniture at all. The place was an empty shell, as evidenced by the echoes produced by their shoes on the bare wood. Jackham's single candle beat back the darkness enough to see that the room they stood in was likely a front parlor. Only heavy dark draperies remained over the windows, giving Phillipa the unpleasant impression that whatever took place in this empty house was never meant to be seen.

Phillipa cleared her throat. "What are you waiting for?"

Jackham didn't speak. He didn't even look at her.

Now that was odd. Phillipa had not had a great deal of experience with villains, but she'd always imagined them a garrulous lot, determined to tell all before they did their victims in.

Or perhaps she'd simply read too many tawdry novels.

Finally, something else intruded on the silence that had begun to beat on Phillipa's ears like a drum. A click and rattle signaled the opening of the front door. A rectangle of dawn light fell into the front hall, making Jackham's candle dim.

It was later than she'd realized. Soon someone would become aware that she was missing from the club. She only wished she could be sure that James would understand that she was in danger. Yet surely Agatha and Clara would see to a search being made?

Hope threatened to shrink further at the realization that there was no way for them to find her. She was a mere ant in a teeming hill.

And Lavinia stood smirking at her from the doorway.

Another pub, another message from Feebles. James felt his heartbeat trying to speed the cabbie's horse on its way. *Faster. Onward.*

Every slackening in speed, every slow-moving milk cart that crossed their path, every moment seemed to stretch forever.

Another pub. Another message. "West. The Black Lion."

He ought to wait for Dalton, who likely would bring others. He couldn't.

Phillipa.

Faster.

Lavinia flicked a finger at Phillipa's shorn hair. Phillipa slid her eyes sideways. "I bite."

Lavinia snorted but stepped away, turning to Jackham who still had his pistol aimed brainward. "What could she know?"

"She knew enough to search my office." Jackham narrowed his eyes at Lavinia. "I hear she came to see you earlier. What did you tell her?"

"Nothing. You know the bargain we struck. I cannot betray you without betraying myself, and vice versa."

Phillipa watched this byplay carefully. So the traitor mistrusted his mistress . . .

"I imagine this is part of the business one seldom witnesses," Phillipa said. "Although now that I think on it, it is quite logical. After all, if he will betray his friends, why would he hesitate to betray you? And you betrayed your own lover, so why would you halt at throwing Jackham to the wolves?"

They turned to regard her with cold gazes. "You speak nonsense." Lavinia seemed very assured, but Phillipa noticed that the woman cast a wary glance at Jackham.

"Do I? Perhaps that is because it is obvious Mr. Jackham doesn't trust you any more than he trusts me."

"Less," Jackham said.

Lavinia lifted her top lip in a feline snarl. "I paid you well for your contribution," she said to him.

"You lied to me."

She laughed. "And my story touched upon your patriotic core, did it? Odd, I thought it was the enormous amount of money I paid you that convinced you to betray them."

Phillipa blinked. "It was you?" She looked from Jackham to Lavinia. "I thought you drugged James—questioned him and tortured him into it."

Lavinia smiled and turned away. A man dressed in the Winchell livery entered the room, bent to whisper something in Lavinia's ear, then straightened and left. Her driver, no doubt. The fact that Jackham held a gun on Phillipa made no apparent impression on the man. Astounding. Truly a sterling example of the serving class.

Lavinia turned, her eyes shining. Oh, dear. Anything that brought this woman so much pleasure surely couldn't be good.

"It seems we have another guest. You must excuse me, Mr. Jackham. Perhaps you might show Miss Atwater to—to the roof. It is under repair, so there is access through the attic, with a view of the street as well. You can keep watch for other arrivals. Yes, that will do nicely. Sound travels a bit too well in an empty house." She reached a hand as swift as a striking snake to take the pistol from Jackham. "You won't be needing that. Now, I must freshen up." With that, she sailed gracefully from the room.

Phillipa watched her go with nearly hysterical wonder. Of course, it was always important to look one's best when committing murder. Apparently, Phillipa still had much to learn about being a true lady. Pity she wasn't going to have the time.

James nearly fell out of the hired carriage at the final pub. The message waiting there gave an address, mere blocks from where he stood. Not bothering to talk the reluctant cabbie into another leg, he tossed the man a pound note and took off at a run.

When he neared the house, he saw a fine carriage parked outside it. The Winchell crest shone boldly in the dawning light. Lavinia.

Of course.

A shadow moved to James's right. He didn't bother to turn his head. "What have you got?"

"I was just comin' in to report when I spotted the limping man—"

"It's Jackham."

There was an instant of silence from Feebles. "Cor," he said. "That clears up the lot, don't it?" Then he continued his report. "Jackham went in with your redheaded miss less than an hour past. She weren't happy about it. The lady went in just a few minutes ago. I think her coachman might have spotted me, for he lit off into the house."

"Ah." He was expected. "Time to dispense with stealth. I've not the patience for it anyway."

He stepped out onto the cobbles, bypassing the coach and the returning coachman without a glance. He flung open the door and marched inside.

Chapter Thirty-six

Jackham pushed open a small door at the top of the stairs and dragged Phillipa from her brief clinging grip on the jamb. Then she clung to Jackham. Struggling now was out of the question. They teetered on the sloping roof next to the gable for a moment, then Jackham hauled her higher.

Suddenly level surface was under her feet and she was able to stand securely. She managed to ease her grip on Jackham's sleeve, and finally even to open her eyes.

She shut them again at once.

The house was in an older style, large and square and flat on top. There were houses to the right and left, though she didn't stand much possibility of being spotted since they were both smaller than this one. There was a large overgrown garden in the back but no trees grew close to the walls.

Jackham released her once she'd caught her balance. He had no reason not to, for he stood between her and the door. That way lay only Lavinia and the pistol, anyway.

Phillipa scuttled closer to one edge of the roof. The house was four floors in all, she knew from the flights of stairs she'd just been dragged up. She peered over the edge. The view made her sink to her knees to resist the odd pull that heights exerted on her.

Who would have thought four little stories would put one so high?

Yet such a height would not bother Robbie at all. If she were Robbie, she would be looking for drainpipes or trellises.

There was a lovely wide ledge beneath the top story, perhaps a dozen feet below her.

"Forget it," came a raspy voice from behind her. Phillipa scuttled back from the edge, out of push-over range. Jackham stood over her, arms folded.

"You might land on the ledge . . . and then you might not. I know for a fact that three stories isn't far enough to kill you for sure. Four? Can't say. Depends on how you land. On your head, you get a nice casket and some flowers. Land on your feet like me, you might die, if you're lucky. If you're not, you'll walk every step for the rest of your life in pain." His voice was matter-of-fact as he gazed fearlessly over the edge. Phillipa guessed that he didn't have much to fear, having already suffered the worst.

Avoiding him, Phillipa moved back to the center of the roof and crouched next to the chimney, cold though it was. At least it wasn't whirling in her vision. She tried to think of some way, any way, out of her predicament that didn't involve vertical descent.

Unfortunately, she couldn't think of a bloody thing.

James found Lavinia waiting in the only room of the house to contain furnishings. That is, if one could call a gigantic bed and a single dressing table furnishings.

The house must be one of her rendezvous points. Rented with treason money and kept for business and apparently pleasure. Only this room was decorated.

Lavinia ornamented it beautifully, for she lay sprawled wantonly on the bed clad in nothing but a chemise trimmed in Brussels lace. Of course she would have black-market underthings. It made perfect sense.

She had never been more beautiful. Her hair was artfully tousled and not a red-blooded man in England would have had the power of speech in the presence of that half-nude body. "Have you come to serve me as you used to?" she said. "Or shall I be your—what was it now?—your harem dancer?" She smiled at him and trailed her fingertips across her décolletage.

James gazed at the bed hangings. "Give it a rest, Vinnie. I've come for Phillipa. I know she's here."

"Do you now? And why would she be visiting me again, when she just came to see me yesterday?"

His surprise must have shown for she smiled in a feline fashion. "Didn't you know? Not that you would likely care, I'm sure. She's an odd creature, isn't she? Almost—*boyish*."

Damn! How did Lavinia always stay one step ahead of him? She wasn't terribly intelligent, though she possessed a certain amount of cunning cleverness. Then again, it only proved that she'd recently spoken to Jackham, didn't it?

"I've no time for games, Vinnie. You cannot win this time. I have evidence against you now. Jackham kept every bit of correspondence, you realize. It seems he's learned something from all his years with us."

Abruptly, Lavinia dropped her lascivious pose of welcome. "That idiot!"

"Then you admit your involvement?"

"Why not? I still hold all the cards. I have your fiancée, do I not?"

"Did Phillipa tell you that?" He couldn't resist a small smile. It was a roundabout acceptance but James decided he was going to hold Flip to it anyway.

"How badly do you want her?"

James considered Lavinia for a long moment. "How badly do you want me?"

Vicious light flared in her eyes. "Are you suggesting a trade?"

"Perhaps. Or perhaps I'm wondering what you're wondering. How much power do you truly wield now that I know your true nature?" He tilted his head. "Convince me to stay if you want me. Unless you don't think you can? I am the one that got away, am I not?"

It was the worst thing that could be asked of him, to put himself in her hands again. He didn't hesitate. A little time was all the Liars would need to catch up.

She couldn't resist the challenge, as he had known she could not. "*En garde,* my love," she said, with a smile as lovely as it was evil.

She stood, sliding off the bed like liquid sex. She approached him slowly. "Did you like my letters, my love? Did you read them and remember? Did you ever feel as though they were written just for you?"

He'd been correct, then. She'd known her letters would be read. She'd known he would be one of those reading them, had virtually *addressed* them to him.

And he had read them and reread them in his search for evidence—as undoubtedly she had planned for him to. Her words had crept into his dreams, poisoning his sleep, toying with his mind.

"You are truly evil, aren't you?"

"You like me that way, remember?"

It was true. He'd dubbed her evil many times in the past. Then, he had said it with bemused arousal. "Now I truly mean it."

"Yet here you are, putting yourself at my disposal. Surely you would not give yourself to me solely for the sake of that scrawny little redhead. I think you want to be here. I believe you have never stopped dreaming of me."

"Poor Lavinia, always wanting what she cannot have."

"I did have you, remember? I had you this way—" She stroked a hand across the front of his trousers. "And that way—" She ran her other hand over his buttock.

James shook his head. "No, Vinnie, that wasn't you. That was the false Lavinia you painted in my mind. The lonely wife of a busy man who was looking for a bit of harmless entertainment. She was worth wanting."

"I wouldn't be too sure of yourself, James Cunnington. You forget. I know you. All of you. I may have kept something back from you, but you gave me all of yourself."

"Not possible."

"Why not?" She breathed it into his ear.

"Because you never had my heart."

She stepped back, her eyes flashing. "I do have it. Your heart and your soul! Why, then, have you been with no one else since I was arrested?"

"Ah. Jackham has been informative, I see."

"He told me of your brooding and your nightmares and that you still call my name in your sleep." She smiled, sure of her ground once more.

"The two of you must be very close. Are you quite sure he'd want you to be here alone with me?"

"I know what you're doing, James. You're mistaken if you think to make Jackham jealous. The only one he hates more than me is himself."

Understandable. "Everyone turns on you in the end, don't they?"

"My husband is still quite under my spell. Oh, there was that incident with the pistol and the safe box, but it only took a moment to convince him that I was out of my mind with the devastation that you caused with your seduction and then spurning of me." She shook a finger at him playfully as she moved closer once more. "Bad James, trying to sway loyal wives from their husbands that way. And for sport too! You should be ashamed of yourself."

"You'll never know how much so, Lavinia. Nor would you understand."

Jackham paced the roof, peering from this side, then that one until Phillipa thought she would go mad.

Finally, she could take no more. "Why are you party to this, Jackham? James was your friend. They all were. They trusted you—"

He turned on her. "You don't know nothing about it! All the years I worked for Simon Rain, and he was lyin' to me all along. I'd wondered if thievin' was all they were up to, had for a long time. But I figured it was only a bit o' business, maybe some blackmail, maybe some wet-work for pay. I figured Simon didn't tell me for my own good, him knowin' I don't hold with that kind of job."

He shook his head. "Then she come. Looking like an angel, but with the heart of a devil. She told me that they'd killed James. He'd been missin' for some time, and I was right worried. I knew he'd had a woman, some married lady, so I didn't have no reason not to believe her. She told me that the Liars had done him in, when he'd gone against their plan to assassinate Liverpool."

He ran a hand through his grizzled hair. "I thought they'd killed James, I really did. So I gave her names, I gave her everything." He closed his eyes. "I sold that bitch my soul."

"But then James came back."

He sighed and took a seat on the lip of the flat roof. Phillipa didn't see how he could bear to be that close to the edge. She pulled her stomach from her throat to listen to Jackham.

"Then James came back. I'd always minded my own business before, but I'd started listenin' at keyholes by then. When I found out what I'd done . . ."

He looked down, letting his hands dangle between his knees. "You could have just left it alone. It was over. I gave her no more names. Why didn't you simply leave it alone?"

Even in her fright, that was too much. "You think it was over," she gasped in disbelief. "Over for you perhaps, and over for those who died, but it will never be over for James."

Jackham shook off that concern. "James is fine. Landed on his feet right well. He's even to become leader someday, as far as I can tell."

"James is a shell, you fool! A walking, talking figment of our imaginations! The man inside is dying by the day and you are killing him!"

Jackham looked at her for the first time. She leaned forward urgently.

"Jackham, if you have had their trust for so long, perhaps they will forgive you. It was Lavinia's hand on the weapon, not yours. But if you kill me, you will be casting such a shadow upon your soul that you will never dare come out into the light of day."

He turned dead eyes to her. "They don't forgive, don't you understand? Can't you see it in James? Can't forgive himself, can't forgive you, though his love is plain to see." His gaze was distant and cool now, almost resigned. He stood. "They'll never forgive."

Lavinia's hands were all over him, as they had been in his dream. She caressed him, explored him—rediscovered him.

James waited for the conflicted feelings of lust and disgust to overwhelm him as they always did. Her touch was poison, aphrodisiacal venom. The mere scent of her made him feel—

Nothing.

Unbelievable. He waited breathlessly to be consumed by hateful need, to be twisted into gut-wrenching knots by her wicked, enticing—

He felt nothing. Not a bloody thing. The only thought on his mind, the only ache in his heart was for Phillipa.

He felt like laughing. By God, he felt like *flying.*

Her touch brought with it no sickening half-guilt, half-arousal. It brought only distaste and a compulsion to bathe as soon as possible.

With great relief, he realized that he was not the slave of his senses after all.

In addition, it seemed his obsession to avenge his friends had quite run its course. He still desired justice, but it was with a cool and deadly detachment that he'd been unable to manage before.

"You do realize," he said conversationally over her musical sighs, which were probably meant to arouse him, "that I am entirely free of you now."

She lifted her gaze to his. "I don't think so, James." Her voice was cold, but he was heartened by the defeat in her eyes. He had won after all. She turned away from him to move to her dressing table.

"Oh, yes," he assured her. "Now I know that even narcotics and torture cannot make me betray my comrades, much less the wiles of one well-used traitor." He took a deep breath of freedom. "You cannot reach me with your tricks any longer, Lavinia. You cannot touch me at all. Phillipa is the only woman who can."

"Then that is too bad for her," Lavinia said, turning back. She held a pistol in her hands. James blinked. He should not have been surprised, after all. She had killed many men, yet somehow he must have believed that her feelings for him would prevent the same fate from happening to him.

More the fool he.

He stepped forward, but she was too fast for him. In a blur, she turned—

And ran from the room.

The sound of someone scrambling onto the roof brought Phillipa to her feet. *He'd come—*

It was Lavinia, pistol in hand. Her lovely face was now a mask, crumpled and reddened with obvious rage. "Get her up!" she choked out. "Take her to the edge and throw her off!"

"What?" Even Jackham was forced to shake off his resignation at that. "Not that."

Lavinia waved the pistol at them both. "You'll do it or I'll shoot you right off this bloody roof. You survived such a fall once, Jackham. Do you think you can survive when you've been shot?"

James appeared behind Lavinia. Phillipa stopped herself from crying out for him, but it was too late. Lavinia heard him and swung about to point the pistol at his heart. "I'll kill you before I'll let her have you." She seemed to calm now that she had everyone under her control.

Jackham pulled Phillipa across the roof to the edge. With weak knees and panicked strength, Phillipa struggled. It did no good. She was dangled over the edge like an unwanted bit of rubbish.

She clung to Jackham's sleeve with her free hand, clutching at him in her fear. She wanted to scream for James, but her throat was closed. She could only watch while Lavinia backed up until she could keep all three of them in sight. The blonde woman half-turned to push a stack of roof slates tumbling in front of the access door, neatly blocking it shut.

"I want you to watch, James. I want her to die before your very eyes." She motioned to Jackham with the pistol. "Do it! Kill her!"

Phillipa heard James, a hoarse, formless shout of protest.

"P-please!" Her voice was only a whisper.

But Jackham's eyes were flat and dead. "Time for you to go."

The man's grip shifted slightly and Phillipa felt one heel slide from the stones. She clutched at him in desperation. "No! *N*—"

Falling. She felt the wool of his clothing slip past her hands. Her reaching arms struck stone. Slid. Tumbled. Stone under her grip. *Hold.*

The fall stopped abruptly and her arms felt jerked from her body, but she held. Her arms were wrapped about a decorative protrusion from the stone. She held it tightly, pressing her cheek to the filthy sooty granite with passionate affection. Her feet dangled and her booted toes scrabbled for some sort of hold in the building's façade.

She found one with her left foot and used it to take some of the strain from her arms, though her embrace of the gargoyle remained nothing less than passionate. The top of the piece was gritty and encrusted with what seemed to be bird droppings. The morning dew had turned the sandy stuff into slime, making her hands slip.

She couldn't hold. Her fingers gave bit by bit.

Please, God, pleasepleaseplease—

She fell.

She was gone.

James gasped. His chest turned to ice with shock. The cold of the loss began to spread, stealing his breath and his reason. James's final thought as he threw back his head to release a roar of grief and rage—

She was gone.

And it was his distrust that had killed her.

Chapter Thirty-seven

Jackham turned back from the edge to face Lavinia, ignoring James's agony entirely. "Made a bit of a mess, that did."

Oh, God. The pain was unbearable. James's mind and heart transmuted it to rage before he went completely mad from it. Red tinged the edges of his vision as he saw Lavinia eagerly step forward to see what she had wrought.

"Is it horrible?" she said. "Is it bloody?"

James moved forward, no longer caring if she held a pistol or not. In fact, he would welcome death, for it would release him from the knowledge that Phillipa lay broken below.

He scarcely registered the fact that Jackham took the pistol from Lavinia as if to help her step up closer to the edge. The fact that Jackham then calmly pressed the pistol to Lavinia's heart meant little to him.

The sound of the shot finally broke through his awareness as he reached Lavinia—only to have her fall at his feet, stone dead.

Jackham cocked his head as he gazed down at the woman who had been his partner and tormenter for so long. "She was as evil as Satan himself, but nobody ever said she was smart," he said.

James stepped over the body as if it were nothing but rubbish, his blood lust still boiling for the man who had thrown his love to her death. "I'm going to kill you now, Jackham."

Jackham moved back a step and held up both hands in a soothing manner. "I wouldn't if I was you, James."

"Why not?" He would kill him and he would *like* it, by God.

Jackham cocked his head toward the edge of the roof. "Because you'll need me to fetch your girl off that ledge she's standin' on."

The words took a moment to filter past the black tempest of his berserker rage. Then James blinked. "Wh-*what?*"

He threw himself flat on the roof to peer over the edge. Just below him was Phillipa, standing on a ledge with her face pressed to the stone and her arms spread, looking for all the world as if she were trying to paste herself to the wall.

James could scarcely breathe, for his heart had swelled to occupy every crevice of his chest. Mad laughter filled him. "Flip! Flip, darling, reach for my hand!"

It did take both him and Jackham to pull her onto the roof, where she immediately began to crawl to the exit. "I'll get you, Jackham, just see if I won't," she muttered brokenly through her gasps. She paused when she reached Lavinia. "Oh, isn't that simply perfect." She sent a disgusted look at James over her shoulder. "She's even beautiful when she's dead!"

James moved past his crawling cursing fiancée and knelt in her path. "Flip, please stand up."

"No!" She sent him a furious glare, but her lower lip was trembling and her face was streaked with tears. "I am bloody sick of being dragged here and thrown there. If I want to bloody crawl, then I'm going to bloody crawl and you're going to get out of my bloody way." She narrowed her eyes at him. "Aren't you?"

James opened his mouth to reason with her. Jackham stepped up. "The Liars are here."

James stood slowly. Even Phillipa sat up, though she kept a two-fisted grip on the gable. She was filthy, her trousers and coat covered in soot and droppings.

"The Liars will kill you, Jackham," James said. "Killing Lavinia will never be enough."

Jackham nodded, then ran the back of his hand over his perspiring forehead. "I—I don't want to die, but I know they'll never let me go."

James felt one of Phillipa's hands wrap around his ankle. He looked down at her bruised and mottled face. His brave and lovely Flip.

She gazed up at him. "He did save me, James."

Jackham shrugged. "Just a bit of a shell game, that."

James looked at Jackham. "You saved her. You also allowed yourself to be used by a French spy, and then you kept her secret. Men died, Jackham."

"I know it. I couldn't live with myself. I'm glad it's over, I am."

"Men died—but Phillipa didn't." He reached one hand to Phillipa and this time she took it to stand beside him. He touched her cheek with his thumb, wiping away a tear gone cold. "Run," he said, still gazing into Phillipa's eyes. "Run, Jackham, and run far."

Phillipa smiled slightly, keeping him still with her emerald gaze. They heard the scrape of Jackham's feet as he ran, flinging himself over the very roof edge that he had thrown Phillipa.

"Can he make it down?" she asked.

"That is entirely up to him. I have better things to think about."

She gazed at him, a slight frown line between her brows. He wanted to know what she was thinking, but he never had the chance to ask.

With a blow to the blocked access door that broke it clear off its hinges, the Liars came.

"What can you be thinking?" James was trying not to shout, truly he was, but the woman he loved was being so bloody-minded stubborn that he was about to pound his fist into a wall.

She didn't so much as look at him, but only kept packing her valise. They stood in her room at the club. James had left her there to rest this morning after her ordeal. It had only seemed the polite, gentlemanly thing to do.

Now he wished he'd rushed her off to Gretna Green while he'd still worn a heroic glow in her eyes.

Rubbing at his face with both hands, he forced himself to calm. Reason was needed here.

"Phillipa, you don't understand. You set me free."

"I understand perfectly. You are proposing out of gratitude. I realize what being absolved meant to you, and I am glad. I simply do not see that as a reason to wed."

"Phillipa, I care for you."

"Nicely said." She continued to fold her things. "I care for you as well, although perhaps a bit too differently for my peace of mind."

"What are you saying? Didn't you hear me? I want to marry you!"

"You think of me as a friend. You like to bed me." She held up a hand against his protest. "I like to bed you as well. And you are grateful for my role in delivering you from the guilt that you have carried." She finished packing and closed the valise.

"That's what I've been trying to tell you!"

She looked at what was left of the things she had been given. "I don't know what to do with Phillip's clothing. Button went to such pains, but I don't think a real gentleman could wear them."

She toyed with a loose thread on the waistcoat. "I ought to mend this, but there is no time." The seam parted in her hands. Phillipa stared at the lining in evident shock.

"Oh, *merde*." She held it out to show James, her green eyes wide. "The money. Bessie's money. She must have sewed it into this waistcoat for safekeeping." She folded the vest carefully. "I stole it after all," she murmured. "I must return it immediately to Bessie's family."

"Bother the clothes! How can you be so indifferent to me?" James tugged the valise from her grip. "Look at me,

Flip! Look into my eyes and tell me that you do not want to marry me!"

Phillipa looked down at the bag in his hand, then allowed her gaze to rise to meet his. Her eyes were clear and somber and as green as spring pine.

"James Cunnington, I do not want to marry you."

Then she pulled the valise from his numb grip and left the room.

Agatha plunked both fists on her hips and glared at him. "You botched it again, didn't you?"

James grimaced. "I most assuredly do *not* want to talk about this."

He sat at the giant worktable in Kurt's kitchen, although even Kurt had deserted his own realm when he'd seen Agatha was in this fit.

"First you proposed 'politely,' which is bloody insulting if you ask me." Agatha made that sound, the one that women had made at men since probably the beginning of time. It always made James flinch. "What did you do this time, Jamie? Plead gratitude?"

Since that was precisely what he had done, this only infuriated him more. "What is so wrong with being grateful? She did something most astonishing for me."

"So does the ashman, every morning, but that doesn't constitute reason to get engaged to him!"

James opened his mouth to dispute her, but then shut it. Was that what he had done? Offered payment for services rendered? He dropped his head into his hands. "Women are—they're bloody *encrypted,* that's what they are!"

Agatha nodded. "Now you're getting it."

Clara entered. She gazed at James with his head on the table and then considered Agatha's pose of disgust. "He botched it again, didn't he?"

James stood, too upset to suffer further at the hands of these women, no matter how beloved. "I am going to the code room, should—should someone send for me."

"Phillipa isn't in the code room," called out Agatha as he left. "There's nothing there but dusty old papers and dusty old Fisher."

James didn't answer. He needed to decipher the woman he loved, and Fisher was the only code-breaker the Liars had.

Phillipa stopped to say good-bye to Robbie. It wasn't easy to walk back into that house again. The very walls seemed to ring of James's presence. Of course, Robbie was playing in the study, the single most painful room.

Denny led her there, his expression sour. "Don't know what you think you're doin' back here. Made a muck of it all—that's what I'd say if someone were to ask me."

"Denny, you simply don't understand."

"I understand that you come in here and you lied, and now the little bloke won't talk to anyone, and the master is all tied in knots." Denny stopped to glare at her. "Things were just fine afore you come along."

Phillipa blinked. "Before? Do you mean when Robbie couldn't read and James couldn't sleep?" Then she stopped herself. There was no point in arguing with Denny. The man had resented her presence from the beginning. Blaming her for the household's unhappiness was as natural to Denny as breathing.

"You've no need to worry, Denny. I'm leaving in a moment and you'll never have to worry about me again."

Robbie was happy to see her at least. "Flip!" He jumped up from his scattered soldiers to fling himself into her arms. "Are you home then?"

"No, darling. I only came to say good-bye."

"You're leavin'?" He leaned back in her embrace to blink woeful eyes at her. "When are you comin' back?"

Phillipa's own eyes burned. This was harder than she'd dreamed. She didn't know how to explain to this little boy who had never had anyone to count on that she was another person walking away.

"I can't stay, Robbie. I can't live here with you and

James. Lord Etheridge has ordered a rescue operation. I am going back to Spain to await my father's return."

"Spain?" He scowled at her, even as his blue eyes filled. "What's in bl-bloody Spain?"

She didn't answer him, for there really was nothing in Spain, not for her. For that matter, there was nothing there for Papa either, but for memories that had kept him from living for far too long. Perhaps, once he'd recovered from his imprisonment, they might consider living somewhere else.

But not London. Never London.

London meant James, and Robbie, and the Liars. London meant more pain than she was sure she could survive.

Still, she found herself unable to walk away just yet. She sat in the big chair behind James's desk with a wilted, grieving Robbie on her lap. His gangling legs dangled ridiculously far and he was heavy, but she treasured the feel of her boy in her arms.

Finally it was time to go. "Kiss me good-bye, darling. My carriage is waiting."

"Not quite yet, my mistress of disguise," a deep voice said.

James stood in the doorway, leaning one broad shoulder on the frame. His hair was windblown and he'd a small streak of ink across one cheekbone. His brown eyes had gone black with intensity and he kept her gaze pinned with his.

Robbie ran a wrist under his nose. "James, Flip says she's goin' away!"

"I intend to take care of that, son, if you'll kindly take yourself off to your room."

Robbie wrapped his arms more tightly about Phillipa's neck. "No. She might leave!"

James looked at his son then. "Rob, a good Liar knows when to turn the mission over to a specialist."

"Oh." Robbie slid from Phillipa's lap and ran from the room before she could get a last kiss good-bye. Her arms felt empty. She stood, keeping the desk between her and James—not from fear, but as a sort of buffer to the powerful draw of his presence.

"I should go."

"Please, stay just a moment. There is something I need your help with." He pulled a folded paper from his breast pocket. "Fisher can't make out a thing. I thought perhaps you might, if you can spare the time."

"Oh. Of course." Feeling oddly deflated, Phillipa took the document and returned to her seat behind the desk. She took a sharpened pencil from the drawer in her hand and examined the paper.

"It seems to be a message, done in a simple alphabetical replacement mode. If we take the most commonly used letter of the alphabet, which is *e,* and we discern which symbol has replaced it—" She looked up at him with suspicion. "Fisher ought to have been able to decipher this easily."

James shrugged, although he did sneak one finger into his cravat to pull on it. Phillipa blinked at that. Was he nervous about something? Then she found herself distracted by his firm square jaw and his sculpted cheekbones and the way his dark chocolate hair curled just so about his ear—

The code. Yes. She swallowed, forcing herself to concentrate. She continued with the alphabet replacement, and then found herself intrigued anew. "There's an interesting numerical twist here," she murmured. "Not difficult, but nicely concealed. Whoever composed this was quite good."

James made a noise, causing her to look up. She scowled at the interruption. "Do you want me to decipher this or not?"

He nodded, seeming most earnest.

She went back to work. The familiarity of solving the puzzle soothed her. She wasn't sure what Papa wanted to do with himself when he returned to Spain, but perhaps they could work together—

The puzzle snapped into place, the words appearing as if by magic. She smiled. "I've got you now," she breathed.

James leaned forward in his seat. "Read it."

She held up a hand. "Don't rush me." Tilting her head, she blinked at it. "It seems to be a sort of poem." She read it silently to herself.

You are the end, and the beginning.
You are what I wish to hold close each night
And what I wish to breathe in every morning.
When I die, my only regret will be that you could
never reside in my heart to hear how it sings when
you touch me.
You are my fancy. You are my friend.
You are my love.

Phillipa swallowed hard, forcing her heart to slow, not daring to believe. She blinked rapidly, until the mark on the bottom of the page came clear. "There's—there's a symbol on the page, a signature. I'm not sure . . . it looks like a lion and an eagle combined, like a—"

"A griffin." His voice was low and intense.

"Ah." Her voice was not trustworthy.

James shifted nervously then. "I did it correctly, didn't I? I didn't accidentally say I wanted to wear your stockings or some such?"

She laughed but in her laughter began to leak tears. He had charmed her heart open too many times for her to resist him now. Still, she couldn't allow him to escape a very subtle revenge.

She smiled at him, the big broad-shouldered blur that he was. "Shall I code my reply? After all, you made me work for this."

"Dear God, no! It took me hours to write that! Don't make me wait."

"Oh, I think you'll be able to read this code rather easily."

She pushed back her chair and stood. Drying her eyes, she walked around the desk to cross the carpet to him. Raising her arms and arching her back, she began to undulate before him as she hummed a very familiar Arabian tune.

James found that puzzle very easy to unravel indeed.

Epilogue

The apples were gone from the trees, all but a few late bloomers. Soon the leaves would fall as well and the estate of Appleby would take on a cozy air of bubbling hearths and apple wood crackling sweetly on the grate.

Still, for now the weather was fine enough for everyone to have made the journey from London to Lancashire in comfort and good time.

The wedding breakfast was done, the huge serving platters bearing only fragments of the feast that had taken place. Nevertheless, the guests didn't seem to want to leave, despite having eaten their fill of apple tart and apple pastries and apple jumble. It seemed the staff at Appleby had a surplus of apples this year.

James stood in the large ballroom—which had been needed to accommodate the entire village at the tables—with Dalton and Lord Liverpool. They were ostensibly discussing business, although his eye was constantly caught by the glint of bright auburn hair twined with pearls. Phillipa looked every inch the woman in Button's creation of ivory silk. Every female there, and there were some beauties, seemed to pale before her vivid glow.

She was copper and pearl and emerald fire. She was a jeweled work of art in feminine form.

And she was his own. Possessive pride swept him. He felt like a king today, like a—

Fingers snapped before his eyes. "James has gone off again." Dalton wore a patient smirk.

Liverpool raised a brow, but merely continued with what he was saying. "A question still remains, that I don't think we shall ever know now. How did Lavinia know to single out James in the first place? She targeted him most specifically."

Dalton nodded. "I've been wondering that myself. There's more as well. I didn't want to bring this up on such a happy occasion, but a body was pulled from the Thames three days past. We think it may be Jackham's."

Dull regret tugged at James. The poor sod. Jackham had never been a Liar, never had the strength of the club behind him to help him resist Lavinia. "Did you identify it?"

"There wasn't much of a face left. You know what the river does. But the corpse was wearing a very distinctive waistcoat."

Liverpool pursed his lips. "Done in by one of your men, do you think?"

Dalton tilted his head. "They say not. I think they'd give me a hint, even if they didn't admit it outright. Still, it is possible."

James knew better. There had been talk, but so far the men had been unable to come to any sort of agreement. No one Liar would do such a thing without a consensus.

Ren Porter traveled through James's mind, but Ren had cleanly disappeared from London that day, never to be seen since. "The other possibility is that he was killed by the opposition."

"Hmm." Liverpool nodded. "Gentlemen, it seems we have not done yet with this particular espionage ring. There is someone running about with far too much knowledge of the club and the Liars." He eyed the circle of women around Phillipa. "If you gentlemen would only take your courting outside club boundaries . . ."

Both Dalton and James felt the need to protest.

"Come now, my lord, one can hardly say—"

"She came looking for me, my lord!"

James might have been mistaken, but he thought he saw Lord Liverpool's mouth give a tiny twitch. Good God, was his lordship *teasing* them? James rather hoped not. Such a thing would unbalance his world entirely.

"Speaking of your lady wife, Cunnington," Liverpool went on. "How do you propose to explain Master Phillip? He–she made quite the impression among the matchmaking set."

James grinned. "Why, Phillipa's dear twin brother has had to leave on an extended journey to parts unknown."

Dalton grimaced. "Twins? Isn't that something of a cliché?"

"I beg your pardon!" came an affronted voice from behind them. The three men turned to see Kitty and Bitty Trapp, clad in matching maid-of-honor gowns, staring at them with arms folded.

James stepped back. So much identical ire. It was quite disconcerting.

Even Dalton seemed nonplussed. Only Liverpool seemed immune. He was staring across the ballroom at a lone fair-haired figure standing in the grand doorway. There was a careful space around him, as if the other guests feared contagion. Few of the Liars really knew the truth behind Nathaniel Stonewell's sacrifice.

"What is Reardon doing here?" The Prime Minister's words were chips of ice.

James squared his shoulders. "Nate is my friend. I invited him to my wedding."

Liverpool turned to him coldly. "Don't you understand? I *want* him isolated. It is the perfect smoke-screen. As a publicly known traitor, Reardon is the bait on my hook."

James worked his jaw. "Well, there are none but friends here today. The Crown needn't fish at my wedding breakfast."

"Stand down, Cunnington," admonished Liverpool. "I'm not about to throw him out by the collar." He lifted a glass of wine from the tray of a passing footman and raised it to salute James. "Now go see to your pretty bride."

Across the room, Agatha turned to Phillipa in wonder. "I do believe Lord Liverpool is mellowing somewhat. I've never seen him drink standing up before."

Surrounded by her new friends, Phillipa smiled at Agatha's obvious cheer. Even Rose was openly happy to-day—except when Collis was nearby, which sent the girl into somber retreat—and Clara was serenely pleased.

"Why is everyone so thrilled by my wedding James?"

Agatha filched a bit more apple tart from a table. "It's the change in him, Phillipa. He's back with us at last and it was you that brought him home."

Phillipa shook her head. "I should love to take the credit, but he came back all by himself. I only held the candle in the window."

She felt powerful arms encircle her waist, tightening with gentle ferocity. "Like a moth to flame." Warm breath brushed her ear. "I missed you," he whispered.

"I saw you not ten minutes past," she teased.

"Too long."

He smiled at his sister and Clara and Rose, but made no apology as he towed Phillipa away by the waist.

They passed Rupert Atwater, who was discussing something with great intensity with Fisher. Phillipa's father had arrived back in England several days before, in good health but strained from constant worry. The rescue had gone smoothly, its method so undetectable that even now reports came of searches still being carried out in Paris.

Atwater, who wasn't nearly as elderly as James had remembered him being, had immediately taken up his old post with the Liars, much to Fisher's joy. In addition, Agatha had installed three new apprentices in the code-room this week. Not a full department, but it was a start.

Now Rupert Atwater, lean and ginger-haired, stood quite comfortably while Robbie hung from his arm like a monkey on a vine.

James grinned at the sight. "I like your father."

"There was a time when you wanted to kill him, remember?"

He nodded, unrepentant. "And I'm sure I'll want to again, since he's to live with us. A full house. Still, Robbie needs a grandfather and I think Rupert might just need Robbie."

"You think that makes a full house, do you?"

He frowned in worry. "Too full?"

"I should say not, although I'm glad you passed Denny on to Collis. I have neither the time nor the inclination to win him over. We have a mission of our own, you know."

"Oh, we do? What mission is that, pray tell?"

She tilted her head back to look into his warm brown eyes. "Our mission is to repopulate the Liar's Club, of course." She slipped his hand over her belly. "Single-handedly."

James's triumphant whoop rang through the hall. He kissed his pretty red-haired wife hard, making everyone present grin knowingly.

The Griffin was back in good form.

READ ON FOR AN EXCERPT FROM
CELESTE BRADLEY'S NEXT BOOK

Rogue in My Arms

COMING SOON FROM ST. MARTIN'S
PAPERBACKS

Sir Colin Lambert had thought nanny duty would be so simple. After all, perfectly idiotic people raised children every day. He was an intelligent fellow, some might even say a brilliant scholar, and he'd considered that a platoon of younger cousins had granted him some experience with children.

So why couldn't he manage to keep an eye on one tiny little girl?

He'd had it easy before, he realized. When little Melody had been left on the doorstep of Brown's Club for Distinguished Gentlemen, there had been two of them to take care of her. Then Aidan had brought in his former lover, Madeleine, and things had gone quite smoothly from there—if one didn't count the homicidal maniac kidnapper lurking in the attic. Which, to be entirely truthful, hadn't been Melody's fault. Not even a little bit.

This mess, however, was entirely of his own doing. When Aidan and Madeleine had left on their honeymoon, Colin had blithely decided to leave the safety of the club and all its convenient and tolerant staff behind and venture out into the world of fatherhood.

Where he now suffered on his own with dear little Baby Bedlam.

The hell of it was, he was beginning to suspect more and more that—inexplicable mulishness aside—little Mystery Melody was his own child. Being a man of logic and forethought—usually—he'd thrown caution to the wind and set out with a tiny child to Brighton in the hopes of finding his former lover who might be Melody's long-lost mother. What he was not quite willing to admit to was the secret hope that when he found the lovely Chantal again was that she would not only confess to being Melody's mother, but she would also accept a proposal of marriage.

First, however, he had to find Melody!

"Mellie! Mellie, I know you're hiding in there! Come out this instant!"

Of course she didn't come. Why should she? He was doing the same thing he'd thought so idiotic when he'd observed other adults dealing with children. Children weren't stupid. Calling them when one was angry was like a dog trying to coax a cat out of a tree.

Fine. Colin took a deep breath and sat down in the shade of the aforementioned tree. He listened for a moment and was rewarded by the slightest scuffling of little boots. Powdered bark sifted down through the moist summer air to ornament his dark green superfine surcoat. He brushed at it in resignation and then tilted his head back and closed his eyes against the leaf-dappled sunlight.

If one had to be stuck on the side of the road, unable to get one's possible offspring back into the carriage after she'd been turned loose on yet another call of nature . . . well, this was most definitely the spot to do it. Even if a one-day journey had turned into nearly three days.

"I was thinking about a bit of lunch, Mellie . . ." He let the sentence fade away unsaid. "Well, you probably don't want to hear about that." He picked at a bit of grass. "Or do you?"

Silence. She was undoubtedly hungry, but she was too stubborn to admit it.

You'll need better bait than that.

He nearly whimpered. *Not again.* He'd only been travel-

ing with Melody for a few days and already he'd told her
more outlandish pirate tales than there had ever been out-
landish pirates! If he had to review the gory details of keel-
hauling one more time, he was definitely going to lose the
last of his mind.

"You see ... I was wondering what pirates had for
lunch ..."

"Fish."

Speaking of fish, his had just taken the bait. He smiled.
"Of course, how silly of me. I imagine they ate a great deal
of fish." He hummed to himself for a moment. "What about
breakfast? Too bad they didn't have any eggs."

"Fish eggs."

He stifled a laugh. "Ah, yes. Why not?"

More bark fell onto his jacket. The scuffling of little
boots was closer now. He was tempted to jump up and reach
for her, but he'd learned his lesson well over the last hour
and a half. Melody might be scarcely three years old, but she
showed an early aptitude for altitude.

So he gave in with a sigh and began the litany that he
must have repeated forty times over the last days. "Once
upon the high seas—" *Damn the high seas!* "—there sailed a
mighty pirate ship. Upon the prow were letters etched in the
blood of honest men and they read— " He waited.

"Dishonor's Plunder!"

"Dishonor's Plunder," Colin affirmed wearily. And the
story was on. Blood ran, gore oozed, and a horridly high
body count mounted. At least three keelhaulings later, he realized that Melody had climbed down from the tree and was
seated tailor-fashion on the grass beside him.

"Hullo," he said carefully.

"I'm hungry."

"I'm not." He was, in fact, ever so slightly nauseated by
his own imagination. If anyone in the Bathgate Society of
Scholars were to hear the dreck he spouted sometimes ...

Well, that would never happen.

He stood and brushed at his clothing. "Right, then. There
should be an inn a few miles down the road. Up you go,

Cap'n Mellie." With that, he tossed her giggling onto his shoulders and strode back to where their still-harnessed horses were manfully striving to mow the entire roadside, despite the bits in their mouths. Colin put Melody into the curricle and vaulted up into the driver's seat.

The horses reluctantly pulled their heads up and began to walk.

So convenient, really, just the two of them making this journey together. No servants, no nattering companions. No one telling them when to start and when to stop—

"Uncle Coliiiin! I gotta *go!*"

Prudence Filby threw her sewing bag down onto the dressing room floor in frustration. Damn Chantal! She put her hands over her face, trying very hard to quell the panic icing her veins.

"She isn't coming back?" she asked the manager of the Brighton Theater even though she knew his answer. "Are you sure?"

The stout man behind her made a regretful noise. "She's gone. Took off with that dandy, sayin' she was in love. I wouldn't take her back if she did return. She might be the most beautiful actress in England but she's also a towering b—" He cleared his throat. "She's a right pain in the arse, she is! The last ten performances, she's only done two! Keeps saying she's too weary, too bored, too good for such a horrid play."

He'd left out spiteful. Prudence raised her eyes to see the dressing room's true disarray. It looked as though a tornado equipped with vindictive scissors had torn through it. Everything was ruined.

Damn you, Chantal.

She looked over her shoulder at the manager and tried to smile. The man had managed to perfectly capture Chantal's petulant tones. "You should go on the stage yerself, sir. You've a right knack for playin' a towering b—"

He smiled, but shook his head regretfully. "It'll do ye no good to flatter me, Pru. I can't get ye another job. Ye can't sew a lick and all the cast knows it. The only reason ye lasted so long was that ye were the only one who could put up with Chantal's tantrums."

Pru nodded in resignation. "Not yer fault, sir. Ye've got the right of it." There was no point in denying it. Not that she was a patient person in reality. She'd simply realized that if she could keep her temper through Chantal's rages and abuses and bouts of throwing breakable objects, she'd be able to keep feeding herself and her twelve-year-old brother Evan. The other seamstresses and dressers had helped her with the actual stitching, grateful that they weren't called upon to personally serve the she-devil.

Now it was over. Chantal had left without paying her for her last month's work and there was nothing left in her pockets but bits of snipped thread and extra buttons.

She couldn't even sell the costumes, for Chantal had shredded them in a last fit of malice.

The manager left her to contemplate her short and miserable future. This was the only job she'd ever managed to get here in Brighton. No one wanted a girl without useful skills—no one but the factories.

Her chest felt heavy with the cold undeniable truth. She was going to have to go into the factories. She only hoped she would be one of the lucky few to someday come out.

All the dressers at the theater had horror stories to tell. Factory work was grueling and unhealthy. Girls froze at their machines in winter and fainted from the heat in summer. Cruel foremen made advances and refused to be refused. Machines lopped off fingers and slashed hands, and there was no law that told the factory owners nay. Despite the grim conditions, as soon as one girl was abused past her ability to endure, another one would be begging for the work.

It was a last resort, but there were many who were forced to take it out of desperation.

Better her than Evan. The children in the factories scarcely ever saw their next birthday once they walked through those doors. She swallowed hard at the thought.

No. She was stronger than her small frame and large eyes

led people to believe. She was smart and careful. Besides, she told herself firmly, ignoring the cold ball of dread in her belly, if she could abide Chantal, she could tolerate anything!

When Colin at last drove the curricle into Brighton, he was exhausted and frustrated. Nevertheless, he nearly turned around and drove back to London at the sight of the sticky seaside crowds with their ludicrous swimming costumes and their whining, sunburned children.

"Summer in Brighton. What was I thinking?"

He'd been thinking that he would see the exquisite Chantal again, that's what. Just the thought of her, so lovely, so sweet-tempered, so delicate, so very, very amorous when he had at last managed to worm his way past her modest and righteous morals—

He gave the distracted and weary horses a small stroke of the whip. *Chantal awaits!*

Except, as it turned out, she didn't.

Colin blinked around him at the empty, shabby velvet seats and the peeling gilt of the stage border—not quite as magical during the day, was it?—then turned back to the stout fellow who claimed to be the theater manager. Melody stood between them, one arm wrapped around Colin's shin, gazing about her in awe.

"She isn't coming back?" Colin asked. "Are you sure?"

The man scowled. "Why do people keep saying that? She ain't comin' back, I don't want her back, and she ain't welcome in any other theater in the city!" He threw up his hands in an Italianate manner and strode away muttering resentfully.

Colin's knees felt ancient as he slowly lowered himself to sit on the edge of the deserted stage. At least the theater was dim and cool, a welcome respite from the dusty road. Melody promptly deposited herself in his lap and rested her head on his waistcoat.

"Uncle Colin, I'm tired. I wanna go back to Brown's. I wanna see Maddie and Uncle Aidan and my room and the garden and . . ." She went to sleep quickly, as she always did. Melody only had two settings: go and stop.

Colin rather wanted to crawl somewhere and sleep himself. All this for nothing? The hours and hours on the road, the nondescript inns with greasy food that Melody refused to eat, the hundreds of exhaustively detailed decapitations?

For a moment he fervently wished he was scarcely three years old so he could fling himself down upon the stage and kick and scream in frustration.

"*No!* I won't go and ye can't bloody make me!"

Colin looked up at the furious voice, automatically covering Melody's ears from any further profanity. His action was not so much to protect her innocence as to limit her extensive vocabulary. There had already been a few embarrassing moments on their journey so far.

From around the back of the stage came a small figure, stomping angrily in boots too large, swinging fists that were none too clean and scowling with a face that had apparently had strawberry jam for breakfast. The person saw Colin watching and glared back belligerently.

"What ye starin' at, ye posh bastard?"

Colin blinked at the miniature vulgarian in dismay. He couldn't be more than twelve years of age, and a poorly grown twelve years at that. However, his large gray eyes showed the shadows of too many hardships and too few childish pleasures.

When had he begun to pay so much attention to children?

"I'm looking for Chantal Marchant," he told the boy. *Why did I share that?* Really, to someone who didn't understand the past that Colin and Chantal shared, for him to come looking for her with the road-dust still on his clothing . . . well, it might come across as just a tad—

"Pathetic, that's what!" The boy spat. Then he turned to face the direction he'd just come from. "There's another fancy blighter lookin' for Herself!" he yelled.

Colin turned to gaze at the shadows behind the half-drawn curtain. He saw a dark figure bend gracefully, deposit something on the floor of the stage, and then stretch her arms above her head like a dancer. Against the backlight, he could see that she was slightly built but there was no hiding the fact that her bosom was lush and full. What a lovely figure!

She lowered her arms and planted her hands on her hips. It only served to show off the narrow dimensions of her waist.

Really spectacular. Colin leaned sideways for a better view. *Chantal?*

A low, velvety voice came from that luscious shadow. "Leave the fancy blighter be, Evan. It ain't his fault he's an idiot."

Colin was so distracted by the sensual richness of that voice that it took a long moment for him to realize that he'd been slighted. In addition, the speech patterns were of an uneducated woman of no social stature, i.e., "not for him." He blinked wistfully at that momentary fantasy as it seeped away.

Still he couldn't help await her entrance into the light. If her face matched that body and that voice—! Well, he simply might have to reassess his standards a bit.

She stepped into the dim daylight streaming in through the great double doors that stood open to the summery sea air. Colin felt a hit of disappointment. She wasn't precisely unattractive . . . more like a bit plain. She had small, pointed features that did not fit his usual idea of beauty—though her large gray eyes were rather attractive.

They matched the boy's eyes, in fact. Ah, her son, obviously. She must be older than he'd first thought.

She gazed back at him for a long moment with one eyebrow raised. He suddenly had the uncomfortable sensation that she somehow knew precisely what he'd been thinking about her.

Then she tossed a bundle to the boy. "Evan, we got no choice. Go ask the coach driver if he'll let us sit on top for a shilling."

Evan smirked. "We don't got a shilling."

She turned back to gaze speculatively at Colin. "We will."

Evan, defeated at last, stomped his way from the theater, but not without a last resentful look at Colin.

The woman approached him and stood there, looking down at Melody in his lap. "You're lucky," she said, indicating Melody with her chin. "That age is easy."

The very thought of it getting harder made Colin's spine weaken just a bit. "Really?"

The woman gathered her full skirts and sat down next to him, letting her feet in their worn boots dangle next to his costly calfskin ones. "Oh, sure 'tis. Now she thinks ye hung the moon. Yer the champion. When she gets a bit taller, she'll figure out that ye don't know what the hell yer doin' and she'll never respect ye again."

Colin gazed down at the top of Melody's head in alarm. "But what if I do know what I'm doing?"

"Won't matter. Ye'll never convince 'er of it." She shrugged. It did interesting things to the supple burden within her bodice. Not that he was interested in her—but he breathed, didn't he?

She swung her feet idly for a moment. "So . . ." Her tone was conversational. "Ye know Chantal."

She was a bit too familiar for Colin's taste. "Don't you mean 'Miss Marchant'? She was your employer, was she not?"

Her fingers tightened on the edge of the stage but her response was respectful. "Sorry, guv'nor. I just thought ye'd be wantin' to know where *Miss Marchant* took off to."

Ah. The gambit, at last. Well, he had shillings to spare if she had information. "What'll it cost me?"

She slid him a sideways glance. "Five quid."

He snorted. "Nice try."

"Three, then."

"Shillings or pounds?"

Her lips twisted in reluctant respect. "Shillings, then."

Colin shrugged. It was only money and she looked like she needed it. "You have a bargain. Where is she?"

"Not 'til ye fork over."

He reached into his waistcoat pocket and withdrew three

shillings. He laid them out in his palm and showed them to her. "You can see I have them. I can see you have something to tell me. So tell me."

Her eyebrows rose and she scoffed. "What, an' ye walk away leavin' me empty-handed?"

"Fine. I get three questions, then. I pay as you answer."

She examined his face closely, then shrugged resentfully. "Right. May as well start cheating me then."

Colin nodded, amused. She was a quirky little thing. "Why should I pay you for information? What makes you privy to Chantal's business?"

"Prudence Filby, seamstress and dresser to Miss Chantal Marchant, at yer service." She smiled and dipped her head elegantly. Damn, she was graceful. Too bad she was so plain. And common. And had the boy . . . well, he was here for Chantal, anyway.

He dropped one shilling into her outstretched palm. "See, I am a gentleman. I pay my debts." She snorted at that. He went on. "Second question . . ." An image of the boy crossed his mind. He looked so much like his mother, it was hard to see the patrilineal contribution. "Who is Evan's father?"

Wait, that wasn't what he'd meant to ask!

She paled slightly and drew back. "Why'd ye want to know?"

He cleared his throat and forced himself not to redden. "I'm asking the questions here. Who fathered your son?"

Her eyes narrowed. " 'E's dead."

"You're a widow, then?" Why couldn't he let this go? Perhaps it was Melody and how she'd been abandoned . . .

She gazed down at her very clean, very elderly boots. "I ain't never been wed."

An awkward silence stretched. "Right. None of my business."

She held out her hand without looking at him. He dropped the shilling into it, feeling like a heel.

"Third question . . . where is Chantal now?"

She shrugged. "Can't tell ye that. But I know who she run off with."

"She ran away with some . . . man?" Colin felt a trickle of jealously. "Who?"

"Bertram Ardmore. Him with the pink weskits."

The trickle became a tidal wave. *"Bertie Ardmore?"* Melody shifted in his lap so he dropped his tone to an outraged whisper. "That sniveling pup?"

She shrugged and held out her hand. "Chantal said they looked beau'iful together."

No longer interested in correcting her familiar manner, Colin seethed as he dropped the last shilling in her hand. " 'Purty Bertie.' My God."

The clever miss climbed lightly to her feet and grinned down at him. "Don't take it so 'ard, guv'nor. I 'appen to know Chantal ain't really Purty Bertie's sort. Too womanly, if ye take my meaning."

"I know." He dropped his face into his hands. "That's what makes it so mortifying!" Then he lifted his head. "She must not know. That's wonderful. She'll figure him out and be so disappointed—and there I shall be, on one knee—"

Her gaze turned cold. "Right. Off ye go, then." She turned away to pick up her other bundle. "I've a coach to catch. There's no work for me in Brighton. Evan and me are going to London."

He blinked, remembering what she'd told her son. "You're going to ride all the way to London on top of a mail coach? In the summer? You'll roast!"

Gazing at the poor, small woman before him—a woman experienced with children—a woman who could help him find Chantal—Colin had a wonderful, marvelous, outstanding idea!

"Melody and I have to keep traveling in order to find Chantal, but we'll end up in London. Why don't you and your son come with us?"